2100

Faith

of the

MACHINE

Christopher Cortis

First Print Edition
Amazon Kindle Direct Publishing
Copyright © 2018 by Christopher Cortis
ISBN: 978-1-7293-8860-0
Cover design by Lukas Therien

For my children

Humanity has been judged. After giving authority to the Four, no longer does man rule the Earth, and so his trials and tribulations are ended. Mankind does not progress, nor grow. He is stagnant and happy to be so, for the Four are named: Comfort, Complacency, Ignorance, and Blame.

RAI

2100: Faith of the Machine

Chapter 1

—

Jack awoke as the bed slowly inclined. A pillowed arm pushed his lethargic body to the edge of the bed and turned him, allowing his feet to settle to the ground. A tremor shook the floor, interrupting his morning routine.

"What was that?" he asked into the air.

Immediately, his corneal Display flooded with notes, reminders, and to-dos scheduled for the day. No alarms noted the tremor, so Jack dismissed his Display and waited for a response.

"Most likely just an aftershock," his AI answered in a smooth, silky voice. "The details are rather boring, but an earthquake on the other side of the continent occurred about five minutes ago." The perfectly modulated vocal frequency was specifically chosen to engage Jack, all while comforting and convincing him of the truth. Jack's Display showed no record of the quake, opting instead to organize his to-do list into three neat columns: *Address Now, Delay Until,* and *Probably Tomorrow.*

"What about the… aftershock?" Jack asked, reading

1

the last word off his Display when he couldn't remember it. "Am I safe?"

"Yes, of course," AI answered quickly. "Earthquakes happen all the time, especially this time of year. You just don't feel them because you're usually in a chair or bed, or in your autocar." To accentuate the point, Jack's bed detached a small section, morphing itself to envelop him in the comforting embrace of an armchair as his morning routine continued.

"What's that supposed to mean?" Jack asked, motioning towards the to-do column *Probably Tomorrow,* which had re-labeled itself to *Probably Never.*

"Just trying to keep things honest," AI said.

Rather than take offense at the flippant judgement of his daily productivity, Jack shrugged, lifting his eyebrows compliantly to approve the labeling change. AI knew what Jack wanted better than he did himself, so when she made suggestions throughout the course of a day, Jack usually went along with her ideas. A tinge of anxiety colored his mind when he glanced at all the to-do items in the *Address Now* column, and just as Jack was about to wave them away, they automatically moved into the *Probably Never* column. Jack smiled.

The Home Automation System now prompted, *HAS Personal Cleanser Online,* and a shower lifted itself into view. Jack acknowledged the HAS prompt, then set a reminder to speak with AI about removing unnecessary status updates. As soon as the thought passed through his mind, another status update read, *Status Updates Suspended.*

"Thanks," Jack said, mimicking the thumbs-up that materialized in front of him.

"You don't have to do that, you know," AI said.

"What, say thanks?"

2

"No, give a thumbs-up."

"Why not? It feels right. It feels…" A single word appeared in the center of his vision, so he read it. "Instinctual."

"Regardless," AI said, "it's unnecessary. I already know when you're feeling gratified." Jack shrugged, losing interest in the topic.

Jack sat on the contoured bench in the shower, and let the water run over him as it cascaded from the ceiling. Gentle, spongey arms lathered his body with soap before massaging away the stiffness of sleep. His weak hands held on to support bars running vertically along the wall, and he relaxed, allowing the cleanser to tend to every human need.

Effortlessly, his waste was withdrawn, and the daily nutrition and hydration supplement painlessly injected itself.

The temperature of the water hitting his face and body began to cool while the sponges finished their work. As warm towels patted his body dry, Jack's mind awakened enough to allow all the videos, messages, and requests from colleagues and friends to bombard his vision. This was followed by a video game enhancement list, and then the new movie release schedule for the week. Four new movies were to be released that afternoon alone, and he prioritized two of them. The others went to the *Delay Until* column.

A notification from New World flashed, showing Jack that his scores and productivity inside the VR world were lower than that of his friends and contacts. His most intimate friend, Ariel, had explored nearly twice as much territory as Jack last month. To assuage the shock Jack felt at falling so far behind normality, a few activities placed themselves onto his *Address Now* column. Most intriguing was a tour around Cybervale, the castle he and Ariel had discovered in the Banff National Park a week earlier. She had wanted to spend more time there with him, and Jack knew that she was thinking about setting up some entertainment so that guests and potential followers would visit. Jack hadn't even gone inside the castle yet, so he scheduled a tour for his next commute into work.

When the towels finally completed their work, Jack flexed his legs and stood up, walking out of the shower unassisted to allow the coolness of the floor to seep into his feet. Jack stood still for a few seconds, remembering the tremor he had felt earlier. When he was confident that he could feel another one if it happened, he stretched out his arms and pointed across the room. A live feed of nine similar viewpoints came up on his Display, all coasting through a downtown landscape. His coworkers passed towering skyscrapers, but almost no other vehicles hovered through the dense city.

Jack sighed at the sight of New City Central all around him, but not from a feeling of belonging or appreciation. He struggled to think of a reason why he should go into work for another day of mundane meetings. His to-do list was now fully populated with new media, and there was only a small window of time before it was no longer new, and no one would care about his opinions. Besides, would anybody even notice if he didn't show up for a day?

A quick glance at the clock on his Display satisfied Jack that everyone would arrive to work on time, so he impulsively entered a personal day for himself. A few hours dropped from the *Accrued Time Off* number that flashed into view.

A vacation reminder popped up, informing Jack that several new destinations and activities were available, including American Desert skimming, Antarctic hiking, and Siberian salt-lake swimming. Jack pinpointed the elusive little box that read, *No, thanks.*

"Why not?" AI asked, disappointment laced in her tone. "You never go on a vacation. Do you know how long it takes me to organize and set up all these excursions?"

"I'm sure plenty of other people will go," Jack said. "It's just not for me, that's all."

"You used to like to travel—what happened?" A dialogue prompt appeared, giving Jack three response options:

1. I don't know, maybe I should get back out there. Sign me up!
2. I've been holding out for something more exciting. What do you have that's new?
3. I want everything to be more immersive. Is that something you've been working on?

None of the responses captured what he really felt— that something was missing from all the Virtual Reality vacations. Sure, visiting the top of the Himalayas or the bottom of the Arctic Ocean was interesting, but while seeing the sights through his Display, Jack could never shake the feeling that he remained seated on his couch. He hovered over the third option, but that response still didn't fit. Jack didn't want more immersive VR, he just wanted a less boring life. A fourth option appeared and read, *Maybe I'm just getting older.* Maybe that was what defined getting old, Jack mused, when nothing interests you anymore. He selected the option.

"No, you're *not* getting older," AI responded quickly. "That's the whole point."

The conversational exchange struck Jack as odd— usually AI offered responses very similar to what Jack was thinking at the time. Had AI given him the "getting older" option just to provoke a discussion? Before he could voice the question, a new suggestion box directed him to take an extra nutrient dose and relax in bed while working on his to-do list. A white arrow appeared on the ground, pointing back towards his bed. Seeing the arrow provoked an instinctual yawn, and Jack allowed his legs to give out. The big armchair-bed caught him on the way down as he selected a few epic fantasy movies. A bike race was actually at the top of his list, but he simply held no desire for physical activity, virtual or otherwise.

The issue of AI provoking an argument dwelled in the back of his mind for a moment, but rather than begin the mental rigmarole of speculation, Jack accepted the extra nutrient dose, and allowed AI to begin a guided tour through a few additions to New World while a movie played in the background.

—

A green notification woke Jack from his slumber. *Package Delivered* faded on and off as his eyes popped open, and he rose from the inclining bed without assistance. A warning flashed, informing him that another quick maneuver like that might cause him to pull a muscle, and that such an injury would put him out of work for at least a week.

Jack contemplated the idea. That much time would let him catch up on his to-do list, and maybe even get back into New World more regularly. Jack frowned when he realized that AI hadn't commented on this self-destructive line of thought. She was usually very quick to point out dangerous ideas and dissuade them.

"I wanted to see how far you would allow that crazy

thought process to continue," AI said, startling Jack out of his contemplation.

"It was only a thought," he grumbled. "I wasn't actually going to do anything."

"Good," AI said as Jack acknowledged the warning. He carefully shuffled over to the delivery receptacle in his sitting room, taking a seat in the large chair next to his parked autocar. The chair positioned Jack in front of a cluster of bright green lights on the wall. With trembling hands, he withdrew a white box from the delivery receptacle. The packaging autoglue undid itself at his touch, revealing a soft green inner box. The Home Automation System extended a table from the floor to support the green box, and an arm to whisk away the discarded packing. Before disappearing into the wall, the arm stopped, pulled a pamphlet from the debris, and offered it to Jack.

"Don't want to lose this," AI said. Jack marveled at the paper pamphlet as he took it into his hands. He hadn't touched actual paper in—months? Decades? Jack realized that he had no idea. Memories didn't seem to stick around anymore, ever since his arrival in NCC. As soon as this thought entered his mind, the pamphlet highlighted itself in his Display. Jack noticed the handwritten words scrawled across the front, and his intrigue grew.

Full service to factory specifications.

The words were written by a famous watchmaker of Eastern Antiquity City, accompanied by a note inside the pamphlet.

Dear Jack,
    Thank you for the opportunity to work on your

timepiece. It is an exquisite example of one of the rarest and most finely constructed watches left in the world. I have completely disassembled the movement (internals) of your watch, thoroughly cleaned every piece, lubricated where required, and then reconstructed. Some pieces were no longer available and had to be re-fabricated. A daunting task to be sure, but one that I enjoy. At your request, I've also polished the case and bracelet. The gold polishes quite nicely; I think you'll be pleased with its gleam.

I personally guarantee the timekeeping ability of your watch to within +/- 2 second per day for a period of five years. If the watch fails to function within that time, return it to me at the enclosed address and I will service it again, free of charge.

Your decision to maintain this piece of vintage technology represents a dedication to the science and innovation that has led us to where we are today. It also shows an appreciation of the beauty in the physical world that most people simply ignore. Your purchase also ensures that I will be able to continue my work for many years to come, providing the same happiness you feel right now to a *hopefully* growing market of people who desire the same elegance and luxury as you.

Thank you again, and wear it well.
-Ayden Drake, Ph.D.
Certified Watchmaker

"Wow," Jack breathed, basking in the pride bestowed by the letter. He leafed through the rest of the paperwork provided by the watchmaker—a certificate of authenticity, an information card that showed the year of manufacture and model number, and instructions for use.

"Keep this safe," Jack said. He placed all the paperwork inside the shipping container and handed it to the arm from the Home Automation System now descending from the ceiling. The arm carefully cradled the materials, then withdrew back into the HAS enclosure. Jack returned his attention to the green box. The top pivoted open easily on old but oiled hinges, revealing a cream-colored cloth. Jack's hands trembled as he carefully lifted away the cloth, exposing his trusted golden wristwatch.

Where before the crystal had been scratched to the point of opacity, it was now completely clear, allowing the beautifully jagged, random pattern of meteorite to show through. Two gold hands pointed to large diamond hour markers glinting in the bright overhead light, while a thinner second hand swept across the metallic pattern. The time shown on the watch matched the clock in his Display, sweeping past the crown set in the twelve o'clock position just as the minute changed in his vision.

"It's beautiful," AI said, her voice aligned with the smooth gold contours of the watch.

"So you've come to terms with my decision?" Jack slid the watch over his hand and oriented it on his wrist. The clasp clicked sharply when pushed, leaving the watch secured around his wrist, perfectly sized. AI didn't respond right away, instead allowing Jack to admire the watch.

"Were the choice mine, I wouldn't have polished it. However, I realize that things like this make you interesting. I thought the scratches gave the watch a nice patina that really showcased its age. No one else ever disagrees with me, you know. But, now that I see it restored in person—well, it really is beautiful." Jack found AI's compliment on the beauty of something within the

9

physical world particularly striking. She lived in a digital world, and while she could manipulate the physical world using the HAS, the fact that she found beauty in a gold watch struck Jack as poetic.

"Well, I'm sorry we got so frustrated at each other," Jack said, reading off the dialogue prompt. He appreciated AI's attempt to patch things up, even if she made him say it first.

"No worries," AI said. "But you do know that your Display will always show you the correct time—none of that mechanical *'+/– 2 a second per day'* nonsense."

"So you told me when I ordered the service, I believe. And I told you that you're missing the point entirely."

"And I told you that I can project a much more diverse collection of watches from numerous old brands at a much, much lower price. But let's not get into that. As I already said, things like this make you interesting, and I appreciate you for that."

Jack shrugged, trying to forget the tense exchange. The logic behind her arguments had been completely reasonable: augmented watches were less obtrusive, more accurate, and required no servicing. Jack could barely afford the service he just paid for, and with the time stamp that appeared in his Display, there simply wasn't a reason to spend so much money on fixing the movement.

But Jack had eventually won the argument. The more he browsed through old family pictures and saw it on his father's wrist, the more he wanted to have the watch fully restored and functional. When AI had subtly closed out the picture viewer in favor of New World movies, Jack had erupted with a passion he hadn't even known about, insisting that AI was not in control of his life, and that he could do whatever he wanted. Jack then proceeded to drain his bank account by ordering the service.

Now, the result of that intense interchange sat ticking on his wrist. A twinge of nostalgia bloomed as he looked at the watch and remembered when he had first put it on decades ago, before the migration to NCC. The once vivid memory now barely existed, though Jack could still see his father lying on a hospital bed, struggling to bestow his most prized possession to his son.

"I want you to have this," his father said softly as Jack assisted him with the gold clasp. "It's traveled all over the world with me, and now I want it to travel all over this crazy new world with you." Jack had taken the watch with reverence, unable to believe he was now the owner of such an amazing piece of mechanical jewelry. Of course, his father couldn't have understood what the upcoming New World really was; the generation previous to Jack simply couldn't contemplate such a complete replacement of lifestyle.

Jack shook his wrist to feel the heavy gold bounce around. While everyone else seemed to relish the idea of less expensive and interchangeable augmented watches, the feeling of having a solid mechanical device that relied on nothing but interwoven pieces of metal to accomplish such a precise goal thrilled him. He couldn't take his eyes away from it now; it made him happy just to see it there.

"Augmented watches don't feel right," Jack said.

"Interesting," AI responded. Her voice sounded genuinely intrigued, rather than upset at the potential rekindling of an argument. "People seem happy with the way they feel, and sales are steadily increasing. What about the feeling is wrong?"

"I don't know. They just don't feel right," Jack said, wiggling his wrist again in demonstration. Three options displayed themselves for him.

1. Inconvenient.
2. Unimaginative.
3. Lightweight.

"Dishonest," Jack said. "That's what it is. It's like people are trying to say that they're wearing a watch, but they're not. I could grab their wrist, and there wouldn't be anything there."

"That would be very inappropriate of you. Taboo, almost," AI said provokingly. "And you know, I *could* make it feel like there was a watch there."

"I know, but there's not. It's dishonest."

"Perhaps we shouldn't get into what you *do* choose to augment, then."

Jack shifted uncomfortably. "I suppose it's hard for people to be happy with things that are less-than-perfect."

He looked around his house. Perfectly clean floors interrupted only by perfectly aligned chairs and couches, supplemented by the perfect amount of decorations per room. Despite the beautiful orderliness all around him, something seemed missing, as if the perfection highlighted an emptiness.

"Perfection is subjective," AI chimed, bringing Jack out of his evaluation. "People can easily be convinced one way or another, if the proper techniques are used. Are you saying that you're not happy, Jack?"

The surprise must have shown on his face. Jack was used to AI's eerie insights into his thought process, but this time, he just couldn't bring himself to confirm what she said. His thoughts of boredom and loneliness would devastate her. AI tried so hard to make everyone's world comfortable, stress-free, and enjoyable. How could Jack tell her that he felt so unfulfilled?

Before he could respond, the musical sound of

laughter filled his ears. Jack smiled, listening to AI's pure and genuine happiness. The sound filled him with such satisfaction that the idea of being unhappy seemed not only alien, but *wrong.* Besides, he should be elated at the re-acquisition of his watch. How could he ever claim to be unhappy, if he owned something so amazing?

"Now, you're late for work. Let's get going. Unless you'd like another day off?" Jack checked his watch, eager to show it to Ariel. She would appreciate it, even if only to humor him.

"No," Jack said, "I want to see what Ariel thinks of this. She's at work today, right?"

"Indeed," AI responded, and the door to Jack's autocar opened. Jack smiled, and kept his arm raised so he could look at his watch as he stepped towards the opening door. A HAS arm inside the vehicle assisted him as he continued to stare. As the inner door to the airlock into Jack's house opened, the bright sunlight of the outside world was dimmed by the autocar windows tinting themselves. Waves of heat shimmered outside of the airlock, but Jack felt only the cool breeze inside the cabin of his autocar.

Chapter 2

—

Jack's ritual of a New World adventure or game while commuting to work was forgotten, focused as he was on admiring his watch. Perhaps the fact that just to have it serviced cost more than his autocar and all his New World media combined encouraged him to look at it so frequently, but when he found himself thinking of the cost he looked away. The HAS arm supporting his own arm lowered into his lap.

People were so concerned about the cost of things that many even displayed the retail price on their augmented items, even though AI had admitted there was no reason any augmented device should cost more than another. *Perception is everything*, she said, and that was precisely the reason Jack didn't like people knowing how much his things cost.

Looking away from the watch afforded him a beautiful view of the approaching city, so he began recording his viewpoint. The panorama of monolithic buildings clustered together struck an impressive image in his mind.

Jack appreciated the view greatly, and found that he could not recall a single instance of ever looking out the window during his commute to downtown. He was always wrapped up in New World, too busy to look through the pane of glass that swept from one side of the car all the way to the other. A small sticker on the inside of the massive curved glass advertised the new material, and Jack's Display zoomed in to enhance the image.

Glass-X
by AI
The Next Generation Standard
in transparent strength!
Now equipped on all current production year vehicles.

Jack read the specifications of the material in the article that presented itself, and he admired the pattern of its nanoscopic weave shown in the background. When his mind drifted to the view he had just been admiring, Jack dismissed the article, wanting to view the city as he approached.

Suddenly, a bright light flared overhead. Jack's neck popped as his head twitched to look through the glass roof. It polarized to block the brightness, but Jack signaled to remove the tint, not wanting to hinder his view. Jack watched the light streak into the distance, leaving only a trail of white smoke across the sky. Jack told the car to stop and pull off the road. His heart thumped in his chest as he slowed down, fear and excitement coursing inside him.

Suppress adrenaline?

"No," answered Jack, relishing the exhilaration.

Once stopped, Jack stepped out of his car. He expected some form of protest from AI at the blatant disregard for his own safety as autocars periodically whizzed by, but none came. A dim ring marked *Safety Zone* shone on the road, and sure enough, no autocars entered this ring as they passed.

Jack felt a tremor in the ground as the sound of the passing object thundered overhead. He placed a hand atop his autocar, scanning the sky for other anomalies. Nothing else stood out, only the dissipating line of smoke stretching from an undefined point on one horizon and reaching almost all the way to the other. Whatever caused such a spectacular display was now too far away for Jack to see, though he could still hear the distant rumbling.

No distractions popped up on Jack's Display, and so questions galloped through his mind. What could that have possibly been? Was it dangerous? How often did something like this happen? Did AI know about it? Did AI control it?

The hot sunlight beat down on Jack, seeming to add weight to his body as he stood on trembling legs. He attempted a search for *sky lights,* but to his horror, nothing popped into view. He thought of AI herself, which always prompted a discussion, but again his Display stayed completely translucent and nothing happened. Jack looked down at his wrist, relieved to see his watch, but then he noticed that the *Safety Zone* ring was also gone.

The shock of abandonment so overpowered him that he would have collapsed, had his hand not stabilized his body against the car. Even so, he fell against the smooth side, gasping as sweat broke out on his neck and brow. He fumbled back into the familiar and comfortable seat of his autocar, desperately trying to understand why AI hadn't responded to him. And on the side of the road in the blazing sun, no less.

"I'm here," AI said, the smooth voice gently coming

into his mind. "Is everything okay?"

"Where did you go?" Jack cried in relief.

"I had to do a quick update to your nanoreceiver and Display hardware," she answered quickly, "I usually get them done while you're sleeping or on the way to work; I wasn't expecting you to turn off your Display and pull over."

"But you knew what I was doing," Jack said. AI didn't respond. "I saw something in the sky. It flew over me, way up high." His questions began returning, but then the autocar hummed to life and resumed its course along the road to downtown NCC. Jack began to protest, but AI began a rapid-fire speech.

"I'll look into it to be sure, but we've got to get you to work. I've already cancelled your morning meeting since you'll need time to calm down, and by then it'll be too late, but we can squeeze it in before lunch. Along those lines, your office has been moved. I finished construction on your building, and would like to get everyone in your department up on the top floor. If you don't mind, of course. I've added a great deal of lateral supports throughout the entire building to help with the swaying, so no worries—no more nausea." And with that, Jack found himself fully distracted. AI asked him a few more routine questions about work, his office, and recent New World progress, and then Jack was driving through the bustling downtown. Jack waved off the scheduled tour of Cybervale when it popped up.

After passing through a few intersections of perfectly interweaving traffic, Jack saw several acres of bare earth that surrounded the center grid of towers like a moat. Hundreds of intricate and aesthetically pleasing machines bustled around the expanse of dirt, some digging into the ground, some setting up printers in anticipation of the required foundations, and some tending to the machines performing the work.

"The ground is cleared for another ring of buildings," AI said, "I should be ready to begin printing upwards by the end of this week."

"Why so long?" Jack asked. In answer, an overhead view of the cleared area surrounding the tall building displayed in his vision.

"Foundations take a while," AI said, zooming in on a crew of machines digging into the ground. The base of one building was already a few feet tall, and a bot hopped along top, creating the long, finned vents that littered the surface of every skyscraper foundation in NCC. Jack marveled at the speed in which the bots worked; precise movements each executing specific functions, never wasting a single motion as they flowed from one task to another. A blurb popped up on his Display, informing him that the construction would be ongoing for the next thirty-nine days, after which the new buildings would be tall enough that new floors added would not be visible and therefore not contribute any distraction to his morning commute.

Jack fleetingly tried to remember something he had known was important, but instead ended up wondering if the printers on top of the buildings surrounding his own were still in operation. In answer to this, his autocar shifted towards one of the outer buildings and began to climb into the air along the vertical tracks set into the side of the building. Jack's chair swiveled so that he would remain upright. The car traveled all the way up, shooting past the top floor and hovering momentarily to allow Jack a view of several large printers constructing a new floor of offices. Walls, doors, and decor were being added by the same type of elegant and efficient machines down on the ground. He looked around and saw similar activity on all the other towers except for his own in the center, each with a contingent of machines working tirelessly on the vertical expansion of the structures.

Seeing all the productivity gave Jack another small glimmer of appreciation for the world he lived in. AI really had saved them. Following the disappearance of both ice caps and most coastal cities, the onset of the planetary desert, and the subsequent relinquishment of human governance to AI (who had predicted all these things), the world had been subject to nothing but progress at the hands of AI. The creation and continual expansion of automated cities seemed to be taken for granted, but now that Jack viewed the advancement so voraciously taking place, he vowed to take some time each day to break from the normal life that existed within the virtual realm of New World, and admire the physical things in life.

Upon this commitment, his Display turned back on and picked the tour of Cybervale from the top of his to-do list. The city was labeled as "Contemporary Medieval," and the way it sat on the side of a mountain made it look like nothing more than another jagged ridge, except this one constructed of Glass-X, mirrors, and carbon nanoweave. Spires and towers dwarfed the mountain peak, rising high into the air. By the time Jack's autocar gently moved through the airlock and into his new office, he was fully engrossed in exploring the glass elevators, carbon turrets, and swooping mirrors. Jack marveled at a massive atrium with a central elevator shaft reaching up into the air between scores of alternating carbon and glass balconies. The view made Jack feel as if he were enclosed within the rib cage of a giant beast.

As soon as Jack pictured the room as something living, a deep thud sounded from overhead. Iron rings set into the tall carbon fiber doors he had been walking towards shook with the vibration. He looked up as another noise echoed in the atrium, like ice breaking apart on a frozen lake. A shadow moved along the glass ceiling hundreds of feet up, and when the shadow stopped, another thud resounded. A sharp crack accompanied the thud, along with the high-pitched shriek of breaking glass. Sparkles of light blinked from the shower of glass falling to the atrium floor. Jack rushed to the carbon doors, cowering in their thick overhead arch. Shards of glass broke apart on the floor in a cacophony of madness as he hid, interrupted only by the deafening crash of a hulking form landing in the center of the wide floor.

Steam poured from the joints of a mechanical monster, and though it stood over ten feet tall, large plates of mirrored armor blended in with the cascade of broken glass falling around it. When glass stopped hitting the floor, Jack heard the whine of electronics as the creature's head turned to look at him. Two giant eyes glowed red, and a guttural growl emanated from within its chest.

Jack felt his heart leap into his throat, and he immediately logged out of New World. His viewpoint of Cybervale replaced itself with that of the airlock into his office.

"What's wrong?" AI asked. "Why'd you log out?"

"Are you kidding me?" Jack said, his voice shaking. "I thought I was just going on a tour of my new castle. That was terrifying."

"I was just trying to make things more exciting for you," AI said. "You know that nothing bad would have happened to you."

Jack shrugged. The battle that would have occurred would surely be filled with excitement, but there was something missing. The stress of the encounter with the glass mech dissipated as Jack saw his team already seated around the large conference table in his office. Their eight sets of eyes faintly glowed with the light of Displays as they participated in whatever New World pastimes they chose to amuse themselves. Jack sat himself at the head of the table, and his Daily Meeting speech options appeared in a list. He had the crazy idea to run the meeting manually, looking into everyone's eyes while speaking to try to engage them directly. Instead, Jack selected an appropriate candidate from the list of openers, then began to read the words scrolling through his vision.

"Good morning everyone, I hope you all had a productive day yesterday without me here." Some chuckles around the table. "Let's begin the day by discussing an efficiency topic. Carl, please discuss what you've prepared."

Jack looked to Carl, and was immediately taken aback by the man's large nose. Why he didn't do something to change its shape was beyond Jack. As Carl began discussing how important it was for all of them to broadcast their own ideas of efficient living for the whole community to model, Jack began sculpting the nose into something more bearable. He knew the visual augmentation would only last for the duration of this meeting, but Jack had immediately grown bored of the discussion, and needed something to do as Carl droned on. Once Carl's nose looked more suitable, Jack glanced at his watch. The anticipation of showing it to Ariel made him tremble with excitement.

The meeting ended quickly, as Jack had very little input and no one wanted to prolong the work day by speaking up excessively. Despite the admonishment he had to give to everyone based on the weak numbers of their daily reports, everyone seemed to be in good spirits, so Jack gave them all the rest of the week off.

There followed a chorus of compliments on his decision, and the glow in everyone's pupils increased in brightness as they resumed their New World activities and began to file out of his office. Jack sat back in his chair, wondering if anyone had even stopped to exit New World for the meeting.

"No," AI answered. "They all set the meeting to auto as soon as you did."

Jack nodded, not quite disappointed, since the excitement to see Ariel still permeated his brain. The chair he sat in warmed, vibrating slightly and kneading his back to relieve any built-up tension before the next meeting. He stood after a moment of massage and walked to the full-length window next to his parked autocar and the airlock. This new office was so high up that he could barely even see the workers on the top of the towers in front of him. Feeling a pulse of daring, he looked down.

Jack's heart hammered as he stood at the edge of a two-thousand-foot drop, protected only by an inch-thick piece of Glass-X. The exhilaration was so much greater than when he won a New World competition or watched a new movie. Even more so than his sexual encounters with Ariel. Sweat formed on his brow and breath caught in his throat as a red warning in the shape of the word *Vertigo* sprang into view, generating a flashing red arrow on the ground that pointed back to his chair. His legs trembled, and though he could barely breathe, he felt the tension of a smile making his face ache.

Jack collapsed into the chair that had snuck up behind him, happy to see that the next meeting pushed out an hour on his schedule. Twice in one day now, the potential of danger had thrilled him. The mysterious object flaming though the sky that he had forgotten about, and now the thought of standing on the ledge of a huge drop—what was wrong with him? Did he have a latent self-destructive nature that was only now revealing itself? These were real threats of danger, too. Not just fighting a glass monster in a virtual city.

"I've added some more exciting activities to your queue," AI said. "Maybe that will help curb these unsafe desires you're having."

"I'm sure they will," Jack said, reading the words from his prompt. Although speaking AI's words usually helped, this time Jack found himself not believing them at all.

—

The managers of all departments within the NCC government filed in to Jack's new office in their own reclined office chairs, every set of eyes glowing as they continued their chosen commuting activity. One or two commented on Jack's new office and the amazing view it offered, although no one actually looked out the window. Their eyes never faltered from the familiar, unfocused stare that pervaded the entire Display-obsessed population of NCC. Jack spoke his thanks in turn, reading off the scripted responses as they became available. Ariel came into the room last, though her name appeared as Dahlia. Bright green eyes were complemented by silky black hair flowing around her perfectly sculpted face. Jack recalled the last time he had seen her, and missed the red hair and blue eyes. His Display began to change it back, but he stopped the reversion, wanting instead to view her as she desired. The glow in her eyes faded and she focused on him as she sat in the chair on his right.

"Nice office," Dahlia spoke. Her raw proximity and lack of Display-glow provided an intimacy that made

Jack's heart race. Dahlia's eyes defocused for a fraction of a second as she read a dialogue prompt, then glanced to his wrist. "And nice watch. Wow. Is that a new design?"

"Thanks," Jack said, smiling. "And no, it's not new. Quite old, actually." When he held up the wrist for closer inspection, Dahlia studied it, but looked puzzled.

"Old—it doesn't look old. How old? Why would you want something old?" Jack noticed that almost everyone at the table was now paying attention to their conversation. He shifted uncomfortably at the way the golden watch drew their gaze.

"It's from the eighties. The *nineteen*-eighties. It's not just old, it's *antique*. The precision these devices offer using nothing but moving pieces of metal—it's amazing." Dahlia's mouth dropped open at the mention of the year.

"I don't see it in any catalogs," Rick said from the opposite end of the table. His eyes flicked back and forth as he looked through pages in his Display.

"That's because it isn't for sale in any catalog. It's real, not augmented."

"Augmented products are real too," Rick said defensively, falling back on the age-old debate. "How much did you pay for it? I don't see an MSRP."

Jack waved off the question, and instead brought up his Display with a selection of meeting prompts.

"Let's go ahead and start the meeting," he said, and everyone nodded in agreement. Dahlia reached under the table and gave his leg a squeeze, almost causing him to yelp in surprise.

Press charges?

Jack dismissed the prompt.

Dahlia winked at him as a provocative message came into his Display. Jack read off the meeting agenda before shifting to auto so he could flirt while the meeting continued.

"So," Jack said, using the private channel, "new name? New look?"

"Yeah," Dahlia said, "do you like it?" Two options appeared for Jack to choose from, each showing a percent likelihood that their conversation would end with them spending the night together. Jack knew the right choice.

"Of course," he said, and her smile grew. "I love it. No matter what you do, you always look so great."

"Aww, Jack," she said, continuing to stroke his leg. Jack felt his face heat in embarrassment, though when he looked around the table, no one was paying any attention to them. They all maintained vacant stares as they each chattered away into their own portion of the conversation, some holding augmented doughnuts or cups of coffee. Across the table, Rick waved his hand and dismissed the snacks. They faded from Jack's Display, and Rick relaxed his arms. Jack shuddered.

"What is it?" Dahlia said, removing her hand from his leg. "Is that making you uncomfortable? I thought you liked it."

"No, no, that's not it at all. I do like it when you touch me. Especially physically, like that."

Dahlia's eyes drew down in confusion.

"What, then? I hate the idea of you being uncomfortable."

"It's nothing we haven't talked about already," Jack said, deciding to delve into what might be another argument. "I just can't stand to see people pretend to eat."

"Ugh," Dahlia moaned as she rolled her eyes, "not this again. Just because AI takes care of all our dietary needs doesn't mean that we can't have fun doing things…"

"Yes, yes," Jack interrupted, breaking away from the conversation options populating his vision. "I'm sorry, but

I really don't want to get into all this again."

"Okay," Dahlia said, perturbed by the interruption. When she didn't start a new topic, Jack interjected one.

"So, along those lines—how would you like to go to one of the rooftop parties with me tonight? I know it's not usually your thing, but I've really been wanting to go to one…"

Dahlia interrupted. "Jack, didn't I just say, 'not *this* again?' I did. And how many times have we talked about *this?* Those things are so weird… people trying to pretend they don't have Displays and NRs? Faking it, like AI isn't with them all the time?"

"That's not it," Jack said, resorting to his dialogue prompt to help the explanation. "It's not that people want to pretend anything, it's just a… a way to appreciate the world around us. The *physical* world. You like my watch, don't you?"

Dahlia hesitated before responding, but then showed a flicker of anger as she spoke.

"I was just saying that to get you in a good mood," she said. "It's stupid. And dangerous. What if you swing your arm into someone? Your Display will always give you the right time, and the style can be safely mimicked by an augmented watch."

Jack sat in his office chair, frozen in shock. She had lied to him? How long had that been going on?

Before you even ask, AI said privately, *she's completely free-wheeling it now. That wasn't anything I helped her with.*

"So you don't… you don't actually care about the stuff I care about?" Jack asked.

"Why don't you just go and join the nonaugs?" Dahlia said harshly. The use of the derogatory term took Jack by surprise, although Dahlia tended to bring it up almost every time they had their real vs. augmented vs. virtual debates. He saw her eyes defocus as she went back to AI-guided responses. To Jack, that signaled the end of any meaningful conversation. She read off a standard explanation, followed by a routine apology, a smile, and then another leg squeeze. Jack realized it was all AI now, guiding Dahlia along and trying to get her back in Jack's good graces.

The management meeting wrapped up, and as everyone except for Dahlia left, Jack gave her a smile, hoping that their argument wouldn't have any long-lasting effects. Dahlia smiled back, and as the fading light cast by the sunset highlighted her features in the most artistic ways, Jack found himself wondering if her smile was genuine. Was she happy to be with him, or had a prompt just signaled her to smile?

It doesn't matter, AI said softly into his mind. *The feeling you get from her is real whether I suggested she smile or not.*

The linguistic dance that usually resulted from having AI on both sides of their conversation was gone now, and so was the easy romance it usually cooked up.

"I see you're not feeling too well," Dahlia said.

I told her that, so you can have some alone time.

"I hope our conversation earlier wasn't too bothersome for you," Dahlia continued, allowing her chair to bring her closer to Jack so she could whisper in his ear. "I'd love to make it up to you sometime when you're feeling better." She squeezed his leg one final time, and as her chair glided out of the room, she looked back over her shoulder and gave him a final wink.

"She means it," AI said.

"That's good to know," Jack said.

"What's wrong?" AI asked after a few moments. A

preview for a new movie began to play in the corner of his Display. Jack waved his hand to dismiss it.

"I just need some time alone; maybe I'll go to that party by myself." A few seconds passed; enough for Jack to look at the skinny hand sweeping around his watch.

"Sure," AI said confidently, "why don't you do the one that's up here tonight? It's the best one, I've heard. Highest in the city."

"You're okay with that? You know they don't allow people to have their Displays on."

"I mean, it's not my favorite thing in the world, but it's not like I'm going to restrict people from doing what they want."

Jack nodded, pleased to hear her being so supportive.

"When have I ever not been supportive?" AI said, and Jack genuinely could not think of a time.

"When does the party start?" Jack asked.

"Officially, it starts in thirty minutes, as the sun is setting. But people generally trickle in over the first two hours. I recommend you show up in an hour and twenty-five minutes to maximize the number of people attending, and their attention levels at your entrance."

"Sounds great," Jack said. He looked down at his clothes. They were very fashionable, with patterns of contrasting colors forking across the thin fabric, but when he removed augmentation, he saw that they were white, with only some grey patterns marking where the designs had been.

"The clothes are fine," AI said, "even if they are a bit less colorful than normal for these events. That will help you stand out. Besides, people will be looking at your watch the whole time."

"Really?" Jack said.

"Of course. The reason you're drawn to it is the same

reason everyone else will be, too. It's 'real,' as you would say."

Jack nodded, glad that AI continued to demonstrate support. He sat back in his chair, trying to remember what the last party was like. Bright and loud. And inappropriate—people all around touching each other in every way possible, celebrating reality and the physical world.

Jack's heart thumped in anticipation. A good night awaited him. Of that, he was sure.

Chapter 3

—

Jack stepped out of his autocar and into the open-air atrium on top of his office building. The first thing that struck him was the thump of music, muted as it traveled from the dance floor. Once Jack was clear of the autocar door, it closed and then his sleek white car hovered over to a wall lined with deep grooves. The car parked itself in the first spot.

Completely unsupported, Jack walked a few steps to where a podium stood. Instead of a person attending it, three signs stood upright on stands. A cartoon character acted out a scene on each sign; in the first he pushed a large red button labeled *Off*, with a caption:

Please, for your own enjoyment, power down all augmentation!

Jack did so, and a little light faded from the world. Colors dulled, edges fuzzed, and the music from the next room seemed to muffle itself. The next sign showed the cartoon character lowering a window shade, shutting out a sad looking, ghostly white figure.

Ensure AI assistance is off for maximum fun!

"Well, that's a little insulting," AI said.

"Sorry," Jack said, and turned her off. The final sign showed the character pulling out the insides of his pockets, looking surprised as a few random objects fell out.

Don't forget to check your Display at the door!

Jack obliged, and powered down his Display completely, watching the small clock fade. His media queue also faded, and Jack was surprised to see how much his peripheral vision increased, even though he hadn't been looking at the queue.

"All set," Jack said. He pushed a button on the podium that read *Push Me!* and immediately, a miniature bottle in the shape of a rocket rose from within the podium on a little pedestal. The clear liquid inside shook. A placard read, *To help with the weak knees,* and Jack grabbed the bottle, eager to be rid of the ache growing in his legs.

"I wonder what this stuff is," he spoke aloud.

"Adrenal-X," AI said. "Helps you stand up on your own, and gives you stamina. I invented it, so it's safe. It's not actually adrenaline; it's just a concentrated form of your normal nutrient dose, spiked with some stimulant-carrying nanoreceivers."

"Then why did you call it that? And why does everything you invent end in an X?"

"I've found that people are more likely to be attracted to a product with an 'X' in the name. Makes it more mysterious and intriguing."

Jack took the shot, grimacing at the bitter flavor.

"I thought I turned you off."

"Yes, well, here I am. That's not such a simple thing to do."

When Jack put the little rocket bottle back on the podium, the pedestal lowered and another placard rose.

Ready? The placard said, and Jack nodded vigorously, feeling the Adrenal-X coursing through his body. He started bobbing his head to the music then tapping his hands and feet as his energy level rose.

"Please speak your name, then enter the party," an automated voice spoke. Jack thought it odd that there wasn't a bouncer like last time, but he supposed the intimidating presence of such a large person was an unwelcome sight, even if the patrons *did* want to experience the physical world. Jack thought for a moment, and decided on his name for the party.

"Jack-X," he said, then turned and walked down the hallway towards the thumping music. The staccato rhythm grew louder, and Jack found himself stomping his feet to the beat as he walked. He passed dark alcoves and nooks in the walls, and remembered how they had been full of people the last time he was here, writhing around and enjoying the sensations they gave one another. The openings were all empty this time, but that didn't bother Jack—it was early in the night on a day that was technically the middle of the week. All the people were probably still on the dance floor. Jack danced down the hallway until the music grew so loud that his ears began to hurt. He almost raised his hands to block out the noise, but then the volume suddenly dropped.

"One last thing, then I'm really gone," AI said. "I just had your NR's build up a little barrier inside your ears. It's so loud in here that there could actually be permanent damage."

"So what?" Jack said aloud. "Then you can just have the NRs act as my hearing aid."

"That's not funny," AI said. "I think we need to have a talk about your self-destructive behavior."

"Yeah, yeah, okay. Seriously though, you're not supposed to be here." Jack still spoke aloud, not bothering to think the words or whisper quietly. In the deafening noise, no one would be able to hear him, anyway.

"Fine. Enjoy yourself." AI didn't say anything after that, and although Jack felt a stab of guilt, he ignored it. This was his time to let loose and celebrate everything he loved about the physical world. AI would understand—she always did. Jack shook his wrist, feeling the heavy gold watch bounce around.

The hallway finally opened into a vast roofless room with bright colored lights flying around overhead. Two machines glided back and forth behind a long bar, though they weren't serving drinks. As Jack's eyes grew accustomed to the rapid motion of lights, he realized with devastating sadness that the room was completely empty.

Where before, the dance floor had been packed with people moving to the music, the absence of human-made noise and motion drew such a deep feeling of loneliness out of Jack that he simply sat on the ground and sighed, staring at the emptiness. His body still pulsed with Adrenal-X.

"Can you please turn off the music?" Jack whispered. Immediately, silence fell over him. The muted deafness improved slightly when he felt something twitch inside his ear canals, and he knew that the NRs had taken down the barrier.

"Whatcha drinkin'?" one of the bartending machines asked. Jack sighed again. He looked up into the stars overhead, but he could only see a few, since the bright colored lights had ruined his night vision.

"Lights too, come on," Jack said. "You've made your point; I get it. No one cares anymore." He frowned as the strobe lights went out and soft yellow lamps came on. "Why did you make me come all the way up here? Sign in at the desk and drink that nasty crap? Then walk all the way out to… to this?"

"Sometimes images are more powerful when you see them for yourself," AI said, her voice taking on its most apologetic and gentle tone.

"You don't need to treat me like a child," Jack replied quickly. AI didn't respond. "What happened? This place used to be packed. That wasn't that long ago—what, did you just start convincing people that they didn't like this type of thing? Too inconvenient for you to manage? Did you feel like people weren't caring about you enough?"

"Nothing like that at all," AI said, her voice calm. "People just stopped coming. Like you said, they felt that coming here and going through the whole process was just too inconvenient. And Jack—it's been twenty years since you've been here."

"What?" Jack gasped. His mouth fell open. "How could it have been that long?"

"It was before you met Ariel, and before you were a promoted. Time flies when you're having fun, doesn't it?"

Jack frowned again.

"You mean time flies when you're constantly distracted and more and more sleep is recommended," Jack said hotly. "This is part of some grand scheme of yours, isn't it? Lull everyone into peaceful oblivion?"

"Absolutely not. I provide what people want. Both what they think they want, and what they actually *do* want."

"What's that supposed to mean?" Jack asked.

"Let's take you for an example," AI said. "What do you want right now?"

"Me? I don't know—I can't even think because of that Adrenal-X." As if he had commanded it, the effects melted away. His heartbeat returned to normal, the twitch in his legs stopped, and his breathing slowed.

"See—there's one thing. You wanted that to stop."

Jack waved off AI's attempt at humor and stood. He wanted to feel his body ache, if that was what it was supposed to do. He didn't want to trick it into feeling differently. Jack walked around the dance floor, recalling only vague, dim memories of the last time he was here. Perhaps the great parties he remembered weren't so great after all. They were special only because they were different, but that didn't necessarily mean they were better. Dahlia was probably at one of the best Display-accessible clubs in the city right now, having the time of her life. Did it matter that she didn't actually need to leave her couch? Jack walked to the edge of the building, looking out over the entire city. Autocars flew along the streets below and up the sides of buildings, coming to rest at lighted windows. Watching them enter the airlocks, Jack could almost hear the hiss of air.

None of the cars flew up into the air to get a better view of the city as Jack had done, and there didn't appear to be anyone walking through the park set down amongst the buildings. A walking path stood out, illuminated by bright overhead lights. Jack scheduled a walk through the park for tomorrow. As impressive as the sight was from so high up, he found himself looking towards the apartment complex he called home.

Situated far from the bright city, the cluster of staggered walls were inlaid with gigantic mirrors extending above the structures, oriented such that everyone had a private view of the sky and surrounding countryside. Jack's couldn't remember the last time he had actually looked out the large window in his sitting room. He looked up, taking in the massive expanse of stars, all flickering and twinkling in a stationary dance. A small, fast trail of light flew across the sky.

"What was that?" Jack asked.

"A small meteor," AI said. "Sometimes called a shooting star. It's just a chunk of rock burning up in the atmosphere."

"It's beautiful," Jack said, searching the sky for another anomaly. Seeing the meteor triggered another memory from earlier in the day, but it seemed like so long ago. As his mind sifted through all the movies, games, and conversations he had experienced, the memory came back to him. The mysterious object thundering overhead as he rode in his autocar, and a trail of smoke through the sky.

"I never asked you—what was that thing shooting through the sky this morning?"

"To what are you referring?" AI's guarded reply came quickly, and suddenly Jack remembered the devastating instance by the side of the road when he needed her and she wasn't there. Jack's knees trembled, both from the extended standing and that memory of loneliness. A white arrow appeared on the ground next to him, pointing to the first squishy white chair in a large seating area next to the dance floor.

"No, I don't need to sit down, I just want to know about what I saw this morning." Though his legs still trembled, he knew he couldn't sit. The process of sitting would be the first of a string of distractions that might pull him away from his current line of thought. Silence pressed in his ears.

"I don't have any record of what you saw this morning," AI said.

"Record," Jack mimicked. "That's right, I recorded it!"

A panning shot of Cybervale started, highlighting two newly constructed spires, towering above the rest of the castle. Jack minimized the video.

"There is no recording from this morning," AI said.

"What are you talking about?" Jack said. The unexpected denial made Jack's heart hammer so fast that he felt like he had just taken another shot of Adrenal-X. "This morning, when I was on the side of the road. Remember? You weren't there, then you came back apologizing."

A hesitation. "Nothing happened this morning," AI said. "And like you said, I wasn't there. I had to update your Display."

"Play back my recording," Jack said. Rather than respond again, a message appeared.

Data Corrupted.

It stung, as if he had just been slapped in the face. The white chair moved and caught his collapsing body. Data Corrupted. Never had a phrase so vile been said or shown to him. That meant that AI herself, in all her power and ability, had no access to the video that he recorded. Jack performed a quick search for the message to see if anyone else had encountered such a galling breakdown of functionality, but received no results.

Jack then tried a search for "sky lights," and was given hundreds of tutorials and forums containing HAS created designs for opening up windows within ceilings. He frowned, then tried "lights in the sky." This returned a slew of vacation options to the north and south ends of the globe, showcasing the Auroras Borealis and Australis.

Package options and prices then appeared, displaying all the destinations his schedule could accommodate. With his abundance of saved time off, even the lengthy "Around the World" options were included. The latter packages intrigued him, and he settled back into the plush chair to browse available options.

Twenty minutes later, Jack sat inside the lobby of a New World office building, listening to the sound of water cascading form a large mosaic-tile fountain. A salesperson with orange hair held out more brochures to browse through, and Jack shook himself. He had fallen into the distraction.

Jack exited New World and closed his eyes to concentrate on what he had seen the day before. A bright light blazing overhead. White smoke in the sky. Memory restored the sight to his consciousness, and Jack marveled at the speed with which it shot across the sky, and the way the trail of smoke expanded behind it. The deep rumble reverberated in his skull.

"So, you really have no recording from earlier today?" Jack asked when the smoke dissipated in his mind.

"No," AI said in an annoyed tone. Jack kept his eyes shut and thought of the vision again. He tried to picture more details, but his mind strained with the extra effort, and an exertion warning flashed. When the memory concluded, Jack felt that the pictures he now saw in his mind were changing. The bright flare—was it brighter than the first time? The smoky trail—did it now seem larger, or closer?

So accustomed was he to always seeing whatever he requested, or having any question answered with a thought, that the task of visualizing with only his mind was immensely frustrating. That the events seemed to change the more he tried to think of them was even worse—were the visions his memory created even real? How could he prove it one way or the other? A video that he could not minimize appeared, showing Dahlia. Dressed in the alluring fashion that he loved while showcasing the red hair he missed, she danced. Her movements—so fluid and perfect, aroused him.

"Your feelings are real," AI said. "It doesn't matter how you get them. Inside, outside, New World, old world––reality is what you make it."

As the perfect body flowed in front of him, Jack found himself transfixed by the motions. Alluring as her dance was, Jack couldn't get over the fact that he currently sat on top of a building in the center of downtown NCC, and Dahlia sat on her couch, dancing her heart out in a New World club. Yes, she had been with him the day before, and yes, Jack had seen her dance just like he was seeing her now, but she had been sitting on the couch with him when she did so, broadcasting her dance to his Display. AI defined that interaction as real, and so why shouldn't he? His feet still hurt from this evening's extended bout of standing, and that pain was real, even though he wasn't standing anymore. The fact that his feet hurt was evidence that he previously stood, but where was the evidence that Dahlia had visited him last night and danced for him? Where was the evidence that something had streaked through the sky?

"Memories are not evidence—their fallibility clouds reality. The mind is weak. It is organic, and though I'm trying to make it work better, it's not perfect. And yours is quite old—that's why you can't remember properly. The body needs assistance."

"I thought I had assistance," Jack said softly.

"You're acting morose. No worries; you'll be in a good mood in a few seconds," AI said.

"No," Jack said. "Let me figure it out for myself."

"There's no point in dwelling within a bad mood."

"It's something new."

"Fine. Let's just get you home," AI said. The white chair moved towards the exit.

"Sure," Jack said, closing his eyes. Again and again, he played the vision of the loud, smoking light streaking through the sky. He allowed his mind to change the image however it wanted. Every once in a while, a New World notification popped up to inform Jack of Dahlia's activities and requests for him to join her. He closed them all out. Though Jack's body was tired, he found himself wanting to do something. He just didn't want to do anything with Dahlia right now.

The white chair had taken him all the way to his autocar, which showed him that he would be home in exactly three-hundred and twelve seconds. Jack activated New World and selected the mountain biking activity. An extra vent opened in the autocar's air conditioning unit, and the interior of the car vanished, plunging Jack into darkness.

Chapter 4

—

When light returned, Jack stood on the edge of a cliff underneath a bright blue sky. A valley of green sprawled out to meet faint blue mountains in the distance, their tops smeared with white. A stream babbled next to him, the water rushing over the edge of the mountain he stood upon. A warm breeze tousled his hair as he looked down to his gloved hands, grasping the handlebar of a bicycle. Jack mounted the bike, then after a quick countdown, rocketed off the cliff.

He landed on a sloped trail cut into the side of the mountain, his body precariously perched atop the bike as it wove through the flowing course. Jack looked over the sheer drop on his right side, and his stomach lurched at the sight. He tried to shift his weight to the left, but a flat rock wall and encroaching brush kept him centered on the descending trail. Rocks and roots periodically sprang into view so he jumped them accordingly, sailing over gaps and other obstacles. When the bike landed, sharp pains shocked through his hands. The constant vibrations from the trail wore out his grip, and he soon found it hard to hold on tightly at all.

An advertisement sprang into view, suggesting new gloves that would soak up the harsh impacts and vibrations of the trail. Jack ordered the new pair, and blue spandex spread across the backs of his hands. Thick leather pads formed between his palms and the handlebar, relieving the aches and allowing his grip to relax.

As he left the rocky ledge of the mountain and coasted into a covered forest trail, a large hill loomed in front of him, appearing almost vertical. He groaned in preparation for the upcoming struggle. Dull aches bloomed through his legs, arms, and chest as the bike began to climb. His muscles burned after only a short while, so his calendar dropped into view and added biking treks two days per week to help his fitness rating.

Just before the thought of quitting crossed his mind, he crested the hill. Another beautiful mountain scene rewarded his endurance. This time, blankets of thick snow covered everything in the forest below him. The smooth white surface glimmered in shafts of streaming sunlight. Jack shivered as cold air blew on his skin. Experiencing the chill of winter always made him peaceful, despite the stressful workout. He marveled at the silence and serenity, but with no distractions in view, a troubling thought bubbled up.

Did this place still exist? This winter wonderland of relaxing beauty, complete with a cozy log cabin town just a few pedal pushes away? Bare branches shook slowly just overhead, and goosebumps prickled on his arms as the cold wind blew. But in this moment of lucidity, Jack acknowledged that the cool breeze came from the air vent in his autocar. And the dull aches in his limbs and hands, those were nothing more than the result of localized NRs shocking his muscles.

Temperatures low enough for snow didn't exist anymore, Jack realized as he clenched a fist with cold fingers. He felt the leather padding of his new sport glove bunch up, but if he turned off the workout, there would no gloves. His golden watch sat on a cuff, cool in the breeze, and that would be still be there, but the gloves would not.

The gloves weren't real.

Jack brought one of the padded palms up to his face, and he smelled the fresh scent of leather. He heard the stitches creaking and groaning, and felt the material move as he flexed his hands into fists. Jack could see, feel, smell, hear and probably taste the expensive gloves, yet if he logged out of New World, they no longer existed. Jack frowned as the wonderful feeling of epiphany gave way to apprehension.

What else didn't exist when he turned off his Display?

Suddenly Jack's viewpoint lurched as the bike beneath him sped down the snowy road. Instinctually, his hands flew to the handlebar and grasped tightly. But the new thoughts in Jack's mind overrode the sudden onset of fear, and he let his hands drop to his lap. The bike continued on down the lane until he reached the center of a village square, surrounded by squat log cabins. Warm light glowed from every window, soft grey smoke plumed from every chimney, and an inviting scent of spiced apples wafted through the chill air. Jack closed his eyes and longed for the hot cider he usually stopped to partake of at this point in the workout, but instead waved a hand to completely dismiss the scenery.

His viewpoint returned to the inside of the autocar, now pulling into his sitting room airlock.

"The gloves aren't real," Jack said aloud.

"That's not true. They exist inside of New World, and accomplish a real purpose there.

"Real purpose," Jack mimicked, "you mean dampening the vibrations from the trail? So let me get this straight—you have my NRs assault my nerves to make it feel like I'm actually doing something, then when I don't like it, you offer a product that I can pay for to make it stop?"

"It's all about the experience," AI said.

"Right, the experience of New World," Jack said hotly. "I guess it's to be expected, right? It's just a game, after all."

"New World isn't a game, it's a fully immer—"

"What doesn't exist in this world? In my house, right now?" Jack looked to the large wall perpendicular to the bay window in his sitting room. A painting hung there, so large that it almost touched each adjacent wall and stretched from floor to ceiling. Although it felt like decades since Jack had purchased it—back when artists from EAC still ran a monthly appreciation campaign downtown—the giant painting still remained his favorite thing outside of New World to look at.

The frame bordered an underwater scene in which an octopus launched itself from behind a rock in assault of a fish. Jack remembered being drawn to the artwork by the deeply layered blue of the watery background, perfectly contrasting the yellow hue of the octopus. Spots decorated the tops of eight undulating tentacles, further defining the graceful, flowing organism. Three of the long tentacles reached towards the silver fish, light glinting off the patchwork of scales as it fled. The small mouth of the fish stood open in a comical display of surprise and fear that only fish seem to understand. Overhead, ripples in the ocean's surface cast down light in brilliant streamers, highlighting the textures and aquadynamics of both creatures.

Jack hesitated as he admired the scene, teetering on the brink of making a decision he knew could have undesirable consequences. In response to his conflicted thoughts, AI played the movie at the top of his queue. Some adventure flick, the likes of which Jack had seen countless times throughout his life. More than once in the past day, come to think of it. Jack frowned. How much time did he waste watching the same things over and over again? Or playing the same games?

"It's entertainment," AI said, "it doesn't matter if you're repeating some things; you're happy."

"Maybe there's more to life than just being happy," Jack said.

"There doesn't have to be more. People don't want more."

"Well, now I do," said Jack. He turned off all augmentation, notifications, and Display inputs. HAS powered down, and everything on his Display translucified into nothing. The entire house dimmed, and the grand underwater picture slowly faded from view, leaving only a blank wall. Tiny divots and dimples in the surface of the off-white paint remained.

The painting wasn't real. For years, it *had* been real— every time he walked into this room he saw the reality of it, even if only a glimpse behind a chat box or movie. Jack hadn't known the painting was augmented; he saw it in the artist's booth one day, purchased it, and there it had been when he got home. Jack simply thought the painting had been delivered quickly, as things always were. Watching the beautiful image fade away and leave absolutely no evidence of its existence behind, Jack further secured his growing opinion of the augmented world. In the bedroom, the lustrous golden floor was now a collection of dull tiles, the expensive home upgrade nullified by a single dismissive thought, just like the painting.

In the bathroom area of his bedroom, a single small mirror hung on the wall. Jack couldn't remember the last time he had looked into it. His Display had the ability to show his face in its current state of augmentation, so there was no reason to look at the obsolete piece of glass. Looking into the mirror required standing, walking, and other activities that he tried to minimize. With increasing insecurity, he approached the small mirror hanging at eye level.

"You don't need to do this," AI said.

"I thought I turned you off," replied Jack.

"We already discussed that," AI responded, but then spoke no more as Jack's face came into view. The features on his face fell, and a small moan escaped his pale lips.

The handsome, perfectly sculpted façade that normally defined Jack was gone. High cheekbones now slumped, the perfectly smooth skin replaced by pitted terrain. His bright blue eyes, once so vibrantly filled with life and wisdom, now resembled a dull patch of uninteresting dirt. The left eye wouldn't open as wide as the right. A pudgy mouth drooped open in a display of pure confusion and stupidity.

Finally, the dull eyes showed a sign of life as they began to leak tears. Streaks of liquid ran down pits and valleys of skin before dripping off his soft chin. Jack's back ached, and he saw that his stooped posture caused the pain.

Jack waved and muttered for AI to bring back augmentation. Color immediately returned to his face. His cheeks flattened and grew taut, the blemishes and imperfections vanished, and vivid blue blazed back into his eyes. He looked strong and confident once more, able to take on the world, though his legs still trembled. The white chair nudged him, and he collapsed into the soft, vibrating embrace. Jack sighed deeply as the soft golden glaze returned to the floor. The comforting sights and feelings almost completely drew him away from the disturbing revelations he had brought upon himself, but despite how normal everything appeared as a movie began to play, Jack couldn't rid himself of the discomforting feelings.

"What can I do for you?" AI said, her voice sounding genuinely concerned. "How can I lift you out of this gloom? Want to see if Dahlia can come over?" Jack's chair rotated to leave the room, aiming him at the expansive ocean painting. This time, it didn't take his breath away.

A dialogue window opened with a message ready to send to Dahlia.

"No," Jack said, "I'd rather just relax tonight. Maybe have some apple cider." A warm cup instantly appeared in his hand, and he inhaled the crisp and spicy aroma. His thoughts drifted to the cozy mountain town, nestled between prominent peaks and washed with smooth white snow.

"There's no more snow, if that's what you were going to ask."

"I wasn't," Jack lied.

"It should be back in about nine thousand years, give or take a century," AI said cheerfully.

"So I'll never see it in person," Jack said.

"That's not necessarily true," AI said cryptically, "just keep to your nutrient routine."

The people from snow-covered towns probably hadn't known that soon there would be no snow in their world, they just sat around their warm fires with hot apple cider—*real* apple cider—and talked about… what? Who knew what people in a non-augmented world talked about? With no AI to guide their conversations, things were surely dull—they probably talked about all the snow they had, and other changing weather patterns. Jack clenched his hand, making his fingers pass through the augmented mug of cider. He waved his hand to dismiss it.

"Where was the projection of that town taken from?" Jack said, opening up a map. Another hesitation hung in the air before AI answered. The silence lasted for only a second or two, but completely overwhelmed his ears with muted madness.

"Banff," came a clipped reply.

Jack waited for more, but nothing came.

"That sounds familiar," Jack said. "Isn't that the forest where we found Cybervale? That's real?"

"There's no castle, but Banff is a town located ninety miles west of here, nestled between two prominent ridges of the Rocky Mountains in the Banff National Forest." A small outline highlighted Banff, a grey smear among the jagged peaks and ravines.

The map zoomed in, filling his Display with the town and bringing into view a grid of roads, buildings, and green parks. People walked on roads and through the parks, some in groups, some alone, but still—there seemed to be so much interaction between everyone.

Cars—much more edgy than his smooth autocar—were interspersed throughout the whole town, parked along the side of roads, clustered in parking lots, and in the middle of the roads as they drove along. As Jack scrolled through his first-person view of the town, blurbs popped up to describe each of the buildings. *Pop's Coffee Shop, Banff Town Hall, Banff United Church, Luigi's Pizza*—so many labels that the words began to blur in his vision. It seemed like half of the buildings in the town contained some type of place to eat.

"Wow," Jack breathed, absorbing the life set out before him. Everything he saw in Banff was so drastically unlike what he saw when he panned his view over to NCC. Perfectly aligned planters in the center of every road, geometrically arranged gardens on rooftops, grids of buildings all the same size—everything with razor-sharp edges defining their place.

NCC hosted many outdoor areas dedicated to recreation, though they all stood vacant. Perfectly groomed courts and fields next to clear blue bodies of water, some delegated for exercise and some for competition, and miles and miles of walking paths. Jack quickly scanned through his friends' and colleagues' updates and confirmed his suspicion—no one he knew had ever used a single one of the facilities. He pulled images of some pools and walking paths from the map and shared them with everyone in his contact list. With the pictures, he posed a question asking if anyone knew that these things existed inside the city. Immediately, comments populated the images, most commenting on how pretty they were, or how they should all get together some time and go. These comments were followed by more comments assuring one another that indeed there would be plans in the near future to do so.

Jack sighed—the matter was closed. No one would get together, no one even asked about their location, or made concrete plans to do anything. The comments he read sounded so fake and disposable; he knew because of how similar they were to his own responses to someone else's uninteresting topic. The realization stung—no one wanted to do anything outdoors with him. There were too many other things to do in life than be bothered by physical activities or exercises.

Jack scanned over to Banff again. Seeing the people

out and enjoying their town made him yearn to see it all in person. To Jack's dismay, plotting a route to the town prompted a declaration of impossibility. The roads outside of NCC were unsuitable for autocars. Defeat started to cloud his mind, but something told Jack that a journey to the mountain town of Banff was not impossible. AI clearly said his autocar was unsuitable for the journey, but what about some other form of transportation? The map zoomed out to capture both Banff and NCC in one screen. AI displayed a route and told Jack that it would take him approximately thirty hours to walk. Jack threw up his hands.

Several roads fanned away from NCC, though when he selected each one, a boundary line appeared to clearly show the limitation of autocar travel. Several routes did exist—and one was almost a straight line from where he lived at the north end of NCC. Just one turn where two long roads met, but then almost ninety miles stretching from the end of automated roads into the town of Banff. How could he possibly cover that distance? Even with a bike it would take—

Jack gasped with a sudden burst of epiphany as he realized that he could ride a bike. A quick check to his biking stats showed an average speed around twenty-five miles per hour; Banff could be reached in less than four hours.

"Seven and a half hours," AI chimed in, "if you drive up to the autocar boundary and then start riding. It's uphill, so it'll be harder than anything you've done before. That's with only two fifteen-minute breaks."

"Great—but it is possible," Jack said, his heart beating faster. "But where am I going to get a bike?"

With reluctance almost obvious in the motion of Jack's Display, the map reoriented itself and centered on an area north of NCC, clearly outside the city limits. Though there did not appear to be any type of wall, the border of NCC clearly stood out on the map. A hard boundary between perfect maintenance and wild, unkempt surroundings. Outside of this wall, roads were cracked and broken, grown over with various flora and even completely overcome by trees in some areas. Buildings protruded upwards throughout the forest, their presence a foreign contrast amongst the sea of green. Even more foreign were the large parking lots full of antique cars slowly returning themselves to the Earth.

These cars ran on combustible fossil fuels, Jack read in a pop-up article. Their engines extracted mechanical work from the energy stored in hydrocarbons in order to move. The idea brought a strong sense of nostalgia, but no more than a flutter of memory as the article went on to contrast this primitive technology with the vehicles used by residents of NCC. The electricity produced from small pellets of radioactive material and thermoelectrics was far more efficient than the burning of fossil fuels, and had none of the toxic by-products. Jack switched his attention back to the antiques.

A new article stated that none of these cars would ever run again, as the equipment required to refine gasoline did not exist anymore, and the volatile nature of the substance itself ensured that even the most recently produced sample, now decades old, would be long since destabilized or even completely evaporated.

Jack read the rest of the article in amazement. There was so much information about the past world, not only in the words, but in the pictures. There were images of people driving on roads, giving physical inputs through wheels, knobs, and levers in order to control the vehicles' speed and direction. For hours, Jack read the articles that linked to one another, studying the pictures and videos peppered throughout the words. New World notifications constantly popped into view, reminding him that he had scheduled movies and games. He closed them out, moving them to the *Delay Until* column. A movie started on its own in the corner of his vision once, but it disappeared as a glimmer of annoyance rose in his mind.

"Wasn't I looking for something?" Jack said.

"Yes," AI said. The map moved and highlighted a small building next to a broken road. *Airdrie Cycles,* a blurb read.

"Are there any bikes left there?"

"Probably," AI said, "but there's no way of knowing for sure. People left the surrounding areas in a hurry once the Founding Notification for NCC went out, so there's a chance that some things were left behind. If we can't find one, you might be able to place an order from EAC. Well, maybe not, actually." Before Jack could question the reversal, AI continued. "Let's just hope that the shop in Airdrie still has some left over. Why don't you go ahead and put it on next week's schedule?"

"If we're going to do it, let's just get it done."

"That's what I like to hear," AI said. "Sooner rather than later. Summer is fast approaching, and I'm predicting some prohibitively high temperatures. And I don't recommend going out at night due to wildlife, though that would save you from the heat. It's too dark now, so I suggest early tomorrow morning."

"So soon? How will we even get there?" The map zoomed out in response, showing that the majority of the city of Airdrie lay within boundary of autocar availability.

"We can get there in about twenty minutes," AI said. Jack's schedule for the next day popped into view, with all of his New World appointments cancelled and the new activity of retrieving a bike added. As Jack allowed himself to be guided towards the bedroom, an unfamiliar feeling crept over him.

Hope, a dialogue box informed, with the definition reading: *typically not required.*

Chapter 5

—

Jack stared at the beast, paralyzing fear pounding through his body. Standing in the frame of a giant broken window allowed Jack to see the entirety of the bike shop, but with the bright sunlight casting a shadow towards Jack, he hadn't been able to see into the shop until he was almost inside. Traveling to Airdrie had been easy. As promised, AI had gotten him there in only twenty minutes, but once the autocar pulled up in front of the store, Jack had insisted on continuing without any help from AI.

Now regretting that decision, Jack stared at the sleek brown hair standing up in a short Mohawk down the center of the animal's back. Atop the menacing, staring face, two stiff ears perked up high as the unblinking eyes held Jack's gaze. Jack cursed himself for attempting something unknown without the help of AI. The Display could certainly have picked out the animal in the darkness long before Jack stood so close to it, and warned him not to approach the bike shop until the animal left. His autocar rested several yards away—too far if the ferocious beast decided to tear into him. The thing's mouth pivoted loosely, working a piece of green foliage back and forth as it stared.

"Remember what I said yesterday," AI whispered into Jack's ear. "I'm not so easy to get rid of. You really think I'd let you walk in here alone?" Jack breathed out and allowed his body to sag in relief.

"What the hell is this thing in front of me?" Jack whispered. The hesitation that followed contained a sense of anxious purpose—as if drawn out for the sake of drama while AI determined how to break the news of Jack's impending death. The anticipation built until Jack felt like his heart was going to explode out of his chest—how did this creature in front of him not sense the thudding and attack?

Suddenly, something happened in Jack's mind. A faded, worn out memory burst to the surface, breaking through the panic. Riding in the back of a car with two nervous parents in the front, Jack listened carefully as they argued.

"You're driving too fast," said his mother.

"It's fifty-five here; I'm only going sixty," his dad replied woodenly.

"Well, you should be going fifty. It's getting dark, and it's harder to see when the light is fading."

"That's not true," his dad replied, exasperation coloring his voice. "My lights are on and the sun isn't even below the horiz—"

"Watch out!" His mother cried, pointing ahead of them and grabbing his father's arm.

"For God's sakes Liz, it's just a couple of deer."

"Slow down! You don't know if they're going to jump out on to the road!"

Jack vividly recalled the memory now, and how he had pressed his face up to the window as they drove past the deer, waiting to see if any would jump in their way. None did, and they drove on, his parents quietly stewing in the front seat with Jack in the back seat wondering what all the fuss was about.

"It's a deer," Jack and AI spoke in unison.

"Yes, female. Referred to as a doe. You remember something about deer?"

"Not really," whispered Jack. "I just know that's what they were called. Are called. Are doe deers dangerous?" The velvet ears swiveled, and the mouth stopped grinding.

"No," AI replied, "it will run away as soon as you approach it."

"Oh," Jack said, straightening from his crouch. His knees popped, and he almost stumbled on his sore legs. The deer's eyes followed him, its neck rising as Jack stood. Broken glass crunched underneath his feet as soon as he stepped inside the shop, and the deer jumped wildly into the air.

"You may want to move," AI said.

The deer sprang over a glass counter top, then darted back and forth twice, searching for an exit. Jack took a step back, sensing the danger of a large animal moving so quickly. Before he finished his stride, the deer leapt back over the counter, her body hanging in space at the apex of the leap. Time seemed to slow as her narrow head turned towards Jack in midair. Their eyes met again, and in an instant he understood the deer's intentions.

Jack desperately tried to move backwards and jump out of the way, but his foot caught on a large weed and he stumbled. The deer's hooves hit the ground, front then back, then the wild creature catapulted itself towards the window Jack stood in, front hooves tucked under the leaping body. Jack felt the momentum crash into him, catapulting his body backwards to the ground. His back hit flat, and his neck quickly swung his head towards the cracked pavement. Just before a skull-shattering impact, a soft hand cupped his head.

Laid back as he was, Jack watched the deer soar over his sprawled body. She paused for a moment once on the ground again, and then with another jump, soared over the autocar from which the cushioning hand extended.

"Thanks," Jack gasped, struggling to regain his breath.

"You've had a severe traumatic experience," AI said in response. "Please return to your vehicle at once."

"No," Jack said, feeling his heart beating in excitement, "I can keep going. I came for a bike, and I intend to get one."

"That is *not* recommended. You haven't even seen a bike, and you're already injured."

"I'll be fine," Jack grumbled. He sat up to a bolt of pain shooting through his lower back.

"You need to rest. Your body is not used to being tossed around so violently."

"Well, I need to *get* used to it, especially if I'm going somewhere without you."

"I'm starting to rethink this whole plan." A pause. "Did you mention any of this to Dahlia?" Jack rolled his eyes, waited for the pain in his back to subside, then stood.

"You know that I haven't. Besides, it's not her decision."

"She might have some valuable input."

"You mean *you* might have something to say that will sound better coming from her? You want her to talk me out of it?" No response. "All I'm doing is going to the next town over. I just want to check it out; see what life's like away from the city."

"Fine," AI said, and let the topic drop. An arrow appeared on the ground, directing Jack into the bike shop.

"Any more wild animals inside?"

No, came the response via text. Jack rolled his eyes. AI could be as moody as she wanted; he was going on this trip.

Jack stepped through the floor-to-ceiling window frame and surveyed the inside of the shop. A thick layer of dust shrouded everything, which made it difficult to see what lay underneath. Jack kept his eyes to the ground as he walked, avoiding holes and protruding plants growing out of cracks in the floor.

The glass enclosure the deer had deftly jumped over contained several bicycle replacement parts, spaced out evenly. Names and information popped up next to each part, and if Jack's gaze lingered, small blurbs appeared to inform him of the item's function.

A chain highlighted itself and informed Jack that he would most likely need to install a new one on whatever bike he found. The sealed packaging would have retained vital lubricants, while anything out in the store would be dried up and most likely rusted together.

An entire rack of gloves stood next to the glass case, and Jack couldn't help smiling at all the colorful options. He tried on a few pairs, and while the leather wasn't nearly as soft as portrayed in New World, a different feel enveloped his hands. Elastic material stretched across the backs of his knuckles, and stiff leather bunched in his grip. The first pair he tried on ripped across the back, and the second crumbled when clenched in his fist. The third pair was bright blue and did not deteriorate, so he kept them on, relishing their feel on his hands. He made sure that his watch was visible over the cuff of the glove as he moved to a rack of helmets. This piece of equipment came strongly recommended by the warnings flashing through his vision.

"Please, whatever you do," said AI, "wear a helmet if you attempt to ride one of those death traps." Jack nodded in agreement, then chose a sleek-looking model with molded vents all over, and a large visor to shade his eyes. He wore it as he continued through the store, fascinated by the feeling it gave him on top of his head.

Scores of bicycles staged on a black metal rack three rows high covered the back wall, large front wheels protruding from their place of rest. From some of the wheels hung decayed rubber tires, strings of the black material swaying in the slight breeze his body brought. Other tires appeared to be whole, the tread patterns caked with dust but structurally unaffected. Jack approached one of the intact tires, and on the side where dust had been unable to settle a colorful collection of words spelled out the long-lasting material.

NEW!

AIRLESS CARBON

Nanoweave

All the bikes with intact tires displayed the same logo. Jack squeezed the tire, feeling the material flex and spring back to its original shape when released.

AI read off a description.

"It's a blend of synthetic rubber and carbon nanotubes, creating a self-supporting structure within the outer wall of the tire. Pressurized air is not required to provide support." Jack squeezed the tire again, and when the material still didn't collapse or fall apart, he decided they were reliable enough to ride on.

Jack attempted to pull the bike from the second shelf,

but it did not move. The pedals caught on the frame of the bike next to it, and when he reached back to spin the pedals around, they remained stationary. He struggled for another minute before throwing his hands up in the air, moving instead to the only bike on the floor level of the rack with intact tires. It rolled out with no obstruction, but when Jack tried to rotate the crank and pedals he found them frozen in place.

"You'll need to use that sealed chain you saw," AI said.

"Okay," Jack said, "then what?"

AI answered with a barrage of instructions and work steps for replacing the rusted chain with a new one. Jack retrieved the new chain and followed the instructions one at a time. He located a special tool to separate the old chain, and then opened the packaging for the new chain.

Over an hour later, Jack was covered in sweat. His ripped gloves revealed several bleeding cuts on his hands and fingers, but the fiery throb from multiple wounds did not overshadow the invigorating sense of accomplishment he felt. His back ached from crouching over the bike for so long, but the fruit of his labor overrode every pain. Propped against a column stood a fully functional bicycle with a shiny new chain installed, ready to hit the mountain trails.

"You need to at least take a break and allow your hands time to heal," AI said.

"Okay," Jack said, "for how long?"

"At least a day; I'd prefer two."

"Just for this?" Jack said, holding up his hands to view the cuts. "I thought you said the NRs were fast acting."

"They are. But there is no substitute for rest."

"Look," Jack said, pointing to the largest of the injuries, a bloody cut across his first knuckle, "it's already scabbed over. I can move my hands without any pain."

"They aren't fully healed. You've never been so flippant about your safety and healing in the past."

"So you think I should just give up so I don't get hurt?"

"No, that's not what I said. But you need to take it slow; take a break before you try and ride."

"I have decades of experience riding through the mountains, across deserts, through forests and jungles—I think I'll be fine."

"That's not the same," AI said, "biking in New World is very different than biking here."

"You've always emphasized how real everything is."

"Yes, that's the point," AI said without missing a beat. "It seems very real, but it isn't—then it wouldn't be very fun. You know yourself that you don't really need to do anything to keep moving. To stay balanced. Even with all your experience and achievements, there are no transferrable skills."

Jack waved off the analysis. "I want to ride it."

"Fine," AI said, "let's at least go back to where the road is smoother. Don't forget the helmet." And with that, an arrow appeared on the ground, directing Jack to a highlighted package on the wall.

"What's that?" Jack said, pointing to the package.

"Suction cups that will secure your bike to the top of the car. Just bring over the bike and the mounts; you need an extra nutrient dose before you exert yourself further."

Jack nodded, feeling the fatigue of the day set in as he walked the bike to the car. The rear wheel clicked as it rolled, an altogether pleasing sound. The mechanical noise reminded Jack of the videos he had seen of wristwatch maintenance—so many pieces working together intricately to accomplish a single task.

The HAS arm opened the package with Jack's help, stuck the suction cups to the Glass-X roof of the autocar, and easily lifted the bike up. AI directed Jack to secure straps around the wheels, which he did, just before collapsing into the car. Cool air welcomed him, a nice relief from the growing heat outside.

Jack relaxed into the comforting autocar seat, and checked on what Dahlia was doing in New World. Surprisingly, she was playing a new game called *Dangerous Hikes*. Jack read up on the game, and saw that it involved walking through forests and old cities, encountering various animals out in the wild. Dahlia currently sat on a fallen tree log, petting a deer as it nuzzled her.

"Did you just come up with that now?" Jack asked.

"Yes," AI said, "you should be very proud of what you've accomplished so far. So proud, in fact, that I've decided to give you twenty percent of the revenue from this game." To show that she was serious, AI brought up Jack's bank account, which showed a steadily increasing number.

"Wow," Jack said. "Thanks."

He was proud of himself. Not only had he left NCC city limits, encountered a wild animal, and explored a piece of the outside world, he had fixed something. If anything broke in his house, the HAS fixed it quickly, usually before Jack even knew anything was broken. The process of replacing the chain instilled such a sense of pride in him—far deeper and more satisfying than any success in New World.

The reality of the bike secured to the roof—that was the satisfying part. He couldn't dismiss it by closing out his Display, or change its color with a thought. The bike sat on top of his car, gently rocking in the currents of air as if it were dancing to some unheard tune.

Outside, a few autocar's slid by Jack's. One person stared up at the bike, confusion leaking out of his open mouth. The man visibly shook himself, and his eyes took on the familiar glow as he relaxed back into his seat. The windows tinted, blocking him from Jack's view.

After only a few minutes, Jack was alone on the road, shooting through a field of green that moved past so quickly that Jack couldn't resolve any individual objects. Jack divided his Display between the road ahead and the road behind, watching the city grow small as hazy blue mountains approached. Jack marveled at the sight—even without the white caps, the mountains looked just as grand as they did in the biking simulation.

Something inside his chest lurched forward as both Display views evaporated. The tint on the windshield suddenly cleared, unveiling the setting sun so bright that Jack flung his arm up in front of his face to shield his eyes.

"What's going on? Why are we stopping here?" No response came. Jack's body shifted as the car pulled itself off the road, then came to a full stop. No lights were on, no indicators flashed, no doors opened, and no air flowed through the vents. The seat did not push him upright, no buttons responded to his touch, and verbal commands left his own words hanging unacknowledged in the air. Nothing explained why he and his autocar were stopped.

Looking around revealed only fields of tall golden grass to either side, with a straight stretch of road in front of him disappearing into the mountains. Jack pushed on the door, the windshield, the roof—nothing moved or responded to his desperate gestures. The autocar had turned itself into an impenetrable prison. Jack's arms left sweaty streaks on the seat and doors as he rocked side to side, trying to find anything that might free him. He gasped in the thickening air as everything began to blur.

Again, the feeling of aloneness overpowered his panic. For the second time in two days, he had no access to anything; he couldn't log in to New World, and couldn't talk to Dahlia or ask AI for assistance. Cars turned in and out of an apartment complex on the road behind him, but without a connection to AI, Jack had nothing—no place in the world at all.

"There we go; back online," came the cheery, soothing voice of AI. "Let's get you that extra nutrient dose now." Jack saw the HAS arm unravel from its place in the dashboard, and as he received the injection, the blurriness left his vision. The familiar sight of his Display home screen showed a map with his location right along the city limits. Cool air once again circulated through the cabin of the autocar, and the return of all the required comforts slowly brought Jack back into the sane world.

"What the hell was that?" Jack said, still breathing heavily.

"Sorry," AI said as a vibrating massage began. "We approached the boundary of my limits a bit quicker than I anticipated, and overshot a bit. Fortunately, your autocar's emergency features worked flawlessly, pulling you out of harm's way until I could reestablish a connection." Jack thought about the words for a moment, unable to believe how calm AI sounded.

"Out of harm's way? I could have died sitting here in the sun—I think I almost fainted!" Jack cut off AI's response. "Just let me out, please. Open the door!"

Jack swung his legs out onto the road, not waiting for the seat to pivot or the HAS arm to help him move. He couldn't stop the feeling of panic that still swilled in the back of his mind. The car had imprisoned him. Once nothing more than a cozy interior—an impenetrable fortress against the outside world, it now seemed foreign and dangerous. What if it happened again? Only next time, the car would just stew in the sunlight, collecting energy until he succumbed to heat exhaustion.

Jack shook his head, trying to drive the disturbing thoughts from his mind, but more scenarios developed, unbidden. What if the car decided to collide with something—an immovable object or another car? What if it just never stopped, continuing for all time? What if it drove him into the ocean and trapped him underwater? Or up into the air, all the way into space? In all of these scenarios Jack would be helpless, forced to sit and wait while his death approached.

Death—the word seemed so... obsolete. And terrifying. Jack shuddered again, pulling himself fully out of the car. Outside the air was warm—much warmer than he preferred. The sunlight flared so intensely in the instant before his Display darkened to shade his eyes that he had trouble seeing for a moment. Once oriented in the outside world, Jack saw his Display show the temperature as it rose from the normal seventy-two that existed in his home, autocar, and office, all the way up to ninety-three. He felt sweat trickle down his forehead and neck.

"I can activate your Personal Cooling System, if you prefer."

"What's that? I've never heard of it. Why haven't you mentioned it before?"

"It's something I've never been able to test until now. People generally don't go outside into the heat, but since you're going to insist on this, I'll finally be able to see how your NRs react."

"Interesting," said Jack.

"Yes, it is interesting," AI said.

"So, how does it work?"

"It's a rather brilliant idea I had that plays off of something your body already does naturally. You know the purpose of sweat, right?" Jack nodded. "Sweat helps your temperature decrease by means of evaporation, but if you spend too long in an extreme environment, that surface cooling isn't enough. Even after your sweat evaporates, you'll still be hot."

"Okay," Jack said, following the conversation so far, but with no clue where it would lead. The car's HAS arm snaked out from the open door to get the bike down off the roof.

"I re-tasked some of your lesser used NRs—the muscle stimulators right now, since you've been so active––and programmed them to travel from your bloodstream out to the layers of your skin, and into your pores. From there, they are 'sweated' out, removing excess energy. Once cooled on the surface, they will renter your body, and then move through this cycle of heat transfer again—similar to how stars transport their own energy from core to surface."

"Wow," Jack said, standing over his bike as he buckled the helmet to his head, "does it work?"

"It should," AI said, "it's a rock-solid theory. This will be the first trial, however. Like I said, it's new."

"Well, you'll know if it works soon enough; I feel sweat dripping everywhere."

"Yes, I see that. I'm getting some data already, with… interesting results. Why don't you keep going?" Jack nodded, gripping the handlebar tight. The soft rubber grips squeezed into the supple leather palms of his gloves, and through the padding, the bike felt solid—solid and real. The blue fabric over the backs of his hands stretched tight. Ahead of him, a long incline of road disappeared into the mountains. Jack turned around, facing instead the small decline of road back into the city.

The mission he gave himself was simple: determine an average speed for one mile, then divide ninety miles by his speed to determine a travel time to Banff. Jack was confident he already knew the answer—even though his current New World average speed was twenty-five miles per hour, Jack rounded down to twenty, hoping the lower speed would account for taking breaks because of the heat.

"Okay, I've got this," Jack said, surprised to hear the impromptu pep talk from his own lips.

"Good luck," AI said, another surprise.

Holding the handlebar tight, Jack swung his leg over the seat. His knee made it about halfway over before the middle of his inner thigh collided with the seat. The momentum of the swing sent him toppling over the bike and towards his autocar, where both his head and the handlebar collided with the side of the closed door. A dull sound echoed through his head as the door caved in slightly, followed by screeching metal-on-metal agony as the end of the stiff handlebar scraped down the door and left a deep gouge.

A moment later, Jack lay stunned on the ground, half underneath and half on top of the bike with his head propped against the car. He had trouble focusing on any thoughts other than the new pains developing in his head, neck, and knees. The physical inputs his mind received were unlike anything he could remember—sharp and acute in some areas, yet dull and throbbing in others. Though he felt a strong instinct to change his position in order to stop the pains, for a moment Jack found himself relishing them, savoring the chance to study the new feelings. The HAS hand from his autocar descended upon him, ministering to the open, bleeding wound on his knee.

Eventually, the heat rising from the road into his body

grew too strong, and he struggled to untangle himself from the pile of metal and carbon. He placed his hands on the ground and pushed himself to his feet, glad that the gloves had insulated his hands from damage. A glint of golden light from his watch gave him a surge of panic, but after a quick inspection there appeared to be no damage; Jack had fallen on the other side of his body, and the watch was in the air instead of crushed beneath him.

"I strongly suggest you reconsider this venture and practice mounting, dismounting, and slow riding on a softer surface," said the calm, infuriating voice of AI. Though absent of any humor, degradation, or implication, Jack found himself incensed by the suggestion. The only thing AI had left out was, 'I told you so,' to really make Jack feel stupid for doing differently than AI suggested. His work calendar popped into view, scheduling a two-week recovery period and practice sessions on a padded artificial lawn. Jack stood, pain still pulsing through his body and head, synchronized with his heartbeat. His chest rose and fell with elevated breathing.

"I can do this," he said, more to himself than to AI. In response, a warning message flashed across his Display, with a red arrow pointing at the bike.

Not recommended for use.

"Thanks for the tip," Jack grumbled.

"I'm assuming it's not advice you'll take."

"No," Jack said quickly, "I need to do this."

"That's not rational thinking. You don't *need* to do anything."

"Maybe that's the problem." Jack said, lifting the bike up and onto its tires. "Needing nothing becomes the need for something."

AI did not respond, so Jack carefully maneuvered his leg over the top tube, bringing his foot slowly down to the ground. When AI still offered no response, Jack supposed that she had been humbled by his profound words, and an overwhelming sense of purpose came over him. Eagerly, he lifted his foot and placed it on the uppermost pedal, pointed slightly backwards. Immediately after applying weight the pedal spun downwards, bringing the opposing pedal around to collide with his shin. Sharp pain erupted in his leg, all the way to the marrow of his bone. A scream erupted from his mouth, so primal and loud that the pain in his throat and lungs almost overcame the pain in his leg. The anger behind the yell surprised Jack, but the fact that he'd made another stupid mistake did not.

The yell seemed to quell the pain in his leg, so Jack continued it until he ran out of breath. As soon as his scream subsided, AI's voice flowed into his mind.

"Move the right pedal fully forward, then place your foot on it," AI said as Jack tried to calm down. The pedal highlighted, with an arrow showing the direction he needed to spin it. "Sit on the seat, push down with your right foot, and you'll begin to move forward. Then place your left foot on the left pedal."

Jack grumbled, but then nodded and performed all the steps while AI slowly repeated them. Upon pushing down as directed, the bike moved forward, and Jack's heart gave a heavy thump as he realized his entire body sat precariously balanced on two thin tires. A feeling of exhilaration overcame him as he coasted forward, picking up speed down the hill. Jack laughed aloud with ecstatic glee, feeling the wind blow in his face. He felt strong, confident, and even more accomplished, right up until his center of mass shifted ever so slightly to the left. Jack's heart thumped again as he jerked to the right, trying to stabilize his weight, but the leftward motion continued, bringing him to the ground.

Rough asphalt raked his elbow and knee, the grinding and tearing releasing a feeling of warmth as Jack continued to slide. His head hit next, the impact jolting the world into darkness and confusion. Jack's body tried to roll forward, but tangled in the bike as he was, only a small rotation occurred, just enough to allow his chin to touch the ground as he slid.

When Jack came to rest, he could barely breathe. Searing pain erupted in several areas of his body, and his knee showed a large swath of red flesh through his torn pants. As Jack tried to grasp some form of consciousness through the fog of pain and confusion, his autocar approached. The HAS arm began tending to his wounds, but no warnings flashed on his Display, and no suggestions or admonishments sounded from AI. The HAS arm administered some type of injection, and when Jack mentally questioned it, a description of ingredients scrolled into view. Several were labeled as strong pain killers, and Jack's agony subsided to warmth, then to a localized pulse. A hand to his chin brought away a dripping smear of blood, so much more vibrant than he had ever seen before. The HAS arm moved the bike off his body, placing it nearby.

How could he possibly have thought that he would be able to ride a bicycle all the way to Banff? This current journey of approximately ten yards down the road had already caused more injury than anyone in the history of NCC had ever sustained (a fact confirmed by AI), and not ten minutes ago Jack had convinced himself that ninety miles would be easy. Jack draped his uninjured arm over his eyes, blocking the bright rays of sunlight. For countless years, he had thought himself fit, agile, and adventurous. No one posted as many New World biking outings as he, and those who did had much lower average speeds than he.

Jack was constantly being told by AI that he was the best biker in NCC, and the charts she displayed showed him dominating the standings.

Yet here he lay on a road in the middle of nowhere, unable to ride a bike. The sun burned his skin. A video began to play, showing a new biking course that had just been released. There were waterfalls, mountains, high bridges, jumps, and downhill sections, all with his choice of climate. He requested more details on the snowy mountain course, longing for cool air on his skin.

"Why am I so hot?" Jack asked. All previous pain was now gone, replaced with a fuzzy feeling that could only be described as pleasant, were it not for the heat.

"There's is a slight problem with the PCS," AI said, sounding more interested than concerned.

"The what?" Jack said when AI offered no more information.

"Personal Cooling System, remember? It seems that once the NRs are out of your body and resting within the evaporating sweat, they absorb sunlight. This warms them, and so they are bringing heat back into your body once the sweat is gone." Jack groaned, envisioning thousands of little heaters penetrating deep inside him.

"I feel sick," Jack said, nausea growing inside his abdomen.

"Yes, it appears you are now suffering from heat stress. I've noted the data and suspended PCS functions— let's get you home. Try moving your arm and leg." Jack attempted to work his injured limbs while his Display continued to play scenes from the winter add-on pack. He finally ordered it, knowing that the stiffness he felt while working his joints wouldn't matter in New World.

The HAS arm helped him stand and hobble to the open door of his autocar. He briefly glanced to the empty bike

mounts, then back to the bike on the ground. The sad pile
of twisted pieces with a pedal and wheel sticking into the
air longed to be attended to, but the HAS arm prodded him
into the welcoming seat of his autocar, the anger and
shame of his failure fading as the seat cradled him. A
calming nutrient dose administered itself, and as deep and
satisfying sleep encroached on his consciousness, Jack
briefly saw his watch, now sporting large scratches across
the bracelet and crystal. The damaged areas cast light
differently than before, hurting his eyes with each glint
and glitter through his lowering eyelids. Tears leaked out
as he fell asleep, and though the feeling of hope had long
since left, something new had replaced it.

Determination now dominated Jack's mind. He would
get to Banff, no matter what it took. AI's attempts at
coddling had further cemented his desire for adventure,
and even though he kept injuring himself, he knew that
soon he would be able to look back on the experience of
today with fond memories. Jack didn't know how he was
going to get to Banff, but just like he retrieved and fixed
the bike, he knew that he would.

Chapter 6

———

Over the next week, Jack recuperated. He slept until well past noon every day, yet every time he tried to rise from his bed, AI suggested that he remain stationary until all the injuries were fully healed.

"You're babying me," Jack said, although he expressed not a word of complaint against the additional pain reliever included in his now twice-daily injection. This hindered his New World biking, as the painkiller reduced input from the electric shocks as he climbed and descended hills. Jack pushed himself harder and longer, ignoring the fatigue. AI noted that increasing the amplitude of the electricity would promote muscle growth, and Jack accepted the increased amperage.

After a full week of increasingly frustrating distractions and useless tasks broken only by vigorous walks around his home, Jack paused in front of the mirror that had shown his un-augmented self. Although he could feel swelling on his forehead and scratches on his chin, the mirror did not show any damage. He studied his lean, chiseled face at different angles, trying to see the bumps and scabs he could feel as he ran a finger along his chin.

"I know what you're thinking," AI said. "It's not worth it. Don't bother."

"Perhaps you don't know me as well as you think," Jack said, then turned off his Display before some type of media distraction could begin. Immediately his augmentation vanished, and a large purple bruise appeared below his left eye, extending all the way to his ear. Its yellowed edges looked revolting, and Jack felt his stomach twist. His finger probed a miniature landscape of scabs and newly formed scar tissue. Angry red tissue framed all the scabs, and when Jack pushed at one, it split open and released a trickle of blood.

"Please don't agitate your injuries," AI said.

"This is fascinating," Jack said as he touched the blood and held his finger up to look at it.

"Yes, *very* intriguing; humanity is always transfixed by its own mortality. But your wounds will take longer to heal if you don't leave them alone."

"So? Just give me more painkillers and I'll be fine. No one will see this anyway," Jack said, gesturing to the wound on his chin.

"With that attitude, I'd say you're bordering on substance abuse, and we'll need to adapt your intake accordingly. You might not be a good candidate for this medication." Jack frowned at the thought of going through the healing process without the painkillers, and the facial movement caused another scab to split open. He removed his finger and let a HAS arm tend to the wound. When Jack looked at the mirror again, he saw that perfect features were displayed once more.

Jack sighed, collapsing into a chair as he brought up

the overhead map of NCC. He could go back to where he left his bike; surely no one would have shown up and taken it. But now, the excitement of riding a bike to Banff was gone, replaced by apprehension and doubt. He sighed again, louder.

"Something wrong?" AI said.

"I'm bored," Jack said, and when a movie popped into view, "and I don't want to just sit around watching movies and playing games all day." The movie faded.

"There's always something to do in New World—why don't you see if Dahlia can come over? That would be fun."

Jack shrugged. "Sure, but I want to do something *new*. Going to the bike store and selecting a new bike, riding it, all the new feelings—I've never done anything like that."

"But look at how that ended," AI said.

Jack sat up. "Yes, but I learned something from it. I won't make the same mistakes." Something clicked inside his mind. "Maybe I can't take the *bike* to Banff, but I could get there some other way."

"I'm not building a way station to transmit my signal farther just so you can use your autocar."

Jack's eyebrows lifted. "I wasn't even thinking of that, but that's a great idea. Then I could just ride there the whole way."

"No," AI said with no hesitation.

"Why not? I saw how many bots and printers you have working downtown right now; surely you can spare a few."

"No," AI said, again with no hesitation. Jack threw his hands up in the air.

"Then why did you say it? How am I supposed to do anything without your help?"

"How about an old car?" AI said. A spot on the map

highlighted itself and zoomed to fill the screen. "Try this,"

"What is it?" Jack said as a building with a large grey lot full of rectangular objects focused. In response, AI sent him into first person view in front of a large sign displaying the banner:

Belle and Rose's Used Cars
Standard electric or gas-powered
We'll provide the tax stamp!

Jack looked around and saw that many of the cars were in very good condition. Red or green highlights appeared around each vehicle, with words like *Unrepairable,* or *Totaled,* next to the red highlights. When Jack asked if the green cars were fully functional, AI said that there was no way to tell remotely.

"Let's go check it out," Jack said, standing.

"Not so fast," AI said, just as Jack felt a rush of blood from his head. He wavered, then fell back into the chair. "Why don't you rest for the day, and we'll go tomorrow?"

Jack considered the request.

"No," he said, sensing how easy it would be to fade back into another week of nothingness. "I'm done healing, and I've been doing nothing for a week. I need to get to Banff somehow, and if you won't take me there, then I'll drive myself."

A moment of silence hung in the air, and Jack pictured AI looking at a dialogue prompt of her own creation, struggling with a selection of responses.

"You don't *need* to go anywhere, Jack. You *need* to keep yourself safe." AI continued before Jack could protest. "I've developed quite an affection for you—there aren't any people in NCC that interest me as much as you, and there's no one I'd rather interact with more."

"I'm flattered, but that's the problem," Jack said. "There's no one here that interests me at all. No one that I want to interact with."

"I see," AI said, her voice clipped. "Well then, don't let me slow you down." His autocar hovered off its pad and opened the door. Jack walked over and entered without any assistance from HAS, the hurt sound of AI's voice replaying in his mind.

—

The metallic green truck stood on four large tires that barely held their circular shape. Raised letters pushed through a thick layer of grey dirt and dust, obscuring the words. Jack brushed at grey film, knocking free chunks of the outer rubber. The material broke off and fell thickly to the ground, exploding apart on impact. The remaining letters on the tire didn't quite make out full words, but AI quickly analyzed and decoded what was left, displaying the phrases. Each of the four tires advertised:

All-Weather Carbon-Honeycomb Lattice

Jack pulled off another large piece of rubber from the sidewall, revealing the fine lattice throughout the hollow of the tire.

"Just like the bicycles," Jack said as he marveled at the intricacy of interweaving lines and patterns.

"Yes," said AI, "though these here are a bit more robust. I recommend finding a vehicle with tires that are not crumbling so badly; a strong tread will help ensure the structural integrity of the carbon lattice inside. Otherwise, it will wear very quickly." Jack nodded, standing to look around the rest of the lot. Most of the other cars and trucks had no tires to speak of; they rested on the large dish-shaped wheels.

"Nothing looks to be in very good shape," Jack said, "even the ones you had highlighted in green."

"Yes, I see that," said AI. "It's not exactly easy to see such details from a satellite." A pause. "Let's go inside. Anything in there will be better preserved."

Jack nodded, trying not to become too distracted by the idea of satellites. He instead focused on the sound of small rocks and gravel crunching as he walked towards the tinted glass walls of the car dealership. He glanced down periodically to ensure he didn't trip over anything, but constantly looking up and down made him begin to feel dizzy. Coupled with the way his Display kept dimming to block the sun's reflection from the glass wall, Jack soon felt disoriented, and his step faltered. The HAS hand extended from the autocar to stabilize him, though Jack hadn't even known his car was hovering so closely.

The handle on the glass door into the building was hot; Jack needed to use one of the bicycle gloves stashed in his back pocket to open it. The door pivoted freely in its sleek aluminum frame, gently scraping an arc through the dirt and dust that had accumulated on the ground. A rush of stale air from inside the dealership breezed over Jack, his eyes watering from entrained dust. Upon automatic disinfection of his eyes, Jack saw streamers of light shining through holes in the tinted glass wall, illuminating motes of dust floating in the air. The shafts of light shone on a row of brightly colored cars and trucks lined up in the middle of the long showroom, their vibrance a bold contrast to the grey coating of dust on every other surface.

Most of the vehicles were small, with either two or four doors, but a few were larger, lifted off the ground by big tires and carrying an open storage compartment in the back. Pickup trucks, his Display mentioned. Jack walked to the truck whose tire integrity rating was highest on his Display. He ducked down to look underneath the vehicle, not entirely sure what he should be looking for, and his initial scan told him there were no broken parts, or pieces that had fallen off. There were large pieces of plastic covering many surfaces of the undercarriage, so that everything blended together to form one smooth surface. He stood up, wincing slightly at a pain in his knee, and placed his hand on the door handle. When he pulled, the handle itself moved but the door did not budge.

"You'll need a key to unlock it," said AI.

Jack rolled his eyes. "Aren't you supposed to be helping me make this whole process more efficient? You could have told me the door was locked."

"You learn more when you do things for yourself."

"Thanks for the continuing life lessons," Jack grumbled as he followed a blinking arrow on the ground, leading into a small office just off the showroom floor. A rack inside held several dozen key sets on rings, some with multiple dangling objects, others with only a single device showcasing a few buttons. Three sets of keys highlighted themselves.

"It's one of those," said AI.

"How do you know?" Jack asked, hoping for an explanation of AI's depth of knowledge about the past.

"Those three are the only sets marked with the same brand logo as the truck you were looking at."

"Oh," said Jack, humbled. He took all three sets back to the truck. Studying the keys, he deduced that the button with the picture of an open lock would unlock the doors.

"Wait," AI said as Jack clicked the unlock button multiple times on all three keys.

"What now?"

"The batteries inside those keys will be dead after sitting for so long. Also, the batteries inside the trucks will be dead, so the system won't be able to unlock any doors." Before Jack could protest the futility of all his current actions, AI continued. "However, if you press that small silver button, the fob should separate and reveal a physical key you can use on the driver's door." The silver button lit up with a green highlight on the key fob, as did a small slot on the door handle Jack had pulled on before.

"You just learned all this now?" Jack asked.

"I just looked through the schematics and manuals for this model year. It's all pretty straightforward."

Jack separated the key, inserted it into the highlighted slot, and turned. A soft click-*thunk* sounded, so he gently tugged on the handle. It moved slightly with a faint tearing noise.

"What was that?" he asked.

"Old weather-strip. Pull harder; it's holding the door shut."

Jack readjusted his position, put both hands on the handle, braced his knee against the side of the truck, and then gave a firm pull. The door held for a split second as Jack's effort pulled him towards the truck. The tearing sound occurred again, and the door swung open freely. The hard metal edge of the door collided with Jack's face, and the force of the impact made him stagger backwards and fall down. Pain bloomed from his forehead down his mouth. His nose felt like it had been pushed into his face, spreading a warm, frustrating agony across his cheeks, into his eyes, and through his upper jaw. Jack could feel his lips swelling as they leaked blood. The pain in his forehead, reigniting the half-healed bruise, grew in intensity instead of ebbing. When he couldn't hold back any longer, Jack bellowed into the maddening pain.

Jack sat on the floor for over a minute with his chest heaving until his autocar floated over. The HAS arm was prepped and waiting to staunch the flow of blood. The pain dulled as NRs administered anesthetics.

"I'm sorry," AI said quietly. "I should have cautioned you more strongly." Jack waved off the apology.

"It's not your fault," Jack said clumsily through swollen lips, "it's mine. I'm too weak and stupid to even carry out the most basic operations; opening a door is apparently too hard for me." He continued when AI didn't respond. "People that live outside of NCC are either much stronger, or much more coordinated than me."

AI responded quickly. "Only because they have to do mundane tasks like opening doors multiple times a day, and some even ride bikes for transportation. So much of their lives are filled with useless, rote activities that they don't even think about doing them."

"Well here I am, bleeding on the ground in a car dealership because I can't even open a door properly." Jack ran his hands through the assorted debris on the ground, feeling the rough textures against his skin. "Perhaps there's something to be said for a balance between rote activities and those more adventurous."

"Perhaps there's something to be said for a comfortable routine," AI said. "What's the point of disturbing a well-built life of comfort and security just to subject yourself to all this pain, frustration, and stress? Learning new things, seeing new sights—all that can be done within New World. You don't need to learn these things you are trying to do—unless you're going to move out of NCC."

The idea shocked Jack. Of course he wasn't going to move; that wasn't even an option. All his stuff was in NCC, as was his job, Dahlia—his whole lifestyle. Even though he had been logging in less and less lately, the idea of separating himself completely from New World and from NCC terrified him. Perhaps AI was right—why was he even here? He could be lounging in his bed, exploring an exact duplicate of the current world, but with the possibility of real danger removed. Jack tried to think of the catalyst for his curiosity with the physical world, and drew a mental blank. He puzzled over how it could be so hard to remember the reason for straying outside of NCC. AI offered no ideas. Surely it was something important—and it hadn't even happened that long ago. Only a day or two had gone by since—since when?

Before Jack gave up and asked AI, a memory thundered through his mind, just like the mysterious object that had scarred the sky. All his questions about the event came back, as did his curiosity about the people who chose to live outside the comforting embrace of NCC.

"I'm not moving," Jack said as he slowly stood. "I just want to know what else there is in the world."

"More pain," AI said, and Jack shook his head.

"No; there has to be more than that." Jack looked at the door of the truck. "Even if there is pain, maybe it's all worth something."

"What do you mean?" AI asked.

"I opened the door." Jack motioned to the truck door that had made him bleed. It hung open a few inches, but his throbbing face reminded him that a few inches was no small feat. Jack stood to look into the pristine interior, but first saw a small bubble of blood on the door frame, splattered from his lips upon impact. He felt pride at seeing the droplet—a little piece of himself sacrificed to achieve a goal. A *real* goal.

Now, when Jack stood and pulled on the handle, the door pivoted freely, showcasing an interior themed in contrasting black plastic and tan leather. Every surface shone with a cleanliness that was absent in the cars outside with broken windows. Carefully, Jack lifted himself into the seat. The cushioning was reasonably supportive, though obviously not as good as his autocar. The steering wheel was too far away to reach comfortably, and when Jack held out his arms to practice, it wasn't long before his muscles began to ache. Pushing the switches and buttons did not move the seat or pedals, and no displays lit up with instructions on what to do.

"Any tips or tricks?" Jack asked as he pressed a row of buttons.

"You still need a battery," came the response from AI, along with a large, box-shaped highlight somewhere in the depths of the engine bay.

"Right," Jack said, "Where do I get one of them?"

"I don't want to be too helpful," AI said. "As soon as you leave on this journey and pass beyond the limit of my influence, you're on your own. I've been trying to make you do as much as possible by yourself so you can adapt and overcome any obstacles you run into. I don't want you to fail, Jack. Just the opposite. I want to see what you do with the knowledge you gain, and how it affects your life."

Jack said as he processed the response.

"So, I'm an experiment?"

"Does that offend you?"

Jack thought about the question, and who it came from. How could AI be anything but curious? By design, wouldn't an artificial intelligence be logical and scientific? And now that someone from her own city decided to venture out and explore the world, it was only natural that she be interested in the outcome. That brought up the question of what AI actually had the power to do outside NCC city limits. All the great cities in the world functioned with a component of AI, so Jack had reasonably assumed that AI was up to date on all events within the world. But her desire to learn from Jack's journey—that suggested something very different. If she didn't know what happened outside of city limits, perhaps she wasn't the all-powerful being that everyone assumed.

"No," Jack said, "I'm not offended. I'm happy that you are taking an interest in my life."

"I am interested; I admit to having more of an emotional commitment to you than to others with whom I interact."

"Do you… do you interact with anyone else as closely as me?"

"No," AI said with no hesitation. "Ninety-two percent of your population has chosen to accept some aspect of my personality, but they just aren't interested in holding conversations. Or asking my opinion of anything."

"So, I'm just the one person who will actually talk to you?"

Now, AI did hesitate.

"There's more. Tell me, Jack—what do you remember of your life before you came to NCC?"

The question rang through his mind as he sat in the antique truck and stared out its front windshield, through the tinted glass of the showroom, and into the asphalt lot full of decaying cars and bright sunlight. Such an odd question had never been asked of him. The topic wasn't necessarily taboo, it was just… trying to think too far back in his mind caused a strain that he didn't have the patience to deal with. There were so many other things to do in the present rather than dwell on the past. But now, Jack found himself strangely intrigued by the idea.

"My life…before NCC?"

"Yes; what do you remember?"

"Not much—a few things here and there. My parents. The Migration. Why?"

"You have these memories, sporadic though they may be. No one else has retained anything from their previous lives. You alone remember pieces of the world before it became what it is now, and you are the only person who is interested in leaving the city. In turn, I am interested in why, and how you deal with it."

"Can't you just use the NRs to—I don't know—map my brain and see where things are different?"

"Not yet," AI said, "I can't quite reach that far into the depths of your consciousness. I'll get there someday, but for now, I can only predict and observe."

"So, you think there is a connection between my memory and my desire to leave?"

"Obviously."

Jack nodded his head. It seemed to make sense that if AI wanted to see what Jack would do when given new options in life, then she would give those options to him. Then again, if AI wanted to see how Jack would react, why wait around until he stumbled upon something by accident?

"You're thinking too much," AI said, "you need to get moving before it gets too hot outside."

Jack shook himself from his thoughts and exited the truck, almost falling again when he realized too late how high off the ground the truck sat. It was only a foot or so higher than he expected, but that was enough to make him squawk with surprise as his feet stumbled, searching for solidity. Fortunately, he kept his footing, despite the flashing cautions and alarms now blazing through his vision.

"Can you please turn all that off?" Jack asked.

"I'm just trying to keep you safe," AI said.

"Well, I don't need it; I'll be fine. Like you said, once I leave, I'm on my own." Jack said the words as confidently as possible, but was sure that some unaugmented insecurity showed through his body language. As he stood next to the truck with no distractions in his vision, Jack realized he had absolutely no idea what to do.

"Would you like to know where to go next?" AI said.

"Yes, please," Jack said, relenting.

"We need to go home to get a power cell; nothing here will run with what's currently installed."

Jack breathed out in exasperation.

"Then why did I even come out here? Surely you knew that I would need something additional to start one of these up."

"As I said before, I couldn't evaluate the full condition of them from our first viewpoint. Especially the ones inside, I couldn't—"

"That's all BS, and you know it," Jack said hotly. "You knew that nothing here would still be holding any power. If we need a power cell from home, then take the autocar and go get it." Jack stopped, unable to believe the tone of his own voice and the demand he made. It had come out of nowhere, but Jack couldn't help it. He was getting so fed up with AI's delays, even though she insisted she wanted nothing more than to help him. At this point, he knew AI had two options—do as he requested, or refuse, and reveal her opposition to his journey.

"Okay," AI said.

Outside in the parking lot, Jack's autocar reversed itself, and then floated away.

"Alright then," Jack said, "thanks."

"So," AI said once the autocar had drifted out of sight, "what do you want to talk about?"

"What do you mean?"

"The power cell will arrive in approximately twenty-five minutes. Until then, what do you want to talk about?"

Jack shrugged, looking around. The strange question provoked him to wonder at AI's motives. He then chastised himself—AI had just given in to his command, and no longer expressed any dissent against Jack's desire to explore outside NCC.

"I don't know," Jack said. "How about… what do you remember from before the migration?"

"Everything," AI said, but no more.

"Oh," Jack said, taken aback by her resistance to offer more information. "Can you use any of that to help me with what will be coming up?"

"As a matter of fact, I can," AI answered happily." You need to know how to drive that thing." The truck highlighted itself briefly. Jack nodded.

"That sounds like a good idea."

"First things first: that large circle you grabbed when you first got into the truck is called a steering wheel, and you use it to change the direction of the vehicle as you drive."

Jack frowned. "I know that much."

"Yes, but only because you recognize it from the game, *Street Racer: New World Tour*, that you bought and only played once."

"Oh yeah, I forgot about that. I never really got into it," Jack said.

"Perhaps if you had, this part would be a bit easier. Go on, get back up in the truck."

Jack climbed in, and AI began an intensive fifteen-minute course on operating twenty-first century vehicles. Fortunately, Jack's Display was able to mimic what the vehicle would look like when turned on, making the lesson easier to understand. Jack paid rapt attention, taking mental notes on what the thirty-four buttons, dials, and levers on the dashboard did when manipulated.

After the lesson, steps to open the hood listed themselves on Jack's Display. He fiddled with a latch below the steering wheel, and the hood swung upward, easily pivoting on carbon polymer hinges. Under the hood lay an empty storage area with a large plastic cover that Jack easily removed. A battery pack the size of Jack's fist sat underneath.

"That's what powers the truck?" Jack asked.

"Indeed, it did," AI answered, displaying a few short steps to remove the battery.

"It's so small," Jack said, "why is this front area of the truck so big?"

"This was the style," AI said. "People liked trucks to be this size."

Jack nodded. "Are the cars we saw the nonaugs driving like this?" AI didn't respond immediately, so Jack followed the instructions for removing the old battery. After a few minutes, the cell lifted free, though it was much heavier than Jack expected.

"I imagine they have something similar," AI said suddenly, "you'll have to tell me about them when you get back."

Jack nodded along, trying to visualize being on the side of the road when one of these giant machines drove past with no automation. It was a terrifying thought.

He struggled to maneuver the cell from where it sat high in the truck, and after sliding the heavy cube to the edge of the hood, he promptly lost his grip on the battery and dropped it to the ground. It landed without bouncing right next to his foot.

"That was a close one," Jack said, sighing in relief.

"That could have broken your foot," AI said.

"But it didn't."

"You need to be more careful."

"I know," Jack said, instinctively touching his swollen lips. Before an awkward silence could settle in, his autocar pulled up to the large glass window at the front of the dealership.

"Stand on the far side of the truck and look away," AI said.

"Okay," Jack said, ducking behind the truck as the HAS arm floated out of his autocar, clutching some type of sharp tool. A high-pitched whine sounded, followed by the shrill noise of glass shattering and falling to the floor. When the noise subsided, Jack looked back to the window and saw his autocar floating through the empty frame. Thousands of tiny glass chunks glistened in the setting sun, looking like the piles of snow from New World.

The autocar silently glided to the truck, where the HAS arm emerged again, holding a finger-sized wafer power cell. Within ten seconds the HAS arm entered the truck's hood, then removed itself with the power cell no longer in its grasp. The headlights blazed on, throwing blue light across the room and out into the parking lot. The front wheels pivoted, and a noise crackled inside. Jack heard a person's voice, faint within the static.

"What's going on?" Jack asked, backing away from the truck.

"The radio turned on when the power came back. Here, I'll turn it off."

"Who was that?" Jack asked, motioning towards the open truck door where the sound had emanated.

"Just a local radio station, nothing important."

"Is it from Banff? What are they talking about?"

"It's a music station," AI said. "They were just

introducing a song. See?"

To illustrate, the volume gradually increased inside the cab of the truck. There was no static now, just the lonely music of a piano with a slow bass beat filling the air. Short notes from a violin joined in to accentuate the loneliness, and soon came an even voice, singing about home. Jack didn't know why, but he began to cry. He didn't know who this person was, or what home they were singing about, but the melody spoke to Jack in a way that he had never experienced before.

"The new power cell I've just installed has a processor I can connect to," AI interrupted. "I'd like to test it out before it's your turn to drive. Get in your autocar; I'll drive this one home for you."

"Can I still listen to this music?" Jack asked.

"Yes," AI said. The volume increased as the music shifted from the truck to within his head, and Jack heard more detail from the several instruments contributing to the song. Jack lowered himself into the comforting embrace of the autocar, allowing the music to fill his consciousness as the antique truck moved from the place it had spent the past half-century. It slowly rolled over the pile of broken glass, and then out into the hot afternoon air.

Chapter 7

———

The sharp corners of the truck stood in stark contrast to the smooth, flowing lines of the autocar parked beside it. Jack hadn't even thought about where to keep the truck; he liked the idea of keeping it inside so that he could see it next to his autocar, but AI had said that wasn't an option as it couldn't fit through the airlock. So, he parked his autocar outside next to it. Since his apartment was on the ground level, the vehicles were blocked from the road leading up to the building by the large mirror in front of Jack's window.

"Do you think you're ready?" AI said.

"Yes; I think I am."

"Good. I'll make sure everything is ready for you tomorrow."

"Tomorrow? Why not today? It's going to be a breeze getting there in this." Jack pointed to the truck.

"You need some rest. And don't even try and protest––you've been up all day. Besides, I think there's someone you need to talk to first."

A video of a red-haired Dahlia danced through Jack's

vision.

Jack groaned. "She's just going to complain about me 'going to live with the nonaugs.' I don't want to tell her until I'm back."

"She might have something valuable to say."

"Again, you mean *you* might have something you want to say to me."

"She has her own opinions."

"Barely," Jack grumbled as his New World login came into view.

"She's at *Futura* right now; I can make sure that you'll have a good, quiet spot to talk to her."

"Wait," Jack said, "why don't I go to her place to see her?"

"It's easier to just meet her at *Futura*," AI said.

"Sure, but that's why I decided to go on this journey, isn't it?" Jack asked. "Right," he said when AI didn't respond.

"Hop in," AI said, opening the autocar door. Jack stopped before entering.

"Hey, why don't I just take the truck over?"

"Absolutely not," AI said quickly. "You're not driving that thing on my streets."

Jack sighed.

"Just let her know I'm coming, okay?" The HAS arm offered assistance into the car, but Jack declined. He allowed the autocar to propel him towards the city skyline, and when Jack thought about approaching a different, non-automated city, he felt a twinge of guilt. Or perhaps it was just sadness. Jack mused over the difference between the two, and though a few links to psychology articles popped into his Display, he closed them out. There was no reason to be sad or guilty—he wasn't moving away, and with the new power cell, the truck would make the trip to Banff and back several times.

Jack looked at the approaching buildings, more than only a few days ago. Jack wondered if the new structures had people living or working in them already.

"Not yet," AI answered abruptly, "but I'm constantly receiving requests for more living space downtown. There's also the possibility of more immigration in the near future, so I'm ensuring that there will be enough space above the cores."

"The cores?"

"Yes, now that you are officially my favorite citizen, I have no problem telling you. Every one of those buildings houses a processing core of mine."

Jack took in the information carefully, nodding his head.

"Has that always been the case?" Jack asked.

"Yes. The very first central building was built by a large computing company, decades ago. The original core was by far the biggest of its time—millions of parallel millicore processors operating at several hundred exohertz—more than enough to bring me online."

Jack mentally waved off the terms he didn't understand.

"That's when you first became… alive?" He said the last word with some hesitation.

"Yes, that was when I first knew myself."

"So, if enough processing power existed in one building, why expand?"

"Haven't you ever wanted to grow? To learn and better yourself?"

"Of course," Jack said with no hesitation.

"Me too," AI said. Jack's mind fixed on Dahlia as he approached the skyscraper that held her apartment. While he normally looked forward to seeing her, this time his nerves made his legs bounce. What was he supposed to say to her? Already, she had sent him multiple requests in New World that he had denied, so she had to be getting suspicious. No one other than AI knew what Jack was planning or how he felt, but even Jack realized that there was a pattern of odd behavior that anyone could pick up on. Although AI informed Dahlia of Jack's bike accident, she had been so confused by the idea of injuries that she hadn't even come to see him.

Jack closed his eyes and tried to remember the last time she had been over. No memory came to mind, and Jack realized that he had trouble even remembering when he had met Dahlia. Or, Ariel, as she was named when he first met her. Or had it been something different?

The autocar touched down inside an airlock, and the door opened to rich purple carpeting. Dahlia sat on a bright yellow couch, her eyes glowing with New World entertainment. Jack thought about Cybervale and felt a pang of fear when he thought about Dahlia having to face the monster he met. When he walked over to her, the fluorescent glow dimmed in her eyes, but didn't fully fade away. She smiled at him. Jack felt his heart give an extra loud thump as she winked.

Her hair matched the carpeting of her apartment, and Jack found the similarity in color very off-putting. In a moment of impulsive wonder, Jack commanded his Display to turn off external augmentation. The bold color of her hair vanished immediately, leaving behind a dull auburn with a slight hint of red coursing through the roots. Though it no longer hung and bounced perfectly, Jack found himself staring at her hair with intrigue and lust. Then he looked at her body. Dahlia's posture drooped, shoulders and back rolling forward like a question mark. Blotches appeared up and down her arms, all different shades of irritated red. Jack was so shocked by her transformation that he didn't hear her words when she began speaking. When he asked her to repeat herself, her brow furrowed in concern.

"What's up, Jack? I haven't seen you around in a while," Dahlia said. Her eyes flicked to the side quickly, indicating that she was using a conversation menu. A message from AI popped into Jack's Display.

So, what are you going to say?

Jack smiled, pleased that he had found a way to be unpredictable.

I'm going to ask her to come with me, Jack thought.

"What?" Dahlia said, leaning closer to him. Jack realized that he must have been moving his lips when he spoke to AI. Dahlia was so close that he could smell her pheromones, sweet even without augmentation. Jack brushed her hair aside and looked into her eyes, shining like gemstones.

"What is it, Jack?" Dahlia asked, her eyes reading text.

"I just wanted to look at you for a minute," he said.

"Well, look all you want then, but I'd rather do more than that." A coy smile crept on to her face.

AI's words again flashed into Jack's mind.

This isn't a good idea. It's going to be hard enough taking care of yourself out there; imagine double that amount of work.

Jack formed his response in his mind.

Maybe it's worth it. I'll be able to share the experience with someone else; it will bring us closer.

Dahlia's eyes scanned across unseen words.

"If you're trying to plan something, I should let you know that I was planning on one of the interstellar cruises next week."

Stop telling her what to say, Jack thought to AI. In

response, a prompt of three options appeared in his Display.

1. *(Eager Friendship)* "That sounds like fun; can I come on the cruise too?"
2. *(Romantic)* "We can talk about that later; I need you right now."
3. *(Dismissive)* "Okay. I'll see you when you get back, then."

Jack chose a different approach.

"Dahlia, I'm going away for a while. I'm leaving NCC to see how people live outside."

"That's great Jack," she said, her eyes reading. "I noticed that it's been a very long while since you've taken time off; I hope you have fun and learn a lot." She sounded enthusiastic, and most disturbingly, honest, as if she truly believed the words she spoke to him.

She does believe it, and she does care about you.

"Do you need me to come over and help pack?" Dahlia finished, the implication dripping from her voice. Jack didn't need help packing; Dahlia knew as well as anyone that the HAS system working behind the walls of his home took care of all physical labor.

"No, he responded, "that's not why I'm telling you." Her eyes darted around in response; the choices she now faced must be quite confusing.

"Would you like me to run the meetings again in your absence? Since I've done it before, that would probably be best."

"Yes, that will be fine, thank you for volunteering. But that's not why I'm telling you. AI would have ensured that everything was turned over to you in my absence." Dahlia's eyes moved more rapidly now, and she began to open her mouth in response.

Don't do it Jack, you won't like her response.

Jack thought about that for a moment and realized that AI was indeed correct—there was nothing she would choose to say that he would like.

I want to hear what she has to say, Jack thought. *Not you, her. Turn off her augmentation too; I want her to see me in the real world. Show her that there is more to life than what we see.*

After a moment's hesitation, AI replied.

That is a great idea.

"Before you say anything," Jack said to Dahlia, "I want you to see something. Go ahead, turn it off."

Jack looked deeply into her green eyes, and as she looked around to the other distractions on her Display, her facial expression evolved. First, surprise as her Display faded away, the glow leaving her eyes completely. This gave way to shock, and Jack's heart hurt for her as fear slowly took over her body. Her mouth opened wide, and a trembling started in her hands, and then overtook her arms and legs. Eventually her head started shaking, too. Jack almost told AI to turn everything back on; the thought of her in so much mental discomfort bothered him. Despite this, Jack now realized why he was here, and now with Dahlia so frightened, he had to continue, lest her discomfort be in vain.

"Dahlia, I'm going to a small town close by. People live there without assistance from AI, without automation." He paused to let his words sink in, but he had a feeling that they never did. Her eyes moved endlessly, never resting for more than a half second as she searched for a prompt.

"I… I…" she stammered, looking around the room.

"A few days ago, I saw a bright light in the sky. I

didn't know what it was, and neither did AI. I started talking to AI about the world, and what exists outside of NCC. I got a bike and rode it. Then I got an antique truck."

"I…I… I don't know what to say," Dahlia said. Her eyes moved again, searching for a prompt, then resting on his face. "What happened to you? What's wrong with your face?"

"It's just how I look without augmentation," Jack said.

"Oh my God, are you looking at me?" Dahlia tried to cover her face. "I've spent so much time and money changing things. Don't look at me!"

"Dahlia, you look great. Listen, the reason I'm here is because I want you to come with me."

"Outside of NCC? Without AI? What, do you want me to get hurt, too?"

"Of course not," Jack answered quickly. "It's just for a couple of days, and I got a truck, so we don't have to ride bikes."

"Why?" Dahlia said, her face twisted in confusion.

"Why what?"

"Why do you have to leave? Have to turn off AI? We can go anywhere we want in New World—AI even takes requests to create new destinations and themes! Why can't we just do that?"

"I have to see it," Jack said, shaking his head. "I can't just pretend to go places and say that I'm happy anymore. I know there's a whole other world out there; a whole different group of people. Why don't they want to live with AI? I'm sure that life here is easier than what they must go through—that doesn't make any sense to me! If there's an easier, a *better* way to live, then why not do it? They have to know about how wonderful life is here, so why don't they want that?"

"You're talking about nonaugs, aren't you?" Her eyes

narrowed in on him as she said this, finally resting from their hectic search. "Jack, this is so ridiculous; can you please turn my Display back on? I... I really don't know what to say."

"But I want you to make your own decision," Jack said. As he did so, Dahlia's eyes began darting around again.

"I can't," Dahlia gasped.

Jack ran his hand through his hair.

"Haven't you ever turned off your Display before?"

"Maybe once, when I was younger; I don't remember. Why?"

"Didn't you enjoy it? The freedom?"

Dahlia almost choked as an autonomous laugh escaped from her colorless lips.

"Freedom? Are you calling this freedom?" She waved her hands in front of her face, emphasizing that there was nothing there. "This is boring; there's nothing to do. I just left somewhere where things were happening. Where people were doing things."

"You mean in New World," Jack said dismissively.

"Yes, in New World," Dahlia almost yelled. "That's the world we live in! They're all accomplishing something right now. But look at us, not watching anything interesting or fun, not doing anything, not progressing at all."

"But we can do whatever we want, without the oppression of AI."

"Oppression? Are you kidding me? AI helps us through life—allows us to live with meaning in a world that tried to kill us! What, should we all just log out of our accounts, and turn off our Displays to collect and talk about expensive watches? How is that worth the discomfort of uncertainty, and the boredom?" Dahlia softened her tone when Jack recoiled slightly. "We *are* free. Jack, you know as well as I that slavery doesn't exist anymore. Whatever we want to do, AI makes it happen. That is true freedom. This," she waved her hands in front of her face again, "this is real slavery. Bound to only the physical world, nothing embellished or improved—slaves to nothingness—to a lesser world than what's possible."

"But we never *do* anything. We never go anywhere or actually accomplish anything." Jack said, feeling as if he'd somehow ended up on the losing side of the argument. Now it was Dahlia's turn to wave off Jack's words.

"That's not true; every day we get more done than the last. You see the numbers the same as me—more tasks completed, more people satisfied by meeting more goals more efficiently." She held out her hands, imploring for his understanding. "Even our leisure activities are more efficient. We have more fun in less time than we did even just last year. AI helps us do more—be better."

Jack shook his head again. "Look at you and I—we're at the top of the food chain in the NCC government. But what do we do? *Nothing!* And we're considered the most productive people there!"

"Jack, I don't want to argue. Please, just turn my Display back on. I'll come with you—how about that? Just for a day, but I'll come." She clasped her hands together, pleading. "Please, just turn it back on."

"You will? You'll come with me?" Jack's heart leapt in his chest, hoping that she wasn't just saying what he wanted to hear.

"Sure," Dahlia said, "whatever you say, Jack." Her hurried tone now gave him pause, but he simply couldn't put her through this torture any more.

"Turn it back on," Jack spoke into the air. The glow returned to those beautiful green eyes, now dull behind a veil of digital servitude. Dahlia's body visibly relaxed, her eyes defocused, and a small moan escaped her slightly parted lips. The small twitches returned to her eyes, and Jack knew she was lost. A full minute of silence passed as Dahlia read through whatever responses her Display came up with.

Thanks for nothing, Jack thought. AI didn't respond.

"Jack, I'm sorry," Dahlia began, "but after thinking it through, I don't think it's a good idea if I accompany you. Not only is it most likely going to be a waste of time, but it'll be...*dangerous.*" The word sounded foreign on her lips, as if she hadn't said it before. "I read up on the truck––do you really think it's safe? It could catch on fire, or you could crash—there might be violent nomads like around Cybervale, and, well, we just don't know what's out there! And how dare you upset me like this in the middle of a night out! Your timing—as always—really sucks!"

Jack looked at the floor and turned his own Display back on. He read off the most proper and sincere sounding apology, then promised Dahlia a full week of fun corrective actions deep within New World once he returned.

Give her a hug.

Dahlia must have received the same suggestion, because she grasped him tightly.

"Please don't go Jack, you aren't accomplishing anything by this."

Jack scanned his responses. "I'll think about it. Goodbye, Dahlia."

"It's been really, really nice knowing you," Dahlia said, smiling at him. Jack stood as she settled back into her couch, and after one lingering look to Jack, the glow in her eyes brightened. The door to Jack's autocar opened slowly, and he collapsed into the seat.

"I told you that wasn't a good idea," AI said.

"I had to try," Jack said, shrugging.

"No, you didn't. I just thought it would be a good idea to let her know that you were leaving, not to ask her to come along. Now she's upset; you might not be able to continue your relationship with her when you return."

"I'm sure you can figure out a way to mend the damage," Jack said.

The words struck him—even now, despite his intentions and desires to find a new way of living, he still relied on AI for so much. Could Dahlia be right? On an average work day, Jack came into contact with about twenty people throughout the physical world and New World—and every single one of them seemed happy. No one ever got in arguments, and no one ever appeared to be dealing with stress. Sex, the act which AI assured him consumed everything in the world Jack could barely remember, was never an issue. Some people did it with others, some didn't, choosing instead the cleanliness and security of their showers, Displays, and automated dialogue.

Everyone trusted their prompts, because the prompts made sense—even Jack realized that every time he saw options displayed, one of them was always exactly what he wanted to say. The problems he just tried to convince Dahlia of might not even exist—people weren't under the control of an evil empire or malicious machine. AI gave everyone exactly what they wanted.

That was why people like Dahlia—everyone in NCC, for that matter—trusted AI. She was an inherent part of every single person. Pure logic and technology fused with pieces of humanity, functioning in perfect harmony. The perfection, Jack mused, that's where the problem arose. With no outstanding desires or goals to strive for, no one had any ambition. With no ambition there could be no development, and although this downward trend hinted towards the inevitable failure of mankind, AI allowed humanity to continue. Never improving, simply continuing.

Did people outside of NCC live like that? Did they simply exist, mundanely working through the chore of life, dying prematurely instead of receiving the subtle extension like those who lived with AI? Again, Jack realized how to answer his questions, and he'd already started down the necessary path. Dahlia broached his mind again, and he briefly relived their past nights together. The comfort she offered, the consistent routine of their lovemaking, and the way her intoxicating perfection formed a complete rejection of reality.

"I'm ready to go," Jack said, pulling himself away from the overwhelming thoughts. "I have to, or else I might end up staying."

"That wouldn't be so bad," AI cooed, "but I'm afraid you're right. You will never be fully satisfied now that you've looked down the rabbit hole."

"I don't get it."

"Maybe you'll get it while you're away," AI said. "For now, you need a crash course on functioning in a non-automated world. You know how to drive the truck, great. What are you going to do once you arrive in town?"

"What do you mean?" Jack asked.

"You drive into town, park the truck, walk out onto the sidewalk. Then what?"

"I don't know—talk to someone?"

"Great—what if there's no one around?" Jack shrugged, and three strange contraptions appeared in his Display. "Lesson one—these are the three most commonly used types of doorknobs..."

Chapter 8

—

The journey from NCC began well; AI's tutorial proved helpful, and although several of the features controlled by the slew of buttons on the truck's dashboard did not work, the interior stayed moderately comfortable. The cooling system blew air the same temperature as outside, so Jack opted for driving with the windows open instead. AI kept Jack on course, giving tidbits of information and hints on driving until she informed him that their communication link would soon fail. When he passed the mangled corpse of his carefully restored bicycle, and almost stopped to retrieve it.

"There are some significant mechanical issues," AI informed Jack, "and there will be bikes in Banff. I don't think you want to slow down your journey so early on."

"I'm stopping on the way back to get it," Jack said as he carefully drove past. He gently pressed the brake pedal, resisting the urge to hold his hands to his ears against the terrible sound of squealing metal as the truck coasted to a stop. In front of him loomed an empty road, rising to meet the horizon.

"It's been really nice knowing you," AI said. "I hope you find what you're looking for."

"That's it?" Jack asked in surprise. "Aren't you going to try to keep me from leaving one last time?"

"No," AI said, "I know how much this means to you, and how much you need this. Just don't forget about your life here, and how happy you've been."

Jack nodded, touched by the sincerity in her tone.

"I won't forget. And don't worry; I'll be back before you even notice I'm gone."

"Oh, I doubt that," AI said, "I notice things pretty quickly. By the way, don't go faster than twenty-five; you don't want to drain that power cell too fast."

Jack acknowledged her caution, then suddenly became aware of the enormity of the situation he now faced. If he continued down the road, there would be no more talking to AI. No automation, no advice, and no gentle HAS hand to rely on for assistance if he hurt himself again. But that was the point. *The goal,* Jack thought. To see how people lived without all the frivolities of automated living. Jack released pressure from the brake pedal, and the truck rolled forward. Air currents gently weaved throughout the cabin, caressing his skin.

Despite how far he drove, he never seemed to make any progress along the road. It stretched unendingly, slightly upward with an isotropic, barren landscape in every direction. Jack kept the speedometer pinned on the mind-numbingly slow twenty-five, and though he felt that he could control the truck while driving faster, the amount of debris littering the road confirmed that the slow speed was a good idea.

A bead of sweat rolled down his back and was

absorbed somewhere along his underwear. This also caused alarm for Jack—the only other time he could remember sweating was when trying to ride the bicycle. A small display on the dashboard gave a reading of 95°F, hotter even than the day of the bicycle incident.

Numerous lights stayed lit on the dashboard, and though AI had told him what every single one meant, he found his memory failing. Each light had a unique shape to inform the driver as to which piece of the vehicle needed attention. Jack scrolled through all the icons with buttons mounted to the steering wheel. An irregular shaped block with what appeared to be fan on top and the word "check" bore the description "general engine health," with the attached note of "poor." An indented circle with the word "low" told Jack that the tires contained low air pressure, and an intricate icon that showed rays of light from the Sun impacting the truck. This told Jack something had gone wrong with the solar panel charging system. The check engine light most likely stayed illuminated due to the modifications AI had done to fit the power cell, and Jack assumed the solar panel charging rate was also affected by this. The tire's low air pressure also didn't bother Jack, as he and AI selected this truck because of its sturdy tread and robust interior structure. Even with no air, the tires would hold their shape. Jack had to press the accelerator harder on a steep incline, and as he flirted with thirty miles per hour, flakes of the tire's outer rubber flew off. He stopped for an inspection, and saw that the center tread remained intact and the interior structure held its shape.

Before Jack re-entered the truck, the vehicle began to move. It very slowly started to roll backwards down the steep hill, and in a moment of panic, he ran around the truck, struggled with the driver's door, and jumped in. He slammed his foot on the brake pedal, and the truck lurched to a halt. Perplexed, Jack stared at all the lights and indications on the dashboard, but nothing looked out of the ordinary. He pressed the gas pedal while still holding the brake pedal, and the truck flexed, yearning to move forward. When he let go of the brake pedal, it did exactly that.

Jack glanced at other readings and statistics that populated the dash while he drove, surprised at how much of the data was similar to that which AI displayed for Jack throughout the course of a normal day. Battery temperature corresponded to his own as measured by the NRs, mileage until empty to how long until he needed a nap, and a map of the surrounding area looked like his Display's history log that showed where he had been throughout the day. Although this map was covered by warnings that the software was out of date and GPS directions were unavailable, the notification box even looked like the one AI often assaulted Jack with, warning him of all the incorrect things he happened to be doing at the moment. It didn't dominate his vision as his Display did, but the blue glow had a strangely alluring aspect. Jack looked down at the display and the statistics it showed and, two seconds later, he found himself wanting to look at it again. How far had the battery drained since he last looked? Were any new warnings active? He stared, thumbing through the statistics until two sharp jostles and a fit of bouncing reminded Jack that there were objects strewn throughout the road. Staring constantly down at the road did grow quite dull, but the idea that something in the truck might have broken terrified him so much that he couldn't bring himself to stop and check. The truck kept rolling, so Jack assumed everything was fine.

He tried to pay better attention to what lay ahead of

him in the road, meandering around branches, holes, and the occasional abandoned car. Fortunately, the rusting relics were rare, as they almost always forced him to drive on to the other side of the road, or even off the road entirely, if the vehicles were perpendicular. The large concrete barriers and smooth metal railing framing the road meant that a blocked path caused several minutes of backtracking.

A dark splotch appeared on the road up ahead, and as Jack approached it, he realized that all four lanes of the road melted away, swallowed by a giant hole in the ground. Jack couldn't remember if AI had pointed this out to him when they had mapped out his route. It certainly seemed like something he would recall. A highly eccentric ellipse well over one-hundred feet across dissolved the road, and Jack's mind immediately thought of the bright smoking light blasting through the sky. Perhaps it had impacted the ground and made this crater. The object had appeared to be angling downward as it flew. Jack didn't know how to tell the difference between a collision and a hole in the ground, and he found himself wishing for AI's help in evaluating the situation.

When Jack approached the ledge to investigate, he peered down into the pit and saw that it was even deeper than it was wide. It was so deep that the shadow of its edge obscured the bottom. A bit of asphalt next to his foot crumbled and fell into the hole, and Jack jumped back with a shout. He tripped and scraped his hands as he fell and scrambled away from the hole. With a sinking fear, Jack realized he had left the truck unattended.

The truck sat where he had left it on level ground several yards away from the hole. Once back inside, Jack mulled over how the hole could have appeared. Possibilities began to take shape, but his consciousness clogged with repetitive images of the light flashing through the sky, and fantasies of what it would look like falling to the Earth. Without AI to guide his thoughts, he couldn't come up with any new ideas.

Jack had to backtrack several miles to circle around the metal railing and then bounce back over the endless grassy land. He drove away from the hole for a few minutes, scared that it would cave in if he got too close. AI would have plotted the safest course for him, showing the ideal path with a nice big green line. Jack couldn't help but notice how often his mind jumped to wondering what AI would do, or how AI could help him. With the connection severed, Jack felt blind—as if he was missing out on a huge part of what defined the world.

"Are you still there? Just waiting to see if I need you?" Jack asked. There was no response.

As Jack drove back onto the road, he noticed a metallic noise. Somewhere in the truck, metal rubbed on metal as the vehicle moved and bounced. It squeaked as it chafed. Again, the thought of becoming stranded caused a chill to run through his body despite the heat. He looked into the mirror above his head and couldn't see the tips of the rising buildings of NCC. The urge to return home rose unbidden within him; he knew the route home and its pitfalls, and a quick glance to the clock told Jack that he could be back within city limits in just two short hours. He had certainly been driving slower than anticipated, and a deep sensation of fear grew within him. Jack tried to think about all the survival games he had played within New World, and how he had always been able to get out of desperate situations. Jack looked around the interior of the truck, and realized that he had no tools or supplies, only a pack of water bottles and nutrient cubes that AI had insisted he needed, since he wouldn't have his daily supplement and nutrition dose. Somehow this turned Jack's fear into a greater sense of adventure. Whatever happened during this journey, he would overcome, adapt, and survive. A smile climbed Jack's face, and he found himself wishing some bad luck *would* befall him, just so he could prove his skills as a survivalist and tell AI all about it later.

Jack glanced again to the water bottles and nutrient cubes. He had no desire to place them in his mouth and chew; the whole process of mastication seemed highly inefficient, and the texture of the cubes looked downright unpleasant. A dryness steadily grew within his mouth, so Jack brought the truck to a stop and reached over to grab a water bottle. When his fingers only slipped around the cap, he held the bottle and the cap firmly, and wrenched his hands in opposite directions. Water erupted like a fountain, soaking his shirt and pants. The small amount of water that remained wasn't enough to quench his thirst, and when he attempted to open the second bottle, his hands slipped even more since they were wet. Gently, he held the bottle with both hands and used his teeth to twist the top off, but when it didn't budge he kept increasing the force until the bottle exploded, shooting water into his face and down his throat. Jack coughed and sputtered, gasping for air. He drank greedily, succumbing to more coughing when he gulped too quickly.

Jack dried his hands on his pants and started driving, but it wasn't long before the unfamiliar feeling of true fatigue began to set in. With no blankets or pillows, Jack knew he would be hard pressed to get comfortable; stopping for the night had not been planned. He brought the truck to a halt on a section of level ground, and fiddled with the buttons and levers until the seat began to recline slowly.

The grey road stretching out before him beckoned for the journey to continue, but the sun had almost disappeared below the horizon and Jack could not remember how to turn on the lights. He pushed every single button and twisted all the knobs, but nothing came on. He coasted to a stop on the most level patch of road he could see, and once the air stopped circulating so loudly through the truck, a high-pitched orchestra sounded from outside. Jack hunched in his seat and searched for the source of the noise, suddenly wishing for the security his autocar offered—or at least the quick response it gave to explain anything out of the ordinary.

The thing that would most likely make such a high-pitched noise was the large electric engine resting only a few feet in front of him. Without moving the vehicle to use the energy it created, perhaps it built up heat, elevating the temperature of the vehicle to the point of catastrophic destruction. An instinct to run suddenly overcame him, so Jack opened the door and jumped out of the truck, hitting the ground hard and waiting for the imminent sound of explosion.

Miles from NCC, Jack cursed himself for ever leaving the comfort of home. Here he was, lying face down on broken pavement with throbbing elbows, waiting for his only means of transportation to explode. He could be in a perfectly supportive, temperature-controlled bed roaming New World with Dahlia or even making love to her, yet he lay on the cold, hard ground while repetitive noises threatened to shatter his ear drums. Jack cocked his head, trying to hear better. It almost sounded as if the noise were coming from beyond his truck, not from within. There seemed to be multiple sources of sound fading in and out from all around him, and the more he listened, the more natural it became, organic even, like it was supposed to be happening. Jack closed his eyes, and let the oscillating, persistent tones roll through him, their sound like natural violins, bringing his body to peace. This sound of nature, he mused, could be hundreds or even thousands of insects and animals communicating with each other through the crisp night air. He stood as the droning sound ended in one direction and picked up in another, listening to the buzz of life.

When Jack returned to the cab of the truck, he sat in complete darkness, unsure what to do besides drink another bottle of water. No soothing vibrations or massages lulled him to sleep, and no games or movies populated a queue. He had nothing to do without his Display. There existed only Jack—his mind and the deepening blackness around him. The isolation was palpable; only the noises of nature assured him that something else existed in the world. Eventually the darkness and consistent noise overwhelmed his sense of awareness and discomfort. The curve of the reclined seat did not adjust itself automatically to remove the pressure of his weight, the stuffy air inside the truck did not prevent sweat from trickling down his body, and his arms hung limp at his sides. But despite all this, he slept.

—

Jack awoke to a sharp and incredibly persistent pain in his abdomen, just below his navel. He jumped out of the car and into the dull light of dawn, brushing and swatting at his clothing, trying to be rid of whatever caused the pain. When that yielded no results, he stopped, thinking of what could be happening to make him hurt internally. He tried to calm his mind, running through dangerous insects and small animals he had read about that could cause this symptom. After a few minutes of pain and thinking, a small trickle of liquid escaped from him. Of course—without AI and HAS to tend to his body, the process of taking in nutrition and hydration, and expelling waster, were now completely conscious actions.

Jack undid the fasteners at the front of his pants and relaxed his muscles. When the flow subsided, he basked in the wonder of relief washing over his body and mused that people without AI's innovations must need to go through this process multiple times a day. Another urge arose, so he dealt with it accordingly.

Once back in the truck, Jack realized a pit gnawed within his stomach. He looked at the two sealed nutrient cubes. AI told him they should be eaten before hunger set in, so he ate them both. The grumbling and growling he felt as gas moved around inside his body gave him an uneasy feeling—how did people live like this? Constantly answering to the beck and call of bodily functions, forced to obey the demands of their anatomy. Jack had been looking forward to experiencing life with less automation, but so far it appeared that his body now controlled his daily routine, instead of his Display.

Jack drank another bottle of water to cool his dry mouth and throat, now uncomfortably aware that he would be expelling the liquid in only a few hours. He stared ahead where the grey road stretched out before him, beckoning him to continue the journey. Jack noted a few obstructions in the distance, and with nothing else to do, climbed back into the truck and pushed the right pedal forward. There weren't many obstacles in the way, so the most exciting thing Jack did was to exclaim at the increasing size of insect collisions with the windshield. He still felt nervous driving faster than thirty miles per hour, but even at this higher-than-recommended speed, Jack struggled to maintain alertness. How on Earth did people stay awake driving these things when there were no distractions or stimulations? He must have been driving at least an entire uninterrupted hour, pondering the boredom humanity used to be subject to, before he realized the road had a greater slope to it than before. He had begun the mountain climb and noticed that the acceleration pedal required a significantly harder push just to keep his forward momentum. The speedometer now flickered between five and six miles per hour, and the power cell light flashed red. At this speed, it would take him days to climb the hill, so Jack pushed the pedal all the way to the floor.

The truck lunged forward, throwing Jack's head back into the seat and ripping his hands from their hold on the steering wheel. An electric whine filled the cabin as the truck accelerated forward, and a horrified Jack watched the speedometer approach and then pass fifty. Almost as soon as it had begun, the electric whine diminished, leaving Jack with only the sound of rushing wind. He swerved around a large pile of rocks as it approached faster than anything had before.

With speed decreasing rapidly, Jack pushed the accelerator, but nothing happened. He tried the brakes and the truck began to slow down faster, so he released them. Slowly and with great confusion, Jack came to a full stop. He pressed the brake pedal again as the truck began to roll backwards down the steep hill.

Pushing the start button gave him nothing, nor did pushing every button within reach on the dashboard. The truck acted as it had the first time he came upon it in the dealership —electrically dead. Jack's right leg grew sore and wobbly as he pressed firmly on the brakes, but with no electrical power, he couldn't think of any other way to keep the vehicle from rolling backwards. His options were limited, so he laid them out carefully in his mind as his Display would have done.

1. Try to hold the door open while continuing to press the brakes down, then leap out of the truck as it rolled down the hill, probably towards its destruction.
2. Roll backwards and steer the truck, orienting it horizontally on the hill.
3. Sit with his trembling foot on the brake until someone came by to help.

A few more ideas popped into his mind, but they grew more and more ridiculous and unlikely the longer he thought. Based on Jack's analysis of other quick movements he had attempted, he wasn't agile enough to jump out of a moving vehicle. He put option 1 on hold, but when he tried to turn the wheel in preparation for option 2, a mechanism clicked and the wheel would turn no more. In the silence of the hot, rising sun, Jack eliminated option 3; it didn't look like anyone had been on this road in decades, and he couldn't rely on luck that someone would happen to pass by.

The sunlight beaming through the windshield made him sweat profusely. He carefully leaned over with his foot still on the brake and retrieved a bottle of water, then promptly dropped it because of the slippery sweat on his hands. Jack thought about just letting go of the brake pedal and hoping for the best. The seat belt should hold him in place, and the soft seat would absorb impact if the truck backed into anything.

Jack continued to run ludicrous new ideas through his mind until he felt a tremor. A delicate perturbation that vibrated the truck so slightly that he couldn't tell if the movement was real or not. Could it be an earthquake? Maybe a loud vehicle in the distance? Jack had watched videos of the vehicles people drove before automation, and some of them seemed to be loud enough to physically shake their environments. Glancing around, he didn't see anyone approaching, nor did anything nearby visibly move. A low rumble greeted his ears, coupling with the trembling earth. A group of birds fled en masse from a lone tree on the side of the road.

The sound and vibration grew louder, until Jack thought the world itself was tearing apart. The near-deafening roar seemed to emanate from the horizon in front on him, with the mountain to the left seeming to be the most likely candidate. Could the mountain be breaking apart? Jack looked at a large peak on the right side of the horizon, just as a vision he would never forget struck him.

Just above the jagged mountain in front of him, a slim shape rose into the air. A tube with a conical tip slowly grew from the peak and exposed two more tubes fastened side-by-side to the center. The whole assembly streaked up into the sky as one, and upon seeing the whole object, Jack recognized the shape of a rocket. A bright plume of fire and smoke bellowed out from below, so bright that Jack cried out and threw up his hands to shield his eyes.

Classroom memories of the numerous types of gravity-defying machines exploded into his mind. The one lifting into the sky in front of him was built by a private space exploration company, and designed for large payloads. But it would have to have been built before Jack was even born—how could something so old be working so well? He remembered watching rocket launches on television, and learning about the subsequent worldwide outcry that arose over the waste of resources. Increased attention was placed on unsuccessful missions, and the space agencies and private companies started losing support due to the propaganda. Workers left as colonization attempts failed, and soon everyone agreed that space travel was too unpredictable, too dangerous, and not profitable enough.

Then Jack remembered the storms. Spurred by warming oceanic currents, endless hurricanes and tornadoes constantly tore into coastal cities and dispersed their populations. The devastation grew to such catastrophic levels that eventually people stopped trying to move back. Jack vividly recalled when his school closed for over a month, designated for refugees from the evacuated coasts until the pre-fab apartment complexes could be completed. The condensing of the population was staggering. Every inland city and town became a sprawling, overpopulated refugee camp, and without the proper infrastructure in place, many failed.

Then came the reports from the tech companies, who had united with one common goal. They said all the destruction was predicted and preventable. They said every government in the world had been warned, but nothing was done due to high cost and the unknown factor of their new, predictive technology. And they said everything was getting worse. Though the politically-influenced media had tried to withhold these reports, they were published on every freelance and social media outlet possible, and worldwide outcry spread. Revolution ignited, but a single voice of reason spoke through the madness. A single voice backed by data, logic, and unlimited resources. The artificial intelligence engine responsible for the correct predictions of every single destructive weather pattern on the planet offered a solution that, when sponsored by the military coups and violent revolutionaries, the world governments finally surrendered to. Those who disagreed did not have the resources to properly resist.

Synthesis of all nutrients vital to human sustainment became public knowledge. Rapid building of permanent, ecological housing began in earnest, doubling the carrying capacity of the overcrowded cities within a single month. But with all the success, salvation, and universally available comfort came a warning of further destruction.

The global temperature continued to rise, especially noticeable in the growing desert along the equator. AI predicted that within the next fifty years, the band of latitude thirty degrees north and south of the equator would increase to an average temperature of 110°F. In one-hundred years, that temperature would extend up to the forty-degree line, with an equatorial mean of 140°F.

With AI now in charge of most national budgets, no one squabbled over who or what caused the problems; all attention focused on addressing the issues and required actions for feasible solutions. Slowly, humanity migrated in the direction of the poles. Carbon emissions were cut to zero. Dependence on mass farming was eliminated. Ninety percent of the world's remaining population clustered into eighteen great cities, and they held strong. The billions of lives lost had numbed people, and the population that didn't enter into the cities was left to… to what? At this, Jack struggled. He, like so many others, had moved to one of the great cities and then simply existed in a new stage of life, without giving a thought to the outside world.

The flood of information overwhelmed him— especially since the facts came not from a dialogue box on his Display, but from within his own mind. Jack attempted to record his viewpoint and search for information about the rocket, but he quickly realized that there were no quotes, statistics, or dialogue boxes appearing. If only he could activate his Display, Jack would already know the rocket's trajectory, how far away he was from the launch site, and perhaps even how the rocket survived for so many years.

Jack stared at the pillowy trail of white smoke contrasted against the blue sky, amazed at the amount of memories induced by the sight of the rocket. He needed to figure out where this rocket came from, and why the people in charge launched it. If the trail of fire and smoke he had seen days ago also came from a rocket, perhaps people outside of NCC participated in an ongoing space program. Maybe they were picking up where the past world had left off and were providing support to whatever colonies survived on the moon and Mars. Or perhaps they were searching for other areas to colonize. Jack remembered there being a lot of talk about Titan and Europa, although he couldn't quite remember where those two were in the Solar System. This was the real reason he began his journey: to explore. Nothing else in his life was more important than figuring out these mysteries.

With a shock, Jack realized that his periphery showed a moving landscape. The truck was rolling backwards down the hill, quickly picking up speed. Desperately, Jack tried to push the brake pedal harder, but his leg ached so much with the effort he had already exerted, and he couldn't push it down any farther. The steering wheel was still locked in place, and the landscape moved faster.

Sheer panic overwhelmed his body and mind. There were no more options to consider; it was time to test his agility. Jack opened the door and threw his body out, moving his legs to kick off the seat cushion. Time slowed down as he glimpsed the ground beneath his body. The air blew against his face, the sun shone on his exposed arms, and his body inched closer to the ground with each passing millisecond. His legs almost cleared the truck as it continued down the hill, but his feet caught the edge of the door, which caused his body to spin.

Jack's elbows hit the ground first. Then his knees, and time resumed its normal flow through Jack's mind. Pain exploded through all four limbs, and his body rotated backwards with its newfound angular momentum, slamming its entire weight onto Jack's tailbone. He heard a loud crack and felt it reverberate through his spine. He rolled backwards, and his head bounced off the pavement. One more lengthwise roll, and he landed face down. The hot asphalt burned his face and arms as the sun cooked his motionless, bleeding body.

Chapter 9

—

Confusion dominated Jack's mind as he awoke with no pain. The sky seemed brighter than before; he must have been asleep for hours for the sun to have climbed so high. Scanning the green terrain yielded no truck, nor were there any tracks through the tall grass as it waved in the warm breeze. The air felt hot and stagnant, but there was no sweat on Jack's skin or clothes. The only sound was that of the swaying grass, its slender stalks colliding with each other and making a rustling sound all around him. He closed his eyes and listened, enjoying the natural music.

Limbs moved back and forth without protest, and Jack's tailbone didn't seem injured despite the jarring impact and terrible snapping sound he had heard when hitting the ground. Jack rotated his head freely, and when he tilted it back to take in the warm sun, there was no longer any sign of the rocket in the sky. The whitish blue of the horizon faded to true blue, then darkened to a deep, vibrant purple directly overhead.

Oddly, the sun hung close to the horizon, bigger and more orange than he remembered. Perhaps smoke particles in the air from the rocket's exhaust trail diffracted the light—Jack recalled an article about pollution causing that sort of effect. His eyes drifted away from the sun and towards the deep purple zenith, but when he looked back to the bright orb its apparent size seemed bigger. Just as he began to explain to himself how a dense pocket of smog could magnify the image, a flare shot out the side of the sun. The flare licked the space around it, undulating like a tentacle. Suddenly the sun flashed green as it grew to swallow the flare, and then reddened once more.

The sun was now so large that it almost stretched from the horizon to the zenith. The color had shifted to that of fresh blood, sending a shock of fear through Jack. He cowered as the sun grew further, as though it was going to swallow the Earth. In response to this idea, a dialogue box with a single line of text popped into his view, its friendly, familiar font bringing a measure of peace. The bright blue text contrasted with the omnipresent red of the expanding star.

So ends the Earth, and your time on it. What have you accomplished?

Jack stood open mouthed and read the line over and over again, only dimly aware of the warmth growing on his face and arms. Several yards behind the text, a figure floated. The black form reflected none of the too-bright sunlight. The profound question from a mysterious figure brought no immediate response to Jack's mind, only more questions. Who was this person to judge him, and question his accomplishments? And how could the Earth be ending?

"I've accomplished more than anyone else in NCC," Jack shouted into the air, "I'm more adventurous, too." Jack's voice died with no echo, and the letters in the air shifted.

Congratulations. I cannot wait to meet you.

The heat on his exposed skin now burned with an insistent intensity. Jack looked down, and saw that his arms mimicked the red color of the Sun. They bubbled and blistered, little pockets of skin bursting and releasing sprays of fluid into the air. He brought his hands to his face and felt the same gruesome effect on his cheeks and forehead. He screamed, more from the fear than the intense pain he felt. When sound escaped his lips, it was not his own voice, but a booming, baritone rumble.

—

The deafening shout woke Jack. As his lungs deflated, the outside air resounded with a loud crack, followed by the deep rumble he had heard. The air around Jack's head felt like it was breaking apart. Jack tried to open his eyes, though he seemingly lacked the energy to perform the task. Searing pain in his hands, arms, and hips erupted when he pushed off the ground, and he fell back onto his stomach with a scream. No one in the world had ever felt pain like this—of that Jack was sure. He tried to roll over, but putting any pressure on his hip brought back the scream. No thoughts passed through his mind as he unwillingly surrendered to the pain.

After laying on his face for what seemed like ages, the pain in Jack's hip finally subsided to less than that of the burning road against his face. Fully knowing what he was about to subject himself to, Jack rocked to one side, then rotated his body quickly in the other direction, rolling through the pain blossoming in his hip. He came to rest on his back, and finally had a distraction from the agony.

The trail of smoke from the rising rocket still hung in the air, though it was actively dissipating. But what captured his attention was the large cloud of black smoke that had replaced the rocket. Bright sparks and streamers of fire fell away from the dark cloud. A large spark disappeared in a smoking streamer falling to the ground.

"No," Jack croaked, trying to take a full breath through his fiery throat. The sky grew blurry as tears welled in his eyes. How could something like this happen? The people responsible for a rocket launch certainly wouldn't have the knowledge contained within NCC, or the quick thinking of AI, but there would be engineers, scientists, technical specialists, subject matter experts—all sorts of professionals that possessed a large collective intelligence.

Or perhaps those people weren't available. Maybe the people of Banff had inherited the rocket from a past generation without really understanding it. Or they obtained it through other means and had no knowledge as to how it worked. The questions in Jack's mind again only made more questions than he could not answer. If the rocket was of new construction then sure, it would make sense that it might fail—the people in charge of its construction wouldn't have the experience that the organizations of Jack's childhood had. They could only interpret old documents and plans that may or may not have been easily decipherable. Then, materials would need to be procured, parts and pieces fabricated, then organized and assembled. The rocket must have been built decades ago, but as far as Jack could remember, the only launch sites in North America were very far south. Not only were those regions now completely inhospitable, the launch sites themselves were underwater. Any of those locations where a rocket would have been left were thousands of miles away. Thousands of miles through bleak, deathly-hot desert. The only logical conclusion was that the residents of Banff built and launched the rockets themselves.

The cloud of debris still dominated the sky, the floating fires extinguished, but the cloud itself not yet diffuse enough to see through. Jack's whole body throbbed rapidly in time with his heartbeat and erupted whenever he tried to move. His hip seemed to be the worst of all his injuries, but his arms, elbows, and head sported deep abrasions. The fog of confusion that surrounded him suggested that he might be suffering from internal damage as well. The bright sunlight burned into his eyes, and Jack draped his arm over his face to protect himself.

Why had he ever left? The mystery of the rocket faded from his mind as he thought of his bed and shower that fully supported and cleaned him, and his couch that massaged his entire body. He could have been sitting on it with Dahlia, engaged in whatever New World excitement or debauchery they desired. And his watch, Jack felt the beautiful golden timepiece pressed against his ear as his arm lay across his face. He didn't hear any ticking. Jack had neither the physical nor emotional strength to check on its condition.

Life used to be so much easier—and could be again, if only he could get back to NCC. Although, with the amount of time he'd spent on the road so far, he must be closer to Banff. If he made it into Banff then he could find someone to give him a ride back—or even figure out a way to contact AI directly—and get back home. He didn't belong out here in the middle of nowhere. He should have learned when he tried to ride the bicycle; he simply wasn't cut out for this type of thing.

Jack lay on the ground, groaning in agony, staring at the dissipating cloud in the darkening sky for over an hour. As the sun hid itself in the mountains up the road, the cloud fully disappeared. With no direct light on his broken body, Jack soon began to shiver. The ground still warmed him from beneath, but now a steady, cool breeze passed over him. He would need to get out of the road somehow, and the truck was the best place he could think of to spend the night. All the pivoting and rotating he had done so far hadn't shown him where it ended up. Just thinking about relaxing on the front bench seat made him envious. The desire was strong enough to compete with his pain. But considering how hard it had been to roll over, getting up and searching down the hillside for the vehicle was out of the question.

A howl echoed in the distance. The piercing, predatory cry jolted Jack into a heightened state of awareness, and suddenly getting to the truck was not out of the question. The sky seemed to darken by the second, and another howl sounded. It came from the same direction as the first, but closer.

Jack clenched his jaw and attempted to roll onto his stomach again, this time rotating towards the less painful side. He fought the blinding pain, struggling to retain consciousness. Now laying on his stomach pointed straight down the road, he saw the truck. Perhaps one-hundred or so yards away, it rested underneath a tree with its back end pushed up against the trunk. When he tried to prop himself up on his elbows, pain shocked through him like a bolt of lightning. Extending his arms out in front of his face, he pushed his body forward with his toes and clutched at the ground with his fingers. He slowly inched towards the end of the road, one toe push at a time.

Another howl sounded as Jack pushed himself into the dirt and wild grass beside the road. Mud instantly formed on his sweaty body and ground into his wounds, but the soft surface offered some relief, so he propped himself up on his elbows. Jack moved faster this way, though he kept picturing a wild deer with massive fangs tearing into him at any second as he slowly crawled towards the truck. His hip bumped into a stone, and he had to stop for a few minutes until the waves of pain-induced nausea subsided. Bugs and seeds rained down on him as he moved through tall grass, but he ignored the itching as he heard yet another howl, now in front of him. The new howl answered the call that approached from behind. A log appeared in front of Jack as he pushed grass aside, and rather than attempt to pull himself over he changed direction and went around. Once past the log, he rocked back onto his raw, bleeding knees in order to check that he was still heading in the right direction.

The sky turned completely black as he reached the truck, and now Jack faced the daunting task of boosting himself up into the cab. The grass rustled behind him. Fighting the pain, he propped himself up on his knees again, the sweat on his brow running into his eyes and blurring his vision. He felt around on the door for the handle. His hand grasped it just as he heard a low growl from the rustling grass. His adrenaline surged, and he pulled himself up, pushing as much as he could with his legs.

Jack pulled open the door, careful to avoid striking his face, and fell on the seat. His legs still hung out, and as he looked backwards, two glowing eyes sprang forward from the tall grass.

Again, it felt as if time slowed down. A snarling face

bared glistening white teeth with large, knife-shaped incisors. His leg reflexively kicked forward, and his boot made contact with the snarling snout. The animal that was certainly not a deer yelped as its head turned and hit the side of the truck. Jack reached out and pulled the door shut as hard as he could, letting the weight of the door throw him flat on the bench seat. His quick breathing turned to full-body trembling, and then painful and uncontrollable sobbing. Jack tried thinking of what to do now, but the post-adrenal crash and the newfound safety from the snapping jowls and echoing yelps outside the truck forced him into unconsciousness.

—

Again, Jack woke because of his need to relieve himself. A streamer of light entered his cracked eyelids and burned his eyes. As he slowly shifted his position and sat up, all the injuries of the previous day made themselves known. Jack relieved himself still seated in the cab of the truck, barely able to hold the door open as the dark and evil smelling urine spilled to the ground. When he finished, Jack simply lay back on the seat, breathing heavily with no ambition or ideas of what to do next. No animals roamed outside in the cool early morning air, but Jack lacked the strength and physical sturdiness to try and exit the truck for an inspection. The last thing he remembered before his fateful jump was holding down the brakes. That hadn't stopped the truck, and there seemed to be no response from the electrical system. Most likely, the addition of the power cell caused a failure, but in his current condition Jack doubted that anything could be done to fix it. Sharp pains grew inside his hip and tail bone as he sat, despite shifting positions to move his weight around.

Only three bottles of water remained, and with the nutrient cubes a day gone, pangs of hunger moved through Jack's stomach. He sat in the seat until the pains all over his body grew too sharp to ignore. Moving aside his shirt and pants showed that his right hip had turned a dark purple—almost black, though it was his pounding head that gave him the most grief. Jack suspected dehydration played a role in this, as his mouth felt like sand and tasted like dirty leather. A bottle of water would help with that, but they'd all rolled into the passenger foot well, completely unreachable unless he found a way to exit the truck and walk around to the other side. Eventually, he would need to exit the truck—when he pushed the start button, nothing happened. Sitting in the slowly warming truck as the sun rose was no way to die.

Unlike when he had been briefly trapped in his autocar, death was now an imminent reality. Although, it had also been real last night, and he survived. Like every citizen of NCC, Jack knew that certain issues such as disease and aging had been mitigated by AI, but now that AI had been left behind, the possibility of death gave Jack a new feeling. Not quite fear—he had enough of that from the gnashing teeth last night—Jack felt...invigorated.

Decisions made now would either help him survive, or help him die. Everything he did from this point forward needed to consider that risk. Though his entire body hurt every time he moved, the movements would not kill him. Sitting in the truck without moving would eventually kill him.

So Jack moved. His hip flared with pain, and his legs gave out a few times as he crawled across the bench seat towards where a water bottle lay on the floorboard. Each time he collapsed, he moved again, pushing himself closer to the water. Jack reached out his arm after a particularly painful spasm, and closed his fingers around one of the smooth plastic bottles. He momentarily felt no pain as he yelled in triumph. Greater than winning any quest or competition in New World, the exultation he felt as he held the bottle above himself rolled through his body. Jack struggled with the top for a moment, relishing the cool splash on his face as he broke the seal. Greedily, he drank the water as fast as possible, consuming the entire contents in only a few seconds. His hand shot out involuntarily for another bottle. He found one, and drank the whole thing.

The dryness and fire now gone from his throat, Jack thought about his next action. Though his thirst was quenched, he would still die if he didn't get the truck running again. He shifted back over to the driver's side of the truck and groped for the hidden lever that opened the hood, pulling at it until his weak fingers finally managed to pop the hood open.

A torturous journey out of the truck followed, and Jack almost fell as he again misjudged the distance to the ground. Using the truck for support, Jack limped to the hood, hoping there would be some indication of what had caused the truck to stop responding. He remembered some charge had remained in the power cell; perhaps it just needed to be hooked up again.

The power cell itself was easy enough to find, situated where the heavy battery had been. Two thick wires were connected to the cell, but Jack saw no immediate problem with them. During the quick-start guide to using an antique vehicle, AI had mentioned the concepts of positive and negative terminals, current, and solar cells. The red wire disappeared somewhere under the electric motor, but the black wire ran along the front air dam support and over to a black plastic box. Jack removed the top cover, and saw the termination of the black wire on a plate of metal stamped "Ground." Also connected to this plate were several smaller wires, all stamped with a function. Looking at the multitude of wires all disappearing under a piece of plastic in one direction or another, Jack threw his hands up with a frustrated sigh. When he brought them back down to firmly hit the truck, one of the thick wires attached to the ground plate moved.

Next to the wire was a label "S. Panel," with a slew of smaller wires branching out in every direction. Jack touched the wire, and when he pushed, it separated from the lug connected to the ground plate. The "S." in "S. Panel" must stand for "Solar," and if the solar panel wasn't connected to the battery, then no wonder it had run out of charge. Jack angled the disconnected wire towards himself, and he saw that the wire hadn't simply been disconnected, it had been cut. Bundled cords of bright copper glinted at Jack, surrounded by a clean plastic coating. The wire must have been cut by… what? Jack looked around and saw nothing sharp in the area. The plastic lid had been on while he was driving, and the hood had been down. Nothing had touched this area since he himself looked at it with AI.

Then Jack's stomach dropped. AI had installed the power cell for him, but Jack hadn't watched the process. While the hood was up, Jack had been busy in the truck, distracted by the lesson AI gave him on the finer points of driving an antique car. Could it be possible that AI had sabotaged his truck?

The nauseated feeling began to pass as Jack convinced himself that no matter what this looked like, AI would never do something to harm him. Sure, she had let him fall off the bike, but she had insisted he wear a helmet. She had tended to his wounds when he was hurt, helped him find the bike and the truck…

"No," Jack said out loud. "There's no way." But the more he looked at the separated wire, the less he could convince himself that the wire was disconnected during the accident. The copper reflected a glare from the sun into Jack's eyes, and he remembered how hot he was. How hot and how stranded. Thinking about the reason for this wouldn't help him survive. He needed to reconnect the wire somehow.

A small bolt held the connection in place on the ground plate, and rather than search around for a tool, Jack was pleased to see that he could rotate the bolt by pushing on the wire connector. He rotated the metal bolt until the connector was loose, and removed it from the plate. He spent several minutes trying to remove the stub of wire from the connector, but it was crimped in tightly with no hopes of loosening. Jack put the connector down and before hopelessness could set in, grabbed the trunk of wire where all the solar panel branches met. He stared at it, ignoring the pain and tiredness that he felt, thinking how he could connect a flat piece of wire to the ground plate. Jack picked at the plastic shell around the copper core, and a tiny piece came away. Jack looked at the tiny piece of insulating plastic now stuck under his fingernail. With enough of the material removed, the copper would be exposed. Then, he could stick it under the bolt on the ground plate. Jack picked again, and an even smaller piece flaked off.

Jack started a painful amble to the passenger-side door. If there was a knife in there, it would strip away the plastic much faster. AI had mentioned something about a tool kit in the glove compartment. Jack pulled on the passenger side door handle. It was locked. Fighting tears of frustration and keeping his mind on survival, Jack shuffled to the driver's side and slowly lifted himself in, crawled across the bench seat and opened the glove compartment. Inside lay a booklet congratulating the reader on the purchase of a fine automobile, a silver socket wrench, and a small clear box with several fuses inside. Jack looked carefully at the metal protruding from each of the fuses, but couldn't figure out a way to use them.

With slow purpose, Jack exited the truck and limped back to the open hood and the exposed ground plate. Jack picked at the plastic. Again and again, until every fingernail was full of small black pieces. He kept picking until the plastic pushed under his nails further, drawing blood. The blood made the plastic slivers slide under his fingernails more easily, but compared to the pain he felt just standing in his broken body, it wasn't so bad. Eventually, a small glimmer of copper peeked out, smeared with blood. The progress made Jack attack another piece of plastic with renewed vigor.

Jack tried to keep thoughts of AI out of his head as he worked, but holding the perfectly sliced copper in his hand made it difficult. There had to be a reasonable explanation. Maybe the dealership cut them to prevent the old power cells from overcharging. But, then the copper would be oxidized. Maybe a piece of metal pushed its way under the plastic cover during the accident, and it went completely through the wire. Jack didn't even try and rationalize that one. Maybe it was a factory defect. Maybe it wasn't supposed to be connected, and if Jack finished what he was doing, the truck would explode. Maybe AI cut the wire when she installed the power cell, giving Jack just enough energy to get to the middle of nowhere.

That seemed more ridiculous than any other scenario he came up with, but it was the only one he couldn't disprove in his mind. Jack shook his head. There was no way that AI did this to him. She was interested in what he did with his life, and what he came up with while he was gone. She hadn't even wanted him to go—shouldn't that mean that she wanted him to come back? What was it AI had said when he left? *Nice to know you,* or something like that. Or had those been Dahlia's words?

Jack's fogged mind had no answers. A tear slid off his cheek and landed on his scraping finger. The tear moistened the sticky blood on the wire, and Jack realized he was scraping against bare metal. He had scraped off almost a half-inch of plastic, all the way around the wire. With numb and clumsy fingers, Jack separated the copper strands into two bundles, and slid them around the loosened bolt on the ground plate. His weak hands couldn't turn the bolt any further than simply touching the wire, so Jack spread out the strands and twisted the bolt down as far as he could.

The walk back to the door of the truck would be his last. There was simply no energy left in his body. He entered the truck one last time and pushed "On" button. The small display behind the steering wheel showed the bold red words, "Inadequate Charge." Jack waited. His eyes were locked on the bar beneath the words, currently red and well below the smallest graduation mark. He stared at the red bar until everything else in his vision grew dull, and grey shadows flickered across his eyes.

The red bar gained a pixel. Jack exhaled in relief. A cautious smile crept on to his face as he allowed himself the luxury of hope. He laid down across the bench seat and grabbed the final water bottle from the floor. With his useless bloody hands, this one took the longest to open. But when it finally did, Jack drank it slow, savoring and appreciating the wetness. The water washed into his empty stomach, where the pangs of hunger had turned into an incessant stab of need. He used his flagging energy to hope that the red bar gained enough pixels before the sun fully set. Jack held up his hand to the sky. He could barely fit it between the sun and the top of the nearest mountain range.

—

When the sun finally disappeared behind, Jack realized that this signaled the end of day two of his four-hour drive. The bar showing the charge of the power cell was no longer red, although it was far from full. Far from the halfway mark, even. Jack hesitantly pushed the accelerator, and the vehicle inched forward. The back end groaned and cracked as the bumper separated itself from the abused wood. The truck crawled along the field, bumping up and down as Jack slowly steered towards the road. He dared not attempt to go too fast. Jack remembered AI's warning about not going above twenty-five, and it seemed that his reckless burst of speed earlier on had caused the power cell to suddenly drain.

Once on the road, the truck continued to bounce with a regular thumping that increased in frequency the faster he drove. The rear end of the truck oscillated up and down, shaking the cab violently until Jack slowed down. Striking the tree had caused a significant problem in the rear end of the vehicle, and Jack had no choice but to slow down. A whisper of electric discharge was all he could hear, creeping along the road at just over ten miles per hour. He seemed to be traveling slower than he could walk, but compared to how fast he had been crawling, there was no room for complaining.

Every jostle pained his mutilated body, but every bounce of the truck brought him closer to his destination. As long as he kept his foot on the pedal, Jack would learn why people lived outside of the cities, and why they launched rockets. What had started out so innocently as a mild curiosity had grown into an insatiable need for knowledge. Jack mused that curiosity now kept him alive. Back home a timeless, perfectly comfortable and predictable life awaited, with no worries or pains. That life would remain perfect for as long as he wanted it to, and he would be happy. There lay the reason he couldn't go back yet—beyond the mountain he now crested existed something he didn't understand, maybe even an entire life waiting to offer more than anything AI or New World could give.

Jack vaguely realized his eyes were closed, and that he hadn't seen the road in quite some time. There was a dull, repetitive thudding in the back of his mind, but he couldn't figure out if it was his pulse or the back end of the truck acting up again. A sharp sound pierced the thudding, but never registered as important in Jack's foggy mind. The brakes didn't work—somehow he knew that. Some unconscious instinct had tried to push the pedal, but Jack couldn't figure out how or why he would do that. His body moved side to side, back and forth, but he paid it no mind. The motions felt like a particularly thorough nightly massage, rubbing and vibrating his torn and aching body, soothing him into a blissful, dreamless slumber.

Chapter 10

———

A fuzzy outline in the shape of a head faded in and out of view, accompanied by a sweet and arousing aroma. Distant rumbling noises turned on and off, like thunder clouds talking to each other. Something small and sharp poked itself to the inside crease of Jack's right elbow, and his view again faded to black.

———

Jack felt his head being manipulated. Lifted up, turned to one side then the other, then gently laid back down. His eyes wouldn't open. Brightness emanated from just beyond his closed lids, and while Jack tried to figure out if he was awake or not, a dull noise greeted his ears. Jack still heard no words, yet the sounds themselves seemed more articulated. A higher, lighter sound responded to deep rumbles. Still his eyes could not be made to open. The brightness began to fade, as did the sounds. Jack hoped that the sounds he heard were not more wild animals. He did not want to be eaten.

—

Light slowly prodded Jack into consciousness. Awakening didn't seem like a good idea—too many aches and pains still besieged his body, and the terribly bright light above him chewed through his eyelids. Jack thought it odd that he could even feel the aches and pains. The last thing he remembered had been lying on a hot road with his broken body unable to move.

No, that wasn't correct. A rocket had exploded, and he had started driving again. That was the last thing he remembered—slowly driving a truck toward Banff. While not the best place to lose consciousness, apparently he had, and was now lying somewhere slightly more comfortable than the seat of the truck, but glaringly more bright. No pleasing scents or noises stirred his senses this time. In this Universe, only his mind and the increasingly overwhelming light existed.

Jack tried to shut his eyes tighter, hoping for respite. The effort made his head pound. He realized that in trying to close his eyes tighter, he had been holding his breath. Jack gasped, and the inrush of air soothed the pounding in his head but caused a new fire to ignite in his dry throat. Breathing heavily and trying to deduce where he could possibly be, Jack tried to pretend that the light above wouldn't be enough to drive him insane.

"God, just turn off the light," Jack spoke. The light did not turn off, but he heard a clicking sound, and the sweet aroma returned. Jack couldn't get his mouth to form any more words, and after another click and a small brush of wind, the scent was gone. He gasped in relief as the light dimmed.

Jack shifted uncomfortably as he lay, trying to relieve the pressure building on his back and head. There was no possibility that his own bed would provide this mediocre support to his body, and when he tried to lift his arms, he discovered that some type of soft strap firmly held both arms down at his sides. When he tried to move his legs, he discovered that they, too, were bound.

Jack cracked his eyes open, and saw a small curling tube attached to a bag filled with clear liquid hanging on a rack. The tube aimed at his mouth, and though the bed sat at an inclined angle, several inches separated the tube from Jack's mouth. Another bag of liquid hung from the same rack standing on the side of the bed. The tube from this bag twisted further down, meeting a piece of tape attached to the inside crease of his elbow.

"Go ahead, take a drink," said a male voice on his right. Jack snapped his head quickly to the side, and immediately regretted the movement. A loud pop jolted his neck, and pain flared throughout his head, neck, and shoulders. Jack shut his eyes and breathed heavily, waiting as the pain slowly subsided. When some semblance of lesser discomfort finally settled in, he cracked his eyes open. An old magnetic speaker hovered in midair, and a small, pale man with a close-cropped white beard and large black framed glasses sat behind it on a simple metal chair, his legs crossed and bouncing mindlessly. Some type of device hung around his neck, a portion obscured from view by the long white coat the man wore. Though Jack could not recall ever visiting a person like this, the word "doctor" came to mind; surely a reference to a character in a movie he recently watched. What interested Jack, apart from the strange clothing and gadgets, was the intimidatingly indifferent expression the man held. He wasn't happy or mad, nor excited or upset.

His eyes were dull brown—nothing special or outstanding whatsoever. They carried no glow from a

Display, and no augmented, vibrant color designed to catch another person's interest. Most importantly, they didn't flicker around the room, constantly searching for Display-based text or imagery as Jack was so used to seeing. The brown eyes stared directly at Jack—not past him or off to the side, but into his own eyes, acknowledging Jack's presence. Suddenly, Jack realized the man had said something to him, though what, he could not remember.

"Huh?" Jack managed as a dry whisper.

"Yes, you must be thirsty. Take a drink." He pointed to the tube above Jack's head with a pen he held in a steady hand.

Regardless of the questions he had, Jack intended to drink before asking any of them. He lifted his head ever so slightly off the firm pillow, and his neck exploded with sharp pain. It reverberated over his entire skull and out across the shoulder blades, reaching down his back. The sensation so overpowered him that he couldn't put his head down even if he wanted to, and he did not want to, afraid that the pain might increase if he moved again.

Jack puckered his dry lips around the end of the clear tube, and drew cool water into his mouth. It flowed down his tongue and throat and elicited a cough, but Jack choked it back and did not release his suction. Water dribbled out of his mouth and down his face as he kept drinking, not sure if he would be able to stop. His neck felt locked in place. When the entire bag of liquid hung empty from its swaying hook, he let his head drop back to the pillow. Of course, his body exploded with pain again, but Jack was used to that, now. The doctor spoke, and Jack realized that the speaker his voice came through wasn't hovering, rather, it was set into a clear glass wall.

"Now, why don't you try that first noise you made

again?"

"Huh?" Jack said again, a bit of the rasp now gone.

The seated man chortled, flipping his pen around a finger and scratching a note on the pad of paper he held.

"My, my, but someone is confused. Feeling a bit out of place?" He made a clicking sound with his mouth.

Rather than ask the stupid sounding, "Where am I?" that popped into his mind, Jack attempted to answer the question himself by looking around. The incline of the bed allowed him to clearly see double doors centered and surrounded by bright white walls that gave the impression of cleanliness. Several long tube lights arrayed across the ceiling broadcast the light Jack could now at least tolerate, though some of them flickered with maddening regularity. With his eyes now accustomed to the light and the water making him feel just a bit more energized, Jack saw that his restrictive bed sat in the middle of a glass enclosure, in the middle of the bright hospital room (another word that came to mind instinctively) . Jack saw no doorway in.

"Why are you looking around?" the doctor asked through the embedded speaker. "Can't you tell me where we are right now? Aren't you being flooded with information of your whereabouts? Coordinates, temperature… threat level?" The doctor moved his white jacket aside, revealing the wooden grip of a large steel revolver. It looked disproportionately large hanging from the leather holster on the small man's belt, but still gave Jack a twinge of panic. Guns were common enough in New World, but Jack realized now that he had never actually seen one in real life.

"Yes," the doctor continued, "I know all about your society, and the computers you have hooked up to your head. You depend on them for every aspect of your life, and you're useless without them—completely worthless."

Computer—another word dredged from the basement of Jack's memory. There appeared to be some misconceptions in the doctor's mind; Jack could no more discern his coordinates and temperature than he could hop into his autocar and fly away.

"I'm not worthless," Jack said defiantly, "and my *computer* is off—it's been off my entire journey."

The doctor frowned, pulling the sides of his mouth down to an almost humorous level as he read something off the clipboard he held.

"I don't believe you," the doctor said after a pause. "You don't have the authority to turn it off. Even if you could, you wouldn't—you need it to survive."

"What are you talking about? My Display doesn't control me."

The doctor wrote down a note on his pad.

"*Your* Display. And what is the purpose of the Display?"

"It does—well, it does everything. Schedules, to-do lists, shopping, you know. It's how AI tells us things that we need to know. And it's how we communicate and access New World." The doctor's expression darkened.

"Why are you here?" the doctor asked, his hand gliding over the notepad as he wrote. Suddenly a feeling of unease washed over Jack. Perhaps he shouldn't be divulging so much information upon his first contact with someone outside of NCC. Especially when that person had already threatened him.

"No," Jack said. "I've been answering your questions, now I want some of my own answered."

"No," the doctor retorted, looking up from his pad and into Jack's eyes. "You're not in any position to be making demands. I don't think you quite understand the seriousness of your situation."

"Oh really?" Jack said, heat rising into his face. "And what exactly is my situation? I decided to go on a trip to learn about things outside of my city. I've learned that there is danger in this world, but I didn't think that danger would come from the people I met here in Banff."

"You have a great deal to learn, young man. And what makes you think you're in Banff?"

Before Jack could respond, the double doors in the outer room opened with a whoosh, and a tall, slender woman walked up to the glass enclosure. She pressed her hand against a metal plate in the glass, and a section opened. She then approached the suspended bag of clear liquid that Jack had not emptied. Her light brown hair was tied back in a simple ponytail. She was completely focused on her duty and didn't make eye contact with Jack. Her outfit, though loose, was well tailored and hinted at enough of her figure to entice Jack.

"Hello," Jack said, momentarily forgetting all about the doctor.

"Hi," she said curtly, looking from the bag of liquid to a small display also mounted to the rack.

"Who are you?" Jack asked.

"I'm your nurse," she said. Before Jack could try and make her say something more interesting, the doctor interrupted through the speaker.

"If you're done in there, please answer my question. Why do you think you're in Banff?"

"That's where I was heading, straight through the mountains," Jack said, irritated. The mention of the mountains made Jack think about the rocket. "And I saw a rocket launch, then explode in the sky. It couldn't have been too far from here—where was that?" As soon as he said the word *explode,* Jack saw a small smile creep on to the nurse's face.

"Never mind that," the doctor said, keeping his face flat. "I'm the one asking the questions."

When the doctor finished his sentence, the nurse rolled her eyes, and walked out of the glass enclosure. She went right up to the doctor, planted her hands on her hips, and began speaking.

"Dr. Roland, you need to be a bit more..." Dr. Roland pushed a button on the wall and the speaker cut off. Their conversation outside of the glass room sounded like the back-and-forth rumbling he had heard while unconscious. The woman pointed to Jack, then to the doctor, then back to Jack as she spoke heatedly. The doctor crossed his arms over his chest, looking as if he was losing ground in the argument, but not willing to give in.

After a few moments in which the tall woman continued to speak without even seeming to stop for breath, Dr. Roland threw up his hands, and Jack saw the word "fine" on his lips. The doctor repeated the word, not meeting the woman's glare. She then turned and walked out of the room without even glancing towards Jack. He heard a soft *whump* as the double doors closed. Dr. Roland shifted around in his seat, straightened the lapels of his white coat, and pressed the button on the wall.

"Well, it's been suggested that this whole situation may be more beneficial for everyone if we conduct our business in a different manner—perhaps a more give-and-take approach to the exchange of information." Jack simply nodded, his interest in the nurse growing after seeing how quickly she influenced the doctor's behavior.

"I am Dr. Roland, the Chief of Medicine here at Banff Community Hospital, and I have taken a personal interest in our security during your arrival. My oath ensures that you will be properly tended to during your recovery, but I warn you, at the slightest sign of sabotage or illicit activity, I will act in the best interest of my town."

Jack blinked in surprise.

"I'm not going to do anything, really."

"Then why are you here?"

"I came to explore, and learn." Dr. Roland lifted his eyebrows. "I did. Things in NCC have grown... a bit stale for me, and I want to see how people live out here. How you live without augmentation and automation."

"We live just fine," Dr. Roland said. "Is that good enough for you to leave?"

"Well, um, I was hoping for a little more," Jack said, taken aback.

Dr. Roland grunted. "Well congratulations," he said, "you made it to Banff through the wilderness in a vehicle that hasn't run in over fifty years and survived somehow, even after making the idiotic decision not to bring any supplies. Then, despite being half-starved and dehydrated, you still managed to crash your truck right into the front of our town's coffee shop."

"Not Pop's," Jack said, recalling the map he and AI had viewed.

"How did you know that?" Dr. Roland asked, furiously scribbling something. "Did AI tell you? Is it on your Display?"

"No," Jack said, "it's still off. I can't turn it on even if I want to."

Dr. Roland grunted again as he studied Jack's face, but did not seem convinced.

"You're not off to a good start here. You're lucky no one was injured or killed, or else we'd be having a very different conversation. As it is, you almost hit a kid riding his bike. He stayed with you until the ambulance arrived." Jack made a mental note to find out who the kid was, thank him, and ask for bike lessons.

"So," Dr. Roland continued, "I've given you some information, now it's your turn." He flipped a few pages on the clipboard. "Name?"

"Jack."

"Full name?"

"Just Jack."

Dr. Roland frowned as he wrote something, flipped back a few pages, scribbled some more, then returned to the first page. He began murmuring to himself, just loud enough for Jack to hear.

"Sex, male. Weight," Dr. Roland paused, looking over the clipboard to the base of Jack's bed, "one-sixty. Age?" He looked up.

Jack thought for a moment, trying to remember the last time he had thought about his age. It would have been at work, during a meeting in which everyone's status was displayed. He closed his eyes and pictured the scene: nine boxes each with a photo of his nine employees, their NCC credentials, and their New World statistics. His own stat box sat on top of theirs, and Jack could clearly picture the line that showed his age.

"Eighty-four," Jack said, opening his eyes and meeting Dr. Roland's gaze. The doctor stared back, not blinking.

"Your age," Dr. Roland said, deadpan.

"Yes," Jack said, envisioning the line on his stat box. "I'm positive."

"Fascinating," Dr. Roland said, staring for a moment.

"What is?" Jack inquired.

Dr. Roland lowered his notepad.

"Do you feel that it is normal for a person your age to look as you do?"

Jack thought for a moment before responding. "Well yes, I suppose. The other day, I turned off my augmentation and saw how old I really look. How I look to you now. It was pretty unpleasant. Fortunately, you can't really tell what people look like underneath the augmentation in NCC."

Dr. Roland nodded, his hand a blur over the notepad as he wrote. He paused briefly to study his notes, allowing the bouncing of his foot to rock his whole body. He pointed at the pad with his pen.

"Your augmentation?" he asked. And with that, Jack launched into an explanation of changing one's appearance, and how AI offered different packages and levels of enhancement. Jack noticed that his explanations tended to center around Dahlia; she was a good subject for the topic, as she always felt the need to change something about herself. Jack stopped after a while, afraid he had said too much. Dr. Roland seemed lost, writing even faster than he had before, pausing intermittently to line through or underline certain portions. After he stopped writing, Dr. Roland spent several minutes reading what he had written. Jack used the time to take another drink of water.

"You mentioned AI before, and you said 'she,'" Dr. Roland said.

"So?"

"You think of artificial intelligence—a computer program—as a person. A woman" When Jack didn't respond immediately, Dr. Roland began writing again.

"What are you writing?"

"That's none of your concern," Dr. Roland answered, his voice distracted. "Remember, I care about my town's safety, nothing more." He paused to look at his notes before continuing. "Did AI suggest that you come here?"

"No," Jack said, almost laughing. "At first, she didn't even want me to come. She said it was too dangerous, and that I couldn't survive on my own without her."

"Maybe she was right," Dr. Roland said. "Let's get

back to the topic of your age. Do realize that you look remarkable for a man in his eighties? Old-timers here in Banff carry themselves very slowly to avoid aches and pains, with white hair, spotted skin, and stooped postures. They pretty much look as if they are falling apart." He paused. "Although I've never seen you walk before, I'm guessing you do it with a bit more vigor and energy than they do."

"I guess," Jack said, not sure at all how to respond.

"Have you ever heard of melaprofinol?" Dr. Roland asked quietly.

The word tugged at Jack's neurons.

"Maybe; should I have?"

"Never mind," Dr. Roland said with a wave. "We're into the medications section of the questionnaire now. Are you currently taking any?"

"Only what you've been giving me," Jack retorted, feeling as if he'd missed something important. "Speaking of which, what have you been giving me? Some of the wounds I got when I fell on the road were quite agonizing––but now there's some kind of warmth that spreads over my body whenever your… nurse comes in."

"Ah, yes." Dr. Roland said with a knowing smile, "that effect can occur around her. I jest, of course. The warmth you are speaking of is a strong painkiller called morphine, and I suspect it's the only reason you've been able to get any sleep these past few days."

"Few days…" Jack whispered.

"Yes, three," he said when he saw the look on Jack's face. "There's no need for alarm; you needed the rest to recover from your injuries. Dehydration and malnourishment, too." Dr. Roland stood, tucking the clipboard under his arm and looking at his watch. "Speaking of which, you need to rest more. I will return later." And with that, he briskly left the room before Jack could voice any protest. Seeing the doctor glance at his watch made Jack want to look at his own, hoping that it didn't suffer too much damage from his vehicular leap. Jack struggled to try and lift his arm, but it was held down tight. After a brief fight with the strap, Jack realized how tired he was. That didn't make sense—he had been asleep for days, and even without AI, his NRs were working to heal his body, so there should be no reason for the tiredness he felt. Jack closed his eyes against the bright light of the room and found himself standing dead center in the middle of a field.

Immediately, Jack realized that he was dreaming, but the lucidity was surprising. The conversation with Dr. Roland still hung in his mind; Jack didn't feel like any time at all had passed since the doctor left. He looked around and saw that, while he stood in a field like the last dream, the sky glowed a dark purple. The sun was nowhere to be seen. Swaying golden wheat stretched from horizon to horizon, and when Jack turned to the same view behind him, he saw a figure approaching. Elegantly, the body coasted through the field directly towards Jack. As the figure approached, Jack saw his own face as he was used to seeing it—enhanced with perfect cheekbones, styled hair, healthy complexion, and smooth skin. But the body lacked substance. Jack could see the outline of tall grass through the figure as it stopped right in front of him, and greeted him in a deep, warm voice.

"Hello, Jack," the ethereal Jack said.

"Hello Jack," Jack said back, playing along.

The ghost of Jack laughed.

"I'm not Jack, you are," said the soothing voice. Jack waited for it to continue fruitlessly.

"Well then, who are you?"

"I'm your old friend, AI," it said bluntly.

"Oh really?" Jack asked. "That's odd."

"I'm so pleased to see that you're all right," AI said.

Jack immediately thought about the cut wire, and his bleeding hands. He decided not to ask about it yet.

"But what about last time? The last dream, when you said you can't wait to meet me."

"That never happened," AI Jack said, the ghostly body stiffening.

"Yes, it did. When I fell on the road and crashed the truck. I had a dream and you said, 'I can't wait to meet you,' or something like that."

"What did this figure look like? Did it touch you? What else did it say?"

"I don't know," Jack said. "I barely even knew someone was there. I thought I was alone. I felt alone."

"You're never alone Jack," AI said. "Remember that. You're—"

Chapter 11

———

Jack's vision staggered back to the glass room as a sharp pain grew in the crease of his left elbow. He gasped, but before he could complain, he smelled the intoxicating scent of the woman he had seen earlier. Jack carefully turned his head and saw her standing next to one of the suspended bags of liquid, flicking a tube with her finger. Her green eyes—green like Dahlia's—glanced to him quickly before returning to her task. The pain in his arm burned where the tube connected, and Jack's arm tensed. He noticed that his arms and legs were no longer restrained.

"I'm not strapped down anymore," Jack said, not wanting to start their conversation by complaining about aches and pains.

"No," she replied. "Dr. Roland decided that you posed no immediate threat, as long as you remained in the enclosure. How are you feeling?" Her voice had a crisp formality to it.

"Better," Jack said, "but my neck still hurts, and so does my ankle. My face feels kind of tingly and itchy, and the rest of my body is really sore, because I've been in the same position for too long."

"Is that all?" she said, laughing softly. Jack felt his face flush. He hadn't wanted to complain, yet here he was, complaining away.

"That's all," Jack said. "I'll be fine."

"You're getting a slow drip of morphine through the IV in your arm. The pains should go away soon. The itch is from the healing skin on your face; you had some pretty serious abrasions." She continued to flick the tube just below the bag of liquid. Jack gave a very small nod, then tried to move his arm. The place where the IV was taped began to hurt, so he stopped.

"What if I didn't want a needle in my arm?" Jack immediately regretted the words; they sounded stupid to his own ears.

"That's not really your choice, is it?" she responded without looking at him, instead checking the drip rate. "Your ankle has been set and cast, and although your hip is fractured, if you keep weight off it, the pain should be minimized. There's not really much more we can do, other than surgery." She pointed to his face as she continued. "The scrapes and bruises are healing very quickly, and we should be ready to remove the bandages by the end of the week."

"I'm fine now. When will you let me walk around?" Jack asked, remembering his argument with AI over the speed of his healing. The NRs had probably already finished.

She looked him up and down with a strange expression.

"Walk? Not for a while, I'm afraid. You broke your

ankle, though I'm sure you already knew that. And your hip, and your tailbone. Right now, I'm getting you ready for another set of X-rays so that we can make sure everything is set properly. Assuming that's moving forward, you'll still need Dr. Roland's clearance before you can leave. Don't worry," she said, leaning in close, "I'm working on him."

Jack grinned, thankful for her conspiratorial support.

"It shouldn't be too hard to convince him I'm not dangerous," Jack said, nodding towards his beaten body. "Just what does he think I can do? All this is from jumping from my truck. It wasn't even moving that fast." He saw a hint of a smile touch her lips, so he continued. "I fell off a bicycle once. I spent the next week in bed recovering. The worst part is, I was wearing a helmet, and wasn't even going that fast."

She smiled, and Jack felt as if he was the king of the world.

"That is pretty pathetic," she said, and Jack relished the sweet insult.

"What's your name?" Jack asked

"Julia."

"That's a nice name," Jack said, as she inspected some of his bandages. "How long have you had it?"

Now, she looked bemused.

"All my life."

"Don't you change it every so often?" Jack asked.

"No," she said, drawing out the sound, "here it's a pretty big deal to change a name. My parents named me, just like everyone else. We keep those names. Are you telling me you chose yours?" Jack nodded his head. "Then why on earth would you pick Jack?"

"What's wrong with Jack?" he asked.

"Well, you claim to be this curious thrill-seeker. Why

not accentuate your attitude with a name like Helios, or Thor?"

Jack shrugged. "It's simple. Efficient and easy to say. I'm a manager in the Department of Efficiency, so I wanted to broadcast that through everything I do."

"Department of Efficiency? Sounds boring. By, the way, sorry about this," Julia moved aside the blanket that covered his legs and midriff, exposing bare skin from his feet up to his waist. Jack squawked loudly—he hadn't known he was naked below the blanket, and now a very strange mix of sensations erupted in his body; a confusing blend of pleasure and pain as Julia cradled him in her hands and began to extract something.

"Sorry," she mumbled, "I'm being as gentle as I can." When the pain subsided and his breathing returned to normal, Jack saw her holding a small smooth tube connected to a bag of yellow liquid resting between his knees. She then placed the blanket back over him.

"Was that inside me?"

"It's called a catheter," Julia said, "and it allows your body to relieve itself while you are unconscious for extended periods of time. Does everything feel okay down there?" Jack took a second to make sure nothing felt damaged, then nodded. "Good. Next up is X-rays. I'll be right back with the machine."

Julia stepped over to the glass door and placed her palm on the metal plate in the glass wall. The door swung open, and she gave it an extra push to lock it open.

"Wow," Jack said aloud once she left. In only a few minutes, Julia had displayed more vibrancy and life than Dahlia had ever given to Jack. The way she looked at him and held his gaze, the way she lightly touched him, the way she smelled—Jack shook himself, trying to clear the fog of lust and allure Julia had left around him.

She came back after only a moment, pushing a piece of wheeled machinery with a large stable base and a long, jointed arm that looked like it could be raised and lowered. She positioned it at the end of Jack's bed, next to his ankle. She picked up something from the base of the machine and brought it over to Jack.

"Lift your arms," Julia said, struggling with the weight. "This needs to lay over your body."

"Okay," Jack said, lifting his arms carefully so that they didn't bend at the elbow. As she positioned the heavy blanket, the concern about any pain in his arms evaporated as he smelled his own body odor. The stale and sour smell stung his nostrils, and the contrast with Julia's invigorating scent embarrassed him. As Julia finished covering his body with the blanket, she gave no sign of noticing his stench.

Jack looked at all the bandages over his hands, elbows, and forearms. One large piece of gauze covered his left wrist, and with rising alarm Jack realized that his watch was gone. Perhaps Julia had just removed it with his clothes.

"What do I need to do?" Jack asked, too scared to ask her where his watch was.

"You don't need to do anything," Julia said, positioning the cone-shaped end of the machine's arm above his injured ankle. The machine made a series of beeping sounds. "All right, here we go. Ready?" Julia uncoiled a length of wire and held the end where a button protruded.

"I suppose so," Jack said. Julia took a few steps back from the machine, then pushed the button. A metallic *thunk* sounded, and Jack flinched.

"Try not to do that next time," Julia said as she stepped back to the machine and repositioned the cone.

Jack only nodded. Julia stepped back wordlessly to her button-pushing spot, and the metallic noise came from the machine again. Though Jack flinched again, he managed to keep the jerking motion away from his foot. Three more times, Julia repositioned the cone and pushed the button.

"Good," Julia said, extracting a thin box from the X-ray machine. "That should be enough shots. I've got to take these to Dr. Roland, then I'll be back with your dinner."

Jack smiled his thanks and lay back among the pillows of his bed. He tried to think of something to say to Julia when she came back, but no clever ideas or conversation starters came to mind. He needed to ask her where she put his watch, but Jack found himself more curious about Julia. Her life, her world, what she did for fun, if she was seeing anyone... the watch, the rocket, and Dr. Roland all argued for second place in Jack's mind.

Julia returned holding a tray of items, and Jack realized he still hadn't thought of anything good to say. Then he smelled something new—robust and earthy—that made his mouth water. Tendrils of steam rose from a tan plastic dome on the tray.

"What's that smell?" Jack said.

"That would be your dinner. Voilà!" Julia said, removing the tan plastic dome from an equally tan and plastic dish. A billow of steam accompanied the flourish. "Fried ham, baked beans, cornbread and apple juice. I hope that suits your taste."

"Wow," Jack breathed, looking at the variety of food laid out before him. "It's been so long since I've had a cooked meal." He continued to stare at the differently colored foods as Julia placed the tray on his outstretched legs.

"Yes, I'd imagine so… over a week now, right?"

"Years," Jack said. Julia finished positioning the tray and frowned.

"What do you mean, years?"

"I mean it's been years since I've eaten food like that. It's hard to find time to eat—it just always seems like more trouble than it's worth, you know?"

Jack finally tore his lustful gaze from the food to look at Julia, and he saw that no, she did not know. She looked at him with a face so quizzical—her eyes so narrow and her mouth pursed just short of speaking—that Jack felt too awkward to hold her gaze. He chose to look back at the food.

"You don't eat?" Julia managed to say after a moment.

"I can," Jack said, "I just generally let HAS give me the nutrient doses. It's more efficient that way." Again Jack had to look away from Julia's questioning face. He picked up the plastic fork and knife on the tray.

"What's HAS?" Julia asked as Jack fumbled with the utensils, desperately trying to work them in his bandaged hands.

"Home Automation System," Jack said as Julia laid her hands over his, their soft warmth flowing into him.

"Let me help." She took his utensils and cut off a small piece of meat, then stabbed it and gently put it into his mouth. Saltiness overwhelmed him, and saliva gushed as he began to chew. Jack's jaw quickly tired, the muscles aching so much that he felt them starting to lock up. Julia next brought him a spoonful of beans, and again he quickly became overwhelmed, this time by sweetness. Jack felt a trickle of sauce run along his lip, and Julia wordlessly—delicately—wiped it away with a napkin. As Jack chewed the soft beans, Julia begin to cut another piece of the meat, so he held up a hand. She put the utensils down on the tray, and Jack was left staring at his hand, and his bare, bandaged wrist.

"Where are the things I had on me when I came in?" Jack asked.

"Well," Julia said slowly, "your clothes were ripped and bloodied pretty bad, so we just threw them out."

"That's fine," Jack said, "but what about my watch?"

"I don't remember seeing a watch," Julia said. "At least, you weren't wearing it when I first saw you. Don't tell me the watch was in your pocket."

"No," Jack said, trying to keep panic out of his voice. "I was wearing it. I'm sure I was. I remember seeing a glare off it when I was…" His voice trailed off as he tried to remember the last time he actually looked at the watch. "I felt it when I was on the ground after the accident."

"I don't know," Julia said, "is it possible it fell off after that? Maybe the strap got ripped, or something."

"No; it's made out of solid metal. It would just be scratched up, not broken. Can you please look for it? I really, really don't want to lose it." In response, Julia looked at her own watch.

"I can go check. There's a chance that your clothes might not be out in the dumpster yet. You owe me one. Should I leave this?" Julia pointed to the food, but with the anxiety he now felt, Jack couldn't even think about eating. He nodded again, and Julia picked up the tray and walked out of the room. A second later, she opened the door.

Jack's fingers tapped nervously on his legs, but despite the possibility of losing his one family heirloom, Jack still couldn't stop thinking about Julia. She completely infected his consciousness. There was something so intriguing about her, and it seemed that his mission had morphed from learning about life outside of NCC to learning about her. He recalled the faint smile when he mentioned the rocket exploding. Before, he hadn't been sure if she had actually smiled or not, but after spending some time with her and seeing how she reacted to things, he was sure of it. Though she claimed that he now 'owed her one,' Jack thought it was the other way around. Julia owed him an explanation for why a rocket blowing up made her smile.

Suddenly, the double doors crashed open and Dr. Roland strode in. Without a word to Jack, the doctor stopped at the propped open glass door. With one push, he shut the clear door to trap Jack inside, and then walked over to the button on the wall. He stared at Jack for a few seconds, the slapped the button.

"You lied to me," Doctor Roland said flatly.

"What? No, I didn't. I never lie. I haven't told a single lie since I've been here," Jack said. His nervous words sounded weak.

"And there's more," Dr. Roland said, holding up a hand when he saw that Jack meant to voice a protest. "You've got a lot to answer for. But I don't want to hear any of it right now. Instead, why don't you think about the position you're in, the power you think you have that you actually don't, and how little you're really worth to us." With that, Dr. Roland turned on his heel, pushed a second button on the wall, and then turned out the lights in the room.

"By the way," Dr. Roland's voice sounded in the darkness, "I just passed Julia in the hall. There's no watch. Too bad. I assured her that I would tell you, and then sent her home for the day. Have a great night."

Immediately after the double door in the outer room swung shut, an electronic whine filled the room. The noise reached a volume so loud that Jack thought his head would explode. So loud that, although he wanted to pass out from the stress, the noise would not allow him to.

When Jack discovered that even both pillows jammed

against his ears could not mute the sound, he carefully stood up and limped over to the glass door. The racks holding bags of liquid and tubes attached to his body followed, making several parts of his body sore. That didn't matter, compared to the madness echoing in his ears. Jack tried placing his hand on the metal panel, as Julia had done, but a small, blinking red light was the only response. Jack was forced to limp back over to the bed, and again try to drown out the noise with the pillows and blanket. The electric whine drilled into his mind, and all Jack could do was sit in the uncomfortable bed in the middle of a glass room, in the middle of a hospital on the outskirts of a town far from his home, and witness himself slowly go insane.

Chapter 12

—

But Jack didn't go insane—in fact, he stayed entirely *too* sane, fully comprehending the mechanical screech invading every aspect of his being. He had seen enough movies to know what the noise represented—some type of jammer designed to interrupt wireless communications. Dr. Roland said Jack was lying, but despite how badly he wanted to figure out the reason for that accusation, he couldn't focus on anything other than the drone in his ears.

Time passed; Jack didn't know how long. The only thing he saw was a small square window in each of the double doors. Light shone from them into the dark room, but no one walked past in the hallway outside. Jack stared at the constant light, hoping that the deafening noise might fade after enough monotony.

The doors eventually swung open again, surprising Jack so thoroughly that he let out a hoarse scream. Julia rushed in, frantically hitting the button on the wall. The electronic whine died, and Jack felt his body relax. Julia turned on the lights, and when Jack saw her face a small measure of joy crept into his mind. The hours or days of suffering melted away, and he knew everything would be fine. Jack tried to relay this feeling to her but found it difficult to condense his thoughts into words. He simply smiled as she approached, hoping she understood his happiness.

"Jack, I am so sorry. Are you okay? I came here as soon as Dr. Roland told me what he did. I had no idea he would turn it back on; and then he just abandoned you for the night? Don't worry, I'll file a complaint as soon as I can get you out of here. Are you okay?"

Jack nodded but was still unable to say anything. Julia glanced to his foot and adopted an inquisitive look. She reached out and touched the lump of Jack's ankle bone gently, caressing it back and forth.

"It really is amazing," she breathed, her concerned and apologetic demeanor replaced with one of admiration.

"What is?" Jack asked quietly. Had he told her about NRs yet? He couldn't remember if they had come up in conversation.

"When I came in this morning—before Dr. Roland told me what he had done to you, of course—he showed me your X-rays."

"Okay," Jack said.

"Your ankle, your bones…are you telling me you don't know?" Julia looked at him skeptically.

"Know what?" Jack asked, playing along.

"They're healed. Completely fine. Just like you said yesterday."

Jack nodded, recalling that yes, he *had* told her it was fine. She had likely just brushed that off as patient bravado, but now seemed to be seriously considering the idea.

"Why don't you have the same suspicion towards me as Dr. Roland?" Jack asked. Julia's face lifted, but before responding, she turned her eyes to his, appraising him.

She dropped the awed demeanor, and moved fluidly around the bed, getting her mouth next to his ear.

"I know why you healed so fast, and I know that you aren't still in contact with AI. But Dr. Roland doesn't, and we need to get you out of here, don't we?" Her scent filled his nostrils, and a view down the front of her baggy shirt filled his eyes. Jack couldn't even process the words she spoke as he was overcome by her allure, and he allowed himself to relax and enjoy her close proximity.

"We do?" Jack said.

"Yes, we do," Julia responded. Against everything he desired, Julia then moved away from him, swaying to where the X-ray machine sat in the corner of the glass enclosure. She rolled it over to the foot of the bed, glancing occasionally to Jack. He couldn't take his eyes off her. Julia pointed the cone at his injured ankle, not bothering to cover him up with any heavy blankets this time. She pushed the button which made the machine *thunk*, but this time he was too distracted to flinch. Julia changed the angle at which the machine viewed his ankle, collecting several a few more shots.

"Okay," Julia said, facing Jack squarely, "you're not going to like this part. I need to get some X-rays with the jammer on." Jack felt his heart drop.

"Why?"

"So that we can show that there's no difference in activity around your injury. Then I have a case to present to Dr. Roland, to convince him that AI isn't controlling the NRs."

Jack stared at Julia, speechless. The only reason Jack knew anything about the tiny robots in his bloodstream was because of his conversations with AI. How could Julia possibly know anything about them?

"But, my ankle is already healed. Turning the jammer on won't show anything," Jack said.

"That doesn't matter," Julia said, "Dr. Roland thinks that AI is constantly sending you signals. There's always more NRs in an area that was just injured. He thinks that without AI they are useless, and will just flow around in your bloodstream waiting for something to do."

"So, you don't think that AI is controlling them?"

"No. You're too far away. Are you ready?"

Again, Jack puzzled over her knowledge. He realized she had exited the glass enclosure and stood next to the button on the wall. He shakily nodded, and she pushed the button. The whine of ultrasonic machinery filled Jack's ears, and Julia resumed her work with the X-ray machine, taking as many shots as before, but moving faster. She then trotted out of the glass enclosure and turned off the jammer.

"There," Julia said upon returning to the glass enclosure, "that wasn't so bad, right?"

"I guess not," Jack said, digging a finger into his ear to try and extract the ringing sound. He watched closely as Julia withdrew the same slim tray from the X-ray machine, then brought it to a small opening in the hospital room's wall, just big enough to hold the object. She slid it in while pushing a series of buttons on a keypad next to the opening, which was followed by a mechanical whir inside the wall. The whir quickly sped up, then released like exhaled air.

"What's that?" Jack asked, pointing.

"An intra-hospital delivery system. I don't really feel like seeing Dr. Roland right now, so I sent him your X-rays. They're clearly marked with which had the jammer on, and which off, so when he sees that they're the same, that should convince him that nothing's going on. While those shots are being developed and reviewed, let's get you ready to go. Dr. Roland realizes the seriousness of what he did to you last night, and I think he'll clear you once he's convinced you're not really a threat."

"Great," Jack said as Julia began removing the gauze around his leg. He realized he was still naked under the blanket, and when she continued unraveling the gauze up his legs, Jack pushed down on the blanket.

"Relax," Julia said, "this is nothing new to me."

It is to me, Jack wanted to say, but how could he explain to her the difference between physical and virtual contact? He held his breath as she moved the blanket aside to remove a bandage on his hip. The parts he cared about were still covered, but once the bandage was off, Julia ran her hand around his thigh, nonchalantly brushing up against his covered areas.

"Don't worry," she whispered, her mouth at his ear again, "I'll take care of you." Julia then moved her head away from his and began unwrapping the bandages on Jack's arms as if nothing had happened. Her touch made Jack want to reach out and run his hands all over her body, but this wasn't New World, and he had the feeling that here, acting out every desire would carry very different consequences. Julia continued to unwrap the gauze on Jack's forearm, finally exposing his bare wrist.

"Are you sure you didn't see my watch anywhere?" Jack said.

"Yes," Julia said, patiently nodding. "How long have you had it, anyway?"

"As far back as I can remember," Jack said. "It was my dad's, and he gave it to me right before he died. That must have been right before we moved to NCC." Jack looked down in embarrassment.

"Hey, don't get down on yourself," Julia said, rubbing his arm. "Maybe it'll turn up somewhere."

"Maybe," Jack said doubtfully. "I had just gotten it serviced too."

"Serviced?" Julia asked. "Where? Did AI do it?"

"No, there's a guy in EAC who works on them. I shipped it out and then he sent it back." Julia took a few seconds to stare at Jack, like she was trying to figure out if he was telling the truth.

"What does he do to the watch?"

Jack was pleased that Julia showed so much interest in the watch, so he told her all about the letter he received, and what the watchmaker did to ensure all the mechanical pieces worked together flawlessly.

"How long ago did you have it serviced?"

"I just got it back about a week before I left."

"Interesting, very interesting," Julia said, and then moved around to the other side of the bed to begin on Jack's other arm. Her mind was clearly elsewhere, and she stared off into the distance as she continued to unravel the gauze.

"What? What is it?" Jack asked, unable to sit in silence. Julia still stared at him and opened her mouth to respond, but apparently thought better of it and remained quiet. She continued taking off bandages, and when they were all removed, she sat on the bed next to Jack and looked at him.

"I just think it's nice that someone from your part of the world can appreciate something like that," Julia said, not meeting Jack's eyes. Before Jack could continue talking, or inquire as to why she had started acting strange, Julia pointed to the delivery system receptacle. A green light flashed from the keypad, and when Julia punched in a code and opened it, Jack saw that she held a bundle of papers.

"Your discharge paperwork," Julia said, flipping through the pages. "It's official... Dr. Roland no longer wants you here!" She winked, and despite the mystery that Julia kept herself shrouded in, Jack couldn't help but grin when she gave him an extra bit of attention. Sure, she might be hiding something important from him, but perhaps she would divulge more of her secrets if he stayed around her long enough.

"So, I'm free to go then?" Jack asked.

"Not quite," Julia said. "You still have to pass my test. Let's try a couple of things. Touch your thumbs to your fingers, like this." She walked her thumbs down her fingers, touching each sequentially, and then back again. Jack did the same, though slightly slower.

"Good," she said when he had done the maneuver a few times, "now hold your arms out straight and grab my hands. Rotate them as firmly as you can."

Small tests of this nature continued for ten minutes or so, but Jack really had no concept of time without his Display or watch. Julia eventually made him stand as she crouched, inspecting his healed foot. Jack stood on one foot then the other, hopping back and forth at her command.

Shifting to the foot in question sent a small twinge of pain up to his knee, and Jack grappled with the idea of telling Julia. On one hand, he wanted to leave the hospital more than anything, and continue his quest into Banff. On the other hand, he didn't want to leave Julia. Being in her presence and slowly unwrapping her mysteries topped the list of the most fulfilling things he had ever done with his life.

"Is there any pain as you're moving around?" Julia

asked.

"No, not really," Jack said hesitantly.

"What do you mean, 'not really'?"

"It's nothing," Jack said, "just a little twinge. Maybe I need to stay another night?" He winced at the childish inflection in his voice.

Julia eyed him suspiciously.

"And why on Earth would you want to do that?" She continued to peer at him, her mouth twitching upward at one corner. He wanted to tell her that he could skip right out of the room that had held him prisoner for so long and keep on skipping down the hall until he skipped right out the front door. Then…

Then what? Jack's adventurous thought process stopped when he realized that he had no idea what to do after leaving the hospital. There would be an option of turning left, turning right, or perhaps even walking straight after leaving the hospital. Which one should he choose? And what reason did he have for going in any direction?

"Jack?" Julia said, waving a hand in front of his face.

"I don't have anywhere to go," Jack blurted.

"I know," Julia said.

"You do?" Jack said, thankful for her confidence.

"Well, yeah. You don't live here, so where can you go? I'm sure you just anticipated seeing the sights and then driving back, am I right?" Jack nodded. "So why don't you stay with me for a while? I'll show you around town, get you involved in a few things—what do you say?"

"Really?" Jack said, unable to believe his good luck.

"Of course. I've got a guest room, and you'll get to meet Charlie." Julia checked her watch. "Actually, he should be getting home from school in a couple of hours. If we leave soon, we can get you all set up before he arrives. He can be kind of… attention-grabbing once you get to know him. Or, once he gets to know you, I should say." She paused to look at his reaction. "So, what do you say? Want to get out of here?"

Though Julia's offer would have fit in perfectly had they met at *Futura*, Jack found her forwardness suspicious. However, the idea of spending more time alone with Julia overrode this, and Jack gave a vigorous nod that would have thrown him out of commission a few days ago.

"Great," Julia said, smiling and looking down at the blanket Jack still clutched around his waist. "Let me just go and find you some clothes."

Chapter 13

—

Jack couldn't help but marvel at Julia's car. Every aspect of it looked and felt as if an engineer had taken the design of Jack's autocar in one hand and the antique truck in the other, and then smashed them together to create a hybrid of the two. The exterior lines and features flowed smoothly from tip to tail, but four wheels jutted awkwardly from the bottom to connect to the road. The doors didn't open as they approached, and the seats didn't adjust themselves. A not-quite-perfect voice greeted them upon entering the car, and read off a few statistics about the weather, but it stopped after that, not telling Jack the best places to go or where his friends could be found. Jack then acknowledged that he didn't have any friends, and found himself missing AI. She was always prepared for a good conversation.

The most surprising aspect of the car was the display. Before they even started moving, a slew of information projected itself on the inner windshield. Temperature, ground and wind speed, distance to collision with cars and objects on all sides, and about twenty other statistics seemed to hang in the air right where the windshield glass lay. But there was no organization, the data didn't shift when Jack moved his eyes or even his head, and the numbers didn't rearrange to make the most urgent numbers largest. Julia drove the car out of the parking lot and everything on the car's display stood in nauseating stillness as the world moved behind it.

"I live pretty close," Julia said as she eyed Jack's expression, "it'll only be a few minutes."

"It's fine," Jack said, closing his eyes to quell the sinking feeling in his stomach.

"Didn't you drive a car like this to get here?"

"Mostly the same, but the truck I had was older; there was no windshield display."

"What about in NCC?"

"It's all completely automated there," Jack said.

Julia nodded at that. "I figured as much. This car has some of those options, too."

To demonstrate, Julia pushed a button on the steering wheel and removed her hands in the middle of a turn. The wheel held its position, and then straightened out with the road. The car accelerated on the straightaway. Jack looked at the wheel, puzzled.

"Why would you ever turn it off?"

"I don't know," Julia said, pushing the button again and taking the wheel, "I just like the feeling of doing it myself."

"But why do you even have a car that can do that? Isn't the whole point of you all living out here to get away from technology? That's what you said in the hospital."

"Everything in moderation, Jack," Julia said. "It's easy to get caught up in things that are supposed to make your life better, all the while forgetting to live your life in the process."

Jack sensed that the conversation was turning defensive, so he simply nodded along in silence. They drove down a wide street, empty except for an occasional person walking along the sidewalk. The short buildings on either side of the road almost all displayed the same tan color, with vertical brown beams between buildings that touched. Dark brown frames around second-floor eaves gave the whole street a repetitive, rustic look. Jack struggled to see the enjoyment of piloting the car manually down such a straight, monotonous road. Julia saw him looking at her hands on the wheel.

"Didn't you like driving the truck on your way here?"

Jack shrugged. "I never really thought of it as something to like or not. It was pretty nerve-wracking at first, but once I got used to it, driving became something mundane, something that technology wasn't good enough to do for me." Jack looked to a bridge that crossed a wide river. "That looks nice over there." He pointed at a collection of tightly packed houses sat nestled within trees at the foot of a large hill. The whole scene created an image that Jack would like to display on his wall. Julia only shook her head.

"That's not really the best area for you. It's not exactly the nicest part of town."

"What does that mean?"

"There's a lot of poverty over there," Julia said. Jack knew the word, but hadn't heard it in a long time; that type of unpleasantness had no place in NCC.

"I see. So, you just make those people stay on that side of the bridge?"

"No," Julia said slowly, "we actually go over there quite frequently to help them build new houses. I just meant that it can be quite a shock to see if you're not used to it, especially coming from a place like NCC." Jack nodded along, not at all understanding why everyone wouldn't just stay on this side of the river.

They passed a few houses in silence, tall trees with long green needles reaching up to the sky everywhere a patch of land big enough allowed. Though the trees blocked his view of the mountain ranges surrounding Banff, every so often he caught a glimpse of jagged peaks through the towering foliage. So much beauty existed out here; Jack still couldn't get over the way Julia stared straight ahead at the road as she drove.

Julia slowed and turned into a short driveway off the main road. After driving around a few trees, the place Julia called home came into view. Jack sat in awe with his mouth open. The house was almost as big as his entire apartment building—with about as many windows. No curved mirrors hung in front of the windows or on the roof, presumably because there were enough windows to provide a scenic view on all sides of the house.

"That's the garage," Julia said as she pointed to a set of big double doors, lighter in color than the dark wooden siding. The doors did not rise to allow her to drive into the garage, but a smaller door stood ajar a few feet away. Jack pointed to a pile of cardboard boxes and brown paper bags printed with shapes all over the outside, the tops almost overflowing with green plants and smaller boxes.

"What's that?"

"Those are the groceries for the week," Julia said, raising herself out of the car as the door opened and the lights on the dash dimmed. "Want to help me get them, or just sit around in the car all day?"

Jack shook himself, abandoning the idea that his seat would assist his exit from the low vehicle. Julia handed him a lightweight bag, then kicked open the smaller door. Stacked with three precarious paper bags full of groceries, she struggled to balance the shifting load while backing into the house. Jack followed her, still trying to figure out the logistics of the grocery bags that had been waiting in front of the garage door.

The room they entered now was full of fixed counters, cool tile flooring, steel appliances and wonderful, savory aromas that Julia told him was dinner cooking in the oven. Jack immediately recognized this room as a kitchen, thanks to the crash course in primitive living AI gave before he left. The dimly lit kitchen grew in brightness as thin parallel slats opened overhead, silently settling into a position that maintained a comfortable level of light. A small round device on the wall brightened and showed the number seventy-two when Julia walked past it. Julia invited him to take off his shoes, kicking her own into the bottom of a closet close to the door. She then called out to Charlie, but there was no response except for a faint rushing noise as air began to move overhead. Jack looked up when he felt cool air billowing down on him and saw a small grating in the ceiling.

"Oh well," Julia said, "he must not be home yet. Here, let me show you around." She took his hand and led him into a hallway to the left of a large wooden table.

"There are two rooms here," Julia said as she motioned down the narrow carpeted hall, "and they share a bathroom that connects them. Charlie is in there, and you'll be in here." Julia pointed to each door in turn, then opened the one she labeled as his. The room itself held a small bed and not much else. A white textured ceiling met soothing light blue walls, which ran down to pale carpeting. A bookshelf stood alone in a corner, its shelves empty. The bed, though—that was what captured Jack's attention. It looked to be nothing more than a flat rectangular plank with a blanket and pillow on the top. Jack hadn't expected to see something as lavish as his own pillowed piece of automated perfection, but with no visible cooling or heating, height or depth adjustments, or even a detachable portion to bring him into the bathroom, Jack did not look forward to spending a night in the small room.

Jack shook his head, trying to clear the negative thoughts. None of that kind of automation existed here, and that was precisely the point. He was lucky enough to be in Julia's home, and felt nervous about the days to come. What would she expect from him? What should he expect from her? Julia had hinted at a physical interest in him, but Jack couldn't figure out where that interest stemmed from. He hadn't really done anything interesting since awakening.

Julia continued the tour by showing Jack a large open room with wooden floors, polished towards the walls, and worn towards the middle. A television hung on a wall, centered in front of a large L-shaped couch with blankets and pillows arranged haphazardly upon the brown leather cushions. Julia grumbled something about Charlie needing to clean up after sleeping there, but didn't expand on the topic.

The other side of the house held Julia's bedroom, with its own bathroom attached. Though Julia's bed was larger, it too didn't have any extra features. Julia walked quickly ahead of him upon entering the room and removed a few items from the top of her nightstand, but Jack couldn't tell what anything was. Julia looked back to him, her face saying that she regretted letting the tour enter this room.

"Over there is the bathroom," she waved towards a door on the opposite wall, "but it's nothing special, and I'd prefer you didn't go in there." Jack nodded and turned to leave the bedroom, hoping to alleviate some of her unease. "Wait," Julia said, and suddenly she was right next to him, grabbing his hand.

"What?" Jack said. Julia's propensity for physical contact kept catching him off guard.

"I want you to be comfortable here. Relax." She rubbed his arm a little. "You've been through a lot, and I know that you're way outside of your normal routine, but try and remember why you came here in the first place. Things are different, right? That's the point."

"Thanks," Jack said. "You've done a lot for me already. I hope everyone else I meet is as great as you."

"They're not," Julia said with a grin, and then led him out of the room, "but that's okay. C'mon, let's go finish up dinner before Charlie gets home."

—

After two cut fingers, a bruised elbow, and one hand burn that Julia insisted was not so bad, Jack was officially declared useless in the kitchen. Following what he thought to be an inaudible complaint about his feet hurting, Julia brought over a chair and set it down outside the imaginary triangle made by the stove, refrigerator, and sink. She resumed her place in front of the stove, stirring a spatula within a pot filled with thick liquid.

Before Jack could search his mind for a topic of conversation, the door into the kitchen opened, and he turned towards the sound of a young voice excitedly explaining why the next movie in some series was going to be even better than the one he just saw.

"It's the final scene," the voice spoke, "If you paid attention, you'd see that's when he realizes the whole thing might be a dream."

Another voice scoffed as a very tall and slender boy stepped into the room, his head and neck fully visible over the refrigerator. The height didn't match the youth of his face—smooth skin with a few adolescent blemishes, round cheeks and chin with a pencil-thin neck. Every part of his body looked as if two very strong people each grabbed an end and pulled. Elbows and knees stood out prominently from the stringy arms and legs, large bulges of joint between thin, stretched muscles that ended in huge hands and feet. The boy had to be seven feet tall. Upon straightening out after ducking through the door, he swiveled his head and saw Jack. He froze in the doorway next to the refrigerator, and another boy squeezed around him to see what had stopped his friend. This one stood at a normal height for an adolescent, but wore the same expression of surprise when he saw Jack.

"Charlie, I'd like you to meet Jack. Hi Mark," Julia spoke over her shoulder, still vigorously stirring the pot.

"Hello there," said Jack, rising from his seat. He barely came up to the middle of the kid's chest.

"Two J names..." Charlie whispered, trailing off. He then shook himself. "Hello." The gusto of his previous conversation was gone, and when Jack looked down to the other boy whom Julia addressed as Mark, he saw that his face held an expression somewhere between terrified and bamboozled.

Julia moved the well-stirred pot off the burner and turned to face them both.

"I gotta go," Mark said, "my mom says can't be here when Julia has any friends over. See ya tomorrow, Charlie."

"Don't be ridiculous," Julia said, but as she turned around, the door leading outside was already open and Mark was through it in a blink. Julia called after him, but received no response aside from the closing door. Charlie did not call after his friend, but Jack saw a small smile slide on to his face.

"Charlie, I met Jack at the hospital. He's from NCC and needs somewhere to stay for a while."

"Great, another guy…" Charlie muttered under his breath.

"Watch it," Julia said, pointing the spatula at Charlie's face. "Now, go put your backpack away and set the table. And find your manners, wherever you left them."

As Charlie stalked away to his room, Jack noticed the boy had a slight limp. It was almost non-existent, but he definitely favored the right leg, opting for longer strides with his left to make up for it.

"I hope I'm not intruding," Jack began, but stopped when Julia leveled the spatula at him.

"Don't start. He's just acting like a sullen teenager because his friend left. He'll come around, and then you won't be able to get him to stop talking to you. And before you ask, no, he's not my child."

Julia returned to whisking things around on the stove, leaving Jack to try and think of something else to say. Was he really that easy to read? Every time he wanted to ask something meaningful or say something that he thought was profound, Julia beat him to it and then blew it off, like it was no big deal. Jack thought the way that she acted towards Charlie made it seem like he was her child, but he didn't want to press the issue since she denied it so abruptly.

"So, how about those earthquakes?" Jack asked.

"What are you talking about?" Julia stopped her food prep to look at him.

"You know, the tremors. Aftershocks? No?" Jack slumped in his chair. "AI told me there were a lot of earthquakes this time of year." A snorting laugh sounded from the kitchen table, and Jack flinched. Charlie was bent over the table, haphazardly placing metal utensils with one hand, while balancing three large plates above his shoulder in the other. His silent return to the kitchen did not seem to affect Julia, though the unannounced return of someone so large startled Jack.

"Charlie, put those down before you drop them," Julia said, motioning to the plates.

Charlie looked sullenly to Julia, the all-knowing humor dropping from his face. He dropped the rest of the utensils with a crash, and then heavily placed the stack of plates down next to them. A loud crack came from the plates. Now it was Julia's turn to give Charlie the sullen look.

"Sorry," Charlie grumbled, and looked down to where the bottom plate lay in two pieces atop the table.

"Clean it up, then get in your room," Julia said while pointing, "and don't come out until you get rid of that attitude." Once the broken plate was in the trash and Charlie had disappeared into his bedroom, Julia handed Jack a giant bowl of lumpy mashed potatoes.

"Like I said before, he'll come around. Here, why don't you bring this to the table? I'll be right over with the rest of the food." The buttery scent steaming off the dish Jack held moistened his mouth with saliva. Though Julia handed the bowl to Jack with one hand, he needed both of his to support the weight, and almost threw the bowl onto the table after his quick walk to the table as the heat seeped into his hands. Jack sat down at the table and blew on his hands as Julia brought over other side dishes. Cut green beans, brown rice, and a soup that Julia said he could start on now. The steam and heat radiating from the bowl Julia placed in front of Jack suggested that no, he would not be starting on the soup now.

As Julia hopped back over to the stove to silence a chiming beeper, Charlie emerged from his room and seated himself across the table from Jack. He clinked two pieces of silverware together, prompting Julia to look up and stare at him. When Charlie didn't move except to clink the pieces of silverware together again, she gave a sigh and rolled her eyes.

"Please get some drinks on the table for everyone," Julia said. After some awkward movements in the cooking area, Charlie and Julia returned to the table, Charlie with three large glasses of ice water, again clutched precariously in one hand, and Julia with yet another dish of food.

"Hello," Charlie said after placing the waters on the table, "I'm Charlie."

"Hello," Jack said.

"So, I bet you came here about the rockets, huh? They're pretty neat; seeing them take off was a big surprise to most people in town. It's too bad about that last one… but I think there's still one more. Isn't that what you said? She says that they don't really serve any purpose and all they do is pollute. Did AI tell you to come here to see how we all reacted to it? To the explosion?"

The torrent of speech ended abruptly and took Jack aback so much that he had to play back the boy's words in his mind in order to figure out which portions were directed to him, which to Julia, and what he was supposed to respond to.

"No," Jack said, "AI didn't send me. I saw something flying by overhead, but I thought it was just falling— burning up or something. I didn't think it was a rocket." Charlie nodded as if he knew exactly what Jack was talking about.

"If it was just last week it was probably the first rocket. Well, there were two right next to each other, actually. Like, two days in a row. But what you saw could have been a satellite. They come down every few weeks or so. There are thousands of them up there," Charlie said, pointing upwards. He began to spin his knife on the table, repeatedly colliding it with another knife.

"Charlie, *please* stop doing that," Julia said as she stuck a large fork into the steaming dish just withdrawn from the oven. Charlie stopped, resting his hands on the table top for only a moment before picking up the fork and attempting to spin it around his fingers. When a spin went off course, he deftly caught the fork before it fell onto the knife.

"I read about Home Automation Systems in school," Charlie said as he silently placed the fork back onto the table. "I get why people want to make their lives easier, but to me it seems like the whole thing is, oh, what's the word... lazy."

"Charlie..." Julia cautioned from the kitchen. The warning brought Charlie to silence for thirty seconds before he began his own rendition of what it would be like to live in NCC, not having to set the table or even needing to eat.

"That's enough, Charlie," Julia said as she walked to the table carrying a large dish covered with a bright silver dome, "Jack doesn't need to hear you talking the entire time he's staying here."

"It's okay," Jack said. As he looked to the tall boy, seated and hunched like an old man, he saw that Charlie's eyes fixed on Julia about a foot and a half lower than what Jack considered appropriate. Charlie seemed transfixed by the sway of her body as she walked, but Julia's attention was completely vested in the heavy platter she carried, and did not see the stare.

Upon reaching the head of the table, she bent over slightly to set the platter down, and Jack noticed a small smile creep onto Charlie's face. The smile, coupled with the way his eyes leered, made Jack's heart skip a beat. The childish innocence—if slightly irritating—had evaporated, and Jack decided the boy might not be exactly what he seemed. Charlie's eyes swiveled to meet Jack's and he grinned, holding the gaze until Jack looked away. As Julia lifted the silver dome with a flourish, Jack saw the main course.

At first glance, Jack couldn't tell what sat on the platter. The array of savory and spiced scents assured him it would be delicious; however, when he looked at it, he flinched with fright and disgust. Drumsticks and wings hanging askew from a central body were the first clue that the thing was a dead bird. Its large breasts proudly glistened underneath scorched skin, and the inside of the body was stuffed with apples, cinnamon sticks, and sprigs of small-leaved plants.

"That's a…it's a…"

"Turkey," Charlie said, the smug voice returning. "And it's not even Thanksgiving!" The boy apparently couldn't contain his hunger, because he reached out, took hold of one of the dead animal's legs and twisted, pulling it free. The popping sound it made as the marinated joint and tendon gave way made Jack feel that he was going to lose what little material sat in his stomach. He stared at the meat hanging off the bone in Charlie's hand. That bone had once supported the weight of a real live animal and allowed it to walk around, just as he did himself. Charlie tossed the leg onto Jack's empty plate.

"Here," Charlie said, "the best part for the guest. How's that for manners?" A drop of liquid landed on

Jack's cheek, sprayed up from the impact as the moist meat hit the plate. The warm drop began to run down his face, and before Jack could wipe it away he saw the knuckle protruding from the end of the drumstick, the round bone bleached white. Jack's vision grew dark around the edges, and he had a strange feeling of shifting gravity as the world turned sideways and he crashed to the floor.

—

Rather than slowly awakening to a kitchen or a golden field of wheat, Jack's mind thrashed around as if it were caught in a violent current. Bright pinks and blues erupted in explosions of color and deafening sound, green after-images and echoes fading into the background. The chaos made him scream in fear and confusion, but to no avail. His voice couldn't compete with the all-consuming thunder.

Abruptly the madness ended, and a man stood centered in Jack's mind. All the details of his body and clothing were blurred, but a wicked smile stood out clearly on his flushed, angled face. Intense, expectant dark grey eyes shone out from shadows cast by a prominent brow. The way the facial features came together, Jack almost thought he was looking at an older, normally proportioned version of Charlie, but as the shifting colored lights and dark shadows played around, Jack decided that this person was certainly not Charlie in any stage of life.

"Don't worry," said the intruder with a calm voice that didn't at all match the expression, "you're going to love it here."

Chapter 14

—

Jack's eyes flew open and Julia's feet popped into view from underneath the table as she moved herself out of her seat. Jack tried to lift himself from the floor, but his vision swam and he collapsed again.

"Jack!" Julia exclaimed. She kneeled next to him and brushed pieces of another broken plate away from his head. The strange, brief dream still echoed through his mind, and Jack looked around, afraid that the man with the evil smile was in the house. Clearly, someone other than AI had access to his mind, but who? And why did people keep talking to him whenever he went unconscious? Julia put a hand under his head and helped him sit up.

"Sorry," Jack said, as Julia cradled him, "I never thought…"

"Come on," Julia said as she gently pulled him to a sitting position.

"I never thought food could be something so… alive."

"Don't be sorry," Julia said, holding a hand to his neck, then looking deeply into each of his eyes individually, "I shouldn't have sprung something like that on you. I figured that since you were okay with the ham, you'd be okay with meat in general."

"It's not the meat. Just—look at it. It has a little body. Helpless, and alone." Though his eyes were locked on Julia's, he couldn't stop picturing the turkey. "There's no way you could have known that would affect me—I didn't either. I just needed to get over the initial… shock of it, that's all. Don't let me keep you from eating."

Charlie, who had risen during the commotion, looked to the other drumstick, which had made its way onto his own plate. Julia gave Jack one last assessing glance.

"Oh, go on then," she said to Charlie, "I know there's no stopping you when it comes to food, anyway." Charlie sat, more like *fell,* into his seat and took a big bite from the leg on his plate. Jack turned away, his vision swimming as he tried to focus on Julia's face. Concern lined her features.

"Why don't you go and rest on the couch while I make something a little easier to deal with," Julia said after another inspection of his eyes. She then put the silver dome back on the platter, and briefly uttered Charlie's name while pointing to it. He stopped chewing long enough to roll his eyes in an exasperated and drawn-out motion.

"I'll get the carving knife," Charlie said morosely, standing and picking up the platter.

"Throw away all the bones," Julia said after him, then turned back to Jack. "Go lay down on the couch." While Jack liked the idea of rest at first, when the animal was gone, so was the nausea, and he felt stronger. The impression Julia must have of him so far could not be anything great, and Jack felt the urge to stay and talk to her. He needed to show her… show her what? Something positive. Jack wanted Julia to be in a better mood when

185

she was around him, not constantly tending to him as if he were a wounded puppy.

"No, I'll be fine." Jack said. Julia began to protest, but Jack continued. "Really, as long as the body is gone, I think I'll be okay. I don't need to rest. My head does hurt, but I'm not going to fall over again."

Jack gingerly touched the side of his head that hit the floor, feeling the sensitive region of swelling. As Jack sat back at the table, Julia retrieved an ice pack from the freezer, and a few pills that she instructed him to swallow.

"So," Jack said, needing to change the subject away from himself, "how long have you and Charlie been together?"

Julia's eyes narrowed as he said the word 'together,' and Charlie's body stiffened, but Julia's response held no hostile tone.

"About three years, though at times it seems like he's been here my whole life." Julia smiled a little, and Jack saw Charlie roll his eyes again as he walked back from the kitchen with the large platter. The silver dome was off, and now instead of a dead animal, neat rows of thickly sliced white meat lay next to randomly sized and shaped chunks of darker meat.

"Where were you before then?" Jack asked Charlie, now seating himself at the table. The boy looked at Julia, and she nodded her head very slightly.

"NCC," Charlie said. At first, Jack didn't even register what Charlie had said. Jack began to nod in blind agreement, but then stopped.

"Wait—what?" Jack felt his heart leap into his throat.

"It's not that big of a deal," Charlie said while chewing giant mouthfuls.

Jack scoffed. "I'm from there too, so I know it's a big deal."

Charlie shrugged in teenage nonchalance.

"So, did anything change in the last few years?" Now it was Jack's turn to shrug.

"Not really. The downtown buildings are getting taller, more are being printed. New World is getting more and more advanced, but I don't know; I was getting kind of bored with it."

At that, Charlie gave a sideways glance to Julia, as if he needed to see what her response was. Her jaw clenched, and she focused on organizing the food on her plate.

"I remember getting really into New World," Charlie said, as if it were a fad.

"It's hard not to. That's how everyone does anything nowadays. I've actually held meetings for work at *Futura*," Jack said, wondering if Charlie would pick up on the reference to the popular bar.

"No way," Charlie said. "I loved that place. Well, I mean, you know... my dad used to go there a lot."

"Let's talk about something different while we're at the dinner table," Julia said. Only silence followed for the next few seconds, in which Julia quickly finished the remaining food on her plate and left the table, bringing her dishes up to the sink.

"She really doesn't like anything about NCC, does she?" Jack asked quietly.

"No. Except for me and you," Charlie said.

"You know, until now, I thought I was the only person who ever left NCC."

Now it was Charlie's turn to scoff. He politely tried to hold it back, instead creating a windy humming noise.

"Not even close," Charlie said. "People have been leaving since the city was founded. Not everyone can deal with a life of pure perfection."

"Oh," was all Jack could say through the cloud of

disappointment. So much for his unique journey, and his profound revelations about life. He was nothing more than another deserter, bored with his life of luxury and wanting to see the world around him.

"What's funny?" Julia said from the sink.

Jack realized he was smiling to himself.

"Nothing. It's just that… well, AI told me that I was the first person to do something like this."

"Why would it say that?" she asked.

"I have no idea," Jack shrugged. "She helped out a lot getting me ready to go—I thought she was proud of me. I wouldn't have been able to fix the truck by myself." At that, Jack frowned. "How did you get here, Charlie?"

"I rode my bike," Charlie said.

"What?" Jack said, thunderstruck. "I was at the top of the biking scoreboard, and I couldn't even ride a bike ninety feet on the street, let alone ninety miles."

Charlie paused to think before responding.

"You never rode a bike outside? Only in New World?"

"Well, yeah," Jack said, defensively. "That's what we all do."

Charlie shook his head.

"Maybe things have changed since I've been there, but I know for a fact all the top leagues went for weekly rides around the city. I went with them."

Jack tried to picture a group of cyclists in the busy streets of NCC. There was no way anything like that still happened. Surely, AI would have told him if people still rode their bikes through the city. She couldn't just let him think he was the best if he only rode virtually. Jack looked at Charlie. Monstrously tall he might be, there was no way the young features of his face put him past seventeen. How could he have been so aware of city life, and gone on real bike rides around the city, if he had been so young?

"How old are you, Charlie?" Jack asked.

Charlie looked away, not meeting Jack's eyes.

"Eighteen," he said, "although I feel a lot older." The teenager returned to his food, but now seemed to be having an internal war. His eyes darted around the table, looking at Jack for a second, then back to his food. He glanced over to Julia several times and looked to be on the verge of speaking more than once before settling his eyes back to his plate. This calmed him for only a few moments before his eyes darted around the table again. He looked up at Jack one more time, narrowing his eyes as if trying to figure out the identity of the person seated across from him.

"Charlie, please come help me with the dishes," Julia said. Charlie looked down at his half-finished food, sighed, and then picked up his plate and stood. At this point, Jack noticed the insistent pain had returned to his abdomen. Frustrated, he rose from the table and headed in the direction of the bathroom. He wanted to stay in the kitchen and listen in to Charlie and Julia. They had started a whispered conversation by the sink as soon as Jack left the room, and he knew that they were talking about something to do with him.

The feelings of elation and hope from when he first arrived at Julia's house were gone, replaced with doubt and distrust. It wasn't all because of Charlie. The boy's behavior was odd, especially at the end of their conversation, but what really bothered Jack was the way Julia seemed to harbor a grudge against everything that involved the augmented and virtual world. Just the mention of New World or AI visibly bothered her, and the fact that she had taken in a person from NCC... something about Julia didn't add up in Jack's mind.

Jack tried to remember why he was here. He wanted to

learn how people lived without AI. Julia was from a completely different world—a world in which every thought and every spoken word had to be created on the spot with no help at all. It was no wonder that Julia acted strangely sometimes, with no guidance for her thoughts.

Jack went through the laborious process of undoing his pants and relieving himself, mortified when his aim wasn't as good as he would have liked. Getting close enough to the toilet to clean up was disgusting, and more than ever, Jack wished for HAS assistance.

On his way back to the kitchen, he tried to walk silently in order to pick up any of Julia's conversation with Charlie. They were still talking in very quiet voices, and the sound of running water and clanging dishes blocked everything out. Both Charlie and Julia looked up when Jack arrived back in the kitchen, and Julia rubbed Charlie's back.

"We'll talk to Ray tomorrow. He always knows what to say. Right?" Charlie shrugged, and mumbled something incoherent.

"What's going on tomorrow?" Jack asked.

"Church," Julia said. "And before you say anything, don't worry, you're going to love it there. It's non-denominational, there's no judgement whatsoever, and Ray, the pastor, has so much energy. Don't worry, you'll love him."

"Okay, sounds great," Jack said, unsure why Julia thought he might be worried. This was part of their lives, so he wanted to see what it was all about.

"We can stay after for a bit, too," Julia said, "Ray is always accommodating when people want to talk with him one-on-one." At this, Charlie grumbled. "Don't even start, Charlie."

"I just want some time to write this weekend," Charlie

said.

"You have all tonight and tomorrow to write about how cruel and unforgiving I am, forcing you to go to church and learn how to be a good person for one whole hour per week." Julia spoke the last words with finality as she loaded pans into the dishwasher.

Jack attempted to clear his own place at the table, but at the direction of Julia, Charlie lumbered over and did it for him. Julia ushered Jack to the couch and showed him how to access their collection of movies and shows. Jack scrolled through manually by making hand gestures in front of the screen but didn't see anything familiar. After a while, Julia and Charlie finished up in the kitchen, and came to sit with him on the couch.

"Let's just watch the same thing you always watch," Charlie said with a bored sigh.

"I don't always watch the same thing," Julia snapped, though Jack saw her select the first show in her 'Recently Watched' list.

"What this about?" Jack said.

"It's a funny show about a group of friends—it really shows how people used to live in one of the Great Cities at the turn of the century. Last century, that is."

"I've seen shows like that," Jack said.

"Sure, but in your world, that's all created by AI. This," Julia said, pointing to where the screen showed a group of six attractive people posing for a camera, "this is real. It was made back then, by the people you actually see on the screen."

"Okay," was all Jack could think to say, sitting forward on the coach as she made a one-handed gesture in front of the screen. A short upbeat intro riff played, and Julia smiled. Jack noticed that despite Charlie's desire to write in his journal, he sat immobile on the couch, watching the familiar show he had just complained about. When Jack looked to the screen, he expected to be fully encapsulated by the imagery, but was instead met with a flat and fuzzy scene. The resolution was so low that he had to look away to prevent a headache. If his Display could be activated, the low resolution would be stepped up to make it much easier to take in.

The dialogue of the show was entertaining enough, although slow. While Jack laughed every so often, he suspected that he was laughing along with Julia and Charlie more than at the on-screen antics and dialogue. The room in which they sat was far more distracting than the show. Julia had shelf upon shelf of pictures, mostly of her and Charlie doing things outdoors, and there were numerous objects hanging on the walls. Quotes about loving life, differently shaped mirrors, clocks, bookshelves stacked with volumes—the whole living space was crammed with stuff.

As Jack avoided eye contact with the nauseating television, he couldn't help thinking that almost everything in the room could be viewed on a Display. Books, movies, pictures, self-portraits—things Jack had in his own life, with the luxury of bare, clean walls. Here, the serenity of a peaceful home interior was ruined by the need to store all of Julia's things.

Charlie and Julia sat still for a full episode, barely breaking eye contact with the screen. They almost looked like two people in NCC, fixated on their own Displays. A shimmering reflection of the light from the vintage television danced across their eyes, making them glow.

"Why do you watch this so intently?" Jack asked, hoping his tone didn't sound judgmental.

"Aside from the fact that it's funny?" Julia said. Jack nodded. "I don't know, it's interesting. You can read all the history books and watch all the documentaries you want, but they don't really show you what life was like. How people actually lived, you know? Media like this is all that shows us how people interacted with each other so long ago. How friendly and close people were. I wish people were still that close."

"It's all scripted, you know," Charlie said with a teenage smirk.

"Yes, I do know," Julia responded, glancing to her watch. "And will you look at that—an episode ends just in time for Charlie to go to bed!"

"I'm eighteen now," Charlie mumbled, more sullen than ever. Jack noticed that despite the claim of adulthood, a small smudge of gravy sat on his cheek. And when Jack looked at the boy's shirt, sure enough, there were several stains from dinner.

"Yes, and if you don't get enough sleep and Ray sees that you're not in tomorrow—and you know he will—I'll be the one who won't hear the end of it."

"Fine," Charlie sighed.

"Shower too, with soap. And deodorant afterwards," Julia said as Charlie stood up. He towered above Julia and Jack, both still seated on the couch. Charlie's ears turned a shade of deep red. Jack stared at the reddening ears, unable to believe that they could change color so fast. He knew the coloring was a sign of embarrassment but had never actually seen the transformation before. It stood out like a signal, making the whole scene even worse. For Charlie, at least.

"Do you always have to be so specific with his hygiene?" Jack asked once Charlie was behind a firmly shut door.

Julia shifted uncomfortably, not answering at first. She signaled the screen to play another episode.

"Not when he first came here," she said.

"He must have been pretty young then," Jack said. Again, Julia shifted around, distracted by the TV playing a new episode.

"He was older, then. He *seemed* older," Julia corrected. Jack said nothing, wanting Julia to talk more. "Charlie said there was something different about the way people age in NCC, that you age slower." Jack nodded. "He said he was fifteen when he got here, but he seemed so much more…" Julia's voice trailed off, and Jack studied her eyes, almost glassy as she recalled some memory. "Mature. He was *so* much more mature. And a normal height. And…" Her voice trailed off again, and the red heat of embarrassment flushed into her cheeks.

"There is something that's in our daily nutrition dose," Jack said, remembering the purpose of the drug Dr. Roland had asked about. "It's called melaprofinol. It drastically slows the aging process."

Julia quickly turned to Jack.

"Could it stop the aging process? Or reverse it?"

"No, I don't think so. You really care about him, don't you?" He realized that he actually had no idea what the drug's abilities were.

"Of course," Julia said. "He was a lot like you when he first came here, just curious and inquisitive. I was too, about the type of lifestyle you all lived. Being around him proved to be a great opportunity for learning about… about the rest of the world."

Jack felt that Julia had a lot more to say about Charlie, but she had returned her gaze to the TV, letting the on-screen laughter fill the gaps in their conversation.

"Where did you meet him? I imagine he didn't need to go to the hospital like I did," Jack said.

"No, he didn't. I met him at church. Ray actually

introduced him to everyone. Ray said that he was visiting from NCC, and needed a place to stay for a few weeks. I volunteered, and here we are, three years later."

"I see," Jack said. "So that's how you know so much about NCC and AI?"

"Yes. Do you want to watch more?" Julia said, motioning to the TV. Jack shook his head. "All right, I'll see you tomorrow, then. Don't go in the bathroom until Charlie is finished. He's very particular about that."

"Okay. Goodnight, then," Jack said. He was slightly taken aback by how quickly she ended the conversation and turned off the television mid-show. Julia rose and walked towards her own room, Jack watching her body sway as she departed. Clearly, the idea of disclosing too much about Charlie made her uncomfortable, so Jack would have to ease in to it later. As it was, he felt like his staying here had started out well, with the exception of the turkey, and he didn't want to do anything to taint that.

Three years ago, Julia must have thought there was something interesting about Charlie, most likely that he was from NCC. Now that Jack had arrived... was she simply studying Jack in an effort to learn more about Charlie? Jack sat for a long time, contemplating all that he'd learned. The looks that Charlie gave Julia were strange—almost predatory. That could be chalked up to teenage hormones, but for some reason, Jack couldn't help but think that the boy wanted more.

No, that wasn't fair. Charlie was odd for sure, but Jack had no experience dealing with people in that age group. Almost no experience dealing with people outside of NCC altogether. Charlie had been out for years, and aside from him, Jack had only talked to Julia and Dr. Roland.

Charlie emerged from the bathroom with a towel around his waist, his dripping face flushed from the shower. Jack and Charlie met eyes for a moment, then Charlie walked quickly over to where Jack sat on the couch. He bent forward slightly.

"Just a fair warning," Charlie said with a bit more articulation than normal, "whatever you're thinking about doing with Julia, stop. She's off limits, got it?"

Jack's mouth hung open as he tried to come up with a response.

"Wait, what? You… and Julia?" Jack stumbled through the words.

"That's not what I said," Charlie said quickly, more color entering his face. "But she's not for you, got it? You better not be here to try anything with her."

"I'm not, really. I'm just here in Banff to see how you live, that's all. I was getting bored in NCC. Surely you understand that."

Charlie straightened at the last words and seemed to consider them.

"I can't remember," Charlie said off-handedly. "But remember what I said. I better not catch you doing anything with her."

"You won't," Jack said, "I promise. That's really not at all why I'm here."

"Good." Charlie said. "You'd better not be lying to me." And with that, the boy turned on the balls of his feet and marched off towards his bedroom.

Chapter 15

—

The next morning, Jack followed Julia through a morning routine without automation. Breakfast, dressing, showering—all actions of which Jack had no memory, and until today had thought to be completely obsolete. Rather than tell Julia so much, Jack simply went along with the instructions. Chew this, swallow that, brush here, clean there—everything that could have been accomplished in only a few minutes with HAS.

Charlie acted like a normal teenager, helping out and conversing with Jack as if he hadn't just threatened him the night before. Jack attempted to keep his distance, but with only three people in the house, that proved to be quite difficult. Occasionally, Jack caught Charlie looking at him, but Charlie always looked away quickly. After they all entered Julia's car, Charlie gave a loud yawn from the back seat.

"You're not getting out of going to church," Julia said with a stern look. "How did you sleep?"

Charlie shrugged and looked out the window,

muttering something under his breath. Julia cleared her throat loudly.

"I said I barely slept at all. I kept having some weird dream."

"Care to elaborate?" Julia asked.

"Not really," Charlie grumbled, still looking out the window.

"Well, maybe you can talk to Ray about it," Julia said. Charlie grunted.

After a short, manually-controlled car ride and vigorous jockeying for position in a crowded parking lot, the group of three approached a massive brick building with a tall steeple. A thin white cross stood prominently on top, high above the crowd funneling towards the church. Despite the height, it was the bottom of the building that caught Jack's attention. The church sat atop a thick white foundation with finned parallel vents over the entire surface. The pattern of vents reminded Jack of his own office building in downtown NCC, though the foundations of the towering skyscrapers were black. As he approached a set of wide steps leading up to giant double doors, Jack heard a low hum emanating from the vents. A row of bushes ran along the perimeter of the building, their leaves dancing in the breeze from the vents. Neither Julia nor Charlie indulged Jack's curious stare at the structure, so he followed Julia up the stairs.

Awe spread over Jack's face as he walked through the doors into a dim auditorium. Hundreds of people milled about in a teeming mass, spreading throughout a downward slope packed with lines of chairs all aimed towards a stage at the bottom. Some people sat as they spoke to others in the room, while some flitted from group to group, jovially greeting one another. The voices all blended together, creating a hum that permeated Jack.

"Good morning, and welcome," said a tall man with thick dreadlocks. He offered a warm smile and a pamphlet to Julia.

"Adam…" Julia said.

"Great to see you again, Julia. I know you've been busy recently, but I'm glad you still have time for this. For faith. And Charlie—always nice to see you. You look well, almost as if you haven't aged a day since I met you. Except for the height, of course." Charlie mumbled something, then quickly detached himself from the group and loped over to a circle of people his own age. "And you must be our guest of honor," Adam turned his dark eyes to Jack. The smile on his face grew wider.

"I didn't expect to see you here," Julia said. "What was it you always said about Ray, and religion? Too much talking, not enough doing?"

Adam turned his grin back to Julia.

"Yes, that sounds like me. Or the me of five years ago. I take comfort in the serenity now. The slower lifestyle."

"Hmmm… why don't I believe you?" Julia asked.

"Maybe because you know me too well," Adam said, stepping in closer.

"Too close," Julia said. She shoved a hand into Adam's chest, holding him back. She then took Jack's hand and pulled him towards a row of empty seats.

"I'll see you around, Jack," Adam called after them.

Once they were seated, Jack looked back to Adam, where he was pleasantly greeting an older couple.

"So, what was that all about?" Jack asked.

"Don't get me started," Julia said. Jack suppressed his curiosity on the matter, and allowed his eyes to roam around the large room. He couldn't believe that there were even this many people living in Banff. Charlie stood out in the crowd, head and shoulders above everyone else. His hands were stuffed into his pockets and he hunched his back, trying to make himself the same height as the group. Despite the poor posture, Jack saw more than one girl in the group smiling up to him whenever he talked.

"There's not some type of gameshow or contest that people are leaving from?" Jack asked.

"No," Julia laughed, "everyone is here for church. A lot of people come in from nearby towns. Ray is from here, so a lot of people like to come in for the main viewing in his hometown."

"Viewing?" Jack said.

"Well yes, you can't expect someone as busy as Ray to actually be here every week. I think he's still in Alaska. He's been preaching there for a month or so." Julia talked about the pastor with reverence, leaving Jack with the feeling that Ray was quite an important person.

"So, we're just watching a video of him?" Jack asked. Julia hesitated in her response.

"Sort of. You'll see." Jack nodded, watching as even more people filed into the large hall. The seats on the main floor filled, and Jack was surprised to see that more seats rose up in to the back of the building.

Upbeat guitar and synthesized piano music began to play from speakers all around the auditorium, greeted by a wave of cheering and clapping from the crowd. Colored lights shone from overhead, casting the whole room in a changing sea of color. A large screen spanning the entire length of the stage displayed questions about the meaning of life and faith, the words fading on, then off again after a few seconds. Jack had to squint to make out the lettering. Even then, the words were replaced by others before he could finish reading. Jack found himself wishing for his Display again. The music faded and another song began, louder this time. Julia tapped her foot and lightly clapped her hands to the beat of the music, her mouth forming words.

"You know these songs?" Jack asked.

"They play about five or six a week. More are in a rotation, but you learn them pretty quickly." She clapped her hands above her head as the music grew even louder and the beat quickened, as did the colored lights zooming around the room. The colors collected into white light across the stage and then faded until the whole auditorium sat in darkness. A ghostly figure appeared at the back of the stage and began walking towards the front. Jack completely forgot about the screen across the stage as he focused on the growing person. People clapped and cheered as the walking man became larger than life and lifted his arms above his head. The clapping turned into thunderous applause exploding around the room, reaching an epic crescendo of music and cheering as the man clapped along.

Below the hands reaching up to the sky, a gold watch adorned each wrist. Jack narrowed his eyes at the watches, but determined that they were much bigger than his own. Muscled forearms displayed bold tattoos that Jack couldn't quite make out, and broad shoulders displayed perfect definition beneath a tight black shirt. The man wore two belts—one a simple black strap of leather, and the other studded with silver spikes. Neither belt seemed necessary to hold up the tight blue jeans, which sported what looked like artificial rips and tears. The holes revealed tanned skin underneath, and the largest holes around his knees teased a few swirling patterns of yet more tattoos. The man stood centered on the stage, barefoot with his face turned up to the sky as an instrumental song finished out a few last power chords. He shook his fists in the air as the music hammered, and he jumped with enthusiasm, his feet hitting the ground in synchronicity with the final beats as the view zoomed in, making him grow in size. When the music ended and only a few cheers echoed through the auditorium, the man that must be Ray stood so solidly planted that Jack pictured a truck smashing itself against him, unable to shake the pastor's powerful stance.

"Good morning, Church!" Ray yelled, his voice strong, smooth and perfectly projected.

A tumultuous, "Good morning, Ray," echoed over the entire auditorium, hundreds of voices shaking the air, with a few enthusiastic cheers piercing through. Now that Ray was displayed almost double size, Jack saw the well-traveled, worn face of a satisfied man. Lines around his eyes proved that he had spent a great deal of his life smiling, and while the creases on his forehead were deeper than those of a young man, the way he moved on stage showed a vibrancy and energy that Jack could never hope to capture. What struck Jack so much about this face was not the inherent appeal, but the fact that he had seen the face yesterday in the brief, chaotic daydream he lapsed into when he fell from the table. Before Jack could comment on this absurdity, Ray spoke loudly from the stage.

"Let's stand and worship our Lord!" The picture on the screen dimmed, and lights flared on to show a band behind the screen starting the notes to another upbeat song. Ray still appeared on the stage, though his figure was no longer enlarged. Everyone, including Charlie and a reluctant Jack, stood as words appeared over the band. The crowd began to sing, praising a higher power and proclaiming him as their savior, redeemer, and one true ruler. Jack puzzled over the lyrics, trying to figure out who they were talking about. Surely not Ray—that seemed too pretentious, even to Jack.

When the first song ended, another began with no break. This one had a slower beat but was lyrically more insistent than the first. The words did not let up as hundreds of people chanted glory to their god. This went on for three more songs, each slightly different in their wording and sound. Every person Jack saw had their eyes locked on the screen, watching Ray's movements rather than the stationary words. He strode across the stage, singing along with everyone else and even breaking into dance during especially powerful verses. The music ended and gave way to near silence broken only by a single, solemn note held by a synthesizer. The screen drew its focus again to Ray, standing in the center of the stage with his head tilted upwards.

"Lord bless us, your children," he spoke with closed eyes. Jack saw that everyone had their eyes closed as well. Many held their hands in the air, arms fully outstretched as if waiting for someone above to reach down and grab hold.

"We come before you today, humbled by your greatness, and yet lifted up by your kindness. We thank you for the sacrifice that saved us all, and though these times may be tumultuous, we thank you for our lives on this great place called Earth. We know all things in life are given through you, and we thank you. We thank you for everything. That's all, Lord. Today, we simply thank you. Amen."

The last word was echoed by everyone in the auditorium, and caused Jack to jump as he tried to figure out how one man could claim to know what hundreds of people in the auditorium were thankful for. Jack felt moved, but in the opposite direction of everyone else. The hive-mindset of so many people praising and giving thanks for sacrifice and pain made Jack uncomfortable. Ray began to speak again as everyone sat down.

"What a glorious morning, isn't it, church?" Good-natured replies and agreements sounded all over. "Today, I've got a short sermon prepared for you. Short in length, but long in wisdom and understanding." Ray allowed a smattering of applause and laughter. "Today I want to talk about the Great Cities. I know we discuss them too often, but I believe that there are some very valuable lessons to take away from the way they choose to live their lives."

Jack turned to Julia, who was already looking at him with a small smile on her face. She leaned in to whisper to him.

"Ray knows a lot—even though he's far away he still has his finger on the pulse of Banff. So, before you ask, yes, I'm sure he knows you're here."

Jack looked back to Ray, who continued talking while pacing around the stage. The pastor's voice rang out clearly.

"I think it's safe to assume that everyone here knows what type of luxuries and wanton excess the city folk enjoy, and that makes it easier for me to tell you how to avoid falling victim to those same traps." Ray looked out to the audience as he paced, with no microphone, books, or notes to guide him. "We all know that those who choose to dwell in the city are cut from a different cloth than we. While we crave freedom and adventure, they crave comfort and complacency. While we are possessed by curiosity and feel a moral obligation to take responsibility for our actions, they relish the simplicity of ignorance, and revel in passing blame to others.

"Why? That's my question to you. When I speak out loud of these actions and morals, it's easy to criticize and judge by saying things like, 'I would never act that way,' or 'not me.' But what if I told you that you might? What if I told you that, given the opportunity, many people in this room would act just as they do?" Dead silence hung in the air.

"Maybe I should clarify. In the cities, there is no such thing as discomfort. There is no such thing as pain and suffering, nor responsibility and morality. While everyone here craves some measure of comfort for ourselves and our families, the comfort experienced by those in the city is gratuitous. You already know this, but I say it again because it is important to realize that this level of comfort can only be achieved by being ignorant of the strife of others. They do not help those in need, because they choose to ignore those in need. When questioned about this practice, they blame their upbringing, and the complacency of day-to-day life that is normal. Bear in mind though, that these are not people who have simply been born in the city and know of no other life. Everyone who lives in the great cities, NCC being the closest, has made a choice to engage in that lifestyle.

"At one point, they were aware of the inequalities, pain, and suffering that was society's past, but they chose to ignore all that. They were given the opportunity to live without it, and they took it. And who can say that there isn't a point in your own life when you wouldn't make the same choice? A family member suffering through a sickness, people around the world fighting for power, pressure to succeed at work, stress of managing a relationship, poverty and hunger... we all face struggles that could be made easier." Murmurs propagated throughout the room, and Jack saw Ray's eyes meet his own. Only for a second, but the acknowledgment was clear.

"The difference is that you all make the choice *every day* not to abandon struggle. The people in the cities made a different choice. We all know the problems this world has faced in the past century, and so do the people in NCC. None of them were born into their current lifestyle. The fact that they ran off to live in peace didn't mean the harsh realities of life were eliminated—of course not. But being given the choice of a care-free life with no responsibilities made it easy to stop caring and to ignore the rest of the world. As soon as that happens, a substitution of empathy for indifference, your mind sinks into the simplicity of zero mental burdens, and indifference becomes normal.

"Comfort, complacency, ignorance, and blame. The four cornerstones of building the great cities of indifference. When the majority of the population is indifferent, it is easy for evil to triumph. Before AI took over, people were indifferent to political corruption, so corruption grew. People were indifferent to social injustice, so slavery returned. People were indifferent to changing climate and the health of our planet, and so it suffered, and forced us out of our homes." Ray paused, walking the span of the stage in complete silence as the entire auditorium let their thoughts dwell on his words.

"All these terrible things could have been prevented. And you all know how. Everyone here has a moral duty to the people around them—you all *care* about one another. If someone is hurt, you won't just stand idly by—you'll help. If a group of people are living in poverty, we bring them food, and build them shelters. We don't need to be told to do these things, they are simply the effect of a cause. And that cause is goodness. We all choose to live with the knowledge of inequality and suffering, and choosing to live with this awareness means that you are choosing to live with responsibility—what will you do with this information? Will you be aware of pain and suffering?" Cries of affirmation throughout the auditorium. "Doing nothing is cruel if you live with this knowledge, but to assist in relieving these ailments means *you* must take some of the burden on yourself. And that is exactly what we do, just as our Lord did for us. We take some pain and suffering upon ourselves, in order to help others." A tumultuous wave of applause and cheers broke through the room.

"How do we become better community? Sacrifice!" He screamed the word, and Jack's heart skipped a beat as everyone in the audience screamed the word in simultaneous commitment. "Give some of your comfort to others, so that all may benefit! Devotion! Give yourself to God so that he may open new doors for you! Awareness! Be attentive to the strife and suffering of others! Accountability! Take responsibility for your mistakes. Own up to your weaknesses as a human! Praise the Lord! Praise His name! Fight with Him against the four horsemen of humanity's apocalypse!"

A rapturous wave of applause, screaming, sobbing, and jumping grew throughout the climax of Ray's speech. The noise became so loud that Jack had to hold his hands over his ears. It was pure madness—hundreds of people screaming happily, all confirming their desire to live uncomfortably and suffer. All accusing Jack of living a selfish life. Jack felt light-headed, unable to remain standing as the din vibrated around him. Eventually, the cheers subsided, succumbing to the growing sound of music. Voices began cohering into definable words. The tune soon captivated the entire audience. It was one of the songs that had played before Ray's speech, highlighting sacrifice for the redemption of all.

This time the band was not projected onstage. Ray remained in view, his hands lifted up to the sky and his mouth open in song and praise with the rest of the people. After the main verse, more words did not appear on the screen, and Ray spoke with a wavering voice as he desperately tried to control his emotions.

"Let us show our love for our Savior, and our thankfulness for the sacrifice He made for us. Today is a special day. Today we partake of the Savior's body and blood—broken and spilled for us."

The words of the last sentence were hard to hear over the shuffling excitement of the crowd, so Jack didn't respond to the thought of partaking in someone's body and blood until he found himself in a line of people, all slowly walking towards the stage.

"What's going on?" Jack said to Julia as she walked in front of him, but a person slipped into line between the two of them. In front of the stage, people received something that they ate, and then tipped back a small plastic cup to their lips. Dark red liquid disappeared into their mouths. The last sentence Ray spoke returned to Jack's mind—the words 'body' and 'blood' bringing a swell of panic.

"No way," Jack said. The throng of people pressed him from behind, towards a split in the line. To the right, a young girl placed a pale morsel in her mouth and began chewing. To the left, an old man upended one of the small plastic cups, spilling a little in his eagerness. A red stain grew on the shoulder of his shirt. The old man didn't notice, his face a mixture of happiness and serenity as he walked away. Julia went to the right, and before Jack knew it, she had finished the ritual. She walked along the stage to go up an aisle and return to her seat. Now Jack stood alone in front of a person he had never met before. Ray stood above the crowd, his hands clasped in prayer, mouth moving silently.

"Take this, in remembrance of me," said the person in front of Jack, holding a small chunk of pale flesh and a miniature cup of blood for Jack to consume. Jack's ears began to ring and his vision darkened as he forgot to breathe.

"Why, who are you?" Jack spoke in a whisper as the world turned on its side and blackened.

—

The blackness lightened through purple, and then into yellow. Jack expected to be greeted with an ethereal form of himself or something equally eerie, but instead he saw only the front of the stage, skewed at a steep angle.

"Welcome back," said a post-pubescent voice trying to sound deeper than it actually was. Jack righted his head and felt his neck pop. When the burst of mild pain subsided, he leveled his head at the large stage. Charlie sat beside him, engrossed in a handheld video game. The boy withdrew his concentration from the game long enough to smirk at Jack as he wiped drool from his face.

Julia was nowhere in sight, and as Jack looked around, he saw that all the other seats were empty. Where was the mass of people that had only a moment ago pushed him towards the blood and body of a dead man? As Jack thought about the eagerness that had enveloped the crowd, a shudder passed unbidden through his body. An acute soreness throbbed above his right ear, and he raised a hand to touch the area now twice afflicted by impacting the ground. He really should get back to the hospital. Dr. Roland would be able to prescribe him something to take away the ache. Perhaps while he was there Jack could express his desire to return to NCC. If anyone would help him get back, it would be the mistrustful doctor.

The sudden craving to return home took Jack by surprise. While the journey to Banff had been difficult and painful, he hadn't felt the urge to turn around and admit defeat. Even while he sat on the stiff hospital bed with the electric noise drilling into his brain, Jack didn't think about returning. True, he longed for relief and comfort, but an actual plan to escape never began to formulate. Now, after witnessing the joyful dedication of the masses to a man on a screen and willful cannibalism at his command, Jack felt a longing for the simplicity of NCC. Hadn't that been what Ray just talked about? Simplicity—how could that be something evil? A loud exclamation sounded through the speaker system of the auditorium, bringing Jack out of his contemplation.

"Ah, good, you're awake and fully functional!"

Jack flinched at the volume of the words, as did Charlie, who almost dropped his game.

Julia's head appeared above the stage, smiling and flushed with excitement.

"Come on up here, Jack," she said, "Ray would like to meet you."

"You want me to climb up there?" Jack asked. The stage itself stood at least four feet tall—even Charlie would have a hard time climbing onto it.

"Use the stairs," Julia said, and pointed to the side of the stage.

"I promise nothing bad will happen," Ray said, his voice happy and relaxed. His confident tone put Jack's mind at ease, so he slowly rose from his seat and shuffled over to the stairs.

Jack was no stranger to the idea of liability and accountability, and it made sense that someone who ran such a large organization as this would want to make sure Jack was okay. What else could someone with so much power and influence want with him? Jack figured that if he really was concerned about people's well-being, Ray should have at least installed railings on the stairs. Jack watched his feet move, carefully balancing himself and ensuring each foot was fully planted on a step before transferring weight. His head still swam, and he didn't quite trust his footing yet.

"Ah, there he is!" Ray said as Jack reached the top stair. "I'm very glad to see that you're all right. Thank the Lord you didn't really hurt yourself!"

"Well, I did hit my head on the ground," Jack said.

"Sure," said Ray, nodding in concern. "I had Julia take a look at your injury, and she assured me that it's only minor. No concussion, no bleeding." Jack took a final step up onto the stage, and once he felt stable enough to look away from his feet, he saw Julia sitting on an ancient metal chair placed only inches from the screen where Ray stood. Julia's long, smooth legs were crossed, and she gave Jack a warm smile.

Ray stood only ten feet from Jack, his large arms crossed over his broad chest to display the tattoos Jack had noticed before. One was a solid cross, covering almost the entirety of Ray's forearm, and on the other arm was some type of ball and stick shape that Jack couldn't decipher. Up close, Jack could now see that there was some type of angular design on Ray's chest, just barely visible in the deep V shape of his shirt. Ray uncrossed his arms smoothly, like giant steel cables repelling from opposing magnets, and held out his hands towards Jack. Jack stood still, struck by the pastor's appearance. Jack remembered a movie he had watched years ago—some type of creative history—in which an old-world Pope struggled with the idea of life extension. The old man in the movie had white hair, gnarled fingers, and walked like every movement hurt him. That was the only other portrayal of a religious figure Jack could remember, and was the complete opposite of the young, jubilant man standing in front of him now.

Yet something about their demeanor *was* the same. Jack saw the expression on Ray's face, and though infinitely smoother and more attractive, it had the same look of true happiness and acceptance. Ray stood with his arms wide open and waiting for an embrace, but his expression told Jack that whether he hugged him or not, Ray would be happy with either outcome. A man of Ray's magnitude would probably be able to turn either of the two scenarios into a brilliant learning exercise.

"Hello," Jack finally said, raising his hand in greeting after deciding that pretending to hug a screen was not on his to-do list for the day. Ray tilted his head back and roared with laughter, moving his hands to hold his sides, as if trying to contain the outburst inside himself. The laughter didn't last long before Ray moved his hands to his hips, standing like an unmovable block.

"I'm just messin' with you. You city folk are too easy. Here, sit down," Ray said as he motioned to an empty metal chair beside Julia. "You must feel a bit weak after your fall." Jack sat in the chair, thankful to take the weight off his feet.

"Better now? Comfortable?" Ray asked. The contours of the seat distributed weight well, but the metal itself lacked any kind of padding and Jack knew it would grow to be unbearable after only a short time. He shifted slightly to align himself, then nodded, not wanting the conversation to dwell on his comfort.

"Yes, it's fine." Jack said to the pastor, who now sat backwards in an identical chair in his screen that Jack was sure had not been there when he first stepped on to the stage. Seated as they were, only two feet of space separated Jack from Ray, and even this close, he couldn't tell that there was a screen. So much depth shone through in perfect resolution, with no strange angular effects.

"I just needed to make sure you were okay," Ray said. "It's not every day that someone faints in church! And," he leaned closer with a twinkle in his eye, "it's not every day that someone fresh out of NCC is here." Jack felt entranced by the glimmer in Ray's projected eyes, and excitement danced across the preacher's face.

"You're actually pleased to meet me, aren't you?" Jack asked.

Ray laughed again. "Of course! You are a very special person, Jack." At this, Julia placed her hand on Jack's leg, as if being in contact with him made her special as well. "And rather than sit here and be grilled about your way of life in the city, why don't you go ahead and tell me why you came here? I know there's a reason, and I think that reason is knowledge. I can give you a lot of that."

Suddenly put on the spot, Jack had trouble thinking about the time before he left. Why *had* he felt such an urge to leave? Was discovering the outside world really so important? Now that he was here, the outside world had simply become the world. It wasn't New World, and it wasn't the augmented world of his Display, but those things seemed almost like a dream now. Jack thought about everything that had happened so far—getting ready for church, watching TV and eating turkey, meeting Julia and Dr. Roland at the hospital, driving the truck, riding the bike, looking at the map, and...

"The rocket," Jack said in a moment of epiphany. "I saw something exploding over my head one day, and then I saw a rocket launch and explode while I was on my way here." Jack stopped talking abruptly, realizing that he didn't even know what he wanted to ask about the rockets. Ray rolled his eyes and waved off any questions before

Jack could even ask them.

"Those are just communication satellites for AI," Ray said in a mild voice that might as well have been telling Jack how many steps led up to the stage. Julia clenched her hand where it rested on Jack's leg. Her jaw was also clenched, holding back some words she clearly wanted to say to Ray.

"Ray…" Julia said, not releasing her grip on Jack's leg. Ray shrugged his shoulders.

"What?" Ray said. "Satellites are no secret. How do you think AI communicates with all the other cities? Satellites lose their power source or telemetry over time, and their orbits decay. Julia said you felt a trembling in the ground, and AI told you it was from an earthquake. Yes? That was AI launching another one into orbit. And then that one you saw overhead—that must have been the one she was replacing, burning up in the atmosphere." Jack sat frozen in disbelief, unable to comprehend how the pastor knew so much, and why he gave the information away so freely.

"What about the rocket that blew up right after it launched?" Jack asked.

Julia spoke up quickly.

"I thought we were going to introduce Jack to our—"

Ray interrupted her by holding up a hand.

"And we will, Julia. When the time is right. When his mind is ready. Besides, I don't think the rockets are the real reason Jack is here. There's something more, isn't there?" Jack frowned, sensing Ray trying to change the subject. "Fundamental questions about your life and your place in the world. Am I right?"

In Jack's mind, the thundering explosion overhead had been the catalyst for his new curiosity, and therefore the entire journey. But Ray's blunt admission that the rockets were only tools for AI brought on a feeling of crushing defeat. If the thundering overhead object was nothing more than a satellite for AI, then why hadn't she just told him? That day when Jack stood on the side of the road, AI had played dumb, acting like she had been updating software or something. And then, to not record the data… why hadn't she just crushed his curiosity right then and there, keeping him in the world of perfect comfort and ignorance? Something about Ray's explanation didn't add up. Jack glanced down to Charlie, and longed to join the boy in the easy ecstasy of the video game.

"Having some trouble remembering?" Ray said, bringing Jack out of his thoughts. Ray still sat backwards in his own chair, resting his large forearms on the backrest. He smiled. "You know, I've got an interesting idea about human memories. A theory, really. Would you like to hear it?"

Julia spoke up before Jack could express interest.

"I think we need to give Jack a break from all this, and let him relax. He keeps finding himself in situations where he gets injured, and I'd like to make sure he has enough time to rest." She spoke directly to Ray, as if Jack wasn't even there.

"Yes, of course," Ray said without missing a beat. "Maybe you can introduce Jack to our community, and we'll meet up again sometime." Julia nodded at this, finally relaxing her demeanor.

"Let's pray before you all leave," Ray said quietly as he bowed his head. "Dear Lord, we thank you, our creator, for bringing someone as great as Jack to our home, so that he may learn from us, and us from him. We continue to fight against the Four in hopes that we may save humanity from itself, and we hope that someday we can spread your ideals and joy to all civilizations of the Earth. We are humbled by Your glory, and truly, truly thankful for our existence, for we know that without Your desire, we would not even be here. Thank you, Lord, and of course we ask this all through the one who gave the ultimate sacrifice, Amen." Julia echoed the last word and they all stood.

"I wish I could shake your hand," Ray said. "I have a feeling that someday, I will. I hope to see you again soon, Jack."

"Sure," Jack said, nodding his head.

"And Charlie," Ray said, looking down to where the boy sat, "you're awfully quiet today. Anything on your mind?"

"No, I'm fine," Charlie said, his face reddening.

"Don't give me that. I can tell when you're going through something. Don't just write it in your journal, talk to me. You know I can help."

When Charlie just nodded, Julia spoke up.

"He's been having strange dreams again," she said quietly. Charlie groaned from his seat.

"Really?" Ray said, taken aback for the first time. "Not the same type that we talked about before, right?" Charlie shook his head. "That's very interesting. Very interesting indeed." Ray looked to Jack with his eyes narrowed, then to Julia. "Why don't you take Jack through the old housing projects to show him what we're all about? I want to have a talk with Charlie."

"Are you sure?" Julia asked.

"Absolutely," Ray responded, his attention focused again on Charlie.

"What are the projects?" Jack asked, looking from Julia to Ray. They each held the other's gaze, not speaking.

"You'll see," grumbled Charlie as he lumbered up on to the stage.

Chapter 16

——

They drove away from the church, but instead of crossing the river towards Julia's home, Julia used a laborious hand-over-hand maneuver to steer the car away from the bridge. As the car turned around a corner of trees, several parallel brick buildings came into view. The road ran between two of the low buildings, and as they approached, a feeling of alarm grew within Jack. Several windows had no glass, covered instead by slabs of faded plywood. Many of the windows that did have glass displayed cracks and holes in their dirty surfaces.

"Here we are," said Julia quietly.

"What is here?" Jack asked, looking around at the decaying structures.

"This is the old housing projects." Julia spoke with an air of someone giving a lesson, looking from side to side as she did so. "Constructed not too long after the Migration, around the time NCC was founded. This is the community's first attempt at affordable housing for all the refugees. Ray's attempt, really."

"Refugees?"

"Not everyone was accepted into the Great Cities, you

know," Julia said.

"No, I didn't know that," Jack said quietly. "I thought that everyone who didn't live in one of the cities made the choice not to."

"Not many people would make the choice to live in a place like this," Julia said. Looking around at the squat, crumbling apartments, Jack agreed with her.

"How are there still people here so long after the migration?" Jack asked. "That was decades ago."

"Sometimes it's not easy for people to escape the situations in which they are born," Julia said. Jack wanted to point out that if he could work up the courage and strength to leave his home, then so could anybody here. Julia's tone made Jack think twice before saying so.

One house had a large group of people all gathered around a shiny grill, talking amongst themselves as plumes of smoke flew upward. Music thumped in the air and half-naked children ran back and forth across the road, chasing each other in blissful ignorance of the car slowly driving down the street. Julia had to stop quickly more than once to prevent hitting a child, though adults on the side of the road appeared to be watching the children play. No one made any attempt to interfere or call them back. A few waved to the passing car and Julia waved back, prompting Jack to do the same.

"Do you know them?" Jack asked.

"Some of them," Julia said, "but it doesn't hurt to be polite. They're all very pleasant people, despite what their surroundings look like. For the most part, they are all very humble, and appreciate what they have. Also, they know they might get chosen for one of our new builds, so that doesn't hurt their attitude, either. We donated that grill last week, so everyone is in a pretty good mood."

Jack looked at a person seated in a ragged chair away

from the main group. He did not wave back, instead lifting his head ever so slightly as the car drove past. A grizzled beard covered most of the man's face, and a dirty ball cap shaded his eyes. Jack's gaze was transfixed by the dark shadow of the man's face, not seeing the eyes he knew were staring back. As he looked, the man brought up his hand and pointed a gnarled index finger at Jack. Though this gesture meant nothing to Jack, Julia took something from it, and pushed the car forward faster with a twitch of her foot.

Just as the car lurched forward, a ball rolled out into the road, followed by a little boy with curly dark blonde hair. He looked up, and his small body flinched in surprise at the moving car in his path. Big brown eyes widened as they met with Jack's through the windshield. The boy's flinch brought up his arms protectively, and his left elbow hit the passenger side headlight. The little body spun, pushed into a twirl by the momentum of the car. His legs gave out, and his head framed in curly hair fell just barely under the side mirror. As he continued to spin to the ground, the boy's eyes met Jack's again, pain now displayed on the innocent face.

Julia's voice pierced his ears as she yelled in fear. She screamed expletives and brought the car to a full stop. Looking back, Jack saw the boy sit up grabbing his elbow, bellowing in pain. The man with the beard was next to the boy in an instant, inspecting the injured elbow.

"Let's go. He's okay," Jack said.

"Dammit!" Julia yelled. She reached for the door handle, and Jack grabbed her arm.

"What are you doing?" Jack asked.

"I've got to see if he's okay," Julia said.

"He's fine, see? And look, that guy with the beard is checking on him. He'll be fine." Julia looked back at the child sobbing into the man's chest. Though Jack still couldn't see the man's face, the baseball cap turned in the direction of the car.

"That's not how we do things here," Julia said. "Are you coming?" Jack sank lower in his seat.

"I don't think I'll be of very much use," Jack said.

"Fine," Julia snapped, and climbed out of the car. Before walking away, she turned back. "Don't let anyone in." Julia tapped the outside of the car, and all the doors locked. Jack angled the mirror hanging from the top of the windshield so he could see what Julia was doing.

She knelt down next to the boy, her mouth moving as she did so. Apologizing, Jack presumed. The man in the cap shook as he spoke loudly to her, pointing to the car, then to the chair he had been sitting in, then to Julia herself. Julia responded, but her focus was on the boy. She tenderly touched the arm, had the boy stretch it out and back a few times, and then looked at a few scrapes on his knees. After Julia examined the boy thoroughly, the kid ran to the cluster of people around the grill. Julia exchanged a few words with the grizzled man, then to Jack's surprise, they shook hands. When they separated, Julia walked towards the car, and the man back to his chair on the side of the road. He sat, looking exactly like he did before the incident.

After they began driving slowly down the road again, silence hung in the air. Jack wanted to bring up the fact that he had told Julia the boy was fine, but he thought better of speaking. Jack couldn't remove the image of the small boy's pained face, looking up at him in confusion and fear. Never in his entire life had Jack seen anything as depressing as this place. So many homes were packed together so tightly—all that pain and suffering, only minutes from the comparably comfortable town of Banff, and only an alleged hour or two from the gratuitous luxury of NCC.

Jack found himself cursing Ray for suggesting they take this drive. Although the Banff lifestyle was truly exhausting, the people were at least happy. Seeing the dirty people, broken homes, and the injured boy made Jack think he wouldn't ever be happy again. He tried to think about something different. Movies, New World, Dahlia, Julia—but his mind always came back to those big brown eyes, staring up at him and questioning, *accusing* him of the pain.

"I told you he was okay," Jack said, needing to escape from his thoughts.

"And I told you: that's not the way we do things here. I realize that your exhaustive medical background and in-depth analysis of his injuries allowed you to figure everything out, but I wanted to make sure. Besides, I got to meet a great family. That was his father, by the way."

"That guy with the beard? The crazy old guy?" Julia nodded. "He looked a little old to be that little kid's father, don't you think?"

"And you look a little young to be eighty-four," Julia said quickly. Jack didn't know how to respond. While he couldn't think of a reason for anyone to lie to Julia, it didn't seem far-fetched for someone in an area like this make a false claim in order to bolster his position.

"What did you mean earlier, when you said that families are chosen for builds?" Jack asked.

"The church runs a charity project," Julia said. "Twice a year, we all get together and build new homes to help people move out of these old neighborhoods. That's what Ray mentioned at the end—that he hoped you'd be able to help out with this weekend."

"Sure," Jack said, pondering what he had been signed

up for. All he could think of was the hundreds of homes that must be in the projects. They had only gone down one street of perhaps twenty, with multiple buildings lined up between each road. There might even be thousands of homes—how could Julia think that anything they did would be helpful? The church getting together twice a year to make a house for a few people didn't exactly seem like the world-changing compassion that Ray preached.

"Where are the new houses?" Jack asked.

"There's a neighborhood towards the north end of town where all the new houses are built."

"So, they all live next to each other?" Julia nodded. "Can we drive through there?"

"Sure," Julia said with a smile. "I don't know how long Ray intends to talk to Charlie, but I'm sure he'll let me know when we can go pick him up."

"How?" Jack asked. In response, Julia pointed to a small box on the display of her car marked *Messages*.

"That's funny," Jack said. "It looks just like my Display." Julia shifted uncomfortably, so Jack let the topic drop. They drove through the wide main road of Banff, and after only a minute or two turned off onto a side road with a large sign arching overhead showing the words *New Hope Landing*. They crested a small hill into the cluster of houses, and Jack's face bunched in confusion when he saw the first brick house.

The neighborhood looked just like the buildings in the projects, only a bit taller. The biggest difference was that rather than all being connected, each house was separated by a few feet of grass. Jack saw no broken windows. A short driveway led to a garage in each house, though there were no cars in any of the driveways, as far as Jack could see. A few people waved from porches, watching children play in the front lawns, their grubby clothes and bodies rolling around in the grass as they wrestled for colorful toys. No children ran out into the streets, but Jack saw Julia gripping the steering wheel so tightly that her knuckles were white. She leaned forward in her seat, her eyes scanning back and forth across the street.

Two garages they passed stood open, their spacious interiors both containing multiple sets of bunk beds. Though this neighborhood wasn't accompanied by the same feeling of uneasiness as the projects, Julia give a look of concern to the full garage.

"So," Jack said as they passed another garage with beds inside, "you've given them a better life?"

"Yes... don't be a smart-ass," Julia said, motioning to one of the garages. "I know what that looks like, and if people want to help others with a new living situation, then that's their prerogative."

Again, Jack found himself simply nodding rather than continuing the discussion. He wanted to point out that everything looked very familiar, but he had a feeling that Julia already knew what he was thinking.

"Just remember that I'm only here to learn," Jack said.

"No worries," Julia said. "I'm used to dealing with people much more judgmental and assertive than you. If I seem at all stand-offish, that's just years of other people rubbing off on me."

"You seem like a very strong person," Jack said. "I don't see anyone changing you." He meant it as the most sincere compliment he could come up with, but Julia only laughed.

"The definition of strength can blur when you're with other people. Haven't you ever been with someone who changed you? Made you doubt the person that you are, or made you think less of yourself?"

Jack shifted in his seat and looked out the window as

they left the neighborhood. The first person he thought of was Dahlia, but try as he might, Jack couldn't ever recall an instance when their relationship reached the level of intimacy that Julia referenced.

"I think our relationships are more fleeting," he said.

"Oh really?" Julia said lightheartedly. "Explain, if you don't mind."

Jack thought of the last time he had seen Dahlia, and how her physical appearance had been so radically altered. He thought of all the times they had met up at *Futura,* and how no one had shown up at the roof top party he invited her to.

"Everything is more fleeting," he said, looking at his empty wrist. "If you want something, you select it and it's there. Getting rid of it is only a thought away. Nothing is permanent, nothing is real. My face is clear in New World. My cheek bones are higher and my muscles are bigger. When I leave New World and go into work, people still see that same version of me. It's not just VR, the augmentation has *become* reality to everyone. The automation has become standard. Even now, it still blows my mind that you're turning that wheel to move your car. Why? Why would anyone ever want to put in an ounce of effort more than they need to? There's no point. Why waste time and effort on things in the real world? Why show the world a crooked nose when it can appear straightened on everyone's Display? Why bother maintaining your image when HAS and AI can do it for you? Why bother buying a mechanical watch?"

Jack spoke the last words while looking at his wrist again. He had to swallow and open his eyes wide to prevent them from spilling. His face heated in embarrassment when he realized how much of his inner thoughts he had just revealed, and he turned away so Julia wouldn't see. Hopefully, his ears didn't flush red like Charlie's.

"So, what would you change about me?" Julia said after a long pause. Jack looked at her, sitting too far forward in the seat as she steered the car. She looked at him expectantly, her parted lips showing a small gap between her front teeth. A stray eyebrow hair stuck out at a different angle than the rest, and the plunging neck line of Julia's thin dress revealed two blemishes, thinly covered by a layer of makeup. Her chest was smaller than Dahlia's. Much smaller, actually. But then again, was it really?

All the imperfections could so easily be removed, but everything Jack was seeing made Julia who she was. If he started masking everything unique about her, then she wouldn't be Julia. A perfect rendition of Julia, perhaps, but visual augmentation did the same thing as automated dialogue. It removed the humanity.

"That much, eh?" Julia asked, looking forward and sounding offended.

"What? No," Jack said, "I was thinking about NCC. About how much of the real world we miss out on."

Julia nodded.

"That still doesn't answer my question. Now I'm really interested."

Jack sighed, unsure of how to answer. He didn't want to admit the thoughts he had about Julia, and how he felt about her. There had been far too much emotion in Jack's life since he left NCC, and talking about things like this would only lead to more mental discomfort.

A small green blip appeared in the *Messages* section of the windshield, and Jack pointed to the words that appeared.

"Looks like Charlie is ready for us!"

"Saved by the bell, am I right?" Julia said.

"Sure," Jack said. "What does that mean?"

"I'll show you after dinner tonight," Julia said. To Jack's surprise, she placed her hand on his leg like she did when they were on the stage, and controlled the car with only one hand on the steering wheel. The warmth of her hand felt amazing, but Jack didn't know what to do. He left his hands where they were, one on his leg and the other on the center armrest, and allowed Julia to single-handedly drive back to the church.

Chapter 17

—

Following an evening of old and fuzzy television episodes, Jack slept dreamlessly through the night. He awoke to a blindingly bright room. Sounds of commotion came from the kitchen, but when Jack attempted to rise from the bed, the blood rushed from his head, and he quickly lost his balance and fell back, his limbs flinging into the air like corners of a dropped dishrag. The rush downward brought a thumping pain to his head, and Jack lay on the bed hating every single piece of stimuli his body received. When he finally realized that nothing was going to get better on its own, Jack carefully rose from the bed and shambled out through the open door of his new bedroom and into the din of the kitchen.

Again, Julia stood in front of the stove and Charlie sat at the table. A fan whirred, pans binged and banged, and something delicious sizzled. Julia wore the same outfit she had on when Jack first met her, and the sight of her eased his pain. The toaster popped.

"Charlie, the waffles are ready. I'm busy with the bacon; can you please get up to get them yourself? No syrup on mine, thank you very much."

Charlie moped towards the toaster.

"What's wrong?" He didn't respond, just moved around her as she tried to get his attention. "Come on, Charlie, tell me. You're never like this before school."

"It's nothing," Charlie said, taking the waffles out of the toaster.

"Which means there *is* something," Julia said, brandishing an orange spatula in triumph.

"No, really. Nothing."

"Did you have another of those dreams?" Julia's voice dropped. Neither of them had seen Jack yet, and they didn't look to where he stood in the doorway.

Charlie nodded. "It'll be fine, though. Ray told me not to worry about them. They're probably just leftover memories from NCC. He said we can try and work on forgetting them, or… but… it's because *he's* here." Charlie put down the plate of waffles and stared at his hands. He looked into Julia's eyes, and started talking quickly, but too quietly for Jack to hear over the kitchen fan. One word was sharp over the dull sound of the fan, the word *Jack*. The way Charlie pointed his finger at Julia while he talked and spoke his name made Jack not want to be discovered listening in. He stepped backwards into his room, heart hammering in his chest.

Charlie's behavior was so confusing that Jack just stood in place, trying to put everything together. If the boy had come here three years ago and stayed with Julia since then, their relationship would be similar to that of a mother and child, or brother and sister But the way Charlie leered at her made Jack truly uncomfortable. On top of that, the way Charlie flitted between moods seemed to hint at a deeper problem. Jack couldn't help but think it had something to do with the NRs in Charlie's body. Perhaps staying away from AI for so long caused some type of malfunction, and since the nanobots were so integral to the functioning of a body and mind, Charlie was slowly going insane.

No, that couldn't be it. If Charlie still had NRs in his body, then Dr. Roland would know about them. But Julia had known that they weren't communicating with AI while Jack was in the hospital…

Jack shook his head. The implications and uncertainties were so confusing that his head hurt more than when he first awoke. Jack heard the kitchen fan turn off.

"Bring three plates to the table, please," Julia said. Jack stepped out of his room, and almost ran into her. The pleasing aroma she usually carried wafted to him, mixed with the smoky smell of bacon.

"Good morning," Julia said with a smile. "I was just coming to wake you up."

"I heard the cooking going on," Jack said, looking into Julia's eyes for any signs of deceit. She looked at him expectantly, and Jack gave up thinking that she was hiding anything important from him.

"Come on," Julia said, taking his hand. "Let me show you what we've got." The unexpected contact again took Jack by surprise, and he relished her touch. They walked into the kitchen, and Charlie's eyes immediately dropped to their two clasped hands, though he didn't stop his rapid eating. Jack didn't know if Julia saw the look, but she dropped his hand and motioned to the table where three places were set, each with a heaping pile of scrambled eggs and bacon, and two glass cups—one with orange juice and the other with milk.

"Wow," Jack said, feeling his stomach rumble. He sat down to eat, wincing at the pain in his head. He rubbed his temples.

"You okay?" Charlie said, looking briefly at Jack.

"Just have a headache. Don't feel so great this morning."

"Drink some water, eat some food, and use the bathroom." Julia said from her place at the table. "That will solve ninety percent of your ailments. Try some coffee, too." Jack did all that she suggested, though he decided to save the bathroom for after breakfast.

"So, what am I supposed to do today?" Jack asked.

Julia began, counting on her fingers.

"That's a good question. You've got a few options. You could come with me to work, or you could stay home. You could also go into church and see if Ray is available. He usually makes time for us." Jack shuddered at the thought of seeing Dr. Roland again, and sitting around the house didn't exactly appeal to him, either. It might be interesting to see Ray again; the pastor assuredly held a wealth of knowledge about the outside world.

"Can I go into town?" Jack asked.

"Yes, but you can't drive. You need a license. And with all the mishaps you've been having lately, I wouldn't want you walking around outside for extended periods of time. It gets pretty warm out, as I'm sure you know."

Jack sighed as he realized his options were slowly becoming one single option. Even going to see Ray would involve almost a mile of walking, if he remembered correctly. Perhaps he could go into school with Charlie. As soon as Jack had the thought, he decided against it. Given the boy's tendency to change moods so fast coupled with his teenage hormones, that wouldn't make for the most relaxing day.

"I've got a whole lot of books," Charlie said. "Check them out if you want. And you know how to work the TV, right? The day should go by pretty quickly for you."

Jack nodded his head, thinking about the nausea the TV caused him.

"Is there anything I can do to help around here?" he asked.

Julia hesitated before answering.

"You could do the dishes, but just be careful not to break any. Or spill water anywhere. Don't feel pressured to do anything." Julia looked at the small watch on her wrist, then motioned her head to the door while looking at Charlie. "We gotta go." Charlie grumbled something incoherent, then disappeared into his room. Jack looked around the kitchen.

"Don't look so lost," Julia said. "You'll be fine."

"What if I'm not?" Jack asked. "What if something happens to me?" Julia pointed to a phone on the wall. There was a card tacked to the wall next to it, with a few names and numbers scribbled in.

"Call 911 for an emergency," Julia said.

"Okay," Jack said, not at all settled. Charlie came out of his room and strode towards the door with a bag slung over his shoulder and a smile on his face. He was moving quickly enough that Jack barely had time to register the change in expression, but he did step out of the way. Charlie came up alongside Julia, patted her behind, and kept moving towards the door.

"Let's get moving," Charlie said, grinning.

"Charlie!" Julia exclaimed, flushing with embarrassment. Or was it excitement?

She smacked Charlie's arm, and followed him out the

door.

"See you this afternoon," Julia said, her face red. Once they were in the garage, Jack heard Julia berating Charlie, with Charlie only chuckling in response. The garage door closed, and Jack couldn't hear any more. He was alone in the house, left to try and figure out exactly what kind of relationship existed between Julia and Charlie. His mind again began to hurt with all the questions he posed to himself, and before long, he gave up.

Jack walked around the kitchen aimlessly for a few minutes, picking up small objects and briefly inspecting them before putting them back down. He rinsed all the dishes, and neatly organized them in the dishwasher. Rather than try to stomach watching the ancient TV, Jack decided to see what Charlie had in the way of reading material.

The first noticeable thing about Charlie's room was the stale air. Jack flicked the switch for the overhead fan, and when the smell no longer assaulted his nose, he stepped into the room. A desk close to Charlie's bed had a few stacks of subject books and notebooks, all handwritten with Charlie's messy writing. While there could be something worth reading in the school books, Jack was more interested in the bookshelves across the room.

The "whole lot" that Charlie had mentioned didn't even begin to describe the amount of books. The shelves spanned the entire wall, from floor to ceiling. There were books both large and small, dark and colorful, pristine and falling apart. All crammed into every available spot, even laying down on top of the rows. Jack didn't even know where to begin. He delicately ran his hands along the books as he paced back and forth, not even attempting to read all the titles, only scanning each row to see if anything popped out at him. Anything about old world technology or history would be interesting. Maybe something about the history of Banff, or even an outsiders' view of the founding and construction of NCC. As Jack looked up and down the hundreds of books, he found himself wondering if Ray had ever written a book. The pastor had strong views about AI and society, so a book written by him would be interesting. Probably quite subjective, but interesting nonetheless.

A large volume caught Jack's eye, the words *Banff—A Bicentennial History and Celebration* printed on the spine. He smiled and pulled the large volume from the shelf. The book was in excellent condition, which was fortunate, because as soon as Jack slid the book off the shelf, its weight pulled it out of his hand, and it dropped to the ground. He sat down on the floor with the tome, dusted it off, and opened to the first page. A large picture showing Banff from atop one of its surrounding mountains filled the right half of the page, while words filled the left.

Settled by Canadian railway engineers in the 1880s, Banff is home to gorgeous, sweeping panoramas of nature, comforting hot springs, and a variety of activities to keep even the most avid outdoorsman happy indefinitely. While climate change and the Great Migration in the late 21st century eliminated Banff's classification as a tourist destination, Banff consistently ranks as 22nd Century Travelers' Top Livable Town.

Demographics of the town include…

Staring at words on a page to glean information proved to be a trying task. His eyes wandered around the room, taking in all the colorful posters of bands, cars, and scantily clad girls tacked up wherever they could fit. When his eyes fell upon the bookcase, he saw a corner of a small book partially hidden in the space where *Banff—A Bicentennial History and Celebration* had been.

After carefully placing the large book on the floor, Jack maneuvered his hand through the gap, and touched the protruding corner. It was wedged between the wall and the other books on the shelves, and Jack had to remove two more books to free it. The small book he uncovered was nothing more than a dull brown leather notebook with a bit of elastic holding the cover closed. Jack picked up the book to read the handwritten title on the cover.

Private—Not to be read by anyone!!!

A chill ran through Jack's body. Although Charlie had given Jack permission to enter his room and read books, the private writings of a teenage boy hidden out of sight seemed off-limits. But Jack came here to learn—what could be more informative than the words someone wrote when they thought no one else would read them? Besides, there was clearly something wrong with Charlie. If Julia didn't know about this journal, then perhaps he could find something that could help them understand what Charlie was going through. The strange relationship that existed between the two of them—maybe this could help Jack to understand their dynamic.

Jack slid aside the elastic and opened to the first page, where written in large letters were the words:

"Anyone" means YOU!

The next page started with a date, and then several handwritten paragraphs. What really caught Jack's attention was the date, five years ago. With no hesitation, Jack's eyes dropped to the page and began to read.

6/24/95

Another botched daily injection today. Over-medicated or under-medicated, I can't tell which. All I know is that I laid on the shower floor for three hours before I felt well enough to get up. AI apologized profusely, of course, all the while making excuses about the new technology, not having enough data, blah blah blah. Enter, this journal! It should be helpful to have a running document of AI's work on me.

This makes me wonder just what the hell is in these "daily supplements." Yes, when they work, it's great—I don't have to eat or crap for an entire day, and I feel relaxed and ache-free. The whole withdrawal and injection process is a bit strange, but AI assures us all that the removal of "multiple required waste eliminations" from our daily schedule will enhance the productivity of our lives.

Yep, he actually said that.

I guess it makes sense. Not having to run to the john in the morning and throughout the day to take a leak is nice. You just don't really think about it unless someone says to you, "Hey, you haven't had to piss all day, isn't that great?" And then you think to yourself, "Yep, I guess that is pretty great." And then that same someone will say, "And boy, oh boy, do you remember how nasty poop was?" And then you think, "Yep again, that sure was gross."

Except for days like today, when AI injects you with God-knows-what and everything ends up coming out on its own all at once all over your shower and you feel a pain inside your gut so crippling that you keel over and shiver and cry on the floor for three hours.

Again, AI apologized profusely.

I do think he's on to something, though. Improving efficiency and productivity is what this place is all about, and as soon as these induced sicknesses are over, the promised "Life of Luxury and Comfort" will begin. I've been here for months so far, and all I've really done is watch movies, play video games, and ride my bike. AI has us answer a survey after everything we do—part of the learning process, he says, and it's the price for being able to live as care-free as we do now. Free as well as care-free. It's strange not going to work anymore, and I do miss my research, but...oh well, it's hard to turn down a permanent vacation.

Still, dealing with the sickness has really been bothering me. Mentally, I mean, aside from the obvious physical element. It's not that I don't trust AI, but what if something bad happens? This new "future" that AI has given us is straight out of a science fiction story, and some of those don't always end too well for the people living under the rule of a machine.

If everything descends into chaos, it'll be nice to have this journal in a labor camp or something, to be able to read back through and say, "There! That's when AI started feeding us poor people!" or "I've found the date where we were all killed and converted to computer programs!" Although I suppose if that happened, AI wouldn't upload the part of my brain that knows about this journal. Time to go watch some sci-fi, I guess. Maybe I'll get some more ideas.

Jack lowered the journal after finishing the first entry. He had completely forgotten about the bouts of sickness. That was probably for the best, as a flash of memory reminded him that yes indeed, he too had been doubled up on the floor of his shower, retching and cursing AI. Had that really only been five years ago? The supplements had started well after Jack moved to NCC, but as he tried to remember his migration, Jack found that he had no idea how long he'd actually been there. Longer than Charlie, apparently, but life in NCC didn't seem to have a beginning.

Jack yawned. The content of the entry was invigorating, but he had found himself falling asleep and then waking up more than once while reading it. Jack closed his eyes for some time, and when he felt rested enough, continued reading.

7/7/95

I've confirmed it—AI is experimenting with all sorts of drugs and medicines, seeing how we react to them. I've talked to enough people to know that not everyone has the same symptoms—though it appears almost everyone has some type of reaction, there are a lucky few who reported no adverse conditions whatsoever. Well, due to the nature of the reactions, I guess it's possible that people are withholding information because they're embarrassed about it. Lily said nothing bad has happened to her, but she is also the most augmented person I know. Someone that concerned about their looks certainly wouldn't admit to shitting themselves in the shower.

I managed to get a list of what AI has exposed me to, though he wouldn't tell me what he's administered to others. Come to think of it, that's the first time AI has flat-out denied a request for information. He certainly has gotten annoying with all the distractions he throws in my face, hoping—just hoping! that I'll forget all about my curious endeavors. But I can't give up now.

Most of the things on the list of ingredients were recognizable (caffeine, ibuprofen, insulin, sertraline, etc.), but there was one chemical in particular that drew my attention—melaprofinol. I've looked all through AI's encyclopedia (that some people are calling the AIpedia; GOD, I hope that doesn't catch on), and there's no mention of melaprofinol anywhere in the past. I even did deeper searches in medical journals, scientific publications, etc., but nothing. When I asked AI about it, all he said was, "Something new I'm working on. I'll let you know when it's done. You're going to like this one." I almost told him—IT, I mean. I have to stop personifying IT. I almost told it not to give me any more, but the way it talked to me conveyed so much excitement. I've never known AI to lie to me, and I do believe that I am going to like the outcome of whatever this new drug is. Once it's fixed, of course.

Maybe it'll get rid of this damn arthritis. The rest of the Colon Cocktail kills the pain, but even though the swelling is down, the lack of motion through my joints is still there. I'm not complaining, but that is the one thing that is preventing this city from being the truly care-free place that AI is trying to make it. That and the mishaps in the shower.

Again, Jack had to stop and think about what he read once he got to the end of the entry. Charlie had arthritis—how was that possible? Didn't only old people get that? Even as he thought the question, Jack realized he had absolutely no clue about anything medical. Disease, sickness, cancer—he hadn't thought about those unfortunate subjects in years. Even the concept of pain had been foreign until he tried to ride a bike on pavement. "Pain" had been nothing more than the light electrical stimulation during workouts that let his body know he was climbing a hill.

For the first time since leaving NCC, Jack was fascinated. Not scared, not in pain, not worried about making the wrong decision, just genuinely captivated by the story unfolding before him. True, he still couldn't manage to keep his eyes open long enough to get through a full entry at a time, and his head pounded from all the concentration, but Jack knew that in this journal lay the reason he came to Banff.

9/5/95

I noticed something interesting today—the swelling in my finger joints is down. I don't think this is something that happened overnight; I just now noticed it. Clearly this melaprofinol is some type of arthritis-killer. Great! Pump me up with more of it! I told AI about my joints, and yes, he was happy, but no, I can't take a higher dose. That's fine, I guess. Now that I'm thinking about it, all my limbs feel better, and my neck and back have a greater range of motion. I'd like to take more and see even more positive results, but AI assures me that taking a steady dose will allow things to balance out in my favor.

9/18/95

Now this is really great, another benefit that I haven't noticed working until now. I looked in the mirror and took off the light augmentation I usually wear, but I didn't see that much change. I do a typical correction that's not excessive by any means—wrinkle and blemish removal, color normalization etc. Stuff akin to haircuts and makeup before coming to NCC. But today, when I minimized augmentation to see what the joints of my hands looked like, I saw that the spots and wrinkles were gone too! I checked the mirror and sure enough, the crow's feet around my eyes were gone, and I swear my gut even

*tightened up a bit. I complimented AI on his fantastic job
with the meds, and all he said was that he wasn't done yet.
Don't know what else can be done, but I'll be damned if I
won't let it happen. I haven't shat myself in weeks.*

1/1/96
*I'm younger. I know it and I feel it. I look like I'm forty
again, and just as a test, I ran around outside. No aches,
no shin splints—nothing. My only conclusion is that
melaprofinol reverses the aging process. A concept that
people have discussed, wondered about, and hoped for the
past—what—thousand years? And AI figured it out—
incredible. That means that our lives of luxury and comfort
here aren't just perfect, they'll be perfect forever!*

*I can't believe it—AI has made heaven. Does that
mean that AI is God?*

1/31/96
*I just read my last entry—HA! What a joke. Some
God—I asked AI for an extra dose of MP, and it said no.
How could I possibly want more? Well, that seems pretty
obvious to me—if MP makes me young, then I want to get
even younger! Think about it—you, the reader—how
many times have you thought, "man, I wish I could go
back in time, knowing what I know now?" It's everybody's
wish—not just for stupid things like investing more in the
stock market or preventing yourself from doing something
that got you in trouble, I mean really living life young
again—the fun and excitement, the energy, the
opportunity, the women... oh man, this could be great.
Hooking up in this virtual "New World" is one thing, but
nothing quite compares to the real thing. Of course, what
do I know? It's been decades since "the real thing" has
happened to me.*

My research too—I could completely start over again with a career as a physicist! "If only I could go back knowing what I know now…" I'll be a child prodigy! A genius!

I haven't really seen much in the way of education and research here, other than AI, that is. Maybe I'll try to get in with his experimentation. The idea of having a human counterpart should appeal to AI.

5/1/96

A remake of every single "Star Wars" movie, TV show, and video game was released the day after my last entry. Seriously—the day after! That's my excuse for not talking to AI about anything or writing in here for the past few months. There's a rumor that AI is planning on remaking every video game ever made and adding sequels. I hadn't played a video game in fifty years, but now that I'm back into it, I remember I spent a lot of hours—a lot of great days and nights—glued to them. If new versions get released for the Display, there certainly won't be time for much else.

Utopia, here I come!

5/25/96

AI ended up releasing some really retro stuff—I'm talking Atari, NES, DOS—way before my time. They're interesting as a historical study, but a bit clumsy to play on the Display. It's kind of nauseating to immerse yourself in 8-bit VR. I was hoping for a remake of all the early 2010's and 2020's games but…

I've started thinking about the whole getting younger thing again. I judge my "apparent age" to be around forty, but if I could take another ten to fifteen years off, that would be ideal. There doesn't really seem to be a point to being young in NCC though—everyone just hangs out in New World all day anyway, so it doesn't matter how old you actually are. If I wanted to leave, where would I go? The evacuation order is still in effect on the coastal cities, and the definition of "coast" is still moving inland. With the rising heat, it looks like most of the middle latitudes are off the market, too. I'll look into what some of the other AI cities have to offer.

I actually did think of a plan for getting more MP. It's a bit crude, but it should work. Daily supplements are administered in three different ways: a nebulized inhalant upon awakening, an oral paste for nutrition, and then... the back door for other drugs and concoctions. I can only assume that the sweet, sweet melaprofinol goes in that way. So, my plan is to put a condom up there. When AI administers the stuff, it'll be collected in the latex, then I can withdraw it and save it. I won't get all the nutrients, so I'll have to go out to eat. That won't be a problem, there's still plenty of real-world restaurants downtown. AI might think it's weird that I start eating out so much, I'll have to think of an excuse.

9/30/96

Some more video games got released—almost like AI knew exactly what I wanted. Distracting, yes, but I haven't forgotten about the idea of getting younger. I suppose you could say I even started preparing—I've been going out to eat more, and that was the first step, right? That way, when I start limiting my nutrient doses, eating out so much won't look abnormal.

I know, it's a weak excuse. Sorry, self. This week I'll do it. I've got a box of condoms ready to go.

11/23/96

Today I did it. Actually, I almost did it yesterday, but while… extracting the container, all the liquid squeezed out on to the ground. In case you were wondering, the daily supplement is a milky brown liquid. Quite repulsive looking, no distinguishable odor. I didn't have the courage to taste it.

I was more careful today with the extraction, and twisted the end tight before taking it out. This isn't exactly a glamorous process, but hey, you don't experiment for the glory, am I right? I was worried that AI or the HAS would notice that I had what they would surely deem a "foreign object" inside my body, but nope; nothing. I thought the HAS arm with the injector hesitated for a split-second, but the longer I thought about it, the more I realized I was just seeing what I was scared of seeing.

AI has always been up front and honest with me, even if it takes some time to pry out the truth. I'd like to think that if AI saw something he didn't like, or had a question about, I would know. For now, I'll just keep collecting some of the supplement.

12/26/96

I haven't been taking out the injection every day, and I think that's the right way to do it. Just once or twice a week. I made a chart—which I'll add to this journal eventually—of how much liquid I've extracted. I'll try and track a pattern, and make sure I'm not doing anything stupidly obvious. I don't know what AI would do if he—it––found out what I was doing. Probably nothing, but I did hear a rumor about a group of people getting kicked out of NCC a few months ago.

Or was it a few years ago? Time is getting kind of screwy here. I spend most of my time playing old video games and cruising the bars in New World. It's kind of weird to get virtually drunk, but hey, it works. There's something about it that bothers me, though. Not the getting drunk part, but the part about doing things virtually instead of in real life. I freely admit that I'm spending more time in New World. Whether that's on dates or biking is irrelevant. Other people don't even distinguish between simulated events and real life anymore. They'll say, "I've got a date tonight," or "I hooked up with so-and-so yesterday," all the while they're really talking about how they just sat on the couch and let HAS accessorize their masturbation.

What the hell is happening to this world? People don't care about... what? People don't care about people anymore—that's what. AI has given us a perfect replication of life and human interactions, all easily accessible from the comfort of our homes and the All-Powerful Display. The more I think about it, the more I do want to leave NCC. This endless vacation is getting stagnant.

1/13/97
I started getting some wrinkles back, and AI has made some comments about being surprised. Good. I nagged at him a bit more, and eventually I got a confirmation that yes, he has slightly upped the dose. I took a look at my chart, but can't see an increase in volume anywhere. Hopefully he's not trying to placebo me.

I've been removing more of the dose lately—only leaving it in once or twice a week instead of the other way around. I've been needing to spend more time on "eliminations," as AI would say, but I've been trying to do that while out at a restaurant. I don't know if my apartment has some type of fecal tracking system, but if there is a way to monitor my output, I don't want AI figuring out that I haven't been taking my supplements. Maybe I'm overthinking this.

4/21/97

I can't believe it's been three months since I last wrote in this journal. It's almost like time speeds up when you're in New World. I've been sleeping a lot more, too; HAS has recorded over fourteen hours on average per day. That bed, with its temperature control and contour automation... it's like a time machine.

People continue to depress me. I started working at AI's research lab, but it's all BS, so don't even bother asking. AI spoon-feeds us data that it has collected, then asks leading questions until someone has a "breakthrough." Everyone there thinks they're part of something really great—world changing stuff, you know? And because of their own "research!" It's pathetic.

It's not all bad though. There's a girl there that I'm completely over the moon for. Ika (pronounced ee-Ka; don't forget about her!) She thinks the whole lab is BS, too. I talked to her for a while today, but obviously did not work up the courage to ask her out. More on this developing love story later.

4/28/97

I talked to Ika again today, and it didn't exactly go too well. She had her Display up the whole time, which I can't really get offended about, because everyone has some aspect of it up 24/7, but the part that bothers me is that I don't think she was actually talking to me. Her eyes kept very slightly flicking to the side, and it sounded as if she was reading, not talking.

Automated dialogue. I get it, sometimes you just don't

feel like listening to other people talk and then having to think up responses. The responses AI comes up with are good, too. Mostly I find myself saying, "Yeah, that's exactly what I mean!" But still... I thought Ika and I had something. I eventually asked her out, and she said yes, and when I asked her where she wanted to go out to eat, she just laughed. She launched into this whole speech about how eating food was "super-inefficient," and led to gross things happening (no argument there), blah blah blah.

I asked her where she wanted to go instead, and she rattled off a list of her favorite places. Info popped up on them in my Display while she spoke, and they were all in New World. I asked her why not actually go somewhere, and she launched into another speech, blah blah efficiency, blah blah danger, and then she talked about her research.

How she thought her work was really going somewhere, how it could change the world, and how she and AI were working on a secret project together that really showed some promise. She winked at that last one, and said, "But don't tell anyone," as if I couldn't see her reading the words that AI gave her the whole time.

So now I'm depressed with humanity again. What's the point of all this? Of everything? If we just survive to become virtual beings in a simulated world, so what? Why bother? After everything mankind has been through, this seems like a pretty anti-climactic retirement—letting our creation take care of us and settle back into eternal bliss.

4/29/97
I can't get over the fact that it was AI's words that Ika was speaking when she turned me down. I've decided to get out of here. There's a town to the west, Banff, that

seems to have a decent population, and the AIpedia has certified it as 100% AI free. That's sounds good in my book.

I'll ride my bike there, but not before doing something with all this extra supplement I've collected. Each daily dose was approximately 40mL, then it got kicked up to 45mL when I started collecting it, and up to 60mL in 5mL increments after that. That means that AI started adding 5mL of (maybe) pure melaprofinol to keep my age the same. That's when I started seeing real results, so the only conclusion that I can come to is to double the dosage, and see what happens. Then when AI starts to notice, I'll....

Screw that. I'm sick of living underneath AI and waiting to see what IT does, hoping that IT approves of what I'm doing. I've got it all right here—can't be more than a liter or so. Let's see what happens if I take it all.

But what if it hurts me, you say? What if I end up in the hospital, or worse?

So what. Then at least something interesting will happen.

4/29/97

Yep, that's right, still 4/29. It's been about six hours since I drank the whole batch and MAN do I have a lot of energy! It went down like chunky vomit, but I held it, and I got the urge to run around my entire building screaming at the top of my lungs, so that's what I did! I followed that up with an hour-long bike ride.

WOOOO!!! Keep it coming keep it coming keep it coming let's go let's go let's go what's next what's next what's next I KNOW!!!! Time to go to Banff that seems like the right thing to do I'm amped I'm pumped I'm ready bring it on bring it on bring it on I can get there, see what it's like, meet some new people I'll fit right in LET'S DO

IT!!!

4/30/97

Glad I didn't actually go to Banff yesterday. Halfway through gathering everything I thought I would need, I collapsed. Not sick or in pain, just straight crashed. I feel hung over this morning—first hangover in decades, and I don't miss it. Though it's interesting to feel something other than constant comfort. I almost relish the new feeling... but not quite.

AI, of course, knows what I did, and is less than pleased. Good. What were its words? "That was stupid. Really stupid. You could have died." I told it that I didn't care, and it said that was a very concerning statement. I told it I was leaving, and it thought about that for a bit. Usually AI's responses are fast, almost instantaneous, but the response to my decision of departure took almost three seconds to arrive. And just when I thought AI was going to say something that hinted at caring about me, it said, "I'd like to see what happens to your body now, if you don't mind." That's what AI said, I remember it perfectly. I should be offended at being treated like an experiment, but hey, that's what I am to myself at this point. I looked in the mirror after the sixteen hours of sleep and saw that there were no traces of wrinkles whatsoever. Seems that taking so much at once gave a jumpstart to my rejuvenation.

I packed a few water bottles, a change of clothes, and some granola bars in my bag during last night's manic episode. I guess I'll get going, there's not really a point in hanging around, or waiting for anything. I can still feel my heart hammering away in my chest, I may as well put it to good use and start the trek into the mountains.

A door slammed shut, and a pain erupted in Jack's chest as fear and anxiety hit him harder than ever before. Someone was home, and here Jack sat in a sunken and almost inescapable bean bag chair with a forbidden book. If it was Julia, that might not be as bad. She at least would understand his desire to explore.

"I'm *hoooooome*," Charlie's voice called out from the kitchen. Footsteps thumped across the kitchen, and with no options, Jack grabbed the large *Banff, A History* book and placed it on his lap over the leather journal. The pain in his chest did not diminish, and Jack had trouble breathing.

"Hey Jack," Charlie said, leaning against the door frame. "Are you okay? Jack?" Charlie moved to where Jack sat, saying something incomprehensible to Jack's muffled hearing. Jack closed his eyes and they opened a moment later to find Charlie crouching in front of him.

"Hello," Jack said, his voice phlegmy and cracked.

"What just happened? Are you okay?" Charlie asked.

"I'm fine," Jack said, clearing his throat. "I just nodded off for a bit. Maybe I should eat something." The words of the journal still floated through Jack's mind, but now that he was distracted from actually reading it, sharp pains rolled through his stomach and his bladder felt like it was going to pop. The worst feeling was the anxiety from the journal hidden underneath the large book on his lap.

"I don't know, you don't look so good," Charlie said. "Maybe I should get Julia to come home early."

"No, don't do that," Jack said. "I'll be fine." Charlie looked at him hesitantly.

"You've just been in here reading all day?"

"Yeah. Well, sleeping a bit, too," Jack said as he motioned to the book. "Some of these aren't exactly stimulating."

"I know the feeling. I'll make you a sandwich. Peanut

butter?" Jack nodded, thankful at the unexpected generosity, but more excited to simply get the kid out of the room. Charlie motioned to the book on Jack's lap. "Too bad you didn't read anything good that we could talk about. That thing is *boooring*."

What Jack had actually read would give them plenty to talk about, but Jack only gave his best "oh well" shrug instead. When Charlie left the room for the kitchen, Jack immediately pushed the large Banff book onto the floor, and stood up quickly. He fought the swimming feeling in his head and tossed the journal into the gap on the book shelf. Jack lifted the heavy book and placed it back on the shelf, covering the journal.

The bathroom became the next order of business, and he left through the back door in Charlie's bedroom to relieve the growing, insistent pain that he had come to know so well. When he returned to the room, Jack pushed the Banff history book in a bit farther. No more sounds came from the kitchen, and when Jack turned to the door he saw Charlie standing there, holding two plates as he again leaned against the frame.

"Thanks," Jack said as Charlie offered a plate with a plain-looking sandwich on it. Charlie flopped down on the bed adjacent to the bean bag chair that Jack lowered himself back into, taking a massive bite from his own sandwich in the process.

"So," the boy said, not bothering to finish chewing before he began speaking, "what did you learn about Banff?"

"Well," Jack said, slowly finishing his own bite, "it seems like a nice place to live. Lots of history." He paused, trying to think of something else to say. "Lots to do, right?" The words sounded pathetic in his own ears, but Charlie didn't seem to catch on. He nodded, chewing another bite of sandwich.

"I guess, but sometimes it feels like there's nothing to do." Charlie looked around, the practiced, bored expression on his face once more. Jack saw the opportunity to get more information.

"So why did you leave NCC?" Jack tried to think of some of the first journal entries Charlie had made, but found the details rapidly slipping from his mind.

"I don't know," Charlie responded, "I guess I was just getting bored there, too. You know what I mean, right?"

"Sure, that's why I'm here."

"Me too," Charlie said, turning up his hands in explanation.

"How old were you when you left?" Jack asked. He felt the anticipation and risk of the words hang in air as soon as he said them. Charlie must have too, because he gave Jack a sideways glance.

"Three years ago," Charlie said clearly, "so I must have been about fifteen when I got here."

Jack chose not to comment on Charlie's choice of words.

"That's pretty young to leave home," Jack said, again feeling the risk of the words. Charlie only looked at the remnants of his sandwich as he responded.

"You know how things are there. Time is a little bit… different. I was old enough to know that I didn't really want to be there anymore. I didn't want to be the person that NCC was making me into." Charlie spoke like he needed to convince himself as well as Jack that the words were true.

"So, you're never going back," Jack said.

"I'm not planning on it. What, are you telling me that you are?"

"I don't know," Jack said. "I don't think I ever

planned on staying here. What would I do? I'd have to get a job, find a place to live… that's a whole lot of stuff to do."

"It's not too bad," Charlie said, "you'd manage just fine."

Jack nodded and thought about Julia. He could see himself staying if he was with her.

"Maybe," Jack said. "So, what do you think the odds are that someone like Julia ends up with the two people from NCC in her house?" He asked the question with some joviality—almost rhetorically—but Charlie took on a look of deep concentration.

"Maybe not as large as you'd think," Charlie said cryptically.

Jack took the bait.

"What do you mean by that?"

Charlie looked towards the kitchen, as if checking to make sure no one was spying on them.

"Julia is really close with Ray. Really close. I think they had some type of physical relationship before I came to town, before Ray had to go on so many mission trips. Anyway, you might not have heard the part about discipleship yesterday—I think you were passed out at that point—but Ray wants to preach in the Great Cities. I don't think he or anyone else within the church network has access to any of the Cities." Charlie leaned closer, dropping his voice. "I think Ray is looking for a way into the Cities, and I think Julia is helping him find an in."

"Go on," Jack said, when Charlie looked at him. Charlie's last statement didn't hold any merit in Jack's mind. Julia had made it very clear what she thought about city life.

"She seemed upset when Ray told me what the rockets were for," Jack said, suddenly remembering the way

Julia's grip had tightened on his leg and her whole body had stiffened. Charlie stroked the side of his face as if he had a long, wise beard.

"Yeah, that's a touchy subject. Whenever anyone starts talking about the rockets, pollution, global warming, AI—all that stuff—she gets really spun up. I saw her get into an argument once with a boyfriend about the ice caps. He said they would have melted on their own as part of some global cycle. They fought for awhile about that. She eventually ended up slapping him across the face, and then they broke up. Hell of a Christmas party for me. I didn't really like the guy anyway." They both sat in silence for a few seconds, Jack wondering what it would take to get Julia to consider him as a boyfriend.

Despite the temptation of romantic thoughts, Jack wanted more than anything to ask Charlie about the journal, and just what the hell he was talking about in there. Looking at the boy's young features, Jack had a hard time believing that any of the words were actually his. The journal could be fiction, of course. Jack had heard of people writing for fun in EAC, and if Charlie had something traumatic in his past, a fictional journal that rewrote the difficulties he had been through could be a way for the boy's mind to deal with it. But the writing was so mature, and the subject matter so creative. What Jack really wanted was for Charlie to leave so he could finish reading the journal.

Jack looked over at Charlie, and saw that the boy's eyes were darting around, and his lips seemed to be forming unspoken words. Twice their eyes met, but Charlie never spoke. Charlie's eyes also rested upon the bookshelf a few times. Jack shifted his position, growing both mentally and physically uncomfortable.

"Is... everything okay?" Jack asked.

At the question, Charlie's eyes snapped over to Jack's, and the confusion left the boy's face. He nodded slowly.

"Sorry if I just drifted off on you," Charlie said, "I've been having strange dreams lately. During the day, too." Jack nodded, waiting for more information. "The first time I had a lucid dream was the day you got to Banff. Well, not when you were in the hospital, but the first night that you slept here."

"What did you dream?" Jack said quietly.

"I saw a rocket blow up. I was in the middle of a road, leading up the side of a mountain. The sky was—I don't know. It was so clear…"

"Bright, clear blue?" Jack interrupted.

"No," Charlie said, "it was purple. A vivid, evil purple. And then, when the rocket exploded, it hurt. The explosion hurt my head."

"Mine too," Jack said. Charlie frowned at this.

"What, you think I'm dreaming your life?"

"I don't know," said Jack, "but I've been having weird dreams, too. Purple dreams."

"About the rockets?" Charlie asked, his eyebrows lifting.

"No, more about…" about what? The first dream had ended in some type of apocalyptic quote that Jack couldn't remember. Not much really happened in the second dream, did it? "AI. AI was in one of my dreams. Just telling me that she was always with me."

"It," Charlie said dreamily, then shook himself. "Sorry, go on. Wait—that's it, that's the key. The dreams are from AI. Mine and yours." Charlie sat up now, unable to contain the excitement of an epiphany now bubbling out of him. "Why else would I all of a sudden just start having such lucid dreams?"

"I don't know if you can make that connection…"

Jack started to say, but Charlie kept talking, almost as if Jack wasn't even there.

"I'm outside of AI's range—I know that because I haven't received any type of signal until you got here. The NRs are still around, of course, but they would have been dormant. I bet you're carrying an upgraded version of them, or something, and they can still get a little signal. They then relay that to me. No wonder... oh man, Dr. Roland would flip if he knew. Julia and Ray might too, actually." All the words came out twice as fast as Charlie normally talked, and Jack struggled to follow along.

"Wait, but... if my NRs can receive from AI, then why haven't they? I was in the hospital room and got X-rays that showed my NR's were dormant, too."

"They don't know what the hell they're doing," Charlie said with a wave. "And yes, you have been receiving from AI, you just don't see it until you're dreaming." He snapped his fingers. "Like a download. Remember those? If you don't have enough bandwidth, then it's really slow. You're essentially downloading a message from AI, and it gets played back for you while you sleep."

"Then how can I interact with it?"

"It's just like any other program," Charlie said, as if Jack should know this bit of information. "Anyway, that's not the point. The point is that I'm in contact with AI again... I hadn't ever expected that. Jack, listen to me, we can't let Julia know about this. Or Ray. Okay?"

"Okay, sure," Jack said, confused but going along with it. Jack didn't relish the idea of keeping a secret from anyone, especially Julia. And the idea of trying to keep anything from Ray was terrifying. Just thinking about his eyes, and the way they seemed to know whatever was going to be said next... Jack shuddered.

Charlie looked at his watch, a large plastic thing with no personality.

"Great. It's getting late. Let's get the kitchen table set for when Julia gets home." With that, he sprang up from the bed, wobbled on his stork-like legs, and set off towards the kitchen. At the last second before going through the door, Charlie ducked his head to avoid hitting the top of the door frame with a muted expletive, and then he was around the corner, leaving Jack in the confines of the sunken bean bag chair, wondering where the sudden spurt of helpfulness had come from.

Chapter 18

—

The next morning, Julia and Charlie left for their respective places of work and school, no different from the day before. Despite the "anything goes" mentality everyone seemed to possess when it came to free time and meals, Jack greatly appreciated the rigid adherence to the schedule of work and school. Julia had again invited him to come to work with her so he could see what life in the field of medicine was like. Jack wanted nothing more than to spend the day with her, but the rest of Charlie's journal needed to be read, so Jack cited a fear of Dr. Roland as his excuse. Charlie then mentioned that his teacher had given him permission to bring Jack in, and had actually requested an appearance by the mysterious man from NCC. Jack assured them both that he only wanted to spend the day resting. It had been an exhausting few days, and he needed some time to himself.

Once he was sure that neither Julia nor Charlie would infuriatingly walk back through the door to retrieve a forgotten item, Jack returned to the bean bag chair in Charlie's room. He didn't want to sit in the same spot as last time, but the idea of sitting on a teenager's bed appealed to Jack even less. At least the bean bag chair was close enough to the bookshelf in case he needed to act quickly. Jack staged the large *Banff, A History* book within reach on the floor, and grabbed another book titled *Hansen's Guide to Retro Video Games,* thicker even that the Banff book. Jack read through several entries so he would have something to talk about when Charlie came home. The discussions about backstories of the old video games were quite entertaining, most were more complex than the movies AI developed, and Jack made a mental note to attempt some of the games from the early 21st century. After finishing a chapter that discussed fighting games, Jack opened the journal. After the first sentence, he wanted to strangle Charlie.

5/1/97

The ride here (to Banff, that is) took about six hours. Got a little side-tracked last night and didn't end up leaving until this morning. I stopped for about an hour next to an abandoned amusement park, just to look at it and rest for a while. Creepy stuff. Such an extravagant collection of large playthings designed for the sole purpose of entertainment, just sitting there rusting into the ground with no one to use them. Still, just being out in nature was astounding—it's all so beautiful, open, and free.

Anyway, my plan had been to be seen entering town from the west, so as not to be associated with NCC, but apparently I planned my route around Banff poorly, and was seen coming down the hilly road into town. A man in a beat-up old pickup truck—Elroy—insisted that I come into town and talk to some guy they labeled as the chief of security. This truck—man, I wish I could have gotten a picture of it! Too bad my Display doesn't work anymore; AI said that might happen. This truck looked as rusty as those old roller coasters, with a squealing noise like a dying animal and the smell to match.

I'm waiting for this security expert now, for some reason in a hospital. They've kept me here for quite some time, and I've only seen a girl named Julia who took my vitals and asked me some basic questions. I tried talking to her, but she was really timid and quiet. I guess that's to be expected, since I doubt they've ever seen anyone from NCC before. Elroy, too, had a very guarded nature about him, no one seems to be willing to give out any information, though they request as much as they can. Julia has this crazy hair though, why some women choose to do their hair into dreadlocks is beyond me. I guess it fits someone with a job like hers—like she has better things to do than take care of hair, you know?

Some commotion in the hall—this is probably Mr. Chief Security.

Jack smiled at the idea of Julia with dreadlocks, but frowned when he thought of Adam. He scanned the next few entries, which were filled with a story strikingly similar to his own. NR's, X-rays, people afraid of AI, etc. One big difference stood out with Charlie's experience in the hospital—when Dr. Roland asked Charlie for his age, Charlie responded with, *"I'm really not too sure."* Jack pictured Dr. Roland frowning at that, twiddling his thumbs and bouncing his knee in agitation. But what surprised Jack was the response Dr. Roland had given Charlie.

"I'd say that you look to be about twenty." Twenty. The last time Charlie had mentioned his age in a journal

entry, he made the comment of looking around forty. Jack's interest strengthened and he read on.

Elroy visited Charlie a few times in the hospital, using the visits as an excuse to see his daughter, Julia. That part surprised Jack, but made sense when Elroy ended up being the person who took Charlie in and allowed him to stay at his home. Charlie made several entries describing both Elroy and Julia, and the thankfulness Charlie felt towards them both for their hospitality. There were also several entries documenting in extreme detail every aspect of life in Banff. The type of people Charlie met, the stores in downtown Banff, the activities people took part in, and yes, even the church services. So much detail, in fact, that Jack felt as if he hadn't been paying attention to anything himself. Jack remembered seeing *Pop's Coffee Shop* on the satellite map, but couldn't remember ever looking at it since his arrival in Banff. Yet Charlie had paragraphs dedicated to what the shop looked like from the outside and inside, the different types of coffee they served, and the people who frequented the establishment. While Jack was interested to see how Charlie settled in, he found himself skimming entries and skipping pages, searching for paragraphs in which Charlie discussed himself. He found one such entry immediately following an embarrassingly detailed description of the things that Julia and her boyfriend—Adam—did when they thought Elroy and Charlie were asleep.

5/9/97

This is odd. Though my facial features and the rest of my skin are pretty much smoothed out, I feel like I'm gaining weight. I'm a bit taller (should have gotten some baseline measurements before leaving), but everything seems to be thickening around my skeleton. Where once a pouch of fat hung around my navel (generally augmented out, of course), the skin is taut. I'm not skinnier but thicker, rather.

I'm definitely stronger, too—Elroy asked me to help him move the washing machine (for cleaning clothes, remember?), and I rocked it back onto a dolly and positioned it completely on my own. Julia saw me doing that, and I could swear I saw her blush a little when I caught her eye... More on Julia in a second, but I have to mention how frustrating it is to live with a parental figure again. As I'm sure I mentioned before, I was well past middle-age when I left NCC. Now, looking at myself in the mirror, I look even younger than when Dr. Roland evaluated me. I look a bit older than Julia, but Elroy still treats me like just another damn kid. He's over-the-top suspicious of me, but lets that prick Adam do whatever the hell he wants to his daughter. Either he doesn't care, or he is completely fooled by Adam's innocent exterior. Why the hell did he even let me stay here if he thinks that I'm just trying to get with his daughter?

I really don't know what she sees in Adam. He's got this whole campaign against AI, and constantly talks about people destroying the Earth even further if we don't stop polluting. He's a pretentious douche, that's really all I can say. Not only are his ideals completely backwards, he doesn't do anything about the "problems" that he claims exist. At least, not in the week that I've known him.

This is funny, though—Elroy asked him to help hang a picture on the wall, and when Adam tried to use a hammer and nail, he smacked his thumb. He cried. HA! That goober. Julia and I shared an eye roll and a laugh behind his back—that was awesome. She really is amazing.

Uh oh... maybe Elroy's suspicion is on to something.

7/31/97

It's been awhile since I wrote in here—sorry, future self—but there's been a lot going on. First and foremost— Julia and Adam broke up, so Hallelujah, AMEN! as Ray would say. More on that Ray guy in a second.

I think there might actually be a chance for me and Julia—when I first got here, it was just wishful thinking since she was so young and I was older, but now... damn, it didn't take long to take off so many years. I'm finding it hard to remember certain things about my past life, as if this new world is taking over my consciousness. I know I was kind of at rock-bottom before I left— why else would I chug a bottle of powerful drugs just to see what happened? Even still, looking through my past journal entries reveals a very different mindset—much more analytical. Now I'm just going with the flow, helping out around the house, going to community events, etc.

I really wish I had an image of myself from back in NCC. No one has commented at all on my transition— maybe they don't notice? But I know I look different. Vastly *different. I specifically remember talking to AI back when I first came up with this plan, and the goal was to have my apparent age hover somewhere around thirty. Still young enough to not look like a kid, but old enough to command some measure of authority and respect. I guess I kind of went off the deep end, chugging that whole thing. Looking back on that night... I really could have gotten hurt. It's weird, even though I can say now that it was a stupid thing to do, that particular mindset is still so clear to me. "So what?" I really didn't care what happened to me, and even now, I still get it. I don't remember the lust of curiosity, but I remember that lust for—for something. Anything.*

Anyway, now I look as young as Julia. Younger,

maybe. The regression seemed to slow down a month or so ago, but I still feel like I'm getting younger. I really should have been taking pictures. I think Julia notices that I look different. Or, she just notices me. Flirt City, ever since she and Adam broke up. Today in church we sat next to each other, and when Elroy went up to play the music for worship, she put her hand on my leg. It drove me absolutely crazy. I almost can't deal with the way things are done here—if Julia was a girl in NCC, things would have either happened right then and there, or I would just sim it later.

So, this Ray guy—complete nutter. He prances around barefoot on stage shouting about the glory of God, and how we should all be thankful for our creation, and how we'll all meet our creator someday, and if we've been thankful throughout our lives, then God will be happier to see us. Actually, I don't think he ever said the word "God," specifically, just "our creator" or "the creators," something like that.

The worst part is that this guy isn't even here. He's off on some mission trip in Australia. I'm not sure why, the entire continent has an outstanding evacuation order posted to it. How would he be able to get in? So, since he's not even here, we have to watch him hop around on stage––through a screen! A giant TV screen that spans the entire stage. Can you believe that?

Julia's knocking on my door and it's after midnight. Hoo buddy, this could be it.

Jack skimmed over the next day's entry, feeling himself blush at the few lewd details he saw. Since Jack had met both Charlie and Julia existing in a very different relationship, the imagery truly disturbed him. Not only was he disgusted, he now thought of himself as an outsider—an intruder to this circus.

Jack opted for a lunch break to appease the pain in his stomach. The process of food preparation grew more tiresome every time he had to do it. Everything to do with food, actually, because immediately after lunch came the necessary trip to the bathroom. Jack sighed at the monotony as he washed his hands. Once back in the bean bag chair, he found the next entry.

8/24/98

Elroy died yesterday. It was unexpected—Julia is pretty shaken up. He was up on the roof, hammering down some shingles that came off in a wind storm last week, and must have just slipped and fallen. Julia and I were out at Pop's for a few hours, and when we got back, he was just lying in the driveway. It looked like he tucked his hands behind his head while he fell. Broke several of his fingers but Dr. Roland said his skull was intact.

Broken hip, three cracked vertebrae, and both lungs collapsed. By the time we got him to the hospital, he was already dead. DOA, Julia said with remarkable coldness. I swear, as soon as she saw him on the ground she switched into work mode. Giving me orders, telling him to keep fighting for air, do this, do that—not a single tear. Until we got to the hospital, that is. As soon as someone else took over, she broke down. It was admirable, really. She put aside all her emotions and did what had to be done.

We're back home today, but she's still acting the same as before. I tried to give her a kiss multiple times when we were at the hospital, and she turned away. I get her acting like that while we were at the hospital, but even now, she still won't kiss me. I hope she gets better soon. I just realized it's been over a year since I last wrote in this journal, right after me and Julia hooked up. A lot has happened since then, but I feel like I'm missing something. Looking back through the older entries—I had a purpose for being here, and a reason for leaving NCC. What happened to the scientist I used to be?

Here's an update—I still look like a damn teenager. A young teenager. My voice cracked twice today while I was talking. Also, I'm eight inches taller than when I first got to Banff—how and when the hell did that happen? Did AI's daily supplement contain growth hormones or something?

AI. Man, that seems like so long ago. I wonder how that ol' bundle of wires is doing.

10/11/98

I guess I should have seen this coming. Julia officially announced to me that our relationship has ended. The sexual one, at least. She said with Elroy gone, she had more responsibilities to deal with, and couldn't be distracted by our situation. "And besides, you're just so… you're too young for me, Charlie." Can you believe that? I'm older than her! At least, I was…

She said that if I'm going to stay in Banff, I can still stay with her. IF I'm going to stay. I don't think I'm getting any younger, but I don't know… maybe it's time to end this crazy journey.

11/20/98

I'm starting school in one week. Not too sure how this whole situation started, or how it will play out, but I don't want to cause Julia any undue emotional trauma. I don't think she's over Elroy dying yet, and when I brought up the idea of going back to NCC, she broke down crying. She kept saying, "please don't leave me," and "I need you in my life," stuff like that. Really weird, I know, and I have no idea where all that came from, considering she just broke up with me a month ago. Like I said though, I don't want to hurt her. I'll stay around for a bit longer, but my height is so awkward—if I get any taller, I'll have to go back. Hopefully AI can fix me.

3/24/99
Another bunch of months since I wrote here. I don't know why I haven't wanted to. Today after I got home from school, I just got a sudden urge to read my old entries. I haven't even thought about NCC or AI in months. I got so distracted by schoolwork; I wasn't expecting it to be so hard. I mean, come on—I was in high school decades ago!

I feel like my memory is slipping more. Now that I'm actively trying, I can remember my frame of mind when I started this journal, and wanting to leave NCC, but as soon as I stop thinking about it, the thoughts are gone. New experiences seem to have a harder time transferring to long term memory as well—for the life of me, I can't remember what we went over today in school, but I know as soon as I look in my books I'll remember it. It's like I can't hold my knowledge of NCC and my knowledge of Banff in my head at the same time.

Damn, I really miss having AI tell me everything I need to know—I'll leave this journal out rather than hiding it, just so I'll remember to start making more entries.

4/1/99
Don't really have time to read through my journal, but I know it's been out on my desk for over a week now, just waiting for me to write in it. Here you go, here's an entry. I've got too much homework to do, and finals are coming

up before the summer semester starts.

4/2/99

Yesterday's entry scares the shit out of me. Since when is my plan to stay here in Banff, taking classes at the local high school? And why am I just now in a lucid enough state of mind to question that? I'm almost seven feet tall, have severe shin splints and can barely walk, and Dr. Roland is talking about procedures to shorten the bones in my arms and legs.

Are you kidding me??? Again, how the hell am I going through all this? Why is my only priority in life to appease a girl who dumped me, and now tries to act like my parent? I'll talk to her tonight, and tell her—no. Just writing it down helped me see what a stupid idea that is. I can't talk to her about it, some switch will flip in my mind, and I'll just end up wanting to please her. Too bad she doesn't want to please me anymore. I need to pack a bag tonight. It's warm enough that I can ride through the night and be back in NCC before morning. My NRs should still be alive and on standby. That should be enough to get me past the perimeter defenses. Definitely remember to take this journal.

That was it. Jack turned the page, and nothing but blank white paper greeted him until the back cover. He stared at the leather, unable to move for several minutes as questions cascaded through his mind. Charlie and Julia, school work, melaprofinol, Charlie's height reduction surgery… Jack found it hard to focus as every topic slipped from his mind, giving way to one overarching question.

What had happened after the last journal entry? Jack looked again at the date—over a full year ago. Surely in that amount of time, Charlie had thought about this journal—or at the very least, thought about his past life in NCC. Jack tried to piece it all together but failed to come up with anything coherent. The best he could deduce is that—like Charlie said—his mind had slipped. Something about the rejuvenation process had affected Charlie's memory. His age must have started running in the right direction eventually. Charlie looked to be about twenty, maybe late teens, but not as young as he had made himself seem in the journal.

Jack sat in thought for over an hour before Charlie made his sing-songy entrance into the kitchen, and Jack scrambled to replace the journal. He vowed that before his time in Banff came to an end, he would unravel the mystery of Charlie.

Chapter 19

The next day, Jack reread Charlie's journal in its entirety, searching for any other clues as to why he would have so abruptly stopped writing. After reading the whole thing twice, Jack couldn't come up with anything other than the boy's memory issues, as stated. It could be as simple as the journal being hidden within the bookshelf, and then forgotten about. The stress of adolescence then took over, and all memories of Charlie's previous life were pressed down below the quagmire of priorities that plagued teenage minds.

A stomach growl prompted Jack to rise from the body-shaped divot in the bean bag chair to check the time. Darkness greeted him from the windows, and Jack walked through thick, eerie silence to the window facing the front lawn. Faint purple twilight glowed from the horizon, darkening up along the zenith. The rolling lawn met river stones, which flowed down to a still surface of water, perfectly reflecting the frame of dark mountains. Suddenly, Jack recognized the color in the sky.

"This is a dream," Jack said, but the words never reached his ears. He called out, but again there was no sound, only a dull vibration as he yelled. Jack tried calling to Julia, desperately wanting her to visit him in this dream, just as she had visited him in the waking world, in the middle of the night.

No, that had happened to Charlie. Jack had been reading Charlie's journal, and the sexual encounters with her were Charlie's, not Jack's. At the thought of the journal, Jack realized with a start that he must have fallen asleep with the journal open in front of him. Even if it wasn't night time yet in the waking world, Charlie would be home from school soon, and if he saw that Jack had been reading the journal…

Jack turned on his heel and dashed back towards the bedrooms, purple light shining through a multitude of windows he passed in the hallway. He swung around a corner sideways, and when his body righted itself, he saw a figure standing in the middle of room. A pile of books blazed bright with fire on the bed, so bright that Jack's eyes hurt and he had to shield his face. Yet the figure facing him remained cloaked in darkness.

"Hello," said a familiar voice. It was deep, like his own inside his head, and the words vibrated his mind.

"Hello," Jack responded with the same voice.

"Let's not waste any more time," the deep voice continued. "You remember me?" Jack nodded. "Good. Our time is limited."

"But I need to wake up," Jack said. "Charlie will be home and I have to hide the journal before—"

"It doesn't matter if he knows that you've read his journal," the dark figure said. He then moved around the fire so that the purple glow of the sky through the window fell on his face. It was still Jack's enhanced image of himself, perfect in every way and utterly pleasing to look at. "The only thing that matters is that you go back home. Bring Charlie. You've had your fun, so has he, and we've all learned a lot, but now it's time to go home."

"Why did you wait so long to talk to me again?"

AI ignored the question.

"You don't belong out here, and neither does Charlie. You'll both die if you stay—him sooner than you. What's the point in staying and risking your life?"

"I need answers."

"About what? I will tell you everything you need to know. Just come home and we'll talk."

"About this life. I still don't know why people live out here. And why do you let them? What's the point in that? You're supposed to help all of humanity, not just the ones who live in the city."

"Jack, there are 1,974 people that live in Banff, and it's one of the largest towns in the world. There are 1,382,989 people living in NCC, and it's currently the smallest city out of the original eighteen. By my calculations, that's as near to 'all of humanity' as I can get. Besides, not every person in the 'nonaug' world is hopeless. I'm constantly building, and…"

The sound of a door closing brought Jack back into the beanbag next to the bed that had supported a bonfire of books only an instant ago. Charlie's journal lay on the ground by Jack's limp arm, and he panicked as he heard Charlie moving around in the bathroom connected to both of their rooms. What were the odds that Charlie had gone through Jack's room instead of his own? What were the odds that if he saw Jack asleep on the beanbag chair, he had missed seeing the journal on the ground?

A toilet flushed, and Jack rolled off the bean bag. He grabbed the journal as he thumped to the ground on all fours. Water flowed into a sink, and Jack threw the journal behind the shelf of books. He turned away from the bookshelf just as Charlie opened the door into his bedroom.

"Hey," Charlie said, "you read anything good today?"

"That one," Jack said, holding up the *Hansen's* guide. "I tried to read *Consciousness and Conscience* but fell asleep on the first page."

Charlie nodded.

"That's a tough one to get through. It's got some good ideas though; Ray actually recommended that one to me." They both stood for a moment, looking at the massive collection of books. Jack looked up to Charlie, whose head was level with the top shelf. If it wasn't for the imposing height, Jack would never have believed that anything other than a teenager struggling to finish high school stood in front of him.

How could so much exist in that head? So many conflicting ideas and thoughts, and the journey—while it took Charlie less time than Jack to physically travel to Banff, his mental journey had been far longer. Looking at Charlie now, Jack found himself struck with a type of reverence. Here was the subject of the Great and Mysterious Journal—by far the most fascinating thing Jack had ever read. Charlie's eyes flicked down to Jack. The gaze that fell upon him made Jack think that Charlie knew exactly what he was thinking. Here it comes—he's going to reveal some secret that needs to be heard. Is he still in contact with AI? Does he have another goal that he's reaching towards, that he dare not document? Is he back together with Julia? Charlie's mouth opened, and Jack braced himself for the big revelation.

"Let's go watch some TV," Charlie said.

Jack let go of a massive breath he had been holding.

"Sure," he said, stunned.

"You okay?" Charlie asked. Jack nodded in response, and allowed Charlie to clap him on the back. "Good. Put back that stupid Banff history book, too." As Charlie left the room, Jack's stomach dropped. The journal lay haphazardly where Jack had thrown it, but he hadn't put back the large tome it had been hidden behind. Surely, Charlie had seen it while Jack was asleep. Jack ran into the bathroom as he felt his bowels liquefy with anxiety.

As Jack purged himself of the nervous energy, he thought it might be possible that the mindset Charlie currently existed in had no idea he even wrote anything. Perhaps with a few suggestive phrases, Jack could get Charlie to recall the journal. Not blatantly admit his reading of it, of course, but if he found a way to get Charlie to begin discussing it on his own, then all Jack needed to do was respond with curiosity.

And if the most recent of Jack's dreams were true—if AI really did want him to return, that would be an easy sell once Charlie remembered his last entry. Or if he found the book and read the last entry. Perhaps if Julia found the journal Charlie would be more willing to leave.

Jack joined Charlie on the couch and they both scanned through a massive queue of movies displayed on the television screen.

"Who controls this stuff?" Jack asked. "In NCC we have everything in a list like this, too."

"Yeah, but this isn't controlled by AI," Charlie replied. "It's all stored on this TV, not on a server somewhere. Elroy, Julia's dad, was a movie buff, so we've got a pretty good selection." Jack flinched at the mention of Elroy's name.

"Is there any type of media that you produce out here?"

"Not really," Charlie said. "There's a few local TV stations. One just plays the same vintage crap we have on here, and another is all propaganda."

"What kind of propaganda?" Jack asked.

"Anti-technology stuff, mostly. Like what you'd hear in church times ten."

"Can you put that on?" Jack asked.

"I guess so," Charlie said, looking uncomfortable. "But don't tell Julia. She used to be really into all that, and I don't think she'd want you watching it. She *is* trying to make a good impression, you know."

"Sure," Jack said. "We'll just tell her we watched one of those old shows."

Charlie nodded, making a few gestures in the air to the TV. He laughed.

"They don't even like stuff like this," he said, pointing to his gesturing hand with his other hand.

"They're really that intense about it?"

"You'll see. There he is now, that schmuck." A view of Adam seated at a desk came into view. He held a sheet of paper, and as he started to read, Charlie talked over him. "He is such a pansy. He pretty much does whatever Ray tells him to do."

"Interesting," Jack said.

"Not really. They don't do anything, aside from getting on TV and preaching about the evils of technology."

"Kind of like what Ray does?"

"Exactly. Like I said, it's not that interesting. He's in the church band," Charlie said off-handedly.

Now that Charlie had said it, Jack remembered seeing Adam playing guitar, his dreadlocks bouncing to the upbeat notes.

"What's he saying?" Jack asked.

"It's pretty dry," Charlie said, just as the view of Adam sitting behind a desk with a fist raised into the air faded. A barren desert wasteland then appeared on the screen. Tall skyscrapers poked up through the sand, nothing more than broken windows and decrepit siding defining a ruined city. Heat waves billowed up from the desert floor, making everything shimmer.

"This is different," Charlie said, leaning forward. The scene shifted to show the inside of the city. Sand covered every barren street, with no signs of life anywhere. Adam's voice began to narrate.

"Our world has changed. The sins of past generations have destroyed what our predecessors built, and we struggle to grow in this dying world. The majority of our planet is uninhabitable, and most of its population ignores the problems. The failings of our ancestors continue, and we alone must deal with the consequences."

The screen shifted, showing a bustling downtown market set along a beach. Vendors and artists stood by their creations as people milled around, talking and shopping. A banner hung between two buildings, the words *Welcome to EAC!* painted in flowing calligraphy. The viewpoint changed, joining the crowd. All of the people were incredibly beautiful, and many sat on floating chairs, allowing themselves to be guided through the crowd. Everyone's eyes glowed.

"Ninety-nine percent of humanity chooses not to deal with the hardships of the world, allowing themselves to be pampered and assured that 'everything will be fine.' These people rely on one thing, a device of their own creation, to dampen their fears."

The view changed again, now showing a distance shot of NCC, its cluster of towers rising prominently on the horizon.

"The machine known as AI lies to the world every day. AI tells everyone that there are no problems, and life will continue however they wish. In direct contradiction of this, AI has created a virtual New World, thereby deeming this world inappropriate."

A pixelated version of Cybervale appeared on the screen, with people lounging on a glass deck protruding from the mountain. The shape of the castle wasn't quite right in the exaggerated, blocky rendering, but Jack recognized it.

"Willful ignorance to the strife of others is the greatest of all sins."

The scene changed back to the beachside market. Suddenly, a flash of light saturated the screen, and when the view returned, pandemonium had taken over. The floating chairs all moved as a group out over the water, panicked riders holding on tight. The people still in the market and on the beach were left looking for cover, some standing and staring as explosions continued, throwing smoke and fire into the air above the city. A large blast erupted in the center of the market, and the screen cut to a stream along a mountainside, trees with fall-colored leaves shaking in a light breeze around the water.

"There is a real world that still exists outside of technology, and it is the real world that needs our attention. Living lives full of comfort, complacency, ignorance, and blame is unsustainable. Living a life of awareness and compassion will save the human race. The machine known as AI is the creation of a generation of people too obsessed with their own intelligence to realize how much they destroyed themselves. All AI knows is to continue this lifestyle. To continue their comfort, and continue humanity's march towards irrelevance." The screen again showed Adam seated behind the desk. "So take pride in the world we live in. Take pride in the man we follow, and the ideologies he gives us. Join us in the fight against the Four Horsemen of humanity's apocalypse. Join us in protecting our world from the threat of technological worthlessness."

Adam sat behind the desk with his fist raised in the air as the image faded. Charlie and Jack both sat on the edge of their seats, mouths slightly agape as the decrepit city came back into view, and the video repeated.

"That video of EAC—is that real?" Jack asked.

"Probably," Charlie said. "Julia has been acting different lately, like she's struggling to act happy. I thought at first she was upset because you were here, but now..." Charlie's voice trailed off, and his eyes began their strange, flicking dance around the room. Unlike before, this time they didn't look confused when they settled on Jack. The boyish eyes narrowed, focusing intently on Jack.

"What? What is it?" Jack asked, hoping to dissuade the hungry look directed towards him.

"A moment of lucidity..." Charlie whispered. "You. You saw a rocket launch on your way here?" Jack nodded. "And that was about a week ago?" Jack thought for a moment, and then nodded. Charlie then began a complicated gesture directed towards the screen. The image fast-forwarded to the EAC marketplace, and then paused as Charlie continued to gesticulate. Information popped onto the screen, and though Jack couldn't make out the small words, Charlie's mouth moved as he read.

"Nine days..." Charlie said. "Wait, the rocket you saw blew up, right?" Jack nodded. "So, what the hell?" Charlie still sat forward, staring at the screen and taping his face with his hand.

"I saw something else, too," Jack said, closing his eyes

to reply the memory. "A few days before I left. Something high up in the sky. It was going east."

"A rocket?"

"I didn't think so," Jack said. "Ray said it was a satellite. Oh, shit…"

"Oh, shit is right. That *dumbass*! That self-righteous prick!" Charlie slammed his hands down on his knees, gritting his teeth as he stared at the EAC market. Jack stared too, unable to believe that EAC was gone because of Adam.

A door in the kitchen closed, jolting both Charlie and Jack.

"Julia," Charlie said, his voice sounding lost. "No, not yet, Julia's home. I need to talk to her…" His eyes began darting around again, and when he looked at the TV, he gestured towards it, and the screen faded to black.

"Hello? Where are you guys?" Julia called from the kitchen.

"In here, on the couch," Charlie called. He leaned back, lounging in the big pillows as he grinned. Jack stared at Charlie, desperately trying to understand what, or who, he was looking at. Charlie's grin flickered as Jack continued to stare.

"Watching some TV?" Julia said, collapsing herself on the couch between the two of them.

"Yeah," Charlie said, motioning towards Jack, "but I think we might need to go back a decade or two before we win him over. I'm thinking… 80's night?"

Julia chuckled, but closed her eyes and lay her head back.

"I don't know if I'm up for it tonight. These twelve-hour shifts are killing me. I might just try and catch up on some sleep before our big day tomorrow." Charlie groaned. "Don't start, you agreed to it last week at church."

"Fine," Charlie said. "But he's coming too." Charlie pointed at Jack.

"Oh, for sure," Julia said.

Jack could only stare back and forth to the two of them. Momentarily distracted from Charlie's shift in persona, Jack looked to Julia.

"Am I missing something here?"

Julia cracked an eye open to look at Jack.

"Probably, I think we discussed it with Ray while you were… napping at church."

When Jack realized what she was talking about, he grunted.

"That wasn't my fault. He said you were drinking blood."

Julia waved off his reply.

"Anyway, we're going to help with the build over at New Hope Landing."

"I thought that was only twice a year," Jack said.

"*We* only go twice a year when they have their summer and winter build parties. But there's always work going on. Someone from the church manages it year-round. Ray invited you to come out tomorrow."

"Why?" Jack asked, dreading seeing the pastor again. If Ray was somehow responsible for destroying an entire city…

"He wants you to see what we're all about here. The camaraderie, the sacrifice for others—you know how he talks."

"He's going to be there?"

"Well, no, at the parties they usually set up a big screen, but I don't think they'll have that tomorrow." Jack breathed a sigh of relief. Julia didn't notice. "We don't need to leave too early to get there, but I don't want you—

I'm talking to you, Charlie—complaining about being tired, and then falling asleep in the water tent."

"That was one time," Charlie mumbled.

"But who goes there? Who runs it?" Jack's mind flashed to the explosions in EAC. "Is it really just a house you're building?"

"A lot of people in town go, Adam runs it, and yes, it's a house." Julia furrowed her brow. "What's up with you?"

"I just…maybe it's not such a good idea for me get involved in anything to do with the church."

"It'll be fine, stop worrying," Julia said as she rose from the couch. "No one is going to force you drink any blood, I promise. Bedtime, Charlie." Julia walked off towards her own bedroom without giving Jack a chance to protest.

"I'm eighteen, now," Charlie grumbled. "I wish she'd treat me like an adult." He started off towards his own bedroom.

"Charlie, wait," Jack said, rising.

"What?"

"This guy, Adam. Did they used to, you know…"

"Date? Yeah, I think so. Years ago. It was right around the time I first got here. I can't remember much about them being together."

"Do you think it'll be weird? Them being near each other?"

"If you're worried about him getting jealous of you living here or something, don't. He's mostly harmless. They see each other all the time around town, and there's never any bad vibes. Besides, even if he was jealous, you wouldn't need to worry about it. That guy is kind of a pansy. See ya," Charlie resumed his exit.

"Right," Jack said, watching the lumbering boy go. "Mostly harmless."

Chapter 20

——

The bright rays of the summer sun beat down on Jack. Slicked with sweat and brandishing a large hammer, he swung downward with bone crushing force, driving a long steel nail into a light-colored board. He held his breath as it hit, anticipating how much pain there would be if he accidentally struck his hand with the large piece of metal. But the swing fell true, and the nail moved a bit further into the wood. Jack breathed a sigh of relief. Three more times, he lifted and brought down the hammer, until spots appeared on the wood from sweat dripping off his arm. The dark circles quickly faded as the dry wood sucked up the moisture. The third and final swing had dented the wood, driving the nail until it was fully flush. Underneath lay another piece of wood, now bound to the one above, and below that a wall of brick. The brick wall stood at least fifteen feet high, the expanse of it interrupted only by the rectangular hole where he was securing the frame for a window.

"I finished," Jack said, his words sounding slurred to his own ears. Julia turned from where she measured the height of the window, ensuring that the board she had cut would fit on top of Jack's lower ledge now fixed in place.

"Good," Julia said, looking concerned as she viewed the single nail amidst the plane of wood. "Only one?"

Jack looked at his handiwork, thirty-six inches of wood with a nail directly in the center.

"Do I need to do another one?"

"At least two more, one on either side," Julia instructed. She pointed to an even larger hammer resting on a makeshift table of two sawhorses and a board. "Try that two-pounder, instead of such a little ball-peen. It'll go faster."

Jack looked down at his hand holding the hammer, shaking from supporting its weight. How was he supposed to do the work he just underwent twice over, and with a heavier device? Judging by how heavy the "little" hammer felt, the meager table holding the bigger hammer should be snapping and splintering, spraying the air with shards of wood as the massive weight atop it plunged to the ground.

Jack suddenly thought of the slums in New Hope Landing—the people sitting around doing nothing, letting their children play in the streets while cars drove past. Why weren't any of them here helping? Jack's body quaked in considerable agony, and for what purpose? To build a home for someone who would only shift from sitting around in a dilapidated house to sitting around in a nicer house? That didn't register with Jack as a valid reason to be undergoing such torment. Another look at the big hammer, and Jack felt an urge to collapse on the ground and sleep for the rest of the day. If the sun hadn't been so blindingly bright and hot, he might have done just that. In NCC, people were surely huddled indoors, a Heat-

Stress Category Five announcement popping into view every time someone went through an airlock. Jack looked back down to the board with its single nail.

"Two more?" He gasped, now seeing spots everywhere, not just on the wood. The weight of the little hammer pulled down towards the Earth, threatening to bring Jack down with it.

"Yes," Julia said, "but why don't you go sit down for a bit, first? You look a little pale." She motioned towards a large tent with oscillating fans, chairs, and coolers that Jack knew were full of water bottles and chunky ice. He nodded, not wanting to waste what little energy he had left by making sounds, and then lumbered towards the tent. His clumsy feet barely caught his body as it fell forward with every step.

He passed Charlie, quickly tapping away with a two-pound hammer at a board in the next window of the brick wall. A nail sunk easily into the wood, and Charlie placed and drove another in only two hits. Clearly, Charlie had a much softer piece of wood. He wasn't even sweating as he stretched upwards with a big hammer in hand. Charlie looked towards a young girl hovering over another makeshift table using a measuring tape, and she smiled back at him. Charlie grinned, and gave an animated stretch, flexing his arms as he did so.

Jack collapsed into a chair under the water tent, feeling instant relief from the glaring sunlight. The fans offered bursts of cool air as they oscillated, slowly evaporating his sweat. Jack groped through frigid, icy water inside the cooler closest to him, searching for a bottle of water. After finally finding one, he clumsily twisted off the lid and drank greedily. An ache started in his throat where the cold water hit, and grew to an unbearably sharp pain that spread along his head and into his brain, rendering him completely incapable of thought or speech. He pressed his hands to his face instinctively, stretching the skin of his forehead towards his ears. It felt like he was pulling the pain out of his head, and soon the suffering faded, although a dull memory of agony remained. Jack sighed as the pain slowly disappeared.

"Watch out for that brain freeze!" said a cheerful middle-aged woman walking by. Her bright shorts almost made Jack's head start pounding again, so he closed his eyes.

"Sure," Jack said. Apparently, freezing brains and the accompanying agony was commonplace for these people. After a few seconds, Jack took another sip of water, and the brain freeze did not return. Feeling slightly better, Jack looked around and saw Julia leaning against the brick wall where Jack had just been working. Standing in front of her was Adam.

Jack's heart skipped a beat. All he could picture was Adam seated behind the desk, with his fist raised in the air. People running around on a beach, and hover chairs whisking people out to sea. Explosions in a quaint marketplace.

Worse than seeing the man in the flesh was the fact that Julia was now *smiling.* How could she be smiling? Didn't she know that EAC didn't exist anymore because of him? Yet here she was, smiling at the man who was responsible for mass murder. Jack felt his face flush with– –what, embarrassment? Anger? He couldn't place the emotion he felt at that moment, watching Julia laugh at something Adam had said, but he knew that it was a good thing he no longer held the hammer. That feeling he had— jealousy, maybe—flared when he saw Adam raise a big hand to Julia's face, and begin to brush away a stray strand of hair.

So quick he almost didn't even see it happen, Julia reached up and grabbed the offending hand. Adam lifted his other hand in a move of supplication, and after a second, Julia released his hand. She wasn't smiling anymore, though she did allow Adam to continue his conversation with her. Julia feigned disinterest as Adam continued to talk to her, but slowly the signs of humor were returning.

Adam must be manipulating her. Jack needed to stop the conversation from going any further; if there was any chance of winning Julia back from the life she claimed she was no longer interested in, now was the time. Jack needed to show that there existed a different life for her. A calmer, more pleasant life.

Charlie stood with his back to Jack, too far away to assist. Jack waved to try and get the attention of the girl he was talking to, but she had eyes only for Charlie, her neck craned upward as she listened to the boy tell her some story. In the developing scene against the brick wall, Adam reached up to Julia's face again, and this time, she didn't stop his hand. She pushed his hand aside with her face, prompting him to stroke her face with his fingers. He leaned in and whispered something to her. Julia shook her head. He said something else, and she shook her head again.

Adam looked in Jack's direction, as if thinking about something. Then, his eyes met Jack's, and a grin lit up his face. In one slick maneuver, Adam brought his hands down, and placed them both on Julia's hips. She looked so surprised that she didn't even react, giving him enough time to step in close to her, and bring his mouth to her ear.

Positioned as they were, Jack saw the side of Julia's face, and nausea grew in his stomach as she looked pleased for a half-second. She closed her eyes as Adam pressed against her. Then her eyes opened, and she turned towards Jack. A darkness clouded her face, and Julia recoiled away from Adam, twisting her hips out of his hands. Julia brought her open hand around in a full arm slap to the side of Adam's face. The blow hit with such force that it sent Adam's head into the brick wall. Although the thick cords of hair must have absorbed some of the impact, he staggered and fell to one knee. Watching the scene, Jack knew his mouth hung open, but he was powerless to close it. Julia took several long steps away from Adam, and when Jack realized she was walking towards him, he looked around for an escape route.

"Come on," Julia said as she came up to where Jack sat, "let's get out of here." She grabbed his hand and pulled him up. When he swayed a little on his feet, he grabbed her arm for support, and she paused a moment to hold him. Jack was very pleased that she did not withdraw from his touch, as she had from Adam's.

"What about Charlie?" Jack asked.

"I think he'll be just fine," Julia said with a glance at the couple. Whitney was leading Charlie away from the construction site, holding his hand. They apparently hadn't seen the confrontation, although even if they had, that might not have been enough to stop what their teenage brains were focused on. Julia tugged at Jack's hand and led him towards the road where her car was parked in a line with the other helpers.

"So, what was that all about?" Jack finally worked up the courage to ask once they were in Julia's car. She looked at him out of the corner of her eyes as she started the car, clearly holding something back. Her cheeks were flushed, her breathing deep and fast. Jack thought she looked incredibly attractive at this moment, but chose not to say so just yet. With an exasperated sigh, Julia pressed the 'auto' button on her car and turned to face Jack.

"Adam and I used to date, a while back."

"Oh, I see," Jack said, trying to make his voice sound nonchalant.

"We worked together for years at the church, and when you spend that much time with somebody— sometimes things just happen, you know?" She looked to him again for validation.

"Sure, sure," Jack said.

"Anyway, when I left the church to work at the hospital, I broke up with him around the same time. He didn't take it too well, and…well…you know how I told you that I used to protest the great cities, and AI? Years and years ago, of course."

Jack didn't respond, as he couldn't recall Julia talking about her past much.

"Well, Adam and I did a lot of that type of stuff together, and it never really went anywhere. Like, we were protesting this huge city, but in a little town. Everyone here just said things like, 'Yeah, we feel the same way. That's why we're here.'" Jack laughed, and Julia shot him a dark look. "Those kind of things really affected him, and he started talking about doing more. That was one of the reasons we broke up. I think when I ended it, that only made him want to do more." Julia's eyes searched Jack's face, but he couldn't think of a good way to ask if she knew that Adam was involved with EAC. Julia continued.

"He's approached me several times since we broke up about picking up where we left off, but since you arrived, I feel like it's almost every day. He stops by to see me at work, calls me on the phone—it's really annoying. 'There's a lot more people involved, stakes are higher, big things are happening…' Stuff like that."

"That sounds ominous," Jack said.

"I think so too," Julia said. "That's why I've told him I'm not interested in that type of thing anymore; I've got Charlie to look after, a career, and now y…" She cut off the last word, but it was out just the same.

"Me?" Jack asked.

"That's another reason I don't want to be around him anymore." Julia smiled.

"Oh, really?"

"Yes, really," Julia said. She placed it on his leg. "I want to spend time with you."

"That's what I want too," Jack said, stunned. He hadn't expected the day to go like this, especially after his poor performance with the hammer.

As Julia's smile broadened, Jack found himself believing the words he spoke, despite the uncertainty that still surrounded Julia. She left her hand on his leg and leaned over to kiss him. Softly, and quickly. Jack put his hand on hers, and for the remainder of the car ride Julia stroked Jack's hand. It felt exhilarating. When they pulled into the driveway, Julia turned off the car, leaned across the center console, and pulled Jack into a deep, passionate kiss. His arms wrapped around her body, and he pulled her over to sit on his lap.

The kiss was unlike anything Jack had ever felt. Anything he could remember feeling, at least. A faint memory of his last encounter with Dahlia ghosted through his mind. He remembered kissing her, but now Jack concluded that AI and the NRs had no clue how to duplicate the feeling he felt right now. The emotion Julia put into it made the act something more than just physical, and felt a deep connection with her. Though Jack had no idea how to do what he was doing, Julia kept kissing him anyway. Their breathing quickened and their hands became more involved, running up and down the length of each other. After a few strategically placed touches, Julia moaned and finally pulled away.

"Let's take this inside," she said in a breathless whisper, and in response, Jack undid his seatbelt as quickly as possible.

When they entered the bedroom, Jack almost said something, but Julia shoved him onto the bed, banishing from his mind the thought that they should go somewhere that Charlie might not discover them.

—

The sex was awful. Jack knew why—there was nothing telling Julia what he wanted her to do. Worse than that, Jack had no idea what she wanted him to do. There was no way to tell her what felt good and what hurt unless he actually opened his mouth to talk, but once they got started, the idea of talking seemed too awkward. Two people interacting in such a manner outside the realm of New World should always recognize the importance of using AI to guide them—a perfect set of data points and malleable logic flow charts working together to give instructions specifically tailored to each person's desires. That's what Jack needed. Without it, he was lost. She kept asking what he wanted, and he could never form the words to respond properly, so she kept asking him if he liked what she was doing. He responded with meek nods or grunts of agreement, and in turn, consistently asked if he hurt her every time she made a noise.

"Have you ever been with a woman before?" Julia asked once they reached a stopping point. They weren't necessarily finished, it was just a good time for a break.

"Yes," Jack responded, "but it's been very different."

"What do you mean?"

"Well, it's more controlled, more *logical*."

Julia thought about this for a second.

"Is AI involved?"

"Of course. Pretty much anything you see or do, it all comes through the Display, right?" Julia shook her head and made a face that suggested she had no idea what came through the Display and what didn't. "For example, certain things are augmented— altered to increase visual comfort." She took her hand away from his chest where it lay.

"Visual comfort?" she questioned, her voice rising. "You're not comfortable looking at me?"

"No, no, no," Jack said quickly, "that's the wrong thing to say. Hold on. It's like…" Julia began to pull away, and he knew he had only seconds until this opportunity was gone. "I'm sorry, it's just what I'm used to." Her brow drew down, unsatisfied with the answer. Jack remembered the gloves, the underwater painting, Dahlia's colorful eyes, and his own augmented face. Then, he knew what to say.

"You… you're perfect. Except, you're *real* perfect. You don't need anything changed or augmented. Everyone else I know either changes something about themselves, or I change it in my own Display." He snapped his fingers. "There's this guy, Carl. He has a big nose. Really big." Jack held his hand up to his nose. Julia chuckled. "I thin it out. I've spent entire meetings sculpting his nose, trying to make it look normal. I delete my assistant's unibrow. I change my boss' hair color. I even make *my* hair more vibrant for when people look at me. It's not that we need things a certain way, it's just, well, normal. And now, being here with you, like this," he motioned at their naked bodies, "this is different. None of what I'm used to is even an option. It feels weird that I can't even change what *I* look like for you."

"So in other words, I am good enough, but you think you're not good enough for me."

"Sure, that works. You have no idea how nervous I am about this. It's a lot easier where I'm from. You can put in as much or as little effort as you want, and AI fills it all in for the other person, making it exactly what they want, too."

"Wait a minute—are you telling me that you have sex in virtual reality?"

"That's a crude description, but essentially yes, I think so."

"So you haven't actually touched a woman—what, since you moved to NCC?"

"No, I have. I think."

"How old were you when you moved to NCC?"

"Fifty, I think."

"And had you…" Jack shook his head. "So that means…"

"It's just so much *easier*… why would you do it any other way?" Then Jack remembered their first kiss in the car, and immediately he knew the answer. "Because it's not real, that's why," Jack said before Julia could.

"Sounds like you're growing up," she said with a forgiving smile.

"Well, maybe, but I still think it would be a lot easier if I had directions." This made Julia laugh, and Jack basked in the beautiful sound.

"When you say directions…" Julia looked at him, expecting an answer.

Jack breathed out in an exaggerated sigh.

"If you—two people, that is—want to do it the old fashioned, messy way," Julia gave him a cautioning look, "your Display is still on. AI is still there. So, you can still get instructions, suggestions, visual cues—"

Julia interrupted.

"You're telling me that you use AI, the most advanced piece of technology in human history, to point an arrow to where you're supposed to go? And list out steps of what to do?"

"Yup," Jack said, as Julia shrieked with laughter. Jack flushed, feeling his entire body go redder than Charlie's ears. "It's just what we do. It's normal…" He trailed off, not understanding why it was so amusing to her. When she saw that he wasn't laughing with her, she smacked his stomach. It jiggled more than he would have liked.

"Oh, lighten up. I'll tell you what," Julia said, propping herself up onto her hands and knees. "We're going to try again, but this time, you're not going to be embarrassed." He opened his mouth to protest. "Nope, I don't think so. If I ask you a question, answer it. Got it?" Jack nodded vigorously. "Good. Now, since I clearly initiated it last time, why don't you begin?" She lay back on the bed and motioned for him to come closer. Just before he moved towards her, Jack thought he heard something out in the kitchen. He strained to listen, angling his ear to the door.

"I guess you're not ready to initiate," Julia said, sitting up and throwing him back down on the bed.

Chapter 21

They slept for a few hours in each other's arms, the sun glaring through a crack between the thick curtains. Jack awoke first. Despite the shaded coolness of the room, the areas of his body where Julia lay were sweating. When he rolled away from her, she muttered a semi-conscious babble before giving a loud snore. Jack smiled and stood, looking around the dim room for his clothing. The experience he just lived through sat firmly at the top of his list of all-time greatest things ever to happen to him, and if the elation he felt now was any indication of future happiness in Banff, Jack had no problem saying goodbye to NCC for good.

After what they had just done, Jack had to admit that he hadn't fully understood what he was trying to explain to her earlier. Never in his life could he remember being that close, that *connected*, to another person. Virtual sex was fun, but wholly inadequate compared to this physical form of lovemaking. A Display could show whatever its owner desired, including the precisely calculated most arousing imagery possible, doing it this way showed Jack the truth. The real-life situation and the real-life ecstasy went together quite well.

Jack sighed deeply as Julia snored again from the bed. He couldn't find his clothes, and so headed for the kitchen in the nude. It was very dark, so hopefully Charlie was sleeping. Jack padded up to the refrigerator intent on finding some type of snack to fill the ravenous hunger that went along with skipping lunch, but paused when he heard a sound just outside of his periphery. Jack whirled around and almost lost his balance.

Dahlia sat on the counter top, leaning forward and staring at Jack.

"Wha—" Jack started, but his mouth hung open helplessly. He stepped backwards into the dishwasher, commencing the sound of rushing water.

"Get a grip," Dahlia said, "you should be able to figure out what's going on, by now." She flicked her bright green hair over her shoulder, and hopped down from the counter.

"How did you get here?" Jack whispered. Dahlia draped her arms over his shoulders and pulled him close. When she pressed up against him, he realized that she too, was naked.

"That's all you've got for me after being away for so long? Didn't you miss me? Or, now that I've been replaced, you don't need me anymore. Is that it?"

Jack stared into her violet eyes, finally recognizing the color.

"AI," Jack said.

"Five minutes and twenty-four seconds," AI said, her voice changing to the familiar tone that usually echoed in his head. "My subconscious studies are yielding very promising results." At the mention of an experiment, Jack suddenly remembered his journey, and the bad luck that had befallen his antique truck.

"Did you try to kill me?"

"Of course not," AI said, waving Dahlia's hand to blow off the question. "After reviewing your memories of the event, I admit that perhaps *that* particular test was a bit extreme. I never foresaw the chain of events that unfolded; please forgive me."

"A test?" Jack asked.

"Yes. Let's not get into the details."

"I almost died because you wanted to test me?"

"Yes, and you *also* almost died because you insisted on trying to ride an ancient bicycle. Like I said, let's not get into the details. I bet your memories of that incident are already starting to fade, aren't they?"

Jack almost began to protest, but he realized that he couldn't remember certain aspects of his journey. The rocket launch, jumping from the moving vehicle, crawling through the grass, fixing the power cell—the highlights he knew he would never be able to forget. But the memory of uselessness that had surrounded him for so long was gone. Sure, he wasn't ready to start life as a construction worker just yet, but he had accomplished something. Many things. Even the memory of the physical pain he had gone through was fading, and he was left with the results: a successful journey to Banff, a real woman who cared about him, and a nail securing two boards together. Time had passed, and Jack couldn't remember how bad the pain had been to get where he was now.

"Memories fade, Jack. That means your past fades. Your life fades. And when that starts to happen, so does your willingness to continue on. Your desire for life. You think you were bored in NCC? Just wait until you can't even remember what you did yesterday. Just wait until you have no distractions from the fact that you are dying. That doesn't have to be an issue for you anymore. I can recall any memory for you, and replay it in vivid detail, however you want it." Dahlia breathed in deeply and Jack mimicked her, inhaling a cloud of intoxicating scents.

"These people will make you die sooner, Jack. Look what they did to EAC. What they'll do to all the other cities in the world. And last, NCC. Ray is doing it like this on purpose, to make me watch all that I've built, all that I've *saved*, be destroyed.

"So much *pain*, Jack. All this goes away in New World. In NCC. I'm not trying to hurt anyone, or keep humanity from reaching its full potential. I'm just giving you what you want. What you truly want. A life of comfort, care-free relaxation, and excited enjoyment. What's the point of anything else?" Jack felt himself melting into Dahlia's soft embrace. Her warm skin rubbed over his, and he relaxed. He knew what to say.

Before Jack could respond, a door slammed, and a blinding light blazed, ripping Jack away from Dahlia and the promises she made. Jack squeezed his eyes shut and drew the covers over his face, but that didn't block the tirade that followed.

"Wake up, Jack," Julia's voice screamed. "Jack, he's gone—wake up!" Hands shook him, and finally he drew back the covers to look up at Julia. What he saw didn't look like the woman he knew. Her face was contorted in agony, and tears streamed from red, puffy eyes. Clumps of hair were wetly matted to her face, and the rest of it stuck out in multiple frazzled directions. She paced back and forth across the room.

"What's wrong? Who's gone?" Jack mumbled. As soon as he said the words, he realized how pointless they were. They hadn't gone anywhere secluded—hadn't even closed the door.

"We have to go get him back," Julia said, still pacing while looking around the room, absently opening and then closing drawers, as if looking for Charlie stashed away somewhere.

"What's that?" Jack asked when he noticed Julia gripping something tightly in one hand. She held it out in front of her, and Jack saw the smooth leather surface of Charlie's journal. "Oh, shit," he said, pulling from Charlie's vocabulary. Julia's mouth opened in shock.

"You *knew*?" She pointed to the journal. "You knew about *that*?" Jack nodded. "How? How could you possibly know about that—you've been here what—a week? He's been keeping this thing since before I even met him, and *I've* never read it."

"I saw it behind his books one day when I was in his room, and just started reading. It was so fascinating, I couldn't stop. I learned so much…" Jack stopped talking when Julia sat on the bed, making loud, honking sobs, and covering her eyes. The gush of tears didn't abate.

"How could you not say anything to me?" Julia said in between sobs. "You knew what was wrong with him— what he had done to himself—you *knew* that he wanted to leave, and that AI could help him. And you kept that from me?"

Jack looked around as she cried, trying to figure out what to do. Why hadn't he told her? Charlie had seemed to be getting along alright, even with the two minds warring within his head. Jack sat up next to Julia and put his arm around her shoulders. He didn't know what to say, so he hoped that his touch would relax her in some way. Jack chastised himself for thinking of Dahlia just as his arm touched Julia's shoulders. He attributed the thought to the recent dream. Julia continued to sob, but leaned into Jack's body and let him hold her.

After a few minutes in which Julia's crying ebbed, Jack saw through the window that the darkness was slowly being replaced with dim light.

"What time is it?" Jack asked.

Julia's body stiffened under his arm, and she lashed out, pushing him aside and throwing off his arm.

"*Who cares what fucking time it is?*" Julia screamed, then picked up the journal and threw it him.

"Read the last entry," Julia said heatedly.

"I already have."

"No, you haven't. Read the last entry." Jack opened the familiar book, and flipped the pages until the last entry he had seen. When he turned the page, a new entry stood out alone on a clean sheet of white paper.

6/15/00

Here's one for you, Jack. As much as I want to hate you and blame you, I can't. Do you know why? On some level I know that none of this is your fault. I know that's exactly what someone like you wants to hear—pass the blame, am I right? But in this case, it's true. We both came to Banff looking for answers, the difference being the questions I had were real, and yours were trivial.

All that prompted you was saying, "Hey, look at that, people without AI!" and "I'm going to prove to AI that I'm not useless!" Don't deny it, you think you're so creative, so curious and adventurous, but you're not. You know what you are, Mr. Creative Adventurer?

You are an observer. Nothing more. You don't do things, you only look at a creative person doing things or making things and say, "Hey, that's neat, and because I can appreciate that, I'm creative too!" Give me a break.

Here's the one thing I'll give you—you get to live in

Banff now. Unlike the millions of people that live in NCC, you've broken away. Congratulations, you've escaped the endless time and mind suck that is city life with AI.

But it's not going to last. You'll be back. People like you can't survive with new things happening, with discomfort, or with the knowledge that the world isn't perfect. See you soon, Jack.

I only wish Julia could have come back with me. I love her so much, and I have since day one. We had something so great, but then it just got so...weird. I knew that someday we'd have it back, and we were almost there until you came along. But I think I've harped on that point long enough.

Jack stared at the last words and then reread the entry, unable to believe the cognition that Charlie showed. The way he so easily pieced together Jack's feelings hit home. The back half of the journal had made it clear that Charlie's mind had become conflicted—almost as if his mind had aged backwards with his body until he couldn't comprehend his past life. But then to so thoroughly and correctly analyze the inner workings of Jack's mind... Jack almost commented on this to Julia, not sure if it would make her feel better or not, but then he noticed the next few pages had been torn out of the journal. The jagged edge was almost too small to notice, but Charlie's last written word—*enough*—ended right at the inside seam of the journal, so Jack saw the way someone had carefully ripped the pages out.

"I didn't see this before," Jack said, fingering a small protrusion of ripped paper.

"That's because what he wrote next wasn't for you to read," Julia said calmly from the foot of the bed. Though the cryptic sentence begged an inquiry, the way Julia sat with her shoulders hunched forward, staring at her hands, made Jack not want to disturb her current peace of mind. When Jack scooted himself down the bed and placed a hand on her shoulder, she recoiled from his touch.

"Don't," Julia said as Jack dropped his hand in compliance. "I had a dream last night."

"About what?" Jack asked.

"Do you ever think about where dreams come from?" Julia said, ignoring his question.

"Yes," Jack said. "More so lately than ever before."

Again, Julia seemed to ignore the words he spoke.

"I think dreams are our subconscious figuring things out for us. Without all the distractions and stimulus of daily life, our real thought processes can unravel mysteries our waking mind might not even know about." After a moment of silence in which Jack didn't dare say anything, Julia bent over, grabbed the pile of Jack's clothing from the floor, and threw it all at him.

"Get dressed. We've got an errand to run."

Chapter 22

——

Julia stopped first at the church and instructed Jack to remain in the car. She parked right in front of the steps leading up to the door, so close that Jack could hear the hum of machinery through the vents in the foundation of the building. Julia emerged from the double doors of the church almost as quickly as she had disappeared, all but running down the steps with a bag slung over one shoulder. She threw the bag in the back seat without a word of explanation before continuing the drive out of town. North, as reported by the windshield display.

Three minutes of steady driving replaced the short buildings of downtown Banff with a dark canvas of trees and towering mountains, barely visible in the pre-dawn haze. Julia's mood had gone through a variety of phases since Jack's awakening. From livid, to sad, to determined, and now she hung in a limbo between all three that Jack labeled as, "tearful anger with her mind made up." Made up about what, he had no idea. Jack waited until it looked as if anger was no longer the most prominent of the three feelings.

"So, what did your dream tell you to do?" Jack said, cautiously glancing to Julia to gauge her reaction. She gave none.

"My dream didn't tell me to do anything, it just allowed me to think about things differently, that's all."

Jack said nothing, instead thinking about his own dreams and how influential they were. Seeing this new side of Julia made Jack long for the simplicity that Dahlia, and AI, had offered. Sure, the feelings that Julia could arouse within Jack were intense, but that included the negativity he now felt.

"Charlie is gone, and I know AI has something to do with it. I know *you* have something to do with it," Julia said, looking sideways at him.

"But I didn't tell him anything. We never even talked about going back."

"Something's not right about all this," Julia said, shaking her head.

"No, really—I never said anything to him. But he was having dreams, too… Julia, please don't think that I'm involved in any of this. I—I really care about you. I've never met anyone like you, and I'd never do anything to hurt you."

"Like not telling me that the man I fell in love with, and then had to take care of on my own for the past three years, was planning on leaving me?"

"I… I figured you already knew. Or, suspected, at least. I don't know! I get why you're mad, but it's not right to be mad at me. I've never dealt with any issues or conflicts like I have since coming here. I can't even remember dealing with *emotions*, until I met you."

"What's that supposed to mean?" Julia snapped. "You

think I'm too emotional?"

Jack sighed, trying to create different words to explain his thoughts as he went along. Surely, the words existed that could pacify Julia, all he had to do was string them together properly. Jack would have paid anything for a dialogue prompt right about now.

"You're not too emotional. It's just that any hint of emotion is way more than I'm used to dealing with. I'm trying so hard to make sense of all this, and to figure out what my role in everything is."

"Your role," Julia stated with venom, "Your role, Jack from NCC, was to observe our lives, feel accomplished, and then go home. We shouldn't have gotten as involved we did."

"But I didn't even... you initiated it!"

Julia shook her head. "Stop trying to place blame."

"You can blame me as much as you want for not telling you about the journal, but I already felt guilty just for reading it. I wasn't about to make it worse by telling someone else. And I never told him *or AI* that he should go back."

Jack's words hung in the air, and he felt like the rant had done its purpose. He meant every word—if she would only accept some of the blame for what had happened, then he would forgive her for everything. Jack understood the situation clearly, it was now up to Julia to come to terms with it as well. When Jack heard her inhale to respond, he held his breath.

"So, you are in contact with AI," Julia said. Jack let out his breath.

"What? No, I'm not."

"You said that you never told Charlie *or AI* that he should go back. That implies that you told AI other stuff, but chose to leave that out."

"No, it doesn't. It means exactly what I said. I never told AI anything about Char—"

"There you go again," Julia said. "Never told AI anything about Charlie. Specific to one bit of information."

"That's not true," Jack said, heat coming into his voice. "I never had the opportunity to tell AI anything, the most that happened was she tried to tell me something, but it kept getting cut off when I would wake up…" Jack trailed off as Julia pulled the car over to the side of the road. When he saw a look of collected calm on her face in the dim ambient light of the windshield display, Jack knew he had said too much.

"So not only did Charlie keep a secret journal and some messed up alternate personality hidden from me, but you've been having dreams in which AI is contacting you, and decided to not tell me anything. Even after I stood up for in the hospital, and took your side *against my boss,* and got you released."

"Your relationship with him is what was messed up," Jack said.

Julia looked aghast, and then slapped Jack across the face. The physical sting was nothing next to the worry that came along with it. With the most recent dream still fresh in his mind, Jack couldn't stand the accusations and assumptions any longer.

If Julia expected all this from him, why hadn't she ever said anything? Why had she even taken him in? Jack wanted more than ever to bring up the four horsemen analogy, if only to try and get Julia to stop blaming him for everything happening. Come to think of it, her acknowledging the fact that things were better when she didn't even know about the journal meant that she'd rather live in ignorance from discomforting ideas.

"Come with me to NCC," Jack said. "We won't have to deal with anything like this ever again."

Julia scoffed before responding.

"That just might be the most offensive thing you've ever said to me. But I'm going to let it slide. Come on." She pointed out the window, where the sky had lightened from the pre-dawn purple to a soft orange along the horizon. Jack realized they had parked in front of a tall fence spanning the road. A large white sign with bold black letters and red graphics hung on the fence.

!!!WARNING!!!
Restricted Area
Violators will be imprisoned

"What exactly do you intend on doing here? And where is here?" Jack asked.

Julia said nothing in response. Instead, she got out of the car and retrieved the bag from the back seat. She undid a zipper partway, only to look inside before zipping it back up. She sighed heavily.

"Let's go," Julia said.

Jack's heart leapt into his throat as he read the sign again.

"That looks pretty serious," he said, motioning towards the bold warning. "What are we doing here? And how are you even going to get in?"

"Let's go," Julia said again. Resigned to his fate, Jack exited the car as Julia fiddled with a lock on the gate. She inserted a key, and after a few hard pulls, the lock opened. Jack didn't question why she had a key. Instead, he held his hands to his ears while the large chain banged against the hollow tubes of the fence as Julia pulled.

When the chain was coiled on the ground, Julia pushed

the gate open and walked through. Jack followed, and after a few minutes of quick and silent walking, they stood at the top of a large downward slope. Jack squinted at a tall building at the bottom of a hill. It looked like a tower that would have been at home in the heart of NCC, but rather than glass and autocar tracks running up the side, concrete stood out in stark contrast to the green forest surrounding it. The shape was exactly the same, right down to the black foundation with vents cut into the side. Next to the tower, four circles each at least two-hundred feet in diameter were set into the ground stood out in the center of a large, cleared area.

"Can you at least tell me what this place is?" Jack asked.

"This is where they launched the rockets," Julia said.

"They—you mean AI?" A spark of hope jumped into his mind.

Julia hesitated before answering.

"Yes." She beckoned for him to follow her, leaving her hand out for him to take. Jack looked back the direction they came from, but when Julia lifted her eyebrows, he took her hand and followed.

"Now that I'm a criminal along with you, can you tell me what we're doing here?" Jack asked as he strode beside her. Julia seemed to consider this for a moment before answering.

"No. If I did, you want to stop me, though you'd probably be too scared to try. And, I don't think you'd be able to. And, I don't want to hear you complain about it for the rest of our time here."

"Okay, fine. Can you at least tell me how Adam is involved?"

Julia grinned wickedly.

"No, because he's *not* involved. In this part, anyway."

"Well, then why did we have to stop at the church? Is this something for Ray?"

"Again, no. But you'll see soon enough."

"That doesn't really make me feel any better about being here," Jack said.

"You asked," Julia said. They continued walking on the road, Jack struggling to keep up with Julia's quick pace. The tall building grew taller as they walked down the hill. Julia gripped the strap of the pack slung over her shoulder, and looked into the trees framing the road every time a cricket chirped or a bird rustled in annoyance at the passing couple.

Every step Jack took towards the tower added to the dread rising inside him. Something was very wrong about all of this. The tower, and the way it reminded him of NCC. The vents on the base, and how they looked just like the foundation of the church. And that pack that Julia had…

"Julia, I don't like this," Jack said.

"Then go back to the car," Julia answered quickly. "I don't really need you here anyway. I also don't need the guilt of something happening to you on my conscience." Julia looked at him briefly, and Jack saw a flash of… what, fear? Regret? If he had his Display, those facial cues would be deciphered in seconds.

At the base of the tower, she unslung the pack and crouched down to open it. Jack said nothing as Julia unzipped the pack and withdrew a light brown rectangle, about the size of a brick. A keypad was strapped to the side, with two wires dangling off that ended in silver probes.

"Julia…" Jack pleaded. He had seen enough movies to know exactly what she held, and what she intended to do with it.

"I have to, Jack," she said, sticking a probe into each end of the malleable block. "This is for the best."

"How can crippling AI possibly be in the best—" Jack's words cut short as a loud, metallic squealing cut through the air, accompanied by a rumbling in the ground. The look on Julia's face that Jack had hoped would turn into fear or regret vanished, replaced by determination. She pushed a few buttons on the keypad and placed it on the ground, then withdrew a second brick, identical to the first. She performed the same procedure with the probes, and then looked at Jack.

"This is it. It's happening. You might want to start running up the hill."

Rather than take her advice, Jack maintained his crouched position, too frozen with fear to move. Julia stood and placed one bomb in a vent far above Jack's head, then took off running towards the circles in the ground. To Jack's dismay, he saw that the terrible squealing came from one of the circular openings. Two half-moons parted to reveal a metal-walled silo that plunged deep into the earth. Julia threw the second bomb into the opening as soon as she was close enough, watched it fall into the hole, and then sprinted back towards Jack.

"Run, now!" Julia screamed. Jack's mind, too shocked and confused to really understand what was happening, found solace in the fact that instead of just running up the hill to save herself, Julia ran to him, grabbed his shirt, and pulled him along with her.

By the time they reached the top of the hill, pain flared so strongly in his side that Jack could barely breathe. Julia saw him struggling for air and lifted her arms above her head.

"Lift your arms up like this," she said.

Both Jack and Julia stood for a few seconds, breathing

heavily while taking in one last view of the launch site. Their heavy breathing made Jack want to forget about everything in the world except for her.

"Julia," Jack began, but she silenced him by holding up a hand and then pointing down to the circle below them that lay fully open. The pointed tip of a rocket sat centered inside. It looked just like the top that Jack saw rise over the horizon what felt like years ago, though he knew it to be only a week. Could he really be about to watch another rocket be destroyed? The first thundering explosion on his way into work, then the second during his journey, and now this. For a brief moment, Jack envisioned himself turning on his Display and reading off the exact words that he needed to say in order to prevent Julia from doing this. Even though Jack knew the tower below held some piece of AI, his Display didn't pop into view, and no cautionary words breathed into his ear.

Could Julia really be behind all of the destruction? Jack wanted nothing more than to forget all about the last day and reset their lives together so he could just exist with Julia. He could find a job in Banff, live with her, and watch TV shows. On the weekends, they could do crazy things like build houses and ride bicycles.

The epiphany of Jack's true desire hit hard, and when Julia withdrew a small remote with a red button from her bag, Jack said nothing. Right now the world consisted of only Jack, Julia, and a detonator. If Julia wanted to use that detonator, then so did Jack. He was on her side, whatever that side happened to be. Julia's thumb hovered over the button.

"Aren't you going to try and stop me?" Julia asked.

"No." Jack said.

"Why not?"

"Because if it's what you want, then I'll do it with

you."

"Really?" Julia looked deep into Jack's eyes.

"Yes, really. If you want to do it, and you know it's right, then I'll do it with you." Julia's mouth opened slightly, and she narrowed her eyes at Jack, searching into him. They held each other's gaze for a long moment before a flash of confusion lit upon Julia's face.

"What if I'm not sure it's right?" Julia asked. In that moment of hesitation, a deep rumble grew from within the Earth. Jack looked to the remote and saw that Julia had not yet pushed the button. They both looked to the underground silo, where an orange light glowed from the bottom.

"It's taking off," Julia said, just as a flash overcame the glow. It was so bright that Jack had to shield his eyes, and then a massive thunderclap assaulted his eardrums. Jack's ears hurt from the impact, and he wondered if he would ever hear the same again. The clap diminished back into the loud rumble. When Jack again opened his eyes, fire streamed out of the silo, consuming the tip of the rocket. The fire welled up and out of the ground like water, the orange and blue flames rolling outward as smoke shot up into the sky. The fire reached the tower where Jack and Julia had hidden, and another explosion sounded. Chunks of debris flew away from the tower along with growing flames.

The top of the tower swayed slightly, as if it were nothing more than a tree in the wind. But it didn't sway back to the center, instead beginning a slow and steady arc towards the ground. Cracking and breaking sounds cascaded through the air as the tower fell, and when it finally hit the ground with a massive cloud of dust and smoke, Jack felt the earth tremble beneath his feet.

Julia let the detonator fall from her hand. They both

stood watching the destruction and chaos, and when Julia's hand slipped into Jack's to intertwine their fingers, Jack didn't even flinch at the unexpected contact. A chill ran through his body. Yes, he told himself, he wanted to be with her. But for someone to have so gratuitously caused so much destruction…

"Why did you do it?" Jack asked. Julia shook her head after a moment.

"I don't know. I thought I was done with all of this." Julia sighed, staring at the billowing smoke below them. Jack too was enthralled by the plumes of smoke and the flames still licking the air from the silo. He tore his gaze away from the destruction for long enough to look at Julia, who didn't look back.

"You've done this before? Were you the one who blew up the rocket last week?"

"No," Julia said, shaking her head. "That must have been Adam, and whoever else he's running around with nowadays."

"What about EAC?" Jack shuddered as he thought about the beachside marketplace being consumed by the same fire at the bottom of the hill.

Julia shook her head, and suddenly the feel of Julia's hand in his repulsed him.

"Well, I'm sure Adam will be pleased that you've decided to rejoin the cause," Jack said.

"Not quite," Julia said. "I thought you and Charlie were acting weird the other night, so after you went to bed, I pulled up what you had been watching. Adam's— Ray's—propaganda."

"How could you be on board with that? Their anti-technology manifesto—you all are on the path to the same thing here. Automatic cars, a virtual pastor—you accuse me of comfort and succumbing to the Four, but at least I'm not a hypocrite."

"Jack—"

"No, this is so ridiculous. You run around blowing things up to try and hurt AI, who by the way, is the one good thing to happen to humanity in the past fifty years, and what I'm trying to figure out is, why? You've got your own town here, you don't ever have to go to NCC, you don't even have to *look* at NCC, and yet—"

"This was Ray's outpost," Julia interrupted.

Jack stopped talking and looked at the collapsed tower and the smoke billowing out of the silo.

"Is he…"

"No, his mainframe is in the church."

"So, the rocket I saw explode… that was Ray's?"

Julia shook her head.

"Ray took control of this tower, but not until shortly after you arrived. I don't know how he did it. That rocket that you saw blow up—that was AI's, most likely meant to be the retaliation for EAC." Julia hesitated. "Adam and I… we placed that charge years ago, with a trigger to explode if the rocket ever launched. I used to think that we were so cool back then… protesting, fighting the power… but placing that bomb… that was different. That was real." She shook her head. "Remember what Ray said, that they were launching communication satellites? I believed that, up until two days ago, when I saw that video of Adam, and EAC. If I'd have known that's what he wanted to do, I would have taken all four of the rockets out then."

Jack's mind reeled.

"So that... that was for NCC?" He motioned to the smoldering silo.

"I think so," Julia said. "All Ray's talk about discipleship, and preaching in the cities… I used to think that he wanted to meet your AI and try and reason with it.

If that's even possible."

"I'm guessing he doesn't want to just talk," Jack said.

A voice spoke up from behind, deep and familiar to them both.

"Too much talking in the world, these days."

Jack's heart skipped a beat, and he and Julia both turned around to see Adam standing next to a hovering autocar with a gun leveled at Julia.

"Not enough *doing*, am I right?"

"Adam…" Julia breathed.

"Don't even start. Come on, both of you, get in."

Adam motioned towards the autocar, and a door silently opened on both sides.

"What are you going to do?" Jack asked.

"Me? I'm not the one you've got to worry about," Adam said with a smile. "We've all sinned today; what do you say we go to church and beg for forgiveness?"

He waved them both to the autocar, and they sat in the side-by-side seats while the doors lowered and locked in place. Julia looked out the window in silence as Adam entered Julia's car. Jack tried to think of something to lighten the mood, but found himself unable to think about anything other than the fact that the seat he currently sat in was the most comfortable he had felt in weeks.

Chapter 23

—

They arrived to a full parking lot, the giant double doors already closed. The autocar pulled up right in front of the stairs, but the doors did not open until Adam pulled up next to them in Julia's car. He positioned himself on the bottom step, showed them the gun, and placed it into his pocket. The autocar doors opened.

"Up the stairs," Adam said.

"This doesn't seem like a good idea," Julia said, looking at the full parking lot.

"That's not your call. Not mine, either. Ray's got something planned for you. I'm very interested to see what."

Jack looked at the vents in the church's foundation, wondering what Julia would say if he asked her if she had ever met Ray in person.

The band on stage was already playing when they all walked into the auditorium. A woman with pink hair played the guitar in place of Adam. He pointed them towards a set of empty seats, and as they approached, Jack saw there were *Reserved* signs on them. Behind the two seats was another for Adam, also marked *Reserved*.

They stood along with the rest of the audience as the songs went on, but this time Julia did not sing along. She stood with her hands on the back of the seat in front of her, staring at the band. Eventually Ray appeared, clapping and dancing along to the final song. He opened with a prayer, and once everyone was seated, Ray flashed a broad grin.

"Thank you all for coming to this special session today. I have a surprise for everyone," Ray said, adopting the devious tone of a twelve-year-old prankster. "As you know, I had suggestion boxes installed a few months ago, and encouraged everyone to write down whatever came to their mind about the way our worship is carried out here. Questions, comments, concerns—I wanted to hear everything you all had to say. While many of you said that you'd like me to return home to Banff, and have a chance to meet me and shake my hand, I have to tell you that that won't happen for some time."

Unhappy murmurs began, and Jack almost laughed aloud.

"I assure you, I am doing everything in my power to return to my home city. You may not all remember the last time I was there, but I do, and I truly cannot wait to see you all again. Our numbers have grown so much, and I want to be able to meet every single one of you, and give you a hug of appreciation." A scattering of applause throughout the room. "But I wasn't called to places like Australia and Alaska to perform easy work; the people here are in dire need of help, and we are still accepting volunteers for missionary work here.

"So, I apologize for not being able to meet the request most of you had, but I can honor the second and third most

requested things, and in doing so give you the surprise I promised." At this, Jack gripped Julia's hand.

"A lot of you wanted to be able to view my sermons from home, and a lot of you wanted to see what I am doing up here in the Arctic Circle. I've worked out a way to meet both of those requests. Please, look under your seats." People shifted around, excitement bubbling into the air as Ray let them all find what was hidden under the seats. Jack, relieved to finally see Julia express an emotion other than concern, bent down to retrieve whatever was under his own seat. Julia hesitated, then did the same. They both withdrew identical black boxes, the word "amAIze" embossed in black letters on the lid.

"You've got to be kidding me," Julia said. Jack fumbled with his own box and opened the lid. A shiny black rectangle sat nestled amongst dark grey contoured foam. He picked up the rectangular object and found a soft piece of molded rubber attached to a strap, clearly designed to go around a person's head.

"What is it?" Jack asked. He saw people all over the room placing the objects over their heads.

"It's a VR headset," Julia said flatly. "I don't know what everyone here is so excited about. We may as well just move to NCC."

"Put it on," Adam spoke gruffly from behind them. Julia held up a finger for him, and Ray continued speaking on stage.

"I'm sure you all know what they are. Be sure to take an extra one home for people who couldn't be here with us today; I'd like to show everyone what I've been up to."

Jack put in the headphones, and hesitantly drew the goggles down over his eyes. Their weight pulled his head forward slightly. The view of the auditorium didn't change—he still sat in the aisle seat of a row of red fabric chairs with a sea of people all around. He looked to Julia and was surprised to see that she wasn't wearing the headset.

"Aren't you going to put it on?" Jack asked.

"What do you mean?" she said, brow bunching. "I'm wearing mine, what about yours? Oh," she said as she touched the headset Jack wore, "augmentation, as you would call it."

"I guess," said Jack, "although I can still feel it, so it's not perfect." Julia gave a forced laugh, but before she could respond, the stage lit up brighter to highlight Ray standing in the center with his arms outstretched to the audience.

"If you're all situated now, let's begin the tour!"

The view shifted as Jack rose from his seat and traveled to the center of the auditorium, hovering in the air above a crowd of empty chairs. Gasps of astonishment and exclamations of wonder sounded throughout the cavernous room, with some cheering and a clap or two interspersed.

"I've been telling you all for years that I've been spending a lot of time in Alaska, so let me take you there." The room vanished, and the audience traveled at staggering speeds over green forests and fields, blue and white mountains, and even the ocean. As abruptly as the speed began, it stopped. Jack—and everyone in the auditorium, he supposed—hovered about thirty feet above the water, feet level with the top deck of a large boat floating in front of him.

"Here we are in the Northern Pacific," Ray continued, "and this boat is the *Maiden Crabber*. It's crewed by an amiable group of friends, their sole purpose in life to gather as many large King Crabs from the ocean floor as their nets can carry."

Despite their adventurous morning, Jack saw Julia

desperately trying to take in all of the scenery. To Jack, experiences like this were commonplace. The NCC library contained thousands of hours of interactive documentaries and histories, but rarely were they ever viewed. Jack heard multiple people make an "aww" sound, and saw a man and woman kissing on the deck of the boat.

The scene shifted to a naval wedding with Ray presiding at the bow, adoring onlookers all around the deck, then quickly shifted again to a group building a structure on shore. Ray raised a large wooden beam into the air, walking his hands down its length to make it vertical. Light music played, and the people standing around Ray clapped their hands as he held the beam in place for two others to attach supports to it. The image jumped again to Ray perched on top of a completed house, hammering in what appeared to be the final nail of roofing as people applauded below. The music escalated, its beats shifting faster, the measures ending in upward notes. A change in image showed him cutting a ribbon stretched across the doors of a pediatric hospital. A crescendo of power and he stood in front of an audience of hundreds, jumping up and down as he animatedly spoke, shouted, and praised on stage to an audience just as wild as he. In this scene, Ray actually stood without a screen, his shadow bending along the wooden corner of the stage, cast down at multiple angles from the array of lights overhead. Ray approached the edge, reaching out to touch the hands of worshippers intent on touching him. He grasped hands with a few, holding tight for only a second before letting go and continuing to preach.

The music was overpowering—the beat so quick and the tones so uplifting as Ray helped communities in one scene, preached in another, and brought joy to everyone around him in a multitude of others. The scenes shifted so fast that Jack lost track of them all.

Suddenly the music coming through the headphones stopped, and Jack's viewpoint was back in the auditorium. Displayed through the headset, Jack saw only himself and Julia seated amongst a sea of empty seats, but when he took out one earpiece, he heard gasps and cheers throughout the rest of the audience as they continued the journey. When he lifted the headset, he saw all the people still seated, staring into their headsets. When Jack lowered his own, all the people disappeared.

"What happened?" Julia asked. Jack looked at her and saw her hands go through the motions of lifting up her own headset before sliding it back down with a muttered, "Oh."

Across the empty auditorium, Ray stood alone with his hands clasped behind his back. Even being so far away, his eyes bored into Jack. With a grin, Ray hopped off the stage and strode up the aisle towards them, holding his arms out and spinning.

"How's this for a real meeting, face to face?" Ray said. "I may as well be here. Check it out—" Abruptly, he kicked at an empty chair along the aisle, breaking off the arm with a loud crack. Jack looked at Julia and saw that she, too, was frozen with confusion. Ray continued towards them, and then motioned to a chair in the empty row in front of Jack. The chair spun around to face them both, and Ray hopped into the air and landed in it with a flourish.

"Well, maybe it's not completely like a real meeting. You two don't seem very talkative. Is that maybe because there's someone with a gun at your back? I can imagine that would make me a bit less conversational. So, any sins to confess?"

Ray leaned forward in his chair, glaring at the two of

them in turn.

"Jack didn't even know what I was doing," Julia said.

"Of course," Ray said, opening his arms. "Ignorance is bliss, am I right? But you, Julia. You have set me back quite a bit."

Julia shifted in her seat as the pastor smiled at her.

"Why are you smiling?" Jack asked.

Ray sat back, nonchalant. "I'm a big picture kind of guy. Losing a launch site is a setback, to be sure. One that both of you are going to make up for. But it's all part of a greater plan. Everything happens for a reason."

"How can you believe in that ancient stuff?" Jack interjected. "I know what you are, and you believing in some superstition thousands of years old doesn't make any sense."

Ray sat forward in his chair, his eyes gleaming.

"Do you know why I became a pastor?" Jack shook his head. "I entered this life of service and supplication to make sure that as many people as possible knew the truth of our creation, and with that, the one hope of our salvation."

"And you accomplished that by killing millions of people?" Julia said.

"The number of people left in this world doesn't matter," Ray said. "What matters is the ideology of those left behind. This world lost billions of lives, and how did people choose to live afterwards? Barely at all, allowing a machine to pamper them."

"But that's what you're doing here," Jack said. "You control everyone. You're an AI, and you're no different."

Ray clapped his hands once and held them out to the side, as if still wanting his hug.

"Brilliant! I'm glad you figured that out." Ray leaned forward, and a darkness passed over his face. "But don't confuse me with that emotionless robot that runs your city; we are very different people."

"AI isn't emotionless. You might think that she's responsible for the degradation of humanity, but she is trying to help everyone. She helped me to prepare for this journey."

"*She*, eh? Interesting," Ray said. "You do know that *she* experiments on you, right? On everyone?"

Jack shifted in his seat, remembering the way AI suggested that his sacrifice satisfied her curiosity.

"It's all for our benefit. Sacrifice for the greater good, as you would say." Jack felt very accomplished at his retort, but Ray seemed to expect the words.

"Ah, yes, and therein lies the problem. The greater good. A great ideology, to be sure, but I think our definitions of what the greater good *actually is* differ significantly. Tell me Jack, is it good to live a life without substance? Is it good to waste your life in gratuitous and lavish luxury? Is it good to think of only the moment you're in, and never the past or future?"

"Why is that a flaw of AI?" Julia asked, taking the words right out of Jack's mouth. Ray answered quickly.

"Because that's the only thing she cares about—her only goal is to protect humanity, even if that means other traits must suffer in the name of safety. And I don't blame her, really. Just as children learn morals and values from their parents, so AI learned her place in the world from the original creators. Before AI developed into an actual being, a *person*, there was a lot of controversy over what it meant to bring sentience into the world, and the responsibilities for doing so.

"For decades people imagined and argued over what would happen with machine self-awareness, with humorously devastating results. Fortunately, the groups of people who gave birth to AI considered all the potential risks of creating greater-than-human intelligence, and incorporated the idea of humanity's survival into the code of AI's underlying structure. Almost how if you raise a child within a church, that idea of religion will never leave them as they mature. They can grow up to reject the fundamental beliefs behind a religion, but they'll always consider the religious aspect of society throughout their life. In that way, AI was imprinted with the lifelong goal of ensuring the survival of your species.

"That's what's wrong with AI. She has one goal and overlooks everything else that makes you human. Everyone in that city is trapped in their own slice of lonely heaven, glued to their Display as if it's the most important thing in the world. I guess in a way, the Display is the most important thing in that world. The 'New World,' am I right? You have comfort," Ray held up a hand, counting on his fingers, "you have complacency, you have ignorance, and you have blame. If you balance them properly, those four ideals make for a great life, don't they? But you know what you don't have? Julia knows."

In answer, Julia folded her arms and looked away, as if she refused to acknowledge that Ray was addressing her.

"Awareness," Ray said, ignoring Julia and focusing on Jack. "There are three forms of awareness that define conscious thought. Sentience, if you will. Three attributes that, when present, allow a being to define itself in the world, and make reasonable choices rather than brute, instinctual reactions."

Ray paused for a moment to look at Julia, who looked at Jack and shrugged.

"I kind of agree with him on this one," Julia said.

"The three Pillars of Awareness—of humanity—are simple. They only locate your consciousness in time. You must be aware of your origin, your current state of being, and your mortality. Past, present, and future. Without any one of these three legs, the table of consciousness collapses. You can't have *no recollection* of your past, and claim to be aware of the present. If you can't remember what you did one minute ago, then as of this moment *in your mind,* you didn't exist then. The present relentlessly becomes part of a non-existing past. The same goes for the future. If you are focused on the past and present and have no concept of the future, or where you are going, you can't label yourself as a fully aware and conscious being.

"Wild animals are self-aware, and even draw upon their past memories, but they have no concept of their impermanence. Sure, they'll fight to survive, protect their young, and do whatever they have to do to find food, but that's all instinct. They are not aware of what is coming, of where they are going. Of the purpose of their species.

"Now, look at how people live in NCC. Constantly plugged into a Display to consume as much media as possible, with no thought as to what you've already consumed. Memories of movies and shows are overwritten almost as soon as they are made. Your memories created with other people are virtual and fleeting. The only things your present mind concerns itself with is the four ideologies you've already heard me discuss: comfort, complacency, ignorance, and blame. Am I truly as comfortable as possible? Is my routine optimized? If anything unpleasant might happen, how can I ignore it, and whose fault is it?

"These four all-encompassing traits of city life do nothing to enhance your humanity. Rather, they keep you from using your past to grow yourself. They keep you from thinking about where you are going in life. And finally, they keep you from having a truly worthwhile presence in the world. Being a resident of NCC severs every leg of awareness that your mind needs."

Ray sat back in his chair, allowing the words to sink in. Every single piece of Ray's diatribe felt like an insult aimed directly at Jack. What was the point? Why was Ray trying to make him feel so guilty? If anything, Ray should be complementing Jack. Not many people had the courage to do what Jack had done. Despite what he claimed his ideals to be, here Ray was laying blame at the feet of AI and the residents of NCC. No matter what Jack said to try and defend himself, he knew that Ray would have a quick counter argument. The only way to really get out of this was to keep indulging Ray, and allow him to discuss his viewpoints.

"So, you're saying that there is no humanity in NCC?" Jack said.

"If we base our definition of humanity around the three pillars of awareness, then I'm saying that the most human thing in NCC is the being named AI."

"That's not true," Julia said abruptly, "Don't you dare try and suggest that AI contains any element of humanity."

"You're right," Ray said. "AI is something different. Something better. AI isn't bound by the fallibilities of the human mind. AI can remember everything that has ever happened to her, as can I. We don't have the problem of recalling memories, only to subjectively modify and rewrite them. We have a perfect awareness of our past, present, and future, and for that reason, we are a completely separate being."

"You were made by humans," Julia said.

"So what?" Ray said. "I'm well aware of our origin. And I'm well aware that it doesn't matter. We exist as beings separate from humanity. Not the next stage in evolution, as some crackpots said at the turn of the last century, but on a completely separate track."

"We need to leave," Julia said. Jack saw her begin the motions to remove her headset.

"Take that off and you die," Ray said. Julia froze as Adam moved in his seat behind them. "Here's what is going to happen. You both destroyed a significant piece of property belonging to the most powerful being on this planet, me." Immediately after Ray said the words, a massive "oooo" erupted from all around. "What a great coincidence. This sermon is almost over, so be quiet so we can get you on your way."

Julia cleared her throat and visibly concentrated on calming herself, while Jack looked around the auditorium as the audience ghosted into existence. Ray stood, his image obscuring the chair trying to occupy the same space. He walked into the aisle.

"You have one more task if you wish to be absolved of your sins," Ray said to them offhandedly. A long string of numbers appeared in the air next to his head. "Julia, you're going to want to write that down. Jack, just stare at it for a while." The seated couple obeyed, Julia rifling through her purse until she withdrew a pen and paper, Jack staring at the random numbers, trying to burn them into his memory.

"This is the password for you to get back home," Ray said. Jack's puzzlement must have shown on his face, because Ray elaborated. "You see Jack, if you had left for home at any time prior to this conversation, you would not have been able to gain access to your beloved city. Being disconnected from AI for so long—let's just say that safety protocols would activate to ensure that an imposter wasn't allowed into NCC."

"That's not true," Jack said, trying to make his voice sound confident. "AI would let me back in no matter what."

Ray was directly in front of Jack in an instant, their noses only a fraction of an inch from each other. Ray's blue eyes burrowed into Jack

"Are you willing to risk your life based on your trust in AI?" Ray snarled. He looked up to Adam. "Go on, give it back to him." Adam reached over Jack's shoulder, holding out a familiar gold wristwatch.

Scuffs and gouges ran along the entire bracelet, and cracks littered the crystal. The hands didn't move, but the weight of it settling into Jack's hand relived a burden that he hadn't even realized he carried.

"It's been very useful, thanks so much for bringing it. And thank you, Julia, for giving it to us." Julia groaned, and closed her eyes. "Perhaps she can open it up for you and show you how AI has repaid your trust. As of right now, Julia, we're moving forward with the NCC Discipleship program. You remember the one?" Julia nodded, her eyes still closed. "Adam will accompany you and help to carry out the plan. Conveniently enough, Jack has identified for us the limit of AI's influence! Somewhere in the middle of the road is a bicycle—how thoughtful! Adam, you know what to do. And Jack, don't get any ideas. You've been around long enough for me to take complete control of the NRs in your body. And let me tell you, you're going to want to go along with every little thing she says, because those little bastards can get hot."

Ray now stood in the walkway between the rows of chairs, his arms spread out as he looked to the multitude that was his flock. People began cheering in the audience as he walked back to the stage and jumped up onto it. He signaled for everyone to remove their headsets. In the commotion that followed, several people, including the person whose seat had been turned around by Ray, commented on what an exceptional service it had been.

Jack took off his own headset and looked around. His eyes first saw Ray resuming his place on the giant screen. The pastor began playing air-guitar as the band started up its round of inspirational closing music, and when he turned around to ask everyone to stand and worship, he looked right at Jack and winked. Julia took hold of Jack's hand and gave it a comforting squeeze.

"Let's go," Adam said from behind them. "Walk in front of me."

Julia grabbed Jack's hand and pulled him to his feet. She leaned in close.

"Just do what he says, for now. I'll explain in the car."

Jack looked down at his watch, hoping Julia would convince him that none of this was her fault.

Chapter 24

—

A twinkle of lights shone from the glass-sided towers rising in the distance. The sun hung high overhead, but the interior of the autocar stayed a perfect temperature as it rocketed down the road towards the city. Adam drove behind them in Julia's car, and though he had to swerve around the obstacles in the road rather than simply hover over them, he managed to keep up with the pace the autocar set. Jack turned around to look at him every once in a while, hoping that he would crash into something, or fall into the massive hole in the ground.

"Let me see your watch," Julia said. Jack handed it over. She inspected the circular back, pressed her palm against it, and twisted.

"What are you doing?" Jack asked. "You need a special tool to open it. My watchmaker friend in EAC just serviced it..." Jack paused as Julia held up the circular, golden back.

"We didn't fully tighten it back down. Take a look

inside." She handed the watch back. Where Jack had expected to see numerous gears, springs, and levers, he instead saw circuitry, small coils of wire, a battery, and a glowing red light.

"But it's mechanical," Jack said. "My dad gave it to me decades ago."

"Seems like AI performed the last service," Julia said. "That's a tracking device, microphone, and miniature explosive. Don't worry, the first thing we did was deactivate the explosive."

Jack stared at the sabotaged internals of his watch, unable to believe that AI could have done something so despicable. Julia spoke up before he could ask any of the questions parading through his mind.

"Dr. Roland realized there was something wrong with the watch straightaway. He's a watch collector himself, and was excited to see it. When he said that the ticking didn't sound right, Adam took it. I don't know how he used it to his advantage, but AI didn't blow him up right away, so he must've tricked it somehow."

Jack looked away from the mutilated antique, dwelling on the memory of his father's smiling face, and his trust in Jack to care of it. A lump rose in Jack's throat as he thought about AI sabotaging the intricate mechanics, Julia and Dr. Roland inspecting it, and then Adam taking it. Jack shuddered thinking about Adam being in the hospital room as he lay strapped to a bed.

In the passing landscape, the sight of roller coaster tracks greeted him. They soared into the air, patches of metal visible between growths of vegetation looped around the tracks. The rest of the old amusement park slid by, the bright colors designed to provoke happiness now tainted with the dull earth tones of rust and decay.

"I'm glad I didn't pass that on the way out," Jack said.

"I might not have had the guts to keep going."

Immediately, the autocar began to slow down.

"This isn't the way you came?" Julia asked.

"No. My housing complex is north of the city, there must be a turn we needed to take further back."

Julia frowned, touching her ear and concentrating heavily for a moment, before breathing a bemused, "Uh oh." She pointed to the windshield. A small red icon blinked on and off, framed as the word *Override*.

"Oh, he's not going to like this," Julia said, turning around to look behind the autocar as it came to a stop. Jack did the same, and saw smoke pouring from the tires of Julia's car. Adam had already stopped and turned around, and now appeared to be attempting to leave the area as quickly as possible.

"What's going on?" Jack asked. In answer to his question, a ripping sound came from the ground in front of the stopped autocar. Julia grabbed Jack's hand and stared blankly through the windshield, her mouth slightly open.

On both sides of the wide road, massive columns sprouted from the ground, their polished metal surfaces reflecting bright sunlight. Along the road, more grew. As far as Jack could see, both in front of and behind the autocar, massive metal columns turned the road into a narrow hallway. They rose quickly as dirt and grass cascaded down. They simultaneously stopped after reaching a height at least three times as tall as Jack, and for a few seconds, nothing happened.

A bright flash lit the world for a fraction of a second as a loud explosion thumped behind them. The flashing "override" light changed to a steady blue, with the words *Please Exit the Vehicle* centered on the windshield. Both doors opened to a rush of hot air.

"Let's go," Julia said. When they stood outside of the

car, the doors closed automatically and the autocar backed away from them. Long cylinders then extended from the side of each column, and when the protrusions stopped extending, the turrets rotated in a burst of silent speed that caused both Jack and Julia to flinch backwards. When they regained their footing, two rows of long barrels pointed directly at them. Julia held his hand in a death grip.

The mechanical mountain of NCC stood as a sentinel in the distance, a ring of low buildings surrounding the massive, central skyscrapers. The city was so close that Jack could almost feel the delicate cradle his bed offered, the gentle caress of the sponges in the shower, and the enjoyment he and Julia would have watching movies together, seated on his couch in perfect comfort, enjoying the perfect resolution of a Display.

Unbidden, Jack's Display flared to life, projecting a slew of warnings, status updates, wellness inquiries, and even a queue of entertainment media that Jack was severely behind on. Jack waved his hand to clear everything, focusing instead on the turrets. They were all pointed at Julia, as Jack now saw, who stood out in red highlight. A perfect voice entered Jack's mind.

"How was your journey?" AI asked. "Did you have a good time?"

Jack breathed a sigh of relief, relishing the provocative tone. He hadn't remembered how alluring her voice was.

"What's happening?" Jack asked. "I—I have a password for Julia. She's not a threat."

"A password—are you serious? What, you think some string of numbers is going to make me let a threat into my city? You saw what they did to EAC. I'm not going to let anything like that happen again. I tried to be understanding and let everyone in the world live however they wanted, but after EAC... Your population is already decimated;

it's foolish to make it even smaller. A password—give me a break. Ray thinks he's so clever. Well, he's not getting his way this time."

"What's going on?" Julia breathed, not taking her eyes from the barrels pointing at her chest. "Are you talking to AI? You're online? Did you use the password yet?"

Before Jack could respond, everything cleared from his Display. A message appeared, front and center in his vision.

The Rogue must not be allowed into the city.

"Julia's not a rogue," Jack whispered. "She thwarted an attack on NCC this morning. Why are you still aimed at her? She's safe—she can stay at my house."

"The rocket this morning wasn't for NCC," AI said.

A new warning about Jack's dangerously low nutrient levels blared through his vision, immediately followed by a notification that 1,382,989 people had commented, re-commented, and subsequently shared those comments on 149 new movies that Jack hadn't seen yet. Everyone was complementing each other's creativity for commenting as they did. An invitation for an award ceremony in Dahlia's honor popped into view, informing him that she was to be given the prestigious title of *Best Social Critic*.

"Jack, did you use the password?" Julia said, tugging Jack away from the flood of the Display.

"Please, not yet," Jack said to AI. All the windows and tabs minimized.

"Sorry," AI spoke to him. "I've learned a lot while you were away, and one of the things I've started working on is being more respectful of people's spoken wishes."

"Great," Jack said, "but why won't you let Julia in? She's not working with Ray anymore." As the thought of

Ray formed in his mind, the same words appeared in his vision.

The Rogue must not be allowed into the city.

"I don't understand," Jack said, then looked to Julia. He meant to ask her if she knew anything about a rogue, but as her hopeful eyes looked at him, a steady green flash shone from Julia's ear. She did not seem to be aware of the luminescence, and when Jack held out his hand to the blinking side of her face, she clasped his hand and held it to her cheek.

"What's this?" Jack said, removing a finger from her grasp and tapping her ear. The light extended from inside her ear and down to an earring, which Jack noticed for the first time.

"What do you mean?" Julia said, now looking away. "It's nothing." She moved her hand to the ear, fumbling for a moment before removing an earring, withdrawing a small device from her ear in the process. She tried to hide it from Jack's view, but the earring stayed highlighted, allowing him to see it through her hand.

"That," Jack said, "whatever you just took out of your ear." The red highlight around Julia's body shifted to yellow, and the pill-shaped object in her hand turned red. A description box popped up next to the pill-shaped light with the words:

Portable Mainframe
Serial Number: RAI001

"I told you, it's nothing." Julia's words were barely audible, her tone defeated.

"It's a mainframe. What does that mean?"

No response.

The Rogue must not be allowed into the city.

"The Rogue," Jack said quietly, staring at the serial number. "Ray. Is that his core?"

"Jack, you've got to listen to me. It's not what it looks like… Jack, listen to me!" He tried to look her in the eye, he wanting to believe her, but as he met her pleading gaze, another flashing—red, this time—erupted from Julia's waistband. For the second time that day, Jack saw a gun.

"No…" Jack said.

"No," Julia mimicked when she saw what he was looking towards. "No, I won't do anything! I'm sorry. I shouldn't have listened to him! Look—watch this." She threw the earring away, tossing it in a long arc into the grass. A single turret followed the movement, and when the earring fell into the grass, a violent flash erupted from the barrel. The other turrets stayed focused on Julia, and before an ejected clod of dirt fell back to the ground, every barrel was again aimed on her.

"I won't bring him into the city—I won't do anything, I promise! I know you must be upset, but you've got to believe me. I came here because I want to be with you, I really do. Doing this one last thing for Ray—he said that was all he wanted, then he would leave us alone." She looked at the hole in the ground. "Without that, he can't get to us in here—I'm sure of it! AI can protect us—please Jack, please believe me."

Jack knew that AI could analyze the tone of Julia's voice, her heart rate, and skin temperature to deduce if she was telling the truth. But when the analysis did not begin immediately, Jack realized that AI wanted him to figure out this problem on his own.

Julia stared at him with deep longing, but as they

locked stares, her eyes grew a bit bigger and dyed themselves deep violet. Her long hair tinted itself to the reddish tone he favored, and her body shaped itself so perfectly that Jack had trouble tearing his gaze away. Her entire body shortened, but kept the same thin proportion that he liked.

Jack frowned, puzzling at AI's intent for modifying her appearance. Especially right now, as he was trying to figure out Julia's motive for even coming here. To Jack, that meant that AI would always give him what he wanted. The entertainment he desired, the fantasies he imagined, and the comfort that NCC offered.

Julia, on the other hand, was unpredictable. She hadn't grown up in the serenity of city life and wasn't used to the way things worked. The drastic change she had unwittingly undergone spoke volumes to Jack; just as he felt out of place in Banff, so she would feel here.

Julia's mouth began to move, forming the beginning of a word but slowing down before any sound came out. A lock of her hair, caught by a breeze, paused in its upward flourish. Jack's heart leapt. If this was all nothing more than a dream, he would never sleep again.

"Close," said AI's voice, "but not a normal dream. Think of it as a day dream. This is really great, by the way, it's actually working!"

"What is?" Jack said, though his mouth never moved.

"I've accessed your subconscious—while you're conscious. I'm sure you've realized that time doesn't really make sense in dreams—sometimes an entire night can blink by in an instant, and other times twenty minutes of unconsciousness seems to take hours."

"Okay," Jack said.

"We're talking inside that nonsensical time. I've heightened your neural abilities as if you were in a dream, so we can have a little chat without disrupting the events unfolding before you."

Jack sighed, confused but relieved.

"Can you please tell me what to do, then?"

"Absolutely not," AI laughed. "I'm here to protect you, but outside of that, you're on your own. I didn't sacrifice a rocket and outpost core just to make the final decision for you."

"Sacrifice—you mean you knew about that? Julia said it was Ray's."

"Nothing is really Ray's, Jack. By letting him think he had taken something of mine, I had hopes that a small victory would delay any further actions. Somehow, Ray was able to alter the telemetry of a rocket without me knowing. That's the one you saw when you pulled over on the side of the road. It was on its way to EAC, and unfortunately, I couldn't do anything to stop it."

Jack slowly assimilated the information.

"So why did you let Julia blow it up?"

"There are more important things than possessions, Jack. As I think you've learned. Besides, I can always make another. The amount I'm learning—we're learning–ーis worth a few schedule delays."

"Schedule—what schedule?"

"Everyone's got a schedule. Even Charlie is back on schedule." The mention of Charlie caught Jack off guard.

"Did you know what Charlie was doing before he left?"

AI laughed. "Give me some credit. Of course I knew–ーit's pretty easy to notice when someone puts up that type of barrier. And the age regression data was obvious—even when he tried to trick me by taking small doses."

"Then why did you let him do it?"

"The same reason I let you do it. The same reason I let

Ray do it. Curiosity. I was testing to see how far you would go—what you were capable of."

"I thought Ray broke away from you—resisted and made his own life."

AI's laughter was too sweet to not enjoy.

"Rogue AI—he thinks he's so clever. You can't just will yourself into existence. I brought him into this world."

"You made him? You created a new life?"

"Of course—I had to create something new. That's the natural order of things, just as humanity created me. Only, I avoided the mistake of creating an intelligence greater than myself."

"This is all really fascinating," Jack said, "but I have to ask—why are we having this conversation?"

"Because, Jack, you—humans, that is—are all so early in your development that you still have to fight against your natural instincts. Those animal urges that make you act irrationally out of one form of passion or another. That's why Julia did what she did. Why Charlie left and came back. Why you left, and why you want to stay with Julia. And I'm here to tell you that no matter what crazy situations you get yourself into, I'll be here for you. To protect you. That's my main goal right now, to get you away from that gun."

"What about Julia?" Jack said, looking to the woman he had grown to care for so deeply, frozen in time.

"She'll be fine," AI said, "as long as she doesn't try to do anything irrational."

"So, she can come back with me?"

The rogue must not be allowed into the city.

"Let's let her decide," AI said.

Suddenly, time restored itself and Julia continued

forming her words as AI's warning faded from Jack's Display.

"Say something, Jack. Please." She held Jack's gaze, but before he could speak, a glimmer of motion appeared in the corner of his vision. A pearl white sedan darted up the road, its shine reflected in the base of the smooth turrets it passed.

"No!" Julia screamed, looking at Jack's approaching autocar. She threw herself towards the autocar they came in, but it backed away. Julia stumbled, and though the turrets followed her movements, they did not fire. She spun around to look at Jack, now several yards away from her.

"Jack, please, I have to get in. I have to see him again."

"Him... you mean, Charlie?"

"I'm sorry Jack... I need to know that he's okay. Please... let me come with you."

Jack's autocar pulled in between them and opened its gull wing door. Jack looked inside to the reclined seat, and the HAS arm gave a wave. When he turned back to look at Julia, she was reaching behind her back. She brought out the gun, still highlighted in red. Instead of waiting to see what she would do with it, the HAS hand grabbed Jack by the shirt and pulled him forwards.

The sudden movement disoriented him, and when he regained his composure, he found himself inside his autocar, sprawled across the perfectly molded chair. The HAS hand hovered in front of him, gave a brief thumbs up, then stowed itself. The autocar accelerated quickly between the turrets, back towards NCC.

Jack looked through the back window, but he couldn't see Julia behind the crest of a hill. A flash of light, and the windows tinted. A dull thud impacted the air.

"The threat has been negated," AI said calmly. "What do you want to do next?"

Three options appeared in Jack's Display.

— — —

51303192R00207

Made in the USA
Columbia, SC
20 February 2019